ASSASSIN'S PROMISE

THE RED TEAM, BOOK 7

ELAINE LEVINE

Published by Elaine Levine
Copyright © 2015 Elaine Levine
Last Updated: February 12, 2018
Cover art by The Killion Group, Inc.
Cover image featuring Colin Wayne © FuriousFotog Photography
Editing by Arran McNicol @ editing720
Proofing by Carol Agnew @ Attention to Detail Proofreading

Print Edition ISBNs:
ISBN-13: 978-1985826830
ISBN-10: 1985826836

ASSASSIN'S PROMISE BLURB

THE RED TEAM, BOOK 7

Traumatized by her unusual childhood, sociologist Dr. Remington Chase, has made a career out of her lifelong obsession with American cults. Her research often results in pushback from the groups she studies, but not like what's happening now, with the White Kingdom Brotherhood biker gang shadowing her every move.

Is it luck or something far more sinister when a consultant from the Department of Homeland Security makes a surprise visit to her university office, seeking her help in finding a teenager lost inside the group she's studying?

Covert operative Greer Dawson has one objective: find the girl who tried to kill his team leader. He promised to protect her, but he didn't, and now his failure haunts him. He'll fight for the answers he and his team need...and risk losing his heart to a woman with secrets as dark as his own.

∼

Length: Approximately 426 pages
Ages: 18 & up (story contains sex, profanity, and violence)

Assassin's Promise (The Red Team, Book 7) is part of a serialized story that includes nine full-length novels and nine wedding novellas. This series is best read in order, starting with The Edge of Courage.

Join the conversation on Facebook: Visit Elaine Levine's War Room - http://geni.us/hxFk to talk about this book and all of her suspenseful stories!

OTHER BOOKS BY ELAINE LEVINE

For Barry, my best friend, my shelter, my everything.

ACKNOWLEDGMENTS

I was fortunate with this story to be able to consult with my friend, Jeni Cross, Ph.D., Associate Professor in the Department of Sociology at Colorado State University. She's so much fun to talk to. Her stories are addictive, and her love and respect for the field of sociology shines through everything she says. While I strove to honor her and do the field of sociology justice, any errors in the story are mine alone.

I want to make a special shout-out to my in-laws, Mel and Evelyn Levine. They are the best parents and cheerleaders a girl could ever want. And GiGi—I did use the dreaded "c**k" word, maybe too freely. I hope you'll forgive me (just clearing the air so we won't have to chat about it at Thanksgiving).

WHEN WE LAST VISITED THE RED TEAM...

Here's a refresher for those of you who have read the previous Red Team books (skip this and go read them if you haven't yet!). This is where we left our heroes...

* * * * * Spoilers! * * * * *

- Max met Hope, the love of his life, while undercover with the White Kingdom Brotherhood.
- Hope's brother, Lion, revealed King is his father.
- Lion is helping the team find King.
- Jafaar Majid is sending a female to infiltrate the team.
- Blade has found his biological father, Cordell Ryker, and secured his release from prison.

- Cordell Ryker now works at Ivy's diner and lives in the bunkhouse at Mandy's ranch.
- Eden and Blade have gotten married.
- Selena has kissed both Val and Owen and must decide between them…or not.
- Rocco is still fighting the demons of his PTSD.
- Approximately 12 weeks have passed since Rocco met Mandy.

And now, we continue with Greer Dawson and Remi Chase's story in ***Assassin's Promise***…

Greer lay on his bed, naked and sweating, sucking air like a marathon runner. *Can dead eyes still see?*

He shot a look around his room, making sure the ghouls had only been in his dream.

He was alone.

He ripped the twisted sheet away from his legs and walked over to the window. Dawn was still an hour away, but already the sky was a pale lavender. He slid the large glass panel open. Cold air seeped inside, spilling over the windowsill and down the wall to wrap around his feet and ankles like the icy fingers of dead hands.

He pressed his face against the screen and breathed the crisp alpine air through the musty screen mesh. He hated ghosts. They were the rodents of the supernatural world. All they did was mess stuff up. Like his head.

Christ Almighty. *Can fucking dead eyes still see?* he wondered.

And whose eyes had he seen in his dream, anyway? He'd memorized the faces of everyone whose lives he'd ended in case they showed up later in unwanted ways. All of them had been men; the eyes he saw in his nightmare were female. Who was she? Someone he already knew or someone he'd yet to meet?

He straightened, withdrawing from the questions he couldn't answer. Centering himself, he closed his eyes and calmed his racing heart with slow, deep breaths. He could feel his energy pulling back inside of him, closer and closer to his inner core, until nothing was left of him in the outside world. He was invisible, one with the atmosphere, inseparable from his surroundings.

Numb to his body and his life.

He let himself exist in that empty zone for a few more minutes, then shut the window and headed to the bathroom for a shower. Hot water pelted his back from a half-dozen showerheads. He bent his head, letting it spill off the sides of his face as he shed all thought. Or tried to.

The nightmare was beginning to fade, but it left behind the black residue of his panic. This wasn't the only go-round with that dream. He couldn't remember the first time he'd seen the woman. Weeks. Months. Who knew?

Breakfast was almost over before he made it down

to the dining room. His stomach was still twisted from his dream. He didn't eat, just filled a coffee mug so no one would pester him with questions.

He wasn't the only one who was self-absorbed; Max and Hope followed him into the room. They looked tired and happy. Replete. Max nodded at him as he held Hope's hand and led her over to the buffet table.

"We're meeting downstairs in fifteen," Kit announced to the few who were still at the table.

Blade grinned at Eden—now his wife. It was the first day back at work after their big wedding celebration over the weekend. He had no difficulty imagining how Blade wanted to spend those minutes.

Greer took his coffee and walked out the patio door. The joy-joy of the couples echoed uncomfortably inside him. He sipped the black brew and looked across the wide, double-tiered lawn behind the house. The tent, carpets, and furniture from Blade's wedding were gone, but flattened areas on the grass showed where they'd been.

Owen stepped outside and paused long enough to take a read on him. The nightmare had left Greer in a strange pall with sluggish reflexes; he was slow to shutter himself from the boss's penetrating gaze, an invasion that ended only when Greer stopped focusing on himself and zeroed in on Owen —an energy maneuver that, in his early days on the Red Team, always netted him a hundred on-the-spot push-ups. It did its job. Owen pulled away.

When he moved down the patio into the den, Greer followed him, leaving his mug on one of the patio tables.

Man by man—and Selena—the team presented themselves downstairs in the bunker's meeting room. Owen, as usual, leaned against the back wall.

"First things first," Kit opened. "We got the report back on Lion's DNA. His sample had no hits. So it looks as if King isn't in the system."

"Or," Greer said, "Lion's father had himself, and his relatives, erased. I would have done that, if I were playing the game he is."

Kit nodded, then looked over the table to Owen. "Interestingly, your friend, the rogue Red Teamer, Wendell Jacobs, was also no longer in CODIS."

Owen didn't seem surprised. "He's on the lam, and he's covering his trail."

"Maybe Jacobs is King," Kit said.

Owen didn't blink or shift his position against the wall. "While he's capable of being King, I don't think he is. We're getting closer to whoever is King, though. I can feel it."

"Maybe Lion was lied to," Max said. "Maybe King is his father in a figurative sense, the way a cult leader is called 'Father.'"

Kit nodded. "Which leads us to the Friendship Community. Greer, get over there and scope them out. They're involved in this—we need to know how."

"Lion said the community sometimes leaves food and supplies for the watchers," Max said. "He talked of Armageddon, too. Those weirdos are in this up to their necks."

"There's a professor at the University of Wyoming who's been studying cults," Greer said. "She's researching the Friendship Community. I'll go talk to her."

Kit nodded. "Good. What have you discovered so far about them?"

Greer put up some pictures on one of the big smart screens at the side of the room, images of the community he'd harvested from the internet along with a topographical map of their compound. "They've existed where they are for close to one hundred eighty years. They owned over ten thousand acres at one time, but sold half of it off to the federal government in the 1960s when the Department of Defense wanted to build the missile silo complex that the White Kingdom Brotherhood now owns. Most of their land is in a fertile valley protected by the Medicine Bow Mountains.

"When the world began to modernize early last century, they were remote enough that they slipped behind. Rather than catching up, they've stayed true to their nineteenth century roots, eschewing everything from electricity to modern medicine. They're a closed group. They have no currency system and only raise enough funds to cover their property tax bill each year. As a Christian pacifist society, they claim a religious exemption from military service.

"They don't own mechanized vehicles. They make

an annual trek down to Cheyenne during Frontier Days to sell their wares to raise tax money and to acquire the small number of goods they can't directly produce. They aren't polygamists. They govern themselves via a secular council structure. And according to the censuses, their population has been slowly increasing since the 1970s, with the largest increase appearing at the last census."

"Lion said the community nearly died out middle of the last century, but if their population has been increasing since, they may be getting an infusion of new adherents from somewhere," Max said. "He said there are multiple prides. Maybe there are multiple Friendship Communities."

"Look into that, Max. Maybe they're co-located with other WKB camps. Greer, let us know what you find after you talk to the professor."

DR. REMINGTON CHASE, assistant professor of sociology at the University of Wyoming, was lost in thought as she approached the department's side entrance. Took her a long minute—too long—to become aware of police cars parked in a no-parking zone in front of the building...and a couple dozen people standing around the greenspace in small clusters, talking in hushed tones.

She realized they were all staring at her now, with worried eyes. Her stomach clenched as a powerful wave of fear hit her. Had there been a shooting on campus? Her grip tightened on the stack of books and documents she held to her chest, as if a few reams of paper could stop a bullet.

There were only two cop cars. Surely there'd be more if there'd been a shooting? She looked at the people standing in groups. None were crying. Still, she had a bad feeling as she walked around to the front side of the building, toward the crowd, and saw what had them in knots.

Giant red spray paint letters, spanning about twenty-feet of the brick wall, read: "Professor Chase is a lying whore."

Her knees went weak as she stared in horror at the message. The paint had dripped in blood-red tendrils, as if the brick wall had been sliced open and now bled.

Dr. Zimmers, her department chair, came over with the cops. "Do you know what this is about, Dr. Chase?"

She shook her head, pretending ignorance, but her pulse was drowning out sound in her ears.

"Hi, Dr. Chase," Officer Franklin smiled at her.

She latched on to the middle-aged cop's kind eyes and forced air into her lungs. The campus police were competent and non-reactionary, used to the antics of students. This was graffiti. Nothing more. It was paint, not blood. Just paint.

He touched her arm. "Are you okay?"

She blinked, then nodded.

"Any idea who might have done this? An angry student, perhaps?" he asked.

She shook her head. "No. Did the security cameras pick anything up?"

"Not in detail. Two men wearing dark hoodies, baseball caps, and gloves did it about two a.m. this morning," Dr. Zimmers said. "They were on motorcycles."

Motorcycles. Remi's fingers dug into the books she held. Were they from the White Kingdom Brotherhood?

"Their license plates were obscured," Officer Franklin's partner said. "Do you have any enemies? Students who are angry with you? Frustrated parents?"

Remi frowned and tilted her head. "There are always students and parents with their own agendas. For the most part, my students and I get along great. They're good people, active and engaged in their studies." She smiled. "Though I wouldn't put it past any of them to do something as outrageous as this for a social experiment."

"Her students love her," Dr. Zimmers added. "She's one of our most highly rated professors. And though it's still early in her career, she's making quite a name for herself and for the university. In fact, she was interviewed about her research into American cults for a public radio segment—it just aired yesterday."

"Maybe someone didn't like the attention you directed at them," the other cop suggested.

"I spoke in generalities during the interview. I didn't call out any specific group. Still, this wouldn't be the first time I've gotten pushback while actively doing field research," Remi admitted, playing it down, making it all sound rational...as if she weren't close to jumping out of her skin at any moment.

"Which group are you working on now?" the cop asked.

"A local group. The Friendship Community. They're just up the mountain. They don't have motorized vehicles anywhere on their compound. They couldn't have done this." The WKB could have, however—a theory she kept to herself.

"It could be someone lashing out from one of the previous groups you've studied," Dr. Zimmers suggested.

Remi shrugged. The papers she held were getting heavy, and her arms were sweating. "I guess."

"Has anything else odd happened lately? Strange emails? Anything threatening?" the campus police asked.

Remi felt her eyes widen. Yes. So much that she was jumping at shadows. And now this.

Dr. Zimmers answered for her. "No. The summer's been very quiet, actually." The police continued asking her department chair more questions, but Remi had stopped listening.

She sent a look around, checking for something

that didn't belong...someone whose gaze seemed furtive or triumphant, someone watching her reaction. She recognized all of the people standing nearby; she worked with them, or taught them, or had seen them on campus. No one looked out of place.

Her gaze settled on her teaching assistant, Clancy Weston, a doctoral student at the university. His expression was neither friendly nor concerned. While he had the potential to be a great sociologist, the chip on his shoulder weighed him down. He'd been unhappy when the university hired her; he didn't seem to think she was the best candidate for the position.

When the police were finished with their questions, she went straight to her office. She'd been feeling a strange, ungrounded anxiety for a while now —a tension which the graffiti only deepened. It was comforting to fill her mind with other thoughts.

The university would be back in session in a few weeks. She had to get her syllabus and everything for her class finished up today so Clancy could post the info online before the semester began. Then she could spend the rest of the summer coding her field notes and interviews—and make another visit to the Friends before the summer ended.

2

_____

"Dr. Chase?"

Remi looked up from her desk to see a tall man filling the entire space of her office door. Words failed her as her eyes traveled the hard edges of his face. He was clean-shaven. His short brown hair was longer on top than on the sides. It was a little curly and uncombed and sexy as hell. His neck was as wide as his square chin, corded and lean. Her gaze lifted then locked on to his light brown eyes, eyes of a warrior—sharp, clear, direct. She had a lot of students like him.

Sometimes, though, eyes like his were hard to look at.

"Nice billboard out there." He nodded in the direction of the front of the building.

Remi felt heat slip up her neck and into her cheeks. From embarrassment or just a reaction to him, she couldn't tell. Deciding it was the latter, she ignored it. This was not a good day to run into strangers.

"I'm sorry…do I know you?"

"No. And I apologize for interrupting. I was hoping you could help me. If you'd rather I made an appointment, I can do that."

"Are you a student here, Mr.—?"

He stepped into her office. "Greer Dawson." He held a hand out to her.

She stood and took his hand, then lost herself in the feel of it against hers, warm, slightly callused, and big. He didn't crush her fingers, though he could have easily. "I'm a special consultant to the Department of Homeland Security." He handed her his card.

She lifted her gaze to his eyes, a good eight inches above hers. He wasn't the first handsome man she'd run into, but he probably was the hottest. All her senses fired off the same warning: *This guy's trouble.*

"What can I do for you, Mr. Dawson?" she asked.

"Greer's fine. My research indicates you're an expert on cults. I understand you're focused on the Friendship Community right now."

She stayed silent, waiting for his question even as she took a read on his intent.

"I'm hoping you can help me find a young girl I believe is living with the people you're studying."

"Was she born in their community?"

"I don't know."

"If not, it's unlikely she's with the Friends. They don't have an open-door policy to outsiders. If she wasn't born into the group, I doubt they'd let her in or allow her to hang out with them. It's taken me years to build rapport with them—not an easy thing to do." He seemed unconvinced. "What makes you think she's in the Friendship Community?"

"I was with her at the clinic in Wolf Creek Bend. Her 'family'"—he made the sign for air quotes —"took her away in their black buggy. I know she's with them."

Remi folded her arms. "What caused her to go to Wolf Creek Bend? The Friends rarely leave their community."

"She came to kill my team lead."

Stunned, Remi couldn't look away. He was deadly serious. "Greer, you do understand that the Friends are pacifists. Committing murder goes against everything their community has stood for nearly two centuries."

"It happened. I have a lot of questions I'd like answered." He made a face, tightening his lips as he frowned. "Look, it's not a quick story." He shoved his hands deep into his pockets, up to the thin black leather and silver cords wrapped around his right wrist and the heavy tactical watch on his left. "Can I buy you a cup of coffee?" he asked.

Remi glanced down to her laptop. She'd submitted the files Clancy needed to get her course up online. She was working on an outline for her article on social cohesion within the Friendship Community. She could take a break. And reluctantly, she had to admit his problem piqued her interest.

"All right. Let's go over to the coffee shop."

He gave her a small smile. "Thanks."

She nodded, then saved her files and shut down her laptop. She put it in her desk drawer and locked it.

Greer waited at her door, letting her exit first. The school was quiet now that they were between summer and fall sessions, but most of the staff were on site gearing up for the fall semester. Clancy Weston passed them in the hall, giving Greer a once-over that made Remi smile.

"Friend of yours?" Greer asked with a lift of his left brow. And damn if she didn't trace that whole dark line with her eyes before she answered.

"My teaching assistant."

When they got to the stairwell, he held the door for her. Someone somewhere had taught him manners. Outside, the heat of the August day wrapped the sweet scent of freshly cut grass around her.

She didn't open their discussion until they were fully in the anonymity of the outdoors. "So, tell me about this girl."

"Unfortunately, there's not much I know. Her name's Sally. She's blond, average height, somewhere between sixteen and eighteen years old."

"Why was she at the clinic? The Friends have an infirmary on site. They don't generally embrace western medicine. Not because of any religious practices, but because they're fairly sanguine about life and the role death plays in it."

"She'd been drugged. We don't believe she was operating under her own faculties."

Remi stopped mid-stride. "No." She shook her head. "This doesn't sound anything like the Friends I know. What did she do?"

"She came into Winchester's—a bar in Wolf Creek Bend—sat on my boss's lap, and took out a knife to cut his throat."

Remi pressed her hand to her neck. "Why aren't the cops after her?"

"My friend isn't pressing charges."

"What you're telling me doesn't match up with what I know about the Friendship Community. They're pacifists. They wouldn't intentionally take a life. Or use drugs. Or leave their compound." She looked at his implacable face, then rubbed her brow. "The Friends have some kind of relationship with the White Kingdom Brotherhood. I haven't been able to pin it down yet. Are you sure this girl isn't in with the WKB?"

He studied her eyes until a muscle bunched in his jaw. "No, I'm not at all sure about that. Maybe she is. All I know is that people who claimed to be her parents changed her into the homespun clothes of their community and took her away in their buggy."

"Did you go talk to them at the community?"

"Not yet. I get the sense that I have one shot at it.

I don't want to be shut down before I can really try. I was hoping you could get me in."

Remi shook her head and continued on toward the coffee shop. "No. I'm sorry, but I can't blow years of work on your problem. Not when I'm so close to wrapping up my research."

"A girl's life is worth nothing to you?"

"That's not fair. You have no idea if she's actually there. You're asking me to put my research on the line for your hunch. No."

They reached the coffee shop. He opened the door. They made their order, then waited in silence for their coffees. Caffeine in hand, Remi led the way back outside.

"Look, I took a census earlier this summer. If a girl named 'Sally' is on it, I'll let you know. If she's there, I'll give you an intro to the elders and the council."

The guy nodded. "Thank you."

She lifted her cup and smiled. "Thanks for the coffee."

She watched him walk down the path leading to one of the parking lots. There was no way she was going to risk everything she'd worked on for a stranger. She felt his card in her pocket. She'd check him out, make sure he was legit before going any further.

~

Selena came out of the bunker entrance in the closet of the den later that morning. Owen was at Blade's desk, writing something longhand. He looked up as she entered, and flipped the page over.

"Got a minute?" she asked.

He nodded, then came around the desk to lean against the front of it. "What can I do for you?"

Selena sent him a look, then glanced out the patio doors as she tried to figure out the best way to say what needed to be said.

Owen smiled. "Take your time. I'm in no hurry."

She tucked her hands behind her back and squared her shoulders. "With all due respect, sir—"

"Don't 'sir' me."

"—I'd like to request a transfer back to my unit."

"Negative."

"Owen—"

"Is this about the kiss?"

"Yes. I overstepped."

"You didn't. I did. And I don't regret it. I needed that kiss at that moment." She met his eyes. They were so pale and blue, she could drift away in them, like a balloon floating up into a sunny sky.

"I do regret, however, that it took your options away," he continued. "I'm your boss, the only way in or out of this group. That's not fair to you. So, I'd like to give you a choice. Me or the job."

Selena felt her brows lift. "Neither. I told you I want to leave."

"Me or the job."

She met his eyes until hers burned. She lowered her gaze, looking at his chest, then followed the line of his arm to the place where his hands rested against his crotch, his fingers loosely linked. She lifted her eyes to his, ignoring the heat that was creeping up her neck. "What if I chose you?"

"Then I'd fire you and move your things into my room."

She huffed a disbelieving laugh. "Way to move slow, Owen."

"I'm not interested in slow, Selena."

"And I'm not interested in giving up my plans, my ambitions, and all control over my life." She shook her head.

"Then your choice is clear."

"It is."

"Can we put this behind us?"

"Oh, yeah."

"Good." He smiled and nodded, dismissing her. As she walked out of the den, she realized she'd just been handled by an expert. She was half tempted to go back and call his bluff just to see what he would do.

Had anyone ever done that and survived?

FIONA TRIED NOT to let Kelan, who was lounging by the corner of her bathroom, distract her. She'd already moved most of her clothes to their apartment in Fort Collins, so she wouldn't have much to pack when she moved out of the house for the semester. Some toiletries. Her favorite jeans and a couple of tops. Kelan had suggested she purchase duplicates so that she wouldn't have to pack or be without anything she needed when commuting back and forth on weekends. She might do that when she was back in town.

Kelan's legs and arms were crossed as he leaned against the wall. It was impossible not to keep looking at him. His frown never eased up. He was a big guy, powerful and intense. He filled the room with so much electricity that it was hard to breathe around him. She couldn't believe he was hers. She could touch him whenever she wanted, hug him whenever it suited her. Best of all was knowing he wanted her to do those things.

She sighed and looked at her packed bag. "I don't want to go." She glanced at him. "Maybe I should quit school for a little while."

His frown deepened. He uncrossed his legs and straightened. "Maybe you should focus and get it done so we can stop having to separate."

She smiled. He expected nothing but her best effort, always, undiluted, uncompromising. School had been hard once her mom passed. And now, after everything that had happened with her stepdad, well, it was nice having someone believe in her.

She walked to him and slipped into his arms. Though he was much larger than she was, she felt they were a perfect fit. She pressed her ear against his chest.

"Do you want me to follow you down?" he asked. "I could stay overnight and see you settled."

Fiona shook her head. "That would only make this parting the longest one ever. For an entire day, I would be dreading your heading back here."

"I could stay with you and commute to work."

Fiona pulled back to look up at him. "It's more than two hours each way. That's a waste of your time. I'll be fine." Her hand touched his cheek. "And you'll be fine."

He shook his head. "I'll be hollow. My ancestors had the perfect term for that. 'Mahasani.' It means you are the me that lives outside of myself. When you're not near, I'll have nothing."

"That's beautiful. Was that from your Lakota ancestors?"

He nodded.

"Will you tell me about them sometime? I know so little about my own family. It amazes me how much you know about yours."

"I will." He touched the security necklace she wore. "Don't take this off."

"I won't."

"Call me if you need anything."

"You've seen to everything. I'll call you each night."

"Call me anytime."

His hand caught the back of her head as he bent to kiss her. She wrapped her arms around his neck and whispered against his lips, "I don't want to wait, Kelan."

"We have only a little over a month to go. We'll wait."

"I miss you already," she said as he eased her back to her feet.

"Go, so you can come back."

Selena knocked quietly on Val's door, glad as hell the other doors in his wing didn't have peepholes. She heard no sound from inside, but a short moment after her knock, his door opened. Val stood there, shirtless and barefoot, wearing only his jeans.

"Can we talk?" she asked.

He smiled and stepped back, giving her access to his room. "Closed door or open?"

She looked up at him, hesitating long enough for the cerulean pull of his eyes to wash over her. "Closed." She set her jaw and moved through the narrow entrance hall.

"S'up?" he asked, shutting the door and following her deeper into his room.

She faced him. "I don't make friends easily. I don't take on lovers easily, either."

His grin widened. He folded his arms, tucking his hands by his armpits as he spread his legs. "Darlin', if you're gonna fire me or hire me, don't leave me standing in this nether world."

"I kissed Owen."

Val's brows lifted. "Did you like it?"

"It was nice."

"Uh-huh."

She shook her head. "I talked to him this morning. Told him it wasn't going to go anywhere, since I work for him."

"How'd that go?"

"He offered to fire me so that he could move me into his bedroom."

Val laughed. "Bastard."

"I have to say the same thing to you."

He stepped closer, all humor gone from his eyes. This close, she had to look up to see his eyes, but she refused to, focusing instead on his Adam's apple.

"Selena"—he touched the back of his knuckles to her cheek, drawing his hand down her neck—"give me a chance."

She started to shake her head, still avoiding his eyes. "You're smoking hot, Val, but you're more than your looks. You have a big heart. You love this team."

He bent and placed the barest of butterfly kisses on her cheek. "Don't do this, Sel. Give me a chance. I can be the guy you want."

"But I can't be the girl you want." She took hold of his wrist and finally looked into his eyes. "I can't come between you and Owen."

"Fuck Owen."

"It would be different if you and I weren't on the same team."

"I'll quit."

Selena didn't hide the shock that offer sent through her, but reality quickly chased it away. "And do what? Come to resent me for burning your bridges and forcing you to leave the team?"

"I would never resent you."

"I want to be friends, Val. I don't want to cross this line."

He stared into her eyes. She could almost see the doors to his heart and his soul slam shut. He dropped his hands and stepped back. "Got it."

She lowered her head and nodded. She had not expected this to hurt—him or her—as it did. "Okay." She flashed a look at him. "Okay." She sighed, then headed out of his room.

3

Greer's phone vibrated. The caller ID showed it was the professor. "Hi, doc."

"Greer."

"Did you find Sally in your census?"

She took an audible breath. *"No. I'm sorry. But I did find something interesting. Can you come to my office?"*

"Sure. I'll be there in a couple of hours."

"Where are you?"

"I'm camping. Up in the Medicine Bows."

"How are you getting reception up there?"

Greer knew Owen had pulled some strings to get additional satellite relays deployed, but that was need-to-know info. "Who knows? I just am. Couple hours, doc. You gonna be there still?"

"Yeah. Call me when you're here. I'll let you in. They lock the building down early in the summer."

Greer folded his campsite and loaded his things into the SUV he'd hidden in the woods. He'd been camping near the Friendship Community to observe its behavior. He wanted to see how often the WKB members came onto Friendship property, what the Friends did during the day, during the night.

Once he was on the road to Wolf Creek Bend, he phoned Max to let him know where he was headed.

"Need a shotgun rider?" Max asked.

"She's just a professor. What the hell do you think she's gonna do?"

"How would I know? I never expected a certain blond mechanic to drop me to my knees, and yet here we are."

"Yeah, well, you're lucky for that, bro." Greer listened to the silence that met his words. The bastard was probably trying to tune up his wait-for-the-right-one speech. Which was all bullshit. There was no right one for a guy like him. He had thought there was, once. But he knew better than that now.

Fuck, they just had to go there, didn't they?

"You should get off the phone and go be with Hope." Greer didn't mean to snap, but it came out that way.

"Right. Anything happening at the Friends' place?"

"Nada. They're up with the sun and down with the dark. I haven't seen any unexpected visitors. Just hardworking residents doing their thing."

"Roger that. Check in after you see the prof."

GREER PHONED the professor as he walked toward

her building's stairwell door. There were only a handful of cars in the parking lot. He was glad the campus security protocols were in place. She opened the door about the time he reached it.

He nodded at her. She smiled and blinked, then stood a little longer than expected, looking up at him. Those dark green eyes of hers did something to him. If he still had a heart, it might have banged out an extra beat.

He raised a brow, hoping to snap her back to the moment...and himself out of it. He wasn't looking for an entanglement. He'd loved once. That was enough. That shit was toxic.

"Right." The doc cleared her throat and slapped the flats of her palms against her thighs like he was a dog or something. "Follow me."

They went up a few flights of stairs. Greer fixed his eyes on her ass, which was fine—rounded but slim, filling out her jeans like they were sewn on. He imagined those cheeks in his hands, white and soft, her legs spread across his hips...

When they reached her floor, Remi looked back at him. His face flamed. He grinned at her by way of apology.

She should have slapped him for the thoughts he didn't try to hide from her. Instead, her face flushed too. She pressed her lips into a thin line, then lifted her chin and started down the hall to her office.

Papers were spread out on the round table in her office. She indicated a chair. "Please, have a seat." She took the chair next to his. Her knee bumped his thigh as she leaned forward to rearrange the papers. His eyes shot to her face to see if the touch was intentional.

It wasn't.

He cleared his mind, since he obviously was the only one on that page.

She looked at him. "I'm sorry I couldn't find the girl you're looking for. That might not be the name she's using with the Friends. Or perhaps she really is not with them. I don't know."

"She's from that community. I'm certain of it."

The professor looked at him as if she was deciding something important. She took a long breath, then jumped in. "I've done some charting of the population changes in the community over one hundred fifty years. Some interesting things popped out."

"Any of this have to do with Sally?"

"Possibly. Bear with me." She pulled a graph with fifteen bars on it, showing the changes in population over the years from 1870 to 2010. The first census showed a community of one hundred twenty-five people, spread across a range of ages. It declined to barely forty people by the 1930 census. It doubled in each of the next two censuses, then halved again by 1970. In 1980, and each census after that, it grew rapidly until it was now over three hundred people.

This corroborated what Lion had told Max about the community nearly dying out.

"What drove this recent growth?" he asked the professor.

She shook her head. "Until your question, I hadn't focused on the bigger picture of changing population patterns in the group. I'll do some additional research to see if I can correlate the major turning points in the community to economic and/or political shifts in the wider U.S. population."

She set the graph aside and looked at him. "But that's not why I brought you back."

Greer waited for her explanation.

"I dug deeper into the last five censuses. I realized that while the overall population is increasing steadily, the proportional count of adolescents is decreasing. I can't explain this either. In each of the five censuses, the number of children fourteen years and younger is increasing at a pace I would expect as the adult population increases."

"So what's happening to the teenagers? And how can the adult population be growing if there are fewer adolescents coming into adulthood in the group?"

"Great questions. Really great questions. I don't know. I need to get back to the community and dig a little deeper. As closed a community as it is, it would surprise me if outsiders are coming in."

"Perhaps they're swapping people from other communities like theirs. Keep the gene pool fresh."

The professor's eyes met his. He could almost feel the alarm he saw in them as the wheels of her mind shifted into motion. He shrugged. "Just a thought."

"I wouldn't have seen this if you hadn't sent me looking for Sally. And my research would have been incomplete. So to thank you, I made this list."

She moved through the jumble of documents and pulled out another sheet. This was a list of blond teenage girls in the community. Eight of them. "I couldn't find anyone named 'Sally,' but perhaps that's a nickname. I'll be visiting with these families when I make another trip to the community. I can try to find out if any of them is your girl."

Greer lowered the paper and looked at the professor. "Let me come with you."

"No. I have built rapport with them. They trust me. They don't know you. If you're with me, then I fear they won't talk even to me."

Greer pressed his lips together, rejecting her decision. She reached over and touched his forearm. Her hand was cool, her fingers long, her nails neat, topped by white crescents.

"Please. We'll get more flies with honey than a show of force."

"What makes you think I have no finesse?"

"Besides the way you're looking at me now?" She pulled her hand away. "You're kind of scary, Greer. If you want to find out about Sally, this is the way to do it."

He nodded and got to his feet. "May I have these graphs?"

His request surprised her. "Sure. But please don't share them. I haven't published them yet."

Greer shook his head. "I'm not in competition with you, doc. You do your thing, I'll do mine."

The professor also stood. "And what is your thing?"

"Finding Sally."

"And other than that? It can't be your full-time job."

Greer folded the sheets of paper she gave him. "I'll tell you all my secrets if you have dinner with me." He grinned, pleased he'd kept the offer so clean when his thoughts of her were anything but.

"Well, I am kind of hungry." She smiled reluctantly, then frowned. "I don't think I had lunch today."

"There a good steakhouse around here?"

"We have several. My fav is J's."

"Then J's it is. My treat."

He waited while she gathered her papers into a neat stack, then packed them into her briefcase. She closed her laptop and added it. They stepped into the hall. She shut off the lights, then locked her office.

They didn't speak as they went down the stairs. Out of habit, Greer went first. His SUV was parked in the almost empty lot, near the building. "Want to go in my car? Or shall I follow you? The restaurant could be packed." He looked at his watch. "It's prime feeding time. We might not want to take two cars."

"You can drive. If you don't mind."

He opened the passenger door for her. "I don't."

She was looking around the interior of his SUV

when he got in on the driver's side. "It's lighter in here than I thought it would be with all the window tinting. It's kind of gangsta."

Greer grinned. "I'm a gangsta kinda guy, I guess."

Her smile evaporated. "Are you?"

He looked at her as he backed up. "Yeah."

"Are you into illegal things?"

Greer released a long breath. "I'll tell you true, doc, when I find Sally, I'm gonna lay down some heads."

"What if the people she's with meant well?"

He shrugged. "Don't matter. She's underage, in an isolationist community. Whether she went there of her volition or was brought there by whomever she's hooked up with, makes no difference. She isn't old enough to make that decision. I told her I would help her. She should have come to me."

He chanced a glance at the professor. He'd told Sally while she was in the hospital getting the drugs flushed from her system that he'd protect her. And he hadn't. So yeah, he felt as if he'd let his own sister down.

And Christ, he couldn't take on much more karmic debt than the load he was already carrying. He was going to find Sally and move her someplace safe.

Unbidden, the ghost eyes from his dream came to mind. Hell was waiting for him. For sure. But he wasn't going anywhere until he found Sally.

AT THE RESTAURANT, Remi fought to keep things together. Greer was one of the most exciting men she'd ever met. Intense, charming, sexy as hell. His ripped body probably had zero percent body fat, which made her self-conscious about her own curves. He smiled easily and joked frequently, but none of that hid the sharp edge of his intellect.

The only thing she knew for sure was that he wasn't what he seemed—a thing she decided to confront him about after they gave their orders to the waiter.

"I checked you out."

He smiled. "Oh?"

She'd called the Department of Homeland Security—not using the number on his card but the one on their website. She'd vetted him before deciding to share any of her data. "When I called DHS, I was rerouted to a Christian Villa—" she paused on the name, wondering if he knew who she meant.

"—Villalobo? Interesting guy."

"He vouched for you."

"Phew. That's a relief. What did Loco Lobo say?"

"That you were on a case, but nothing else. So I Googled you," she said, spinning the base of her wine glass as she watched his eyes.

His half-smile curled one corner of his mouth. "Yeah? Good. Glad you did your due diligence."

"I didn't find anything other than someone with

your name lives in Fairfax, Virginia. You don't participate in social media."

"No, I don't. Nor should you. Social media data streams feed into databases that store your info. It's how governments monitor you."

"Ah. You're a conspiracy theorist."

"They aren't theories." He took out his wallet and tossed his Virginia driver's license down in front of her. "I am from Virginia."

She looked at his ID. "You're younger than me."

Greer retrieved his license and stowed it. "Not by much."

True. She was only three years older than him. How did he know that? she wondered. "I could have babysat you when we were kids."

He laughed at that. She watched in fascination as his entire face lit up, from his generous smile of big white teeth to those whiskey eyes of his. No, not whiskey. Cinnamon.

"I was never young enough for a babysitter." He tilted his head and looked at her. "By the time you were old enough to babysit, I would have been guarding you."

That set her back. She tried so hard to be normal, to pretend her childhood was as mainstream as any other American kid. Truth was, she could have used a guard. He seemed to know more about her than she was comfortable with.

She took a sip of her Shiraz, pleased she'd been

able to do so without her hand shaking. She changed the subject.

"So what do you do for a living when you're not hunting for Sally?"

"I run a data management system for a company that provides security for its clients."

She studied his eyes, then shook her head. "I can't imagine a big guy like you behind a desk all day."

He shrugged. "I'm not behind a desk—I'm in front of the whole world. Computers connect me to everything, everyone, everywhere."

Their food arrived, his near-raw T-bone, her petite fillet. Baked potatoes. Specially seasoned broccoli.

He cut a bite, then consumed it and two more before he broke the silence that had followed their food. "I've told you about me. Your turn."

She shrugged. "Not much to tell. My dad died when I was a kid. My mom raised me. I was home-schooled until high school. I got my undergraduate degree at Colorado State University, my masters at Stanford, and my Ph.D. from Princeton."

"Mm-hmm." He swallowed another bite. "Why sociology? What about that field called to you?"

She got this question a lot. It was easy to trot out her standard answer. "I'm curious about people. Why they do the things they do, live the way they live, make the choices they make."

"Why?" He dug his fork into the shell of his potato. "Do you think you can fix us?"

"No." All she really wanted was to fix herself. "Don't you think documenting what is has value in and of itself?"

"Dunno. I wouldn't be the one to assign that value." He'd finished his meal, and now leaned back in his seat and looked at her. "I'd think there's a risk of making judgments about those you study, being heavily influenced by your own value system, more so, perhaps, than by the facts you uncover."

"True. I'm a human studying humans. I try to check my biases at the door when I take on a new project. Sometimes it's hard to do. So you don't judge others, then?"

"Oh, I do." He smiled. "But in my world, things are often black and white, and those judgments are easy to make. Usually, they have to be made damned fast."

Remi set her fork down. She'd only eaten half her fillet and the broccoli. She should have ordered a salad instead of the potato. She looked across the table to Greer. He didn't sound much like the data analyst or programmer he claimed to be.

"Are you recently out of the military?" she asked, using the cover of her wine glass to camouflage her interest in his answer.

"Why do you ask?"

She lifted her shoulders. "Something about the way you carry yourself. I have a lot of former military in my classes."

"I was Army."

"I'm glad you're here and not there."

"A war's a war." He shrugged.

"What does that mean?"

"Searching for Sally's a lot like hunting an enemy."

"The people in the Friendship Community are peaceful."

"You keep saying that, and yet their youth abandon the community in numbers big enough to show up in stats."

The waiter came by with the bill. Greer dropped cash on the table. They left and made the short drive back to the university. Her Subaru Forester was now the only one left in the parking lot. He pulled in next to it. The parking lot lights had come on.

They both got out. She set her things in her car, then waited for him to come around. She realized she was oddly reluctant to see him go. Dinner was nice. She'd enjoyed their conversation.

"Where do they go, do you suppose?" he asked as they stood between their cars.

"Who?"

"The kids who leave the community. Where do they go? Maybe Sally's one of the disappearing kids."

"I haven't been able to find any former residents, which is not uncommon. Some closed groups breed so much fear into their residents that none who leave openly admit to having been part of the community. They get new names, change their looks, blend into mainstream population."

"And yet you say the Friends are peaceful."

He stood near her. It felt…nice, being here with him. He asked smart questions.

"I don't think you and I would define 'peaceful' in the same way," he said.

"Cult membership is a complex situation. Often members of a cult don't know they're in one until they're on the outside of it. And then they're assailed with negative feelings of guilt, regret, embarrassment, and shame. All of those emotions hide in dark corners, segregating the cult survivors from the wider population. Sometimes, without the cult identity, they have no identity at all. They break."

"Sounds like you've been there, done that."

Her heart skipped a beat. "I've been studying cults a long time. I often help family members and psychologists deprogram former members."

She slowly became aware of a distant sound. The university was near a busy road. Cars in the small college town, populated by broke students, were often poorly maintained with bad exhaust systems and loud mufflers. She didn't really focus on it until it coalesced into the sound of a couple of loud motorcycles. Greer was on alert too.

"Get in your car, doc."

She fumbled with her keys. The bikes were coming closer. It was so silly having this unfounded fear of bikers. Lots of the students here rode bikes. But the cops thought the graffiti had been left by some bikers. And the WKB had been making her life hell lately.

She had to warn Greer about them.

The bikes were rolling in a tight circle around their cars. Keeping them locked in place. She got a good look at the vests the bikers were wearing. The patches showed the WKB insignia.

"Greer! We have to get out of here. They're from the WKB. They're bad news. They'd as soon kill someone as look at them."

He smiled at her. Smiled! "I'm kinda hard to kill."

She touched his chest, forcing his attention to her while the bikers swirled around them. "You survived the war. You came home. You don't want to die in this stupid parking lot here in Wyoming."

"You're right. I'll be damned if this is my end." He opened the passenger door of his SUV. "Get in. Lock the doors."

She hurried to do as he asked. Her hands were shaking as she called 911.

4

G reer activated his comm unit as he walked between the two vehicles. "Max, you read me? Got a situation here."

Angel's voice came over the line. *"Not Max. I got ops. Go, Greer."*

"Got a couple WKBers doing wheelies around our vehicles."

"Roger that. I'll alert the police."

"Don't need help. Just calling in an update. Tell Kit the professor had some interesting info. I'll be stopping by on my way up the mountain to hand it over. I'm out."

Greer stepped forward just as one of the bikers peeled in close. A quick punch separated him from his bike. Sparks flashed as the bike spun out across the pavement. The biker rolled twenty feet, then lay still.

The professor's car alarm went off. Greer looked back in time to see the other biker lean into the back passenger door. The doc was already out of his SUV and was doing a tug-of-war with the other biker over her laptop case across the backseat of her car…and she wasn't winning.

Greer jumped up on the hood of her car and ran over the top, leaping down on the opposite side to land on the biker's leg, snapping it against the edge of the floorboard. The biker screamed and fell backward, out of the car empty-handed, holding his shin.

The cop sirens were coming close. Both of the gangbangers hobbled over to their bikes and managed to take off. One of the cop cars stopped beside Greer and the professor, and the other went after the bikers.

Greer looked over at the professor, who was clutching her belongings to her chest as if they were injured children. Her face was ghost white, her eyes huge. He leaned her against her car, afraid she'd drop without some support.

The lady cop came over to them, her hand on her service weapon. "Dr. Chase, you okay?"

"Yes," she said, as if realizing the cop wanted a verbal answer, not just the vigorous head nodding she was doing.

"Who's this?" the cop asked, looking at Greer.

"A friend. Greer Dawson. Thank God you were here," she said, looking up at him.

"You want to tell me what happened?" the cop asked.

"Some bikers just came up and started to harass us."

"They were—" Greer started, but the professor spoke over him.

"Just some random bikers," she said as she white-knuckled her belongings.

"Looks like they were after—"

"Like they were looking for trouble." Again she interrupted him. "I guess, since we were the only ones around, we caught their eye."

He frowned down at her, wondering what she was doing. Without a doubt, the bikers had come for her laptop.

The cop looked from her to him, then nodded. She, too, had caught the professor's redirect. "You should probably clear out. Call the office tomorrow— I may need a statement from you. You all right to drive?"

Doc nodded. The police officer got back in her vehicle, but waited for them to go. Greer looked down at the still panicked woman. "Let me drive you home."

She shook her head. "No. I need my car."

"Then let me follow you home. Just to make sure they aren't waiting for you there."

She breathed a relieved sigh. "You mind?"

"Not at all." He grinned at her. "I'm always up for kickin' some asses."

The drive to her house was short. A few miles only. He checked in with Angel on the way. "Yo, Angel."

"Go, G."

"I thought the WKBers were there for me, but they were after the professor's laptop."

"Word from the cops is they gave them the slip."

"One of them has a broken leg. See if he shows up at a hospital. Don't think he can make it all the way back to the WKB compound without medical attention."

"Roger that."

"I'm taking the professor home. I'll stop by Blade's on my way back up the mountain. I'm out."

Greer followed the professor into a newer townhouse subdivision. Each unit had a garage in the back next to a small yard. He followed Dr. Chase down the alley to her unit. She parked in the garage. He pulled up behind her.

Leaving his engine running, he got out to say good night. She locked her car and faced him, carrying her laptop and purse. The bright glare of his headlights made her eyes huge and her face pale. The night had been a drain.

"Good night, doc."

She didn't answer. He wondered what she wasn't saying.

"You gonna be okay?"

Her "yeah" sounded like a "no."

He looked beyond her to the door into the house. "Want me to clear your house?"

"Yes."

He shut his SUV down, then moved in front of her. "Stay behind me, but keep up with me." Inside, the professor flipped the light switch. The basement was unfinished. The stairwell was the only area drywalled. He checked under the stairs, then they went up them, the doc flipping on lights as they went.

Once he'd cleared the main floor's kitchen, dining room, living room, and powder room, he walked her back to the kitchen and ordered her to stay put while he checked out the upstairs. There were two bedrooms and two baths, all of them free of crazed WKBers.

He came back downstairs. The professor was standing exactly where he'd put her, still clutching her purse and laptop bag. He eased them from her hands and set them on the counter. Taking hold of her hands, he rubbed the tension from them.

"Talk to me. What's in your laptop that the WKB wants?"

"Nothing."

If he hadn't been holding her hands, he wouldn't have felt the flash of tension that passed through her.

"Maybe they just thought I was an easy target."

"Uh-huh. Why didn't you want the cops to know the bikers were WKBers?"

She sighed and pulled away from him as she walked into her living room. Greer followed her and perched himself on the oversized arm of her sofa.

"I took the position with UW two years ago so it would be convenient to research the Friendship Community. I have a grant to support my research and my department has encouraged this line of research. Now, for some reason that I don't understand, things are getting a little tense between me and the department. Honestly, I feel as if my annual review may not go well. First the spray painting on the building, now the run-in with the WKB." She folded her arms. "I'm afraid the provost is going to ask me to shut my research down."

"How can he do that? You aren't using university funds. What about academic freedom? Aren't you supposed to pursue your own research interests?"

"He's afraid of the WKB, thinks they'll endanger the university and its students."

"Why?"

The professor sat on the coffee table. Her knees were pressed together, her palms on her knees. "The WKB shares a border with the Friendship Community. They have, it seems, some kind of a relationship. They help one another. I don't yet understand the particulars."

"Have other things happened involving the WKB?"

Her eyes slowly rose to meet his. "Maybe." Her lips pressed together, then a long breath slowly left her. "I didn't connect the dots at first. Outlaw biker gangs aren't always rational organisms. I've had them swarm my car twice, when no one was around. I almost crashed the second time. After that, I saw them everywhere I went. Once, they even followed me into a grocery store."

"Did they ever say anything to you?"

"No. Things got quiet for a while, then the graffiti happened. My department chair said this was why the provost wanted me to stop my research into the Friendship Community. So I'm already on thin ice with him."

"Seems the WKB thinks you have your research on your laptop. Do you?"

"Some of it."

Greer lowered his head and rubbed his forehead as he considered the implications. What had she stumbled upon? Would it help their mission?

"I think your department chair is right. I think you should put a hold on things. For a little while."

She huffed a sharp breath as she gave him a weak smile. "I don't intimidate easily. If I've stirred up a bees' nest, then I'm close to the honey."

"Oh, you're close, all right. Close to being taken out." He caught her gaze and held it.

"The very fact that my life is even in the equation means something's going on there that shouldn't be."

"You keep saying they are pacifists, but it seems you have your doubts."

She sent him a measuring look, then began pacing. "There's an undercurrent in their community that I can't quite identify. It could simply be reticence on the part of their council to have me there. I don't know. Whatever it is, it's discordant with the way they present themselves."

"What's so important about the Friends that it's worth your life?"

"Studying the social behavior of isolationist societies is what I do. I've documented fourteen other groups. I have over four hundred federally recognized societies to go. I want to know everything there is to know about all of them."

"Why?" He stood and moved into her path, blocking her pacing.

She looked up at him. "If we can't study our social behaviors, how can we really understand anything about each other? How do we know what our societal weaknesses and strengths are? Social science helps us see the structures that shape our lives—many of which we're not even aware of, yet they inform our behavior and dictate our choices. Studying them may help us understand how to improve society. What's more important than that?"

Greer reached out and caught a slim stream of her hair. He ran his fingers down its red-brown length. "Your life?"

She shut her eyes and lowered her head, leaning her cheek against his hand. An electric current jumped between them at the contact, one that made his skin tingle and set his nerves on edge.

"Thank you for being here tonight, making sure I'm safe."

Greer sighed. He drew her into his arms. Pulling her close seemed the right thing to do. She was so little, so slight against his body. She was taking on the world, standing alone against the Friends, the WKB, and the university. Hell, the whole damned world was weighing down her shoulders.

"Doc—"

"Call me Remi."

"Remi. Do you have friends or family you can stay with? A boyfriend? Maybe put this project on hold for a little while so things can cool down?"

"No."

Her hands on his hips distracted him. "No to pausing the project or no to the other stuff?"

"All of it." She looked up at him with her dark forest-green eyes.

"Look, I could crash on your couch for a few hours…"

She shrugged. "I have a perfectly comfortable bed upstairs."

He stared at her, wondering if he was mistaking what he saw there. It had been a long fucking time since a woman gave him such an invitation. He touched her face with the tips of his fingers, then bent forward to kiss her. Her mouth was soft against his.

Aw, hell. Maybe she meant her guest room. "Doc —" He hesitated, despite his own throbbing desire.

"Remi," she corrected.

"You're just scared. You don't want this." He held her face in his hands as he offered her a last out and silently begged her to take it.

"You're right. And you're wrong. I am scared." She looked up at him, her palms flat against his ribs, under his shirt. "And I do want this."

He stroked her face, along the edge of her hair. Her skin was warm. Gone was the pallor that had claimed her since the incident at the university. Color now flushed her cheeks.

He smoothed his thumb over her lips, then kissed her in a closed-mouth touch of lips. Hers were soft and full. Still holding her face, he deepened the kiss, waiting for her to shut him down each step of the way, as if she were patched in to his ex's hate and fear.

She didn't pull away.

Her arms circled his neck, and her body pressed against his. When she leaned her head to the side and opened her mouth, he took what she offered.

When the kiss ended, she smiled and said, "You smell like—" her brow furrowed as she sought to name the scents "—cinnamon and vanilla. I like it."

"A gift from a friend."

She drew back and looked at him. "A girlfriend?"

"No. A guy friend. He felt bad about my empty social calendar and thought a new scent might help." Greer grinned, thinking maybe Val had been right after all. "How about you? You with anyone?" She'd said she wasn't a second ago, but he had to be sure.

"No. I don't tend to do relationships."

"Why?"

"They become cumbersome after a while. I'm a workaholic. Not much for partner material."

"Makes two of us."

"So we doing this?" she asked, her voice warm and husky.

Fuck, yeah. This was how he liked it. Sex, clean and simple. Nothing more. Just mutually satisfying sex. She wasn't going to be around him long enough to regret it. She began lifting the hem of his black T-shirt. His heart beat a little faster.

Her hands palmed his pecs.

"I've never been with a guy as big as you." She smiled. "Nor one as fit. I feel like a gym poser next to you."

"You're perfect. I like the differences between us." He drew back to look her in the eyes.

She lowered her head, then began unbuttoning her blouse. Her hair fell forward. He brushed it back behind her shoulder so he wouldn't miss a second of the skin she was exposing. She pulled her shirt free and dropped it, leaving only her bra and a fine gold chain with an enameled yin-yang emblem.

He ran his hands down her neck, over her collarbone, over her chain, down to the edge of her bra. "Tell me you have condoms."

She nodded. "In my purse."

He followed her into the kitchen. She retrieved a packet from her purse. He looked down at the small package she handed him. "One?"

"I have more upstairs."

"I'm gonna need three before we even hit your bedroom."

"You'll have to make it last. It's all I have down here."

"Then we'll do you first."

5

———

Greer leaned forward and kissed her. Remi felt the smile on his lips and couldn't help smiling back. She wasn't a stranger to casual hookups, but none had felt like this. Maybe Greer was right; this was all about the adrenaline release from what had happened earlier. But maybe it was all about Greer…a terrifying thought she didn't want to entertain.

She wasn't looking for anything permanent, had in fact promised herself she'd never settle down, settle for someone. She was good on her own. Safer. This was just sex. No strings. No commitments. Satisfying and brief.

He pulled his shirt off and dropped it on the kitchen floor. No ink colored his skin. He was ridiculously buff. Remi reached for the light furring on his chest. A dark line led from just above his navel down below the waist of his cargo pants. She traced the path it made down his belly. His muscles tightened.

"You must be a body builder in your off-hours."

He shrugged. "I work out."

"I like it." She smiled up at him.

"Take your jeans off," he said. Judging by the tension in his face, it wasn't a suggestion. She was used to setting the pace in her encounters, taking what she needed.

"I'll do it when I'm ready." She was out of her element here, standing half-naked in front of a man as powerful as he.

He shook his head. "You'll do it now."

She looked up into his intense eyes. There was no give in his expression. Only hunger. He wanted her. Took a second to absorb the heat of his desire. She'd never been desired like this. As if hypnotized, she surrendered. Her heart beat too fast. Her stomach clenched at the touch of her own thumbs going to the closure of her jeans. His eyes never left hers. Her body began an unusual buzzing.

She had the sense she'd never been with a guy like Greer. May never again. She wanted him to kiss her, wanted his hands around her, wanted to slow down what she feared would be intense and fast and too soon over. Why couldn't a night last a thousand years?

She felt safe with Greer, safe as she'd never been since she was twelve. No. Safe as she'd never been— period. And that scared the living bejesus out of her.

Sex. This was only sex. Not forever. Not anything more.

Her eyes watered. God, she wanted so much more. More than she would ever allow herself.

Greer blinked as if speared by her thoughts. A muscle knotted the square corners of his jaw. He reached a hand up to her face. His nostrils flared. His eyes darkened. His gaze dropped to her mouth as his lips took hers. His mouth opened. She pushed up, against him, into the kiss. Her arms went around his bare chest, wide, strong. Her fingers spread over his shoulder blades. His body was layered with muscle upon muscle. Incredibly male.

Her breasts were pressed between their bodies. Something about him made something in her feel feminine. Whole. That she excited him as much as he excited her was powerful. She tilted her head so that they could deepen their kiss. She liked the way his tongue moved in her mouth, stroking hers, tempting hers into his mouth. He gave and he took and he gave. She never wanted it to end.

His other hand came up to grip the side of her face. He broke the kiss and started it again, kissing her upper lip. The corner of her mouth. Remi's breath was coming in fast puffs. He leaned his forehead against hers.

"I should go, really. But, Christ, if I do, I think I'll fucking die. Remi, please, let me see your body." He looked down into her eyes, checking her response. Words had left her. She wanted him around her, in her. He reached for her jean's zipper. His big fingers dropped that short fastener. She noticed the vein on his thumb and ran her thumb over it.

He pushed her jeans down her hips, knelt in front of her to kiss her ribs, her bellybutton, one of her hips as he lowered them down to her ankles. She stepped out of them. He pushed them away, then brought his hands around her thighs. When he palmed the back of her thighs, a shiver whispered over her skin. His face pressed against the soft skin of her belly. She looked down at him, bowed before her. Her hands dug into his hair as she watched the play of muscles over his shoulders and arms as his hands stroked her ass.

She didn't even care that her pink panties didn't match her white bra. It certainly didn't seem to bother him. His fingers slipped under the edge of her lacy boyshorts. She sucked in a breath as his fingers went from outer thigh to inner thigh. He looked up at her, watching her reaction as his fingers slipped the whole way to the back.

She was getting wet. If he touched her, he would know how much she wanted him. He smiled up at her. She wanted the ride he was offering, curious to see where it took them. It wasn't like her to be so passive, but she liked how he was making her feel. She bit her lip as she looked down at him.

He touched her thighs. "You have goosebumps."

She didn't answer. She couldn't.

He straightened and unfastened his belt as he

walked over to the sofa. He disarmed his gun, set it on the coffee table, then sat down to remove his boots and socks. Standing, he shucked his cargo pants. He was commando. Her gaze dropped to his stiff erection which stood rigid and at a slight angle from a nest of dark hair. If she had any doubt he was ready for her, it was gone before she thought it.

He closed the distance between them and handed her the condom. "Cover me."

Her fingers tingled as she opened the packet and rolled it over him. It was a tight fit. She looked up at him. He smiled. Her heart jumped. He took her hand and led her over to the stairs. He sat on the second step and brought her up to the first step. Looking up at her, he tugged her panties down her thighs. When they were at her ankles, she stepped free of them. His gaze moved over her body as he had her straddle him, facing him.

"You ever do it on stairs?" he asked. She shook her head. "It's like a sex gym." His cock was between them, resting against her thigh. He reached around her to unfasten her bra. It was a front opening clasp. He traced the band to the front and opened it, releasing all of her to his view.

He swallowed hard as he looked up at her. She wasn't large breasted, but she wasn't small either. She wondered briefly if she pleased him—a concern she'd never had before. He cupped her breasts in his hands and grinned as if he'd just been given his favorite toy.

She arched her back, pressing herself forward, hungry to join with him.

His hands were warm on her soft flesh. He kissed the top of her breasts, the sides, nuzzling them. When he licked her nipples, she drew a sharp breath in. She put her hands on his shoulders, felt him flex as he moved forward to taste her.

"Greer—I need you."

He pulled back and looked up at her. Leaving her breasts to their own heavy weight, he stroked her thighs, then rubbed his cock against her core. She lifted a bit. He held himself to her opening. She slowly lowered herself over him. He was wide and hard. Her slick body took him all the way in. She wanted to push up and down over him, but he held her hips still. He was throbbing inside her. Tension tightened his face.

She moved his hands to her breasts and held them there as she moved over him. She controlled their joining, moving at the speed she wished until he touched her clit and sent her spiraling into an orgasm.

When the waves eased away, he wrapped his arms around her waist, holding her until her breathing returned to normal. She realized he hadn't come yet. He was still like iron inside her. She rocked her hips against his. He hissed a breath, then eased her off his lap. He caught her hand and started up the stairs. At the landing, she moved in front of him.

Halfway up the stairs, he said, "Remi, wait."

She stopped and looked back at him. "Bend over."

"Here?"

He nodded. "Right here. Right now."

She did as he asked. She was sprawled over a couple of steps on the second upward set of stairs. He moved her legs farther apart and entered her. Leaning over her, he knelt on the step below her and braced himself on the step above her. She felt him sweep the hair from her neck, then kiss the back of her neck, her shoulder. Each long thrust into her made her nipples brush against the stair under her. She felt so much of him this way. She didn't want it to end, but she was already close to peaking again.

His hand stroked the length of her back, moved around front, and caught her breast. He moved it down her ribs, going between her hips to play with her clitoris. She never thought she could orgasm like she did right there on the stairs. She cried out, pressing herself back against him.

When he pulled out of her, he was still hard. He led her up to the top step. Her body was still heated and hungry. He sat on the top step and drew her onto his lap. He kissed her chest, her neck, her chin. He leaned her back and bent over her to tongue her breast as he entered her.

She caught the banister and held on to his wide upper arm. "I'm going to fall, Greer."

"Never gonna happen. Not while you're in my arms. Hold on to me and let yourself go."

He filled her completely. When he straightened, he leaned her against him. His tempo increased. One hand held her hip, the other her back, pressing her breasts to his chest. She lifted his face so she could kiss him. Midway through the kiss his orgasm hit. He pistoned inside of her, pumping hard and fast, sending her off again at the same time he found his own release.

He smiled as she came down from the high of passion. She touched his cheek and smiled back. He caught her face, bringing her to him for a kiss, one that promised the night was long from over.

He stood, lifting her with him, keeping their bodies joined as he carried her into her bedroom. He withdrew and set her on her feet next to the bed. "Want me to leave, Remi?"

No. She didn't, and that should have panicked her. Instead, she felt a wonderful warmth she wasn't ready to let go of. "No. I want you to stay."

"Good."

Remi's bed was a crisp white-on-white set of cotton pillows and duvet cover. The air conditioning made the room cool. Greer ditched the condom in her bathroom. When he came back, Remi was in the middle of the bed. He picked the side nearest the door and settled next to her.

She moved closer, draping herself over his chest, twining her leg with his. He kissed her forehead, letting his lips linger there. He closed his eyes, enjoying the feel of her in his arms, warm and sated. Her fingers were playing with his chest hair.

"Tired?" he asked.

"I am. Thank you for staying. I would have been scared alone."

He knew the feeling well. He hated being alone when he slept. "Close your eyes and sleep." He felt the sigh she drew as if it came from his own lungs.

"I hope you're going to be around here for a little while."

"I am. A very little while."

"I'd like to see more of you. While you're here."

Greer smiled as he touched her face. "You've seen all of me."

She shook her head. "I've only seen your shell."

His smile faded. "It's dark inside the shell. Not a place for someone like you."

"Because of the war?"

"Because of my war." He reached for the sheet and drew it up over her shoulder. "Remi—before I leave, can I take a copy of your laptop?"

She pulled the sheet with her and sat up slightly to look down at him. "No."

He touched her arm. "The WKB's like a—" he struggled for the right word "—a flesh eating bacteria. Given a task, they will keep throwing resources at it until it's achieved or until they're ended. You don't know what they're after. Let me try to see what it is they want."

"My laptop has a good amount of my research on it. I can't risk that."

"I'm not going to mess it up. I'll take an image and use some of my team's analytics to figure it out. Your data's going no farther than my team."

She frowned. "You have a team?"

"Yeah."

"Why? What are you working on? What is so important about Sally that she's of interest to the Department of Homeland Security?"

"Sally is a symptom of a bigger issue. She's a lead we're following."

"Villalobo said you're working on a case. What is it?"

"I don't have clearance to tell you."

"You want me to share my data, put my sources at risk—without any information from you. No."

"I'm asking for your help. Have your sources committed any crimes? Are they engaged in treasonous behavior?"

"No. They're pacifists, Greer. They're good people who just want to live their lives."

"Then we don't give a shit about them. I need to know what it is the WKB wants so damn badly that they'll expose themselves to outsiders in order to get."

"The Friends are not involved in anything treasonous."

"They're friendly with the WKB. Makes them guilty by association."

"Don't do this. Please don't do this. I promised

them I would protect them in exchange for opening their community to me. No one, ever, has been allowed as close as I've gotten. My research is unique in my field. The Friends are one of the few surviving utopian societies from the nineteenth century. That's huge."

Greer touched her face, easing a lock of hair from her eyes. "Remi, something very bad is underway. When I said it was a war, I wasn't being dramatic. You know the Friends. I know the WKB. You don't want to be in their sights."

She leaned away from him. "I think you should go."

Greer sighed. "All right." He swept the sheet off and crossed the room naked.

Remi put a robe on and followed him downstairs. He dressed, then holstered his weapon. He looked at her, reluctant to go—and not because he hadn't succeeded in securing her information. "This isn't over. The WKB are going to keep coming at you."

She crossed her arms. "I'm sorry I can't help you." Her hair was still mussed from bed. She was rumpled and bed-warm and sexy as hell.

Greer looked at her beautiful face, and wished things were different.

The life he'd chosen to live had cost him everything so far—his parents, his sisters and their families, and his fiancée —all of his options were owned by the war he fought. He had no latitude for dreams.

"Night, Remi."

"*Goodbye*, Greer."

He nodded, not once doubting he'd hear from her again.

GREER WIPED the last of his shaving cream from his face. He'd managed a few hours sleep after he got to Blade's last night. He was up early so he could catch the team up with the info Remi found.

He heard someone come into his room. He stepped out of the bathroom, naked, to find Max standing with crossed arms at the end of the short hallway into his room. Angel was leaning against his dresser, grinning at him. Val was seated in the armchair by the window.

"You're right," Max growled, looking at him but talking to the others. "He does have a certain glow about him."

"How would you know?" Greer asked.

Max arched a brow. "You think the shower washed it off?"

"We saw you sneaking in to the house on the camera," Angel told him.

"I wasn't sneaking in. I live here."

"Whatevs. Who is she?" Val asked.

Greer sighed, then moved into his closet to pull on a fresh pair of cargo pants. He came out drawing a black tee over his head.

"He rescued a professor last night at UW," Angel told the group.

"Whoa. You're banging a cougar?" Val asked. "Kinda Oedipal, but yeah, go for it."

"Val, you're a sick motherfucker," Greer complained.

"Not me. You're the one doing a professor."

"What makes you think all professors are old?" Greer asked. "And why are you guys so curious about my love life?" His glance swept the three of them. They all spoke at the same time.

"Um…the word 'professor'?" Val answered.

"Who said anything about love?" Angel asked.

"Because you have no life," Max added.

"Her name's Dr. Remington Chase." He looked at Val. "And she's only a few years older than me."

"She have any friends?" Angel asked.

Greer had to think about that. The vibe he got from Remi was that she was something of a loner. He shook his head. "Somehow, I don't think so."

"Way to represent the team," Val said as he stood and crossed the room. "I'm going to breakfast. At least I can satisfy one appetite."

Angel followed him, scowling at Greer as he went by.

Max stayed behind. Greer glared at him. "What?"

"Chasing Dr. Chase?"

"She's a sociologist who's studying the Friendship Community. She did some population analysis that might be interesting to us."

"Like what?"

"She discovered an anomaly in the community which seems to indicate that, while it's growing in size, it isn't doing so from within. They're losing a large percentage of their teenagers. Enough that without outsiders joining the community, it would have imploded long before now."

Max frowned. "She know anything about Lion and his pride?"

"Haven't asked."

"What was up with the WKB and you last night? I almost had to leave a really warm bed to pull your hide out of trouble."

Greer laughed. "Have you ever had to pull me out of trouble?"

"What happened?"

"Couple bikers started doing donuts around us. I thought they were there for me, but seems they wanted Remi's laptop."

"Did they get it?"

"No."

"What was on it?"

"She won't let me look at it—yet."

6

Greer felt itchy with everyone looking at him when the team convened in the den after breakfast.

"How's your research going?" Kit asked. He didn't even bother hiding his grin. Greer sent Max a glare, only to be met with a smirk.

"Remi's got—"

"Remi?" Kit interrupted him.

"Dr. Remington Chase. Are you gonna torture me, Kit?"

"Yes."

Greer shook his head. "Doc Chase has some interesting research on the Friendship Community." He told the team what she showed him, passing her graphs around.

"So where are the new Friends coming from?" Blade asked.

"Don't know. She knows the community has a

relationship with the WKB, but she doesn't appear to know what that association is for." He looked at Kit. "She never mentioned the pride."

"Some of those kids may be going into the various prides," Max said. "Lion said there were several of them."

"Some of the new members may be coming from the WKB, but I didn't see any movement between the WKB and the Friends while I was scoping things out," Greer said. "And the professor seemed to think the Friends had a closed community."

A knock sounded on the door to the den. The room went silent. "Ivy's here. I want to go over the background check that came back on one of her new waitresses. After that, let's do some research into the data Greer brought us," Kit said as he opened the door to let Ivy in.

He led her over to one of the chairs in front of Blade's big desk, which he propped himself on the corner of. "We have the background search results back for your new employee, Candace 'Ace' Myers. They're not what we expected."

Ivy frowned. "How so?"

"I can't put my finger on it. All the requisite info is in her file, but that's all. Her performance in school was standard. She's paid her taxes on time since she was sixteen. She paid cash for her used beater. She uses a prepaid cellphone. She doesn't own a credit— or even a debit—card. She's moved a dozen times since she was twenty-one."

"How old is she?" Val asked.

"Twenty-four."

Ivy frowned. "I don't see what you're trying to say, Kit. She hasn't broken any laws…"

"No. She hasn't," Max said, staring at her beneath lowered brows. "Nonetheless, something's not right with her. Why can't she keep a job? Why move around so much? Why pay cash for everything?"

"She said she was trying to keep ahead of an ex-boyfriend who was stalking her. Besides that, she's a kid. She doesn't know what she wants."

Kit pressed his lips together as a sigh hissed from his nose. "You don't need this trouble. Let her go. We can't take chances right now."

"I don't see her as a risk. I'm not letting her go. I've been in her shoes, struggling to pay bills and feed myself and Casey."

"She have a kid?" Val asked.

"No—she's just one herself. Her fear is real. What I would have given if someone had come forward and helped me when I most needed it. No one did"—she looked at Kit—"until you. I can help this girl. I need to help her."

Greer could see Kit digging in. Before he issued an irrevocable edict, Greer tossed out an idea. "Let Val go talk to her. There's not a woman alive who wouldn't hand over all of her secrets to him if he just smiles at her."

"Not me," Val disagreed. "I've lost my mojo. Let Max go see her."

Ivy vehemently shook her head. "Oh, no. He'll scare the hell out of her and send her running."

"Maybe that's for the best," Max said, looking at Ivy.

"What happened to your mojo, Val?" Greer asked, wondering if he'd won the bet he and Max had running about whether he or Owen would win Selena. "I've never known you not to be a magician with women."

Val sighed loudly. His head dropped back against the top of the sofa. "Don't know. It's just gone. I got nothing."

Greer grinned at Max, who gave him a quelling glare.

Kit shook his head. "Ivy, we've been warned that a woman was going to infiltrate our team. Your history, your profile, everything about you has been wide open for anyone to discover. If our enemies wanted to send an operative to get under your defenses—and through you to us—what better way than to send someone who reminds you of you, someone who immediately engages your sympathies?"

Ivy's shoulders slumped. "I'm not good at this game you play..."

"It's not a game," Kit corrected.

She met his hard eyes. "I take people as they represent themselves. If she has anything to do with what's going on, of course I'll dismiss her. If she really is a scared girl who's down on her luck, then I want to help her."

"Val will go," Kit said. He looked at the blond warrior who was still lost in his dramatic moment. "Strike up a friendship with her. Find out the truth… or at least come back with a gut feeling we can go off of." He looked at Ivy. "Whatever he finds, we're going to live with it, feel me? If she's trouble, we're handing her over to Lobo. I'm not putting you or the team in jeopardy."

Ivy nodded. She sent a glance around the room at the guys. "Thanks. I appreciate your help."

They stood as the meeting broke up. Val didn't look even moderately interested in his assignment. His hands were in his pockets. "So, what can you tell me about your new girl? What does she look like? What shift does she work?"

"The dinner shift, one to nine. She's of medium height. Reddish purple hair, kind of shoulder length."

Max took out his phone. "I slipped a tracker in her purse when I was at the diner yesterday doing some maintenance on the cameras. If you want to run into her somewhere other than the diner, let me or Greer know."

"She usually stops for a coffee a few doors down from the diner before coming in to work," Ivy said.

Val put his arm around her shoulders and walked her to the door. "I'll let you know what I find." He looked back at Kit. "I'm not as certain as you are that I can still trust my gut."

VAL SPOTTED Ivy's girl coming out of the tiny coffee shop straight ahead of him. All of his senses went on alert. A zing of anticipation rippled beneath his skin, across his back, and down his arms. He had no chance to catalog his reaction to her further because she was coming toward him fast, head down as she looked at her phone.

He managed to both trip her and catch her within a single motion. Her coffee went a few feet into the air, tumbled lid over bottom several times before exploding as it slammed into the pavement.

"Geez, walk much?" she snapped, pushing free of his hold. She turned and glared up at him, flashing lichen-green eyes at him beneath the rough fringe of her hair.

Val lifted his brows in an affronted expression. "I believe you ran into me." He looked her over. "You okay? Did it spill on you?"

She looked herself over. "No."

He retrieved the ruined cup. "Let me get you a replacement."

She shook her head and held up a hand. "Forget it. Just forget it."

He picked up the empty cup and lid, then tossed it in the trash. "If I don't get you another, the rest of my day will be a wreck. Cheating a woman out of her coffee is like taking ice cream from a kid; it's just mean. C'mon. Come back in with me and order a replacement. On me."

The girl's eyes narrowed, masking their shocking color. "So you admit you ran into me…"

Val smiled slowly. "Maybe. I tend to lose track of my feet if one of them isn't in my mouth."

That got a little smile out of her. He noticed her canines were angled slightly. And sharp. In fact, all of her was sharp angles. Her chin. Her shoulders. Her brows were dark and overly thin, enhanced with a narrow pencil into an artificial arch. Her nose was straight and narrow. Her box-dyed punk auburn hair blew about her oval face, emphasizing the haphazard way it was cut, as if she'd chopped at it herself. Her eyes were outlined in black, giving her a hint of goth. She was waif-lean and stood in jeopardy of having the stiff breeze blow her away. She looked urban and out of place in podunk Wolf Creek Bend.

She lowered her gaze, but not before he caught a flash of emotion from her. *Pain*. He frowned.

"Fine. Let's just get that coffee," she snapped. She went back to the shop and yanked the door open, neglecting to hold it for him. He followed her inside, watching her walk. Her jeans were skintight. She wore a cheap pair of canvas slip-ons.

At the counter, Ivy's girl—Ace—looked at him, then at the menu board, then selected the largest, most convoluted coffee beverage possible, complete with several customizations. Val ordered a house coffee. And he had the cashier warm up two ham and cheese croissants.

"I'm not eating with you," Ace said.

He paid for their order. "It's not for you." He looked at her. "One for me and one for the homeless guy on the corner by the market."

She looked out the front window toward the market.

"Just kidding. There are no homeless people here in Wolf Creek Bend."

Her eyes met his. She blinked. *Pain.* Like brass knuckles slamming his chest. The hell with Ivy and the team; he wanted to know her story for himself. He was a sucker for a woman in need. He could see why Ivy had had the reaction she did.

Because of the special twists she'd ordered, his coffee and sandwiches were served first. He waited with her.

"You can go."

He grinned. "Dismissing me?"

She bunched one side of her mouth. "Just feeling protective of this cup of coffee. Don't want to get tangled up with you and lose it again."

"Probably a good call." He nodded toward the apron she was holding, the uniform for servers at Ivy's diner. "Look, do you have a minute? I thought maybe we could have our coffee in the garden area. Have you seen it?"

"I've walked past it—"

He smiled at her, his best panty-melting smile, and tilted his head. "It's like a secret garden. A beautiful place to drink coffee."

He opened the door for her. The day was as hot as

any late summer day. One of the nice things about Wyoming was how dry it was. The day's hundred degrees felt closer to eighty. He walked past a couple of cafe tables out front on his way into the sitting garden on the side. He heard her behind him and was relieved she'd followed him.

An iron fence, covered with climbing roses, separated the garden from the sidewalk. Inside the arched entryway was a large patio paved with red bricks. Flowering plants of dozens of different colors and textures, in-ground and in pots, softened the hard edges of the buildings that the garden sat between.

Val picked a small table and set his tray down. He looked over at Ace. She wore an odd mixture of curiosity and ambivalence. She put her purse on the ground and draped her apron over the back of her chair, then moved her chair around the table, letting her sit with a view to the entry gate. She fingered the cardboard band around her coffee.

Val sat and pushed the plate with one of the croissants toward her. "Eat."

"Don't want it."

"I didn't buy them both for me."

"You're a big guy. They're probably just an appetizer for you."

"You're a skinny girl. You could probably eat a dozen of these."

Her lips thinned.

"I'll eat one if you eat one," he suggested.

She drew the thick china plate toward her. "I don't usually do this."

"Do what? Have coffee with a new friend? Have coffee outside?"

"Yeah. All of that." She took a bite of the croissant. He watched, hoping for a sight of her angled canines. Her bite was too careful to show her teeth. She held the croissant in her long-fingered hands. Her nails were short and painted black. They were neatly trimmed, but the paint job was a selfie.

"Been here long?" Val asked after swallowing his bite.

"No." She lifted the croissant to her mouth, then lowered it as she glared at him. "Look, we don't have to talk."

"Prickly little thing, aren't you?"

"Who the fuck cares?"

Val grinned. "Fine. We'll just speak with our eyes." He tried to quit smiling. Christ, it was fun to meet a female who challenged him. Maybe that was what he'd liked best about Selena.

Ace's eyes narrowed. Val's widened. She cracked a grin. "Are you always this noisy?"

Val sighed. "So my friends tell me. You gonna tell me to shut up, too?" The wind fingered her hair, agitating the ragged locks. They looked soft. He imagined them slipping between his fingers.

"You don't seem like you're from around here," she observed aloud.

"I'm not."

"So, what are you doing here?"

"Fishing. Corporate retreat. Team building or some such shit."

"You don't like it here?"

"It's quieter than I'm used to."

She finished her last bite, then got to her feet. "Sorry to eat and run"—she held up her apron—"but I really do need to get to work."

He stood up. "You work at Ivy's?"

"Yeah. You know her?"

"Doesn't everyone know everyone in a little town like this?"

She made a tense smile that was gone as soon as it appeared. She held up her coffee cup. "Well, glad you ran into me!"

Val laughed. He stopped her as she was about to step through the metal arch. "Hey—I don't know your name…"

She looked back at him. *Pain.* He sucked in a breath, trying to mentally unwind the thorny vine climbing through his ribs, reaching for his heart. "It's Ace. Ace Myers."

"I'm Val." He grinned. "Val Parker."

She didn't mirror his humor. She only nodded, then slipped away.

Greer frowned at the screen. It was as if Remi had appeared out of thin air seventeen years ago, the summer before she started high school in northern Colorado. She'd been homeschooled through middle school. No records existed from her primary school years. She flunked three out of five classes her freshman year of high school. She did summer school that year, then managed to carry a 3.5 grade average the rest of her high school years.

Her social security number was issued the summer before high school. Her dental and medical records began that year as well. He couldn't find records for her prior to that summer seventeen years ago.

Her mom's tax returns showed they'd been living in the same house from Remi's birth until she left for college. The whole package had fit so neatly until that detail; the house listed on her tax returns hadn't been built until Remi was ten.

He looked up her mother's employers over the years. All were small businesses that had existed for less than three years. He called up her driver's license. It was issued the year they showed up in northern Colorado.

He blew the picture up and stared into the eyes of Remi's mom. Joan Chase. A chill scraped his spine. Eerie how much she looked like her daughter—he recognized the fear in her eyes. The photo was seventeen years old. She was, in this pic, only a little older than her daughter was now.

What happened to her? She disappeared from all records when Remi graduated from high school.

Remi was as much an enigma as her mom. She

moved on to Colorado State University after high school, graduating with a Bachelor of Arts in Sociology. She took her masters degree in Sociology from Stanford and her Ph.D. in Sociology from Princeton.

Why sociology? Who the hell picked sociology if they hoped to support themselves after school? Maybe her goal all along was to be a professor. She certainly was passionate about her field.

Greer got up from the computer in the ops room and walked away, moving absently through the hall and into the big conference room. He rubbed his face. The eyes of his dream flashed through his mind, sounding an alarm.

Remi didn't exist. Not on paper, only in the flesh. Someone set up her identity. He went back to his computer, determined to find out who she really was.

Six hours later, he had found what he needed to know. He went upstairs through the den. Owen and Kit were there, talking quietly.

"S'up, Greer?" Kit asked. "You look like you have bad news."

Greer frowned. "I checked out the professor. Her identity is an illegal one her mom purchased from a black market vendor seventeen years ago when they left the Grummond Society."

Kit leaned back in his chair in front of Owen's desk. "What's the Grummond Society?"

"A polygamist group in southern Colorado."

Kit looked at Owen, then back at Greer. "Are they connected with the Friends or the WKB?"

"No."

"Didn't she need a criminal background check before the university hired her?" Owen asked.

"Possibly, but she's been in her false identity since she was fourteen. It would have passed inspection since she doesn't have a criminal record in that ID or any other associated with her fingerprints."

"Does she know her identity's bogus?" Kit asked.

"Not sure," Greer said.

"Maybe Jafaar Majid knows," Kit mused. "Maybe it's what he's blackmailing her with so he can force her to be the 'butterfly' he told Rocco about. If her university finds out, her career is over."

Greer shrugged. "It's a stretch to think she's the mole. I went to her. She didn't come to us. They couldn't anticipate that connection before we'd made it. She doesn't want anything to do with our investigation. She's unwilling to expose her data and reveal the confidential sources of her research. If she were being blackmailed, she'd be a whole lot more willing to be helpful so that she could get inside."

"You could be right," Kit said. "We just heard back from Val. He said Ivy's waitress is hiding something. Said she was hyper-vigilant during their chat, kept herself on alert the whole time."

"We have no idea who Jafaar's butterfly is," Owen said. "Could be more than one person. May not even be female. Hell. It could even be Lobo's new boss. Let's just keep our eyes open and be aware."

Greer nodded. "Could be false info he's feeding us

to distract us or to see where it washes out in our network."

"Or that." Kit stood up. "If you think your professor has some useful info, get the scoop on what she knows of her identity."

7

Greer repositioned himself on the ridge overlooking the Friendship Community. He'd come back out to continue observing the Friends, trying to get a sense of their behavior patterns. It was past one a.m. The community had rolled up its figurative sidewalks hours ago. They didn't spend a lot of time awake after dark, he'd learned—if he were to judge by the few cottages that were lit after sunset. In the daytime, they were busy in their gardens and fields, doing laundry, cleaning their cabins. Or baking. Geez, the sweet scents from their kitchens wafted up to his stand every day.

He checked his watch. It was time to rendezvous with the team. The place he'd picked for the meetup was near the community's entrance. The spot was accessible by their SUVs via a forest service road; it would be easy for the guys to get in and get out. He stood and slung his pack over his shoulder.

Something triggered his inner alarm. He went still, channeling all of his attention to what he was hearing…or not hearing. At all hours of the day and night, the woods were alive with large and small game. The forest never slept, but tonight, it was silent.

He wasn't alone. Needles pricked along his spine. Aw, Christ. Not here. Not in the dark nether world of the woods. He watched and waited, calming his rapid breath.

He definitely had picked up a ghost somewhere along the line.

His grandfather had taught him how to calm his pulse, quiet his breathing, open his senses. *They can hear your thoughts, you know, the people you're tracking,* he'd told Greer. *Thought waves go first, tickling the senses. Empty your mind. Silence it,* his grandfather had warned.

Same held true for ghosts.

He and his grandfather had spent an entire summer on self-control. His mind, his thinking, his bio impulses. His grandfather had begun mentoring when he was eight. Puberty had wreaked havoc with more than his body; he'd had to relearn the lessons of an eight-year-old once he'd started his shift into adulthood. The mental facility of a child was far shallower than that of an adult, and the lessons in puberty were intense. Everything that had come before was like kindergarten compared to the real shit his grandfather set loose when Greer's body had reached its full size and power.

And now, in moments like these, he could become

nothing—nothing sentient anyway. Just air and shadows, seeking the source of the disturbance he'd felt, protecting himself from the ghost. He heard a breath, felt a chill on his skin. The temperature in the woods had dropped twenty degrees. A movement out of the corner of his eye caught his attention.

Someone was out there. A woman, maybe. He'd seen a flash of clothes before she slipped behind a tree. A sleeve, or the edge of a skirt. It happened too fast to say. He waited a second, polling his senses for anything else that might be near.

Everything was silent and still.

He moved in the direction of the woman. He caught another flash of clothing, long hair, pale-looking in the moonlight. They were heading down a hill, away from the village. She was moving quickly, as if something had spooked her. Maybe she'd seen his ghost.

Greer sped up, determined to catch her. Why had one of the girls from the village run away? Where was she going? He looked behind him to see if anyone was after her. They were going up a hill now. He topped the ridge and came to an abrupt halt.

A different woman—one that was flesh and blood —was scrambling down the hill, her flashlight bouncing like a laser show. She stumbled once. Greer hurried to help her, but she got to her feet and continued down the hill. They were headed toward the forest service road. When he saw her car, he knew who she was.

What was Remi doing here in the woods at night?

She hadn't come far from her car. Standing in front of it, arms folded, legs spread, were three of the guys. She came to a full stop. Helluva welcoming committee. She flashed her light at them, then turned it on him. She stood to the side, trying to keep herself from being sandwiched between them.

"Greer? That was you?" she asked, relaxing just slightly.

"Yeah. What are you doing here?"

"I was just leaving—I've been here all day."

He hadn't seen her, but he'd spent most of the afternoon in the woods between the WKB property and the Friends'.

"I was almost to my car when I thought I saw a girl."

"You saw her, too?" he asked.

Remi nodded. "I lost her though. I thought, maybe, she was running away. Who are these men?"

He moved closer. "Friends. Val, Kelan, and Angel —meet Remi Chase."

She gave them a long look, then switched her attention to Greer. "Your team?"

"Yeah. Part of it, anyway."

"What are you doing here?" she asked.

"Scoping things out."

"You're on Friendship land." She gave him an injured look. "Greer, don't do this."

"What?"

"Be here…anywhere near here. Please. You put all my work in jeopardy."

"We aren't engaging the Friends."

She put a hand on her hip. It was dark and hard to tell, but she may have stomped her foot. "Greer Dawson, your hand's in the proverbial cookie jar. Don't you dare tell me the Friends aren't why you're here."

"Actually, ma'am," Angel said, "we were going to do some night fishing."

"Want to join us?" Val asked.

"No," she snapped, then looked at him. "This is not a game. If the Friends catch you, they'll think I brought you here, that I've sneaked you in behind their backs."

"I've been here on and off for a week. No one has seen me yet."

He heard the shocked breath she drew. "So that's it? The hell with everything I've worked toward? The hell with three years' effort?"

He stepped toward her. "Bring me in."

"No. They aren't your enemies. They aren't anything to you."

"Let me see that for myself."

"No. Dammit, Greer. No." She moved toward her car. Angel was blocking access to the driver's door. She glared up at him.

"Let her go," Greer ordered.

Angel turned sideways, but stayed in her space. She unlocked her car with her key fob, then quickly locked it again once she was inside. They watched as she pulled out of the small parking lot and headed back down the long dirt road.

"Why's your woman prowling around the Friends at night?" Angel asked.

Greer shook his head. "She's not my woman." He rubbed the back of his neck. "Say, did you guys see her go up the ridge? How far up had she gotten?"

"About where you met her," Kelan said. "Why?"

"Because there was someone else in the woods. She and I both saw her. A girl. I thought she was running away from the village, like most of their teens seem to. I wanted to catch her. She came straight this way. Didn't you see her?"

"There was no one but your little professor." Val hooked his thumbs in the corners of his front pockets of his cargo pants. "You said you wanted to give us an overview of the village?"

"Yeah. This way." He'd had the guys come out so that they could see for themselves the layout of the village. He'd found the best vantage point, the perfect spot for a sniper, should things come to that.

Greer looked over his shoulder to the dark woods down the ridge. Maybe he and Remi had both been mistaken. Could have been the backside of a mule deer they'd been chasing. She—it—ran over the ridge right where the professor was standing. It must have darted away just before breaking out of the woods.

Then again, maybe Remi had scrambled his head more than he'd like to admit.

TWO POLICE CARS were parked out front of the campus building that housed the University of Wyoming's sociology department when Greer arrived the next morning.

He went up the three flights of stairs to the fourth floor. There were several small clusters of students and staff clogging the hallway. He wove his way around them as he headed toward Remi's office. The cops were inside, one interviewing the doc, the other talking to a younger man. The doc's office had been wrecked. Piles of books and papers spilled out of drawers and shelves, furniture was toppled, bits of broken glass crunched anytime anyone moved.

Greer drew back and dialed the team's ops center. He could have used his comm unit, but that would have drawn unwanted attention.

"*Go,*" Max said on the other line.

"Someone hit the professor's office. Looks like it happened overnight. Cops are here taking statements. Can you take a look at their cameras, see what you can find out?"

"*On it.*"

The cops went past him. Some of the people in the hall cleared out, following her assistant, who'd been with the professor. Greer stepped inside her office. Remi was on her knees gathering a pile of papers. She looked over at the metal filing cabinet they came from. The thieves must have used a crowbar to pry the thing open; it was completely unusable. She shook the papers free of glass fragments and looked up. Her eyes widened as she saw him there.

A dozen thoughts raced through her eyes. He felt each of them.

He knelt on the debris in front of her. "Remi—"

She shook her head, stopping him, then resumed grabbing papers.

He started to separate papers from glass, too.

"Why are you here?" she asked.

"I wanted to apologize for scaring you last night."

She paused and looked up at him. Her forest-green eyes seemed to be holding back a monsoon's worth of tears. If he ever wanted to slay dragons, it was hers. Jesus, he wanted to fucking shred them.

"I think you should go."

Greer lifted the corner of her desk and used his booted foot to push some papers out of the way. "I can help clean up—" His eyes begged her to let him.

She shook her head. "I'm in enough trouble. I've been summoned to the provost's office. I don't know why all of this is happening, but it won't be good for me if the university finds Homeland has an interest in it, too."

She got to her feet and set the stack of papers she'd made on top of her desk. She wiped the back of her hand against her eyes. He pulled her into his arms. It was the only thing he knew to do.

She leaned into him. "It's never good when the provost calls you in."

"I'm sorry," he said. "I'll go." Her arms went around him. His hold tightened on her. "Can I call you later?"

She looked up and met his eyes. Something in him snapped—into place or broke, he wasn't sure which. "Please do."

Greer gave her a soft smile, willing her to be strong. Briefly, the tension in her face eased, which further twisted his gut.

A sound behind him startled them. Remi pulled away. A suit stood at the door, giving him a dark look. His gaze shifted over to Remi. "Ready?"

Remi squared her shoulders and drew a breath. "I am." She grabbed a pad of paper and a pen, then shot him a look.

The suit was looking at him again. "You're the one Dr. Chase was with when she was attacked by the bikers."

Greer nodded. "Yeah. I was."

Remi gave him a strange glance. "Dr. Zimmers, my friend Greer Dawson." The two men nodded at each other. Greer felt the muscles at the corners of his jaw tighten. He looked at Remi, whose face was a mask of resolve. "I'll call you later—unless you want me to wait?"

She shook her head. "We'll talk later."

He went into the hall and phoned Max. "What do you have?"

"Cameras showed a medium-height man in a black hoodie and cap come down the hallway from the elevators. He had a crowbar. He was in the professor's office about five minutes. That's it."

"Did he have anything with him when he left?"

"Not that the cameras showed."

"First her laptop, then her office. What are they looking for?"

The air-conditioning system kicked on. Geez, the university had to have it set to freezer. He blew air to see if his breath showed.

"See if you can get her to let you have a look at her data. If the WKB wants it, we do, too."

Greer caught a flash of something from the corner of his eye. He looked down the hall in time to see a young woman's blond head and shoulder slip between two groups of students in the hallway.

"Roger that. I gotta go," Greer said, dropping the connection.

People were moving about the hall, checking bulletin boards, standing at office doors. He moved around them, trying to see the girl. His height was an ally, for he looked the long way down the hall and saw her just as she turned the corner.

He jogged after her and spun around the corner to an empty hall. It was by the bank of elevators. One of boxes was descending. He watched it land on the ground floor, then ran down the stairs. He came out onto the lobby area as the elevator was heading back upstairs.

He looked around the small area, down both hall-ways. No blond in sight. He walked outside. People were moving around. The campus wasn't in session yet, so it wasn't terribly crowded. The girl was nowhere to be found.

He shoved his hands into his hair and squeezed his eyes shut. Lifting his face, all he saw against the red wash of his eyelids were the dead eyes from his dream, judging him. He felt cold in the hot summer sun. He opened his eyes and stared up at the blue, blue sky.

He was either losing his mind or—yeah, he was losing his mind. No fucking way around it.

8

Remi took her plate of scrambled eggs and fruit out to the sofa in her living room. She ate a few bites before setting it down. She wasn't hungry. Couldn't focus. She was numb—gratefully so, too.

She'd worked hard to be where she was. And now she had nothing. Well, not true. She had a mortgage, a car payment, a mountain of student debt, and no income if she decided she couldn't comply with the provost's ultimatum.

She paced. Her townhouse wasn't huge. Just the living room, dining room, and kitchen on the main floor. Only took a minute to make the circuit. She did it again. A third time made her a little dizzy, so she sat on the stairs and looked at her place.

What the hell was she going to do? Sociology professorships weren't easy to come by. And she'd wanted this one in particular so that she could complete her study of the Friendship Community.

She leaned forward and rested her forehead on her knees. The university had been excited about her career when she interviewed two years ago. They looked forward to her research projects. They knew when they hired her that she was researching the Friends.

She thought back to when she started to have problems with her department. It wasn't until earlier this summer that her department chair had begun sending a strange vibe her way. The facade he'd presented to the campus police when she was being questioned about the graffiti was his posturing at its best.

She braced her elbows on her knees, then propped her chin up. The Friendship Community wasn't the first group she studied that did some pushback. Most of them did. That which lived in cults liked ignorance and darkness. Anything that shined a light on it was a threat.

The strange thing was that none of the pushback she'd received on this project came from the Friends themselves. All of it was from the WKB. Even before the spray-painting episode, she'd twice had club bikers flank her car on the ride home, forcing other cars off the road.

Put this project on hold until the campus police complete their investigation. Once we know your work isn't endangering you or the students and staff here, we'll reevaluate, the provost had warned.

She had to comply—too much was at stake. But how would the WKB know she had parked her work? What if it had already gone too far to reverse what was happening? She lowered her face to her palms, wishing for a single thought that didn't cause her distress.

Greer instantly came to mind, with his hard face and soft eyes. There was something in the way he looked at her, the way she felt when he held her. She realized, slowly, she was sitting where she had had the most amazing sex of her life, thanks to him. Heat washed through her, dispelling the chill that had been with her ever since discovering the mess in her office.

Was it only a coincidence that he showed up the same time the trouble from the WKB intensified? And the men he called friends…they all looked like mercenaries. Macho guys like that weren't usually friends by choice. They were too competitive to join up with others like themselves. Usually, only one supremely alpha male existed in a group of men, because, by their very nature, they were a threat to each other.

She left the stairs and moved absently into the living room. She needed a plan. Could she continue quietly compiling her notes, and risk her future at the university? Surely, she couldn't really be fired, could she?

But if she did continue working on articles based on her existing research—even without additional field work—and if the problems escalated, would she be liable? Was she willing to risk that?

And if she wrote the articles but didn't submit them for review at strategic journals until things were clear, would she be derailing herself from her tenure track by not having publishable research?

She heard a motorcycle come down the parking area in front of her townhouse. And another, their engines rumbling loudly in the quiet night. One of her neighbors had a Harley. She assumed he was just getting home, bringing a friend with him.

Over the next few minutes, a few more bikes joined the first. She heard them now from the front and rear of her building. She got up and looked out the back window, over her tiny backyard and garage, to the alley where the bikers had stopped. Three of them, their bikes right at her fence.

As she watched, they kicked in her gate and toppled her lawn furniture on their way to the basement door. Her motion-detecting light turned on, illuminating their gang vests and shaved heads. Oh. God. It was the WKB. Here for her.

She grabbed her laptop case and purse as banging began on her front door. She tore up the stairs. There were two master bedrooms upstairs. In the one she used as a guest room, she'd set up a secret space in its walk-in closet behind a shelf she'd had custom made. There was just room enough for her to squeeze inside and close the panel.

Her security system triggered when the bikers

kicked in her front door. The cops would be there soon. Five minutes. Maybe ten. She just had to stay hidden—and alive—until then.

She reached into her pocket to turn off the sound on her phone. She couldn't risk responding to the security company's confirmation phone call. The phone vibrated in her hand, making her jump. Her non-response would trigger their call to the police.

Men spilled through her home. She heard crashes following their progress, shouting and laughter. Her hands shook. There was no one she could call for help. No one.

Greer's face floated through her mind, and the way he'd grinned and said, "I'm always up for kickin' some asses."

She called up his number, then realized she'd hit call when she'd meant to text him. She was about to hang up, but he picked up before the first ring completed.

"Dawson here."

She held still, trying to hear if anyone was near.

"Hello?"

"Greer?" she whispered.

There was a pause. *"Remi. S'up?"*

"Help me—"

"Where are you?"

The door to her guest bedroom banged against the wall. They slammed into the bathroom. The door banged against the closet wall where she was hunkered down.

"...Max, where the fuck is she?"

"At her house," another voice said, fainter than Greer's. *"Hit the road. I'll tell Kit."*

Seconds later, the bikers were in the guest closet. The light flipped on. She could see a thin line of it beneath the compartment's door. She held the phone to her chest to muffle the sound of Greer's voice. She rocked back and forth in short movements, unable to sit still.

Above the blood pounding in her ears, she could hear the faint sound of a siren. Someone downstairs made a loud whistle. She listened as several sets of footsteps moved out of the bedrooms and headed downstairs. Bikes started up, loud and screaming as they sped out into the night.

She didn't move—didn't know if they were all gone. After a few minutes, she lifted her phone to her ear, hoping he was still on the line with her. "Greer?"

"Yeah. What's happening, doc?"

"I need help."

"I'm on my way, but I'm about a half-hour out. The cops will be there shortly. Stay where you are until they get there."

She nodded, then realized he couldn't see that. "I will," she whispered. The sirens' whine grew louder.

"I'll stay on with you as long as I can. I'm coming down from Wolf Creek Bend. I might lose the connection between here and there. If you need me, call me back. If I don't answer, call again."

"Okay."

"Are they still there?"

"I don't think so. I don't know. I heard their bikes leave."

"Bikes?"

"It was the WKB again."

"Shit."

The sirens stopped. "I think the cops are here."

"Where are you in the house?"

"Upstairs."

"Stay put until the cops come to you, just in case any of the bikers stayed behind."

"Okay."

She heard the cops announce themselves downstairs. She couldn't tell how many there were. At least two. They cleared the main floor, then separated, one going to the basement, the other coming upstairs. The cop announced herself as she came up the stairs.

Remi slipped out of her hidey-hole, leaving her laptop behind. She was getting to her feet as the cop came into the bedroom.

"What happened here?" the police officer asked, her hand on her weapon.

"I don't know." Remi folded her arms. "Some bikers just stormed the house."

"Why your house? You friendly with them?"

"No."

"You dealing drugs?"

"No."

The cop looked skeptical. "Stay here while I check out the rest of the rooms up here."

Remi nodded. The cop went through the other

rooms, making a pass at any place it might be easy for a human to hide. Her partner was coming upstairs.

"Jack," the cop said to her partner. "Let's go downstairs and take her statement."

Remi followed them and told them what she knew, tried to answer their questions. They took her statement, gave her their cards, and let her know a detective would be following up with her about the case.

"You going to be okay here, ma'am? We could give you a lift to a hotel."

"I'll be all right. I have a, um, friend coming over."

Speak of the devil, he was walking up the path to her door. Her mind spun back through their hushed conversation while she was hiding. He moved like he owned the world, as if no enemy on earth could defeat him.

Who was he?

God, was he in partnership with the WKB? A good guy to their bad guys? Were they tag-teaming her? No. Not only did he and his friends not look like bikers, Christian Villalobo at the FBI had vouched for him, for what that was worth.

His eyes were intense. In a single sweep, he took in her appearance, the cops, the shambles of her living room, then returned to her as he stepped into her foyer and came right over to her. He put his arms around her, and she breathed the first full breath she'd had in hours.

"You okay?" he asked in a quiet voice as he rubbed her back.

She nodded. The cops left. Greer pushed the door after them—it was too banged up to shut properly. Greer sent a look around her place.

"Looks like your office." He frowned at her. "You wanna tell me what's goin' on?"

She looked at him, then moved away, stepping into her living room. It wasn't completely a shambles. The bikers hadn't had more than a few minutes to wreak havoc.

"What are they looking for, Remi?" Greer faced her, his warm brown eyes sharp. "They didn't find it at your office, so they came here. Did they get what they were after?"

Remi looked over to the broken secretary cabinet where she housed her fake computer setup. Soon enough, the WKB would know she hadn't accessed that in more than a year. She'd put it there as a decoy.

"They took my computer."

"So they got what they wanted."

Greer was only a foot from her. Impatience rolled off his broad chest like heat off a hot tin roof. "Maybe," she said.

He shoved a hand through his hair and perched on the arm of her sofa. "Talk to me, doc. I can't help you if you keep secrets."

Remi folded her hands together and pressed them to her lips. She paced away a few steps, then turned and looked back at Greer. "There's nothing on the computer they took." She drew a breath and faced him. "Except a screen that has a laughing clown and sends a virus over to their system, if it's connected to a network when they access it, which it likely would be when they start it up." She glanced at the broken cabinet it was in. "And even if it isn't connected to their system when they attempt to copy the data, there's an app that watches for a network connection and self-initializes."

Greer laughed, then shook his head. "Jesus. I think I love you. What does the virus do?"

She lifted her shoulders. "I had a student write it for me. I told him I wanted it to email me as much info as it could about who opened my computer, where they were—anything that might be useful in tracking them down. I don't know what else he might have put in it."

"All right. If you get that email, don't open it. You don't know what hitchhikers they might be sending back to you. Can you tell me what they're looking for?"

"I really don't know."

"You said you'd had pushback from groups you studied before."

"I'm not sure what you know about me—"

"A whole bunch of flat facts that could use some connecting dots. I know you're a professor of sociology at the University of Wyoming. I know your degrees. I know that, though it's early in your career, you're already making a name for yourself as an expert in the sociology of cults." He lifted his brown eyes to her. "And I know that this year, you're focusing on the Friendship Community."

"Yeah. That's me in a nutshell." Hell, that was the whole summation of her life. "Sometimes, these cults have friends in the world outside their little community."

"Can I look at your data?"

"No. I'm close to finishing a paper funded by a grant. I can't have it messed with at this critical stage. I need to submit it for review at a journal as soon as possible."

"Your paper isn't going to get finished if you're dead. And these goons aren't going to stop until they get what they want. Killing you may be part of that plan." He stood up. She wasn't yet used to his height. "Pack up. I'll take you someplace safe."

"I have someplace to go to. And I'm not handing over my data. Besides, I'm not going anywhere until I get my doors fixed."

"How about we make a deal? I'll get your doors fixed, then you and your data come with me."

When she still hesitated, he walked closer to her. "We aren't competitors. You know that by now, right?" His voice was quiet, so much so that she had to look up at him as he spoke to hear what he was saying. "I'm not going to scoop your paper. I don't want any part of your professional spotlight. I want to keep you safe while we find out what info the WKB wants so bad they'll make a scene to get it."

"Who's 'we'? The guys you were with the other night—your team?"

Greer nodded. "There are a few of us, enough to keep you safe while we figure things out."

"You can get my house fixed?"

"Yeah. One phone call."

There was an edge about him that set her senses on warning. It was like standing too close to a big cat whose keepers thought was tame. She stepped back. But of course, she was then distracted by the way his tee molded his ripped arms and torso.

"Deal?" he asked.

Her eyes met his. There was nothing classified about her data. She wasn't afraid of being scooped by another academic; she was the only one she knew who was studying the Friendship Community. She just wished she knew for a fact she wasn't jumping from the pan to the fire by going with him and his friends.

His lips thinned as he waited impatiently for her answer. "If you stay here, I guarantee they'll be back. They could even be on their way back as we speak."

"All right. I'll go with you. I have to be back in a week."

He nodded, then lifted his phone and punched a quick-dial number. "Tell Kit I'm bringing the professor back with me. She's agreed to show us her data. I need someone out here ASAP to fix her doors… Right… Roger that." He hung up and looked at her. "It's done. Bring me your legit laptop, then go pack a bag. If I were you, I'd hustle."

"But my doors——"

"Will be fixed before sunup."

She nodded. "Okay. I'll be right down." She returned with her laptop and handed it to him.

"Log in," he ordered. "I don't have time to hack it."

She sat on the sofa and opened her laptop. He took control of it, opening a command screen. "Go pack."

"What are you doing?"

"Sending your info to my computer." He looked at her. "Just in case."

"In case what?"

"In case we're delayed getting back. Get moving."

9

R emi's hand shook as she dialed her department chair.

"Dr. Chase…is everything all right?"

Remi hesitated. She should have gotten her thoughts together before calling him. She already knew she wasn't going to tell him about what happened at her townhouse, but she felt obligated to let him know she was going to be out of town for a while. "Yes. I just wanted to let you know that I'm going to be away for a few days. Maybe a week or so."

"The provost gave you a week to shut things down. You're not going to, are you?"

"Dr. Zimmers, the university was well aware of my research when I was hired. In fact, it was a deciding factor in my selection."

"Things change. Your work is now putting you and the university in danger. It must stop before someone gets hurt."

Remi held the phone to her forehead, shutting her eyes as she considered what might have happened had she not hidden when the WKB were here. And she wasn't the only person in danger anymore. Her work endangered all the students and faculty at the university.

"I'm leaving town tonight."

"So you'll be stopping your work on the Friendship Community?"

Remi paused. She hadn't yet decided. "I don't know." She wondered if she should tell her department head where she was going, but she didn't know that either. "I'm going to take a break and give it some thought."

"You do understand that your entire career is on the line—"

"I do. That's why it's a decision I can't make without a great deal of thought."

"There's no thought needed. Not for a rational person."

"I just need some time."

"Then I will let the provost know you will voluntarily stay away from the university, and that in no more than one week, we'll have your official response. Understood?"

A terrible thought struck her. "They got to you, didn't they?" she asked.

"Who?"

"The ones behind these attacks. Did they threaten you?"

"That's crazy talk. This is not a big conspiracy. It's some thugs being bullies. Some gang rite of passage. Let the detectives do their work. Let them find out who's behind this. Lay low

until we get some answers. Then we'll revisit things with the provost. The university will be in session in just a couple of weeks. Focus on that."

Remi felt her chest tightening up. Without a job, she couldn't keep the lights on. But without her work, did she even want the job?

"I've made arrangements to stay…someplace safe for a few days." How did she explain Greer and his team? They weren't friends. They weren't allies. Telling her chair she was in contact with consultants for the DHS sounded like a really bad option.

"That's a good idea. I'll call and check in on you. Don't return to the university unless you're ready to comply." There was a pause. *"Dr. Chase, if I don't hear from you in two weeks, I will be forced to place you on leave for the remainder of your current appointment, and you will not be eligible for reap- pointment. Do you understand?"*

"I do."

"Very well. Good night. And be safe." The line went dead.

"How's it goin', doc?" Greer called up from downstairs.

"Fine. I'll just be a moment." She didn't move. She had an awful feeling she'd just lost her position. Choosing between her work and her job was useless. Her work came first. It had to. It was the only thing that helped her make sense of her life, helped others understand what people like her—survivors of cults— went through.

When she looked up, Greer was standing at the

door to her bedroom. Geez, he filled that doorframe, too.

"What happened?" he asked, frowning at her.

"Nothing."

"You're not packed."

Packing. Right. Wait—was this a test? If she went with him, would the university make good on its threat to put her on leave without waiting out the two weeks?

"I'm not going with you." She wasn't going to give up on her work, but she couldn't toss her job away either.

His eyes hardened. "I don't recall giving you an option. You called *me* for help, remember?"

"I'm going to lose my job, Greer."

"That's unfortunate." He looked around for a suitcase, looking in her closet, under her bed. Not finding one, he straightened. "But better that than your life. It doesn't matter a whole helluva lot whether you come with me as you are, or if you pack a couple changes of clothes. Either way, you're going to be out of this house in five minutes."

She stood. "I don't take orders from you."

His mouth formed a thin line. "Have it your way."

He bent and slung her over his shoulder. The room spun as he turned for the door. She pushed up from his back. His body felt like a carved totem pole beneath her hands.

"Set me down. Now." She straightened in his

arms. He held her with an arm around her legs, supported her with a hand at the small of her back as she glared down at him.

"You gonna pack?" he asked.

She studied his eyes. He slowly lowered her to her feet, slipping her body the long way down his. She stepped back, putting a foot of empty air between them. "What, exactly, is going to happen where we're going?"

He locked his jaw. His nostrils flared. God, his eyes were hard. He looked at his watch. "Three minutes."

She shook her head, then pivoted on her heel and headed for her bedroom. She opened a drawer and pulled out some underclothes, which she dumped on the bed. She went to her closet and selected some tops. From a shelf, she tossed out a couple pairs of jeans.

"Greer!" a man called out from downstairs.

Her eyes shot toward Greer, wondering who it was, if more trouble had just hit her doorstep.

"Up here," Greer answered. He pointed to her growing pile of clothes. "Focus," he ordered.

Two men came up the stairs, taking the steps three at a time. She couldn't follow Greer's edict once she set eyes on them. Both were about the same height as Greer. One was blond, the other with olive skin and dark hair. Both dressed head to toe in black attire—black beanie, black tee, black cargo pants, black boots. With Greer, the three of them took up the entire upper landing area.

Weren't they among those she'd seen last night at the village?

The blond one grinned as he looked at her, some kind of automatic weapon in his hands, angled downward. He grinned at her.

Greer moved to block the door. "Glad you're here. They took out her front and back doors. The crew should be here shortly to get them fixed. Seal this place up before you leave."

"Roger that."

Remi realized she was standing on her tiptoes to peek over the side of Greer's arm. The blond guy could have been a model. On steroids. The darker guy's features were carved from granite. His rough shadow beard did nothing to soften his features. His eyes regarded her as if she were an enemy. If a warrior robot became human, he would be this man.

Greer glanced over his shoulder at her, then moved a quarter turn to include her in their conversation.

"Val, Angel, you remember Dr. Remington Chase." She nodded at the men. "They'll be securing your house until the doors are repaired."

She looked from the men up to Greer, feeling a strange mix of relief and concern. Deciding to tamp her fear down, she nodded. "Thank you," she said, in a way that included all of them. Then she stepped away from the door and continued gathering the things she'd need for an indefinite stay away from home.

"Owen wants you to take her to Mandy's," one of the men told Greer.

Who was Owen? Geez, were there more of them? She started to stuff her clothes into a suitcase she retrieved from a cabinet in her closet. The night at the village had been a blur of terror and panic when Greer and his friends caught up with her; she couldn't quite remember how many men had been standing around her car.

She wheeled her large suitcase out into the hallway where Greer was waiting. "Got everything?" he asked.

"I guess so. It's not like I can't come back and get something if I forgot it."

He didn't respond to that, making her think her statement was more of a question than a possibility. He lifted her suitcase and went downstairs, then paused at the door. The dark one was there.

"Give your car keys to Angel," Greer ordered her. "He'll bring your vehicle up when they come back."

Remi looked over at the half-moon table in the foyer where her keys lay. "Um. No. I'll drive my car. I'll follow you."

"Negative. You're with me." Greer picked up the keys from the table and handed them to Angel. "Your car in the garage?"

Her gaze bounced between the two men. She nodded.

Greer pulled her dented front door open, letting the night air into the foyer. Its cool touch matched the cold panic knotting her insides. She was in way over her head. And she was just going along with it. She wanted to run. She wanted to fight. She'd long ago told herself she would never again be subject to the edicts of madmen, yet here she was, letting one make critical decisions on her behalf.

Her phone pinged. Grateful for the excuse to break contact with Greer, she dug it out of her pocket. "Oh, God. It's them. They booted up my computer."

Greer nodded. "Copy that." She wasn't certain he was talking to her. "My teammate saw the message. He'll deal with it," Greer said as he reached over to take her phone and shut it off. "Don't open that message. Now what's it gonna be? You comin' with me, or you hangin' here with my friends for your baddies to come back when the clown doesn't make them laugh?"

Her breathing was shallow. There was no choice to make. No choice at all. "I'll go with you."

He nodded and lifted her suitcase and laptop bag, then stepped over the threshold. They walked down to a big black SUV parked at the curb in front of her house. He tossed her suitcase in the back hatch, then handed her computer bag to her.

"So, where are we going?" she asked

"Wolf Creek Bend."

That was way the hell out in the middle of

nowhere, at the base of the Medicine Bow Mountains. "What's up there?"

He looked out of his side mirror as he pulled onto
the street. "Your last hope in the hell that's become
your life."

10

Remi watched the barren land roll past as they drove west out of Laramie. The moon had finally risen, spreading its sepia light over summer-brown hills. They were heading away from civilization at a breakneck speed.

She looked over at her traveling companion. The muscular lines of his neck and face were lit by the pale green dashboard light. His brown hair was brushed back from his forehead in waves that rippled toward the back of his head.

He appeared rational, calm.

She was bewildered that she'd gone with him so meekly and unnerved that it didn't feel wrong. It made no sense. The only person who knew she was headed away from her home was waiting to make her termination official. She hadn't told her assistant where she was going, a fact that she wondered about now. Clancy was brilliant, and could one day be a phenomenal scholar, but there was something off about him, something that had made her keep him at a distance over the two years she'd been teaching at the university.

"Who are you? For real," she asked Greer.

He looked over at her. The green dash light illuminated his serious face. "Shall I lie to make you comfortable now that your world is standing on its head?"

"No. I need you to be honest with me."

He faced the road. "I'm a consultant in the security industry."

Somehow, she doubted that was good news. "What is your job, exactly?"

"I hunt, find, and kill bad guys." His smile broke into the silence that followed his words.

"Hahaha. You're not really great at calming nerves. You should probably never read stories to children. I think even Humpty Dumpty would sound sinister if you read it."

"True. And that, Remi, is me in a nutshell." The smile ended, falling from a mouth that looked as if it never knew true joy.

Remi's stomach knotted. She faced forward, staring into the dark that swallowed the light from their headlights as the road twisted and rose up into the national forest.

"I thought you were a computer programmer."

"I am."

"So you moonlight as an assassin?"

"'Assassin' is such a harsh word."

"Finding Sally's not your real focus, is it?"

His grip on the steering wheel tightened. "No. She is real, though. And I promised her I would keep her safe." He looked at Remi. "But I didn't."

"So you and your band of merry mercenaries got together to find her?"

He tilted his head as he considered his answer. "Only one of us is really merry."

"Greer," she said, in her best unamused professor's voice. "I need answers."

"You'll get them. When we get to Wolf Creek Bend."

Ignoring the bone he tossed her way, she continued digging. "Are you with the WKB?"

"No."

A more chilling idea hit her. "The Friends?"

"No. Relax, professor. You'll know what you need to know shortly."

She gaped at him. "'Relax'? Really? Your life isn't the one on the line right now."

"The hell it isn't."

She scrubbed her hands over her face, then pressed them against her mouth. "I think I'm going to vomit."

He looked over at her. "For real?"

She focused on breathing, but her skin was growing cold and clammy. She nodded. "It's a panic reaction."

"Shit." He pulled over and stopped the car.

"Don't go running through the wayside. There are rattlers everywhere. Just lean out the door."

She pushed the door open. Cool evening air spilled into the cab. She released her seatbelt and turned to sit facing the open prairie. This was it. This was her only chance to run. She sucked in a few long, slow breaths. Go or stay? Her indecision roiled in her stomach.

Greer had helped her twice already. Surely she could trust him?

Or had he saved her only to preserve her for something much, much worse?

She leaned over and folded her arms about her waist, reminding herself she knew how to survive— just look how far she'd come. A girl with minimal education until high school, no hope in hell of being free. She'd managed not only a diploma, but also an undergraduate degree and two advanced degrees. And now she was a professor at a public university.

For a few more days, anyway, unless she complied. She had no choice. She was going to have to put her research on hold. She could still draft the articles she'd had in mind, just not submit them for publication yet. She'd have to come up with something else to submit to the sociological journals if she wanted to stay on her tenure track, which she could do. She had plenty of primary data from the other groups she'd studied.

Her sigh was deep and long and drew the attention of the madman driving them into the night. He reached over to touch her. His hand was warm and big and comforting on her back. She looked over at him, pleased the nausea was subsiding.

"It's going to be all right, Remi. You're safe now. No one will harm you where we're going. We've been fighting the WKB for a while. Believe it or not, they're a symptom of a much bigger problem."

She watched him over her shoulder. She liked the sound of his voice. Words were just words, but intent was something else all together. Her gut said his intent was solid.

Greer watched her silently, the hard lines of his face stark in the green light. "Let me know when you're ready to go again. I don't want to linger longer than we have to."

She looked at the open field beyond the car door and decided to see where this was going. The panic had crested. For now. She resettled herself in the cab and shut the door.

They soon cut through the edge of Wolf Creek Bend and out again into the dark mountain road, bordered on both sides by tall, slim evergreens. Up, up, up. Her ears popped as the elevation shifted. It seemed they drove a long way out of town, but it was only minutes. At last he began to slow down, then turned right onto a long drive.

The little ranch house he stopped in front of was lit inside and out. "Whose house is this?" she asked.

"A friend's."

They got out of the SUV. She collected her purse and laptop case while he grabbed her suitcase, then they both paused between the SUV and the house. "Greer, I can't exist in a vacuum. I need some info from you," she said as she looked up at him.

He looked down at her. The big farm light that lit the drive silhouetted his face, making pockets of shadows where his eyes were, beneath his cheekbones, under his chin. "I know. It's coming."

The front door opened. A man stepped out onto the porch. His blond hair was sliced off in a sharp flattop. He nodded at them. "Dr. Chase, Greer. Get in here. We need to get started." He went back into the house without introducing himself.

"How many of you are there?" She was pretty sure Flattop hadn't been among those she'd run into at the village a couple of nights ago.

"As many as we need for the job we're here to do."

"Thanks." She started for the front steps. "As usual, that's astoundingly ambiguous."

She walked into the house, then stopped. She could see the living room, dining room, and part of the kitchen, all of it empty of humans but full of old farm furniture. Where did Flattop go?

"Remi, if you'll follow me, I'll get you settled before we begin." He turned and pulled her suitcase behind him down a hallway to the bedrooms. "You have your choice of rooms." He went into the one at the end of the hallway. "I suggest you take the master. You'll be most comfortable here. I'll wait for you in the living room."

She walked into the room, then turned around. "Greer, what is it that we're beginning?"

His face was stony. "Come out when you're ready."

She stepped into the hall, still holding her purse and laptop. "I'm ready." She blinked. "At least, I'm as settled as I'm going to be. Let's begin whatever this is."

He held her gaze for another minute, then nodded and walked back into the living room.

She followed him down the hall and across the living room to the stairs. At the basement door, she paused, sending him a panicked glance.

"I won't leave your side," he said in a voice that was barely a whisper.

This was so cloak and dagger. A sane person would either laugh or run; she was frozen in place. "What's in there?" she asked, delaying the inevitable.

He pulled the door to, giving them a moment of privacy. "An old rec room." His face took on an intensity she'd never seen.

Yeah, that didn't scare her.

"Trust me. Please." He bent his head to the side and gave her a small smile. "And there's a bathroom, in case your stomach complains again."

She crossed her free hand over her stomach. "Am I going to need it?"

"There are a lot of us. And we can be overwhelming."

A blond man with eyes like ice opened the door.

"Dr. Chase, I'm Owen Tremaine. I own the company these men work for. There's nothing here but a simple basement." He flashed Greer a chilling look, then set those steely eyes on her again. "Won't you please join us? There are things we need to discuss that have to do with our work and your safety."

He stepped back and gestured for her to enter. She pursed her lips, but did as the head guy requested. At least the room was just a room. It was large and open, but the number of men filling it made it seem half its size—seven of them, including Greer and his boss. She thought of the two who'd remained back at her townhouse and wondered how many more there were. She stopped just inside the room. The boss nodded to the flattop guy, then crossed the room to stand at a space against a wall to her right.

Greer touched her elbow as he gestured to each of the men, calling off their names—all of which rolled into a big, scrambled lump of information. Usually she was excellent at remembering names and faces and titles; it was a skill she'd learned to rely on when she first entered mainstream America and one she used extensively as a professor and researcher.

She nodded to the men. True to his word, Greer remained standing with her. She would never admit the hint of cinnamon and vanilla that swirled between them was at all comforting. Surely someone who smelled like a cookie couldn't be terribly dangerous, right?

"Please, have a seat, professor." The flattop guy

gestured toward an empty chair. Kit Bolanger—her mind trotted out his info from the introductions that had just happened. He was Greer's team lead. Was he the one Sally had tried to kill? Who would send a young girl to do that job?

The chair she was being offered was sandwiched between two dark-haired men—Rocco and Kelan. Her panic had to be receding if she was able to recall names. She set her things on the chair, then stayed where she was next to Greer.

"I think I'll stand, thank you," she said, letting her expression slip into a mask of bland interest.

Greer stood so close, their arms and feet touched. She could feel his heat. His dominance. It should have inflamed her panic, but it didn't. She hooked her pinky through his, felt comforted when his finger bent to hold hers. She wasn't a coward. Usually. She was just waaaay out of her element.

The flattop guy was talking. She forced herself to focus on him. "You picked a helluva year to study the Friendship Community."

"Actually, I began studying them three years ago, though I hadn't been invited to their compound until this year."

Kit propped himself against the arm of one of the couches. "Well, it seems they have an association with the group we're studying—the White Kingdom Brotherhood." He shot a glance toward Greer. "I understand you've been having some run-ins with them."

"Yes."

"Can you tell us what their interest in the Friends is?"

"I don't know what it is. My focus has been on the community itself, not on peripheral populations." She suspected the WKB was simply touchy about anyone getting too close to their compound. The Friends' property abutted the WKB's longest boundary line. "Frankly, I have no interest in the WKB."

Kit folded his arms and leveled a hard glare at her. "It appears they have an interest in you. I think we can help each other."

She looked around the room. A meaner bunch of mercenaries she'd never seen. Well, really, she'd never knowingly seen a mercenary at all before Greer, but if she had, they'd look like these men.

"No, thanks. I'm not interested. I don't want anything to do with the WKB. And I don't want to put my work with the Friendship Community in jeopardy. It's taken me years to get permission to conduct on-site interviews with them, which they've only just granted this year. I'm very close to being able to draft several articles on their unique society."

"We don't intend to jeopardize your work, doctor. We just want to piggyback on it for our investigation."

Another quick glance around the room. "And who did you say your organization is working for?" She'd checked out Greer, but Mr. Villalobo had provided only a minimal amount of info.

"I didn't." Kit sent a look over at the man leaning

against the wall, who gave him a hint of a nod. "We're a private security company. We've been contracted by the Department of Homeland Security to assist in their investigation into domestic and foreign terrorists operating in this area."

Remi's mouth opened. What the hell had she gotten herself into? These men *were* mercenaries. Oh, God. Greer's big hand took hold of hers—for comfort or warning, she didn't know.

"We're asking for your help, Dr. Chase. Take Greer into the community and help him get some of our questions answered."

Remi nodded. "I'll talk to the elders on your behalf, but I'm not bringing Greer in with me. He's a stranger to them."

Kit smiled, like the warning snarl of a wolf baring his teeth in a silent growl. "True that. To simply have him accompany you would be inappropriate. You'll be bringing your *husband* with you."

Reality screeched to an abrupt halt as Remi's clusterfuck sensors fired. "They know I'm not married."

"Tell them you recently got married."

She pulled away from Greer, and laughed as she reached for her things, which helped unlock her chest and her lungs and calm her terror.

"You're good, Mr. Bolanger." She looked around the room. "All of you, in fact. You had me going there for a minute. Tell me, did Clancy Weston put you up to this? 'Cause sometimes I think he's crazy like that."

That was the best answer for what was happening.

Except her assistant—even as oddball as he was—wouldn't smash her doors in just to set up a joke.

Oh, God. This was real. This was really real.

She stared at her things, trying to figure out how she could unwind the day and have it play out differently. Greer touched her shoulder. She looked up into his warm brown eyes.

"Please, Remi. We need you. A lot of people need you."

"Dr. Chase," Owen said in a supremely calm voice, "please tell us everything you know about the Friendship Community."

"Everything I know about them?" She looked over at the cool-tempered boss. "How long do you have?"

"As long as it takes."

She looked at Greer, who gave her a supporting nod. "I've told them some of the obvious things, but assume we know nothing about them."

Remi moved to the front of the room, deciding to treat the group as she would any other class. For the next hour, she gave the history of the group, from its founding in the first half of the nineteenth century to its current incarnation. Each generation had left its touch on the community, which had started as a secular group pursuing its vision of a perfect society. It was one of very few that survived, in any form, from the original movement over a century and a half ago.

"Why does it still exist?" Owen asked.

"It's come close to collapsing several times. In the 1870s, when there was a gold rush in the Medicine

Bows, they lost a great deal of their population. Fortunately for the Friends, that rush played out rather quickly. It lost some of its population to both world wars. The Great Depression was a boon for them. Their community never stopped its standard practices, although they had started to slowly integrate with mainstream society before the depression. A few dozen drifters, traveling between farms for work, stumbled upon the community and stayed there. They had a small boom in population that got bled off during World War II. They are a pacifist community, but they didn't become conscientious objectors until the Vietnam War.

"Something changed in their community around then. During the Cold War, the group walled themselves in, only leaving the community for their annual trades during Cheyenne's Frontier Days Rodeo. Over the last three generations, they've returned to their root values as an agrarian society."

"And now," Greer said, "there's another small boom in their population, but it's not from within."

Remi nodded. "I've discovered an anomalous trend. Their community appears to be losing teenagers at an alarming rate. Nonetheless, I think they're one of the few groups who could survive a World War III." She didn't miss the look Kit and Owen exchanged.

"How so?" Kit asked.

"They are fully self-sufficient. They only need to raise enough funds from their annual trading to cover property taxes and buy the few things they can't provide for themselves. Otherwise, they grow or raise their own food. Make their own clothes. Build their own houses. Govern themselves without outside influences. They know how to survive without modern services or technology."

"So what's the WKB's interest in them?" Greer asked.

"I'm not sure they have an interest. Their two societies are diametrically opposed to each other. If anything, the Friends provide a nice buffer between the world and the WKB."

"I don't think that's all it is," the one called Ty said. "The WKB bought the land their biker compound's on during the Cold War. They could have bought any of the newly decommissioned missile silos around the country. Why that one?"

She looked around the room, trying to understand the implications of that comment.

"Doc, what's the nature of your relationship with the Friendship Community?" Kit asked.

"We're on friendly terms."

"Good. So getting Greer inside shouldn't be a big problem."

She looked at Greer, whose face was hard and expressionless. Yes, she could go to the Friends' village at will, but bringing him in put everything at risk.

She glanced at Kit. "I don't think you fully understand the impact of what you're asking. The Friends are an isolationist community. They're extremely wary of outsiders, very closed off to strangers. It took me three years to finally gain their trust to the point where I can visit with them not just at Frontier Days, but at their compound, too."

Kit's face was set. "Think of it this way, doctor. You have a choice. You can take Greer in. He'll follow your lead. He'll be respectful of the Friends—and your work. And you'll control the interactions. Or our FBI contact will send in a team of investigators and potentially tear the place wide open. I think our way will net more info and cause less damage."

Remi nodded, horrified at the disruption a bunch of FBI investigators could do—potentially irreversible harm to a community as fragile as the Friends.

She sighed. "I'll do it. But I'll need to bring them some gifts as a sign of goodwill." If they were going to force this issue, then at least she could see to it that the community benefitted.

"Give Greer the list," Kit said. "I want you two out there tomorrow."

Greer met her eyes, his gaze warm and determined. She nodded. This whole thing was rolling forward, with or without her. Hopefully, she could keep it from being a complete disaster.

11

———

Greer fetched a glass of water from the kitchen, then walked back to his room through the darkened house. The only light was the thin beam that came from beneath Remi's door. A shadow crossed it, making the beam blink. Looked like she was pacing.

He went down the hall to her room. "Hey, Remi. You okay?" he called through the door.

The shadow in the light paused. He wondered what was going through her head. Maybe she was going to keep still and pretend she was sleeping. After a long moment, she opened the door.

She crossed her arms and looked up at him. "No. I'm not okay."

"I'm sorry. It's a shitty situation." He took his phone out of his jeans pocket and flipped to his pictures. Holding his phone up to her, he showed her photos of her new doors.

Her nostrils flared. "I was hoping this was all a joke that my assistant took too far."

Greer frowned. "That the sort of thing he would do?"

She handed his phone back. "While I'm not certain he's rowing with matching oars, I don't think he'd go this far."

"Has he done similar things before?"

"Not similar things. He does take practical jokes to an extreme, though."

Greer studied her as he considered that. "Text me his name. I'll check him out."

Her eyes widened. "How can you do that?"

"A little thing called technology." He grinned. "Want some water?"

She took the glass. Her fingers brushed his. He watched her throat move as she took a couple of sips. She pressed the ice-cold glass to her forehead. She caught him staring at her and handed his glass back.

"If you're too warm, I can adjust the air conditioner," he offered.

"I'm not warm. My head is throbbing."

"Okay. That's it. You need some rest." He took her hand and stepped into the room, drawing her over to the far side of the bed. He set his water down, then folded back the covers, holding them up for her. "Get in."

"What's the point? I can't sleep. I'm just going to get up and pace when you leave."

"What's pacing going to resolve?"

"Greer——"

"Bed, Remi. Now."

Exasperation made her face scrunch and huff a sigh. She got under the covers, but defiantly stayed sitting up. He flipped off the light and took his water. He hadn't made it to the far corner of the bed when she said, "Do you have to go? Maybe you could just talk to me until I sleep?"

Greer settled next to her on the bed. She was lying on her side now, her hands folded together under her head. There was such innocence about her. Maybe he could get her in and out of the Friendship Community before everything got even stranger, but given how things already were, his chances were slim.

"Did you do a lot of babysitting as a kid?" he asked, trying to get her mind off their situation. "You said, given the differences in our ages, that you could have babysat me."

"Yes. We lived in a small community. Everyone helped each other."

"Fort Collins wasn't a small community, even back then."

"Our social circle was."

She watched him in the shadowy room. He couldn't see her expression, but he liked how smoothly she dodged his comment.

"What did you mean when you said by the time I was old enough to sit you, you would have been guarding me?" she asked.

"My grandfather was a spy in two wars, Korean

and Vietnam—three if you include the Cold War. He made enemies. They didn't care that he was out of the business when he retired; they had scores to settle." Greer leaned his head back against the headboard, remembering times he thought about too often, events that shaped his life.

"My baby sister was murdered when I was six."

"Oh my God." She pushed herself up to her elbow. "I'm so sorry."

"Not much of a bedtime story, is it? My grandfather made my parents move to a house he'd had specially constructed. Each floor had a panic room."

"Did you ever have to use them?"

"Yeah. One time. But I guess once is enough. He moved in with us. His enemies came again."

"You think his enemies killed your sister?"

"I know it."

"What happened when they came again?"

"He and I got my parents and my two sisters into one of the panic rooms, then we took out the bad guys."

"How old were you?"

"Fourteen. I'd been training with him since I was eight. I was raised to be an assassin." He smiled and looked at her. "So you see, I wouldn't have needed you to babysit me. I never was a baby."

"Eight years old. Greer. Your parents were all right with that?"

"Gramps had worked hard, very hard, to keep his work life separate from his home life. He wanted my mom—his only kid—to have a normal life. She did. She was a kindergarten teacher. My dad was a middle school math teacher. Everything was peaches and cream. My parents thought Gramps was just giving me a break from being around my younger sisters.

"We would go camping, but they didn't know it was survival camping. We met up with other men and their kids at mercenary camps where we were taught how to fight. How to build shelters. How to fish, hunt, and track. It was like the Boy Scouts on steroids. Every summer was boot camp all over again. We never told my parents what actually happened. Maybe they guessed, but they never asked. By the time I actually got to boot camp, it was a cakewalk."

"So you're legit badass."

Greer shrugged. "I am what I've become. Legit or not, definitely badass."

"Am I safe with you, Greer?"

"Yes."

She reached over and wrapped a hand around his thumb.

"I'm glad you're here, Remi. The WKB's ruthless. For some reason, this particular project is attracting their attention." He looked at her, wishing he could see her face better. "Any idea why that is?"

"No."

She answered so quickly—maybe too quickly—to allay his fears.

"You know anyone named King?" he asked.

"I may. It's not an uncommon surname."

"But nobody stands out to you?"

She shook her head. "No. Who is he?"

"We don't know yet. He's someone who has his hands in everything. He's one of the bad guys. If you come across him, steer clear."

"I will."

"Well, enough talking. You need to sleep."

"What about you?" she asked.

"I'll stay until you've dozed off. Good night, Remi."

"Night, Greer."

HE DIDN'T WANT to let go of her hand. Even in sleep, she clung to him. He was glad she was here, safe, and not facing the WKB all on her own. It weighed on his conscience that he hadn't been able to keep Sally safe; he wasn't going to fail Remi.

Something caught his attention from the corner of his eye. A movement in the front yard—a strange light, anyway. He eased his hand from hers, then went to the window. The blinds were lowered but half open. Spreading two slats of the blinds, he looked out…at a face.

Startled, Greer jumped back, then looked again. Whoever it was had turned away and was moving down the driveway. He bolted from the house. There was no time to check the security system or find out why the alarm hadn't triggered. The person was moving fast…or rather, disappearing fast.

Greer moved around the cars and out into the black night at the edge of Mandy's tall farm light, moving farther from the house than he'd intended. The person was gone. Vanished. Another light caught his attention. Blade's dad was coming over from the bunkhouse with a big flashlight. He closed the distance between them.

"Ryker," Greer greeted him.

"Greer."

"Didn't mean to wake you."

"You didn't."

"You saw it, too, didn't you?"

"Yeah."

"What did you see?"

Ryker shrugged. "Don't know. A face in the window."

Greer felt goosebumps on his arms and a tension along his spine. "Was it male or female?"

"Wasn't there long enough for me to see."

"Yeah. I blinked and it was gone." Greer flipped his phone to the security cameras on Mandy's property. Somehow, none of their alarms had been tripped. He looked over at Ryker, glad he wasn't the only person who had seen something odd.

He shrugged. "Nothing on the cams. Guess maybe it was an owl flying too close to the houses."

Ryker looked at him as if he were an idiot. "You don't believe in ghosts?"

"You do?"

"Callum had a lot of them. You get used to seeing them. Question is, was it here for me or you?"

A cold chill blew through Greer, raising the specter of the disembodied eyes that had been commandeering his dreams. "You think it was a ghost?"

Blade's dad gave a dry laugh and shook his head. "It sure as hell weren't no owl."

Greer watched Ryker walk back to his little cabin. He put his phone back into his pocket.

Question is, was it here for me or you?

He had a bad feeling he knew the answer. He turned back to Mandy's house, which was still quiet. Too quiet. Too dark. Too ripe for a visit from his nightmare. Maybe he wasn't awake at all. Maybe this was just part of his dream. He stepped toward the hallway where a white figure moved in the shadows. He stopped and tensed, instinctively preparing for an attack from a ghost.

"Greer, you okay?"

Remi. Only Remi. The air left him in a fast exhale. Fucking Ryker, spooking him. "Yeah."

"You ran out of the house. I thought the WKB had come."

"I saw something out the window. Was just an owl flying low for a mouse or something."

She didn't move as he came toward her. He didn't stop until his bare feet touched hers. He knew what he needed…the only thing that would delay his dance with the devil's eyes.

Greer flattened his hand against Remi's face, keeping still long enough for his senses to take note of her warmth and softness and humanness. She was very much alive.

He bent his head and kissed her, flattening his mouth to hers, pressing in to her as his other hand gripped her back. He walked her backward to the wall. Her hands reached for his face. She lifted herself against his body as her head tilted and her mouth opened for him.

A faint scent of something sweet and spicy drifted to him. He couldn't place it, but he liked it. His nostrils flared as he breathed more of her, felt more of her.

He gripped her hips, her ass, and lifted her as she leaned back against the wall. Holding her legs spread over his hips, he rocked into her. Bumping. Grinding. He kissed her again and timed the thrusts of his tongue with the meeting of their hips.

She arched her back. Her legs tightened against him. He heard the hiss she made as their bodies connected. He broke from the kiss and buried his face in her neck, breathing her in until her scent was locked in his soul.

He opened his mouth and licked the line of her smooth, soft skin. Waves of anticipation throbbed in his cock. Her touch, her moans—all of it stirred him as he'd never been stirred before.

He carried her into his room. She wore nothing beneath her loose T-shirt and panties. Moving one hand to her opposite cheek, he freed his other hand to reach under her shirt and grip her breast. Her lips parted.

The moonlight streaming in from his window let him see how dark her eyes had become. He wanted her shirt off, but didn't want to let go of her.

"Take it off." He tugged at it, then held her as she lifted it over her head. His eyes feasted on the bare skin she revealed. Her nipples were tight. He pressed her against his bare chest, feeling those mounds and the hard points of her nipples. He moved his hand slowly, so slowly, up her spine, pressing her closer to him. When his hand reached her neck, he eased her down onto the bed.

She moaned in complaint at the cool air that separated their bodies. He smiled. Hooking his fingers in the edge of her panties, he pulled them down her hips and legs, far too slowly to please her. He brought her feet up to his chest so he could run his hands over her silky skin from her ankles to her thighs.

He bent and kissed her calf, opening her legs as he did so, then knelt on the floor so he could press his face to the back of her knee. Her thighs were slim. His big hands had complete control of her legs, holding her open for the taking. Her sweet, spicy scent was in the curve of her knee, as it was everywhere else on her.

He licked the space behind her knee. Her body contracted. He grinned and nibbled the tendon next to the soft crease, then continued toward the V of her legs, stopping just short of the dark curls at her core.

Switching his attention to her other knee, he repeated the licks, tastes, and nibbles. When he neared her center again, he looked up at her. She was leaning on her elbows, watching him. As soon as his mouth left her, she hissed.

Forking her fingers through his hair, she brought his face down to her sweet center. Greer hooked her legs over his shoulders. Gripping her hips, he held her immobile as his tongue swept along her seam. Her thighs tightened around his face. He wrapped his arms around them, opening her again.

His tongue slipped between her folds and leisurely stroked the length of her feminine core, from her clit to her opening. He lost himself in the pleasure of tasting her. He could feel in the tension of her legs the waves of desire growing, becoming, thrumming for release. Each time she nearly peaked, he paused, waiting for it to pass, until at last there was no stopping her release. She screamed as it racked her body. He prolonged her ecstasy by penetrating her with two of his fingers, leaving his thumb to manipulate her clit so that he could watch her writhe on his bed.

When the moment slowly eased away, he kissed the inside of one of her thighs. He stood and withdrew a handful of condoms from his go-pack that one of the guys had brought over to Mandy's for him. Dropping his jeans, he kicked them off and covered himself.

Kneeling between her legs, he braced his arms on both sides of her body. "Anyone ever tell you how good you taste?" he asked.

She smiled as she bit her lip. Running her hands up his arms, she said, "Anyone ever tell you you get chatty at the wrong times?"

"Do I?"

"Mm-hmm."

He kissed her shoulder. Holding a breast, he kissed the soft mound. "Sounds like you're in a hurry."

"Sounds like you're not."

"Don't conflate speed and desire. I could happily fuck you all night. Slowly."

She braced her heels on the mattress and pushed herself up against him. "Less talking. More action."

"Or what, professor?" He caught her nipple between his teeth and ran his tongue roughly over the tight peak. "You know, I could make you come half a dozen different ways without any penetration."

"Really?"

"Yep. Want to see?"

"No. I want to feel."

"Not in a hurry anymore?"

"Greer, I'm on fire. All of me hurts. All of me wants all of you."

"Mm-mmm," he growled. "In time."

She caught his face. "No. Now."

He stood and wrapped his hands around her knees. "Now?"

"Greer."

He grinned and lifted her legs. "Put your feet on the bed." She braced her feet on the edge of the mattress. He took hold of her hips and fitted himself to her, then thrust into her, all the way. Her small muscles gripped him like a hot fist. She was tight and slick. He watched their bodies joining, knew the way he was holding her gave her no leverage. She was dependent on him for her pleasure and release.

Still holding her hips, he knelt on the bed and pushed her farther across the bed, making room for himself. Her legs folded on either side of him, gripping his hips. He settled his torso over hers, holding his weight on his elbows to keep from crushing her beneath him.

He was moving slowly inside her now, watching her watch him. She had the most beautiful eyes, deep and mysterious. His thumb brushed her face, and he wondered at the soft texture of her cheek. He wanted to see her in the light, but didn't want to leave her body to turn it on.

He kissed her eyebrow, the corner of her eye, the hollow of her cheek. Then pressed his mouth to hers with soft kisses. Slow sex with her was amazing, but he didn't think he could hold out much longer.

Slipping his hand down her ribs, over her hip, down between their bodies, he fingered her clit. She gasped. Her body tightened like a compressed spring. He joined hands with hers just as she went over the edge. He met her thrusts with his own. She orgasmed twice more before he found his own release.

When the passion eased enough that their breathing calmed, Greer became aware of a stinging near his knuckles. She'd dug her nails into him.

"Did I hurt you?" he asked.

"No." Her eyes watered, her tears like diamonds in the moonlight.

"Why are you crying?"

"I'm not."

"Then do you think you can retract your nails now?"

She gasped and eased her grip on his hands. "Sorry."

His thumbs brushed the moisture from her eyes. He kissed her cheek as he withdrew from her. "Stay with me tonight?"

She nodded. He disposed of the condom, then slipped onto his side, curling his body around hers, holding her with an arm around her ribs. He pulled the quilt up over them.

The eyes wouldn't come to him tonight, not here, in the cocoon he'd made for them. Tonight, he could sleep.

And he had Remi to thank for that.

12

Greer's eyes slammed open. Sunlight poured into the little bedroom at Mandy's house with relentless cheer. Remi hadn't been gone from his bed long—her side was still warm. He turned over, rolling in the faint scent of her that lingered in his sheets. He moved his hips, grinding himself against the linens as he thought about calling her back to bed.

And then he made the mistake of checking his watch. It was just after six a.m. He didn't hear Remi moving around. She was probably still getting dressed. No alarms had been triggered, so he knew she was still in the house.

He took his shave pack from his bag and headed for the shower in the bathroom across the hall. He'd almost made it when Remi's door opened.

He did a once-over to see what she was wearing—

a light green camp shirt, jeans, and a pair of hiking shoes. She looked situated and ready for their trip to the Friends. For some reason, that bugged the hell out of him.

He'd woken in a mood. "Remi."

"Greer." She grinned, then bit her lower lip as her gaze dropped to the raging morning boner that was saluting her, the hallway, and anything else he looked at.

"You didn't wake me," he complained churlishly.

"You were sleeping like a baby."

He rubbed his chest. "I'll be with you as soon as I shower."

"I don't think we're in a hurry to get out there this morning, are we?"

"No. The team's probably still putting together the list of items you requisitioned." He was surprised he could string normal words together. He stepped into the bathroom and shut the door, ending their conversation. He looked outside where he'd seen the figure last night.

He realized anyone who'd been looking in the front windows had to have been more than ten feet tall. Or standing on a stool. After his shower, he meant to check it out.

Ryker thought it'd been a ghost. *Question is, was it here for me or you?*

Greer turned the water on and waited for it to heat up. There wasn't a human alive he feared, but ghosts were an entirely different matter.

After his shower, he pulled on a fresh pair of tan cargos, then went back to the bathroom to finish getting ready. He brushed his teeth, then lathered his face. He'd just lifted his razor when a movement from the corner of his eye caught his attention.

Remi stood in the open door. "Mind if I watch?"

He couldn't stop a half-grin. "It's riveting."

She moved into the bathroom and lifted herself up on the counter.

"Why a straight razor?" she asked with an arched brow.

He looked at her, then back at the mirror. "I can sharpen it as needed, so it's cheaper than disposable. And it doubles as a weapon." The razor scraped his skin, clearing a path through the cream. This was the innocent side of her that he wanted to protect. "Did you watch your dad shave?"

"I never knew him. He died when I was still quite young."

Greer paused mid-stroke to look at her. "I'm sorry."

Remi shrugged. "It wasn't a loss for me. I never knew anything different. My mom was pretty good at wearing both pairs of shoes."

"I can tell."

"How?"

"She raised a strong woman."

"I'm not strong, Greer. I'm curious, determined maybe, but not terribly brave."

He made the last stroke against his skin, then

rinsed the remaining foam from his face. He patted his face dry, then stepped between her legs.

He took hold of her hands. "You should see yourself from my eyes."

Her gaze met his. Her lips thinned. "What do you see?"

"A warrior."

"A warrior?" she echoed with a disbelieving huff.

"Not all warriors wield knives and guns, Remi. Sometimes, simple resistance makes a person a fighter. Refusing to cave to wrongful domination or bullying is the bravest act of all."

She frowned and tilted her head, wary suddenly. She blinked and pushed him back, then hopped off the counter and left the bathroom. He watched her go, wondering what it was he'd said that hit wrong.

He finished gearing up, then went to the living room. She was sitting on the sofa, leaning over her laptop on the coffee table. She didn't look up when he joined her.

"Hungry?"

Her gaze took in his Beretta holstered at his waist, then slipped away as if she hadn't noticed it. She nodded. "Where do you want to eat? There's nothing here."

"We'll go to my friend's house. He has plenty of food."

She collected her purse and put her laptop in its bag. "You're going to raid your friend's fridge?"

"Why not? He keeps it stocked." Greer grinned. "We'll go in quietly. He won't know we've been there." He walked to the door and held it open for her.

"Until his eggs are gone…"

Greer lifted his brows as she walked past him. "Geez. How many eggs do you eat?"

She sent him a glare over her shoulder. "The phone book showed a diner in town. We could go there."

Greer went to open the passenger door for her. "Maybe tomorrow."

She stepped around the SUV, then paused, her attention snagged by the black ravine where Mandy's riding center had been. She walked slowly to the edge. Greer knew it had been too dark to see last night, but the sunlight couldn't hide the stark devastation below. The new construction crew had already started cleaning up the site, but the huge piles of rubble did little to improve the site's curb appeal.

"This wasn't an accident, was it?"

He shook his head.

"Who did it?"

"The people we're after. The ones who have Sally. This is why we're taking your safety pretty seriously."

She looked up at him, her eyes weary, green, and friendless. She crossed her arms. "I was hoping the last few days weren't real."

He didn't look away. Honesty was best served fast,

cold, and straight up. "It happened. Your world's sitting on its head. It's possible, though, that we can put it back to rights."

"Do you really believe that?"

Greer took two long breaths. His nostrils flared as he answered. "Yes."

"Why?"

"Because the bad guys don't get to fuck with the good guys."

The sigh she made relaxed her shoulders. She nodded at him. "Where's my car?" she asked.

"It's at my friend's house."

She got in the SUV. Greer shut her door, then went around to the driver's side and got in.

She leaned back in her seat as she snapped the seatbelt. "I'm going on blind faith right now, you know."

He put his shades on. "Yeah. I get the feeling it ain't your first time on that ride."

THEY ROLLED down the driveway and turned in a direction leading away from town. Before she could ask him where they were headed, he turned onto another driveway. She sent a questioning look his way, but his hard profile revealed nothing. There was no point asking him anything. She wouldn't understand his cryptic answer anyhow.

She faced forward as they crested a hill. A huge,

sprawling mansion came into view. A couple more SUVs were parked in front, along with her car. "This is your friend's place?"

Greer pulled around to the garage. "We'll take the back way in."

"Are we allowed to be here?"

Greer grinned at her. "Try being anywhere else." He parked off to the side. She got out, clutching her purse and laptop bag.

"I don't have a good feeling about this." She sent Greer a worried look, then caught his arm. "Let's not do this."

He pushed his shades to the top of his head. His cinnamon eyes reflected the light from the concrete drive, making them eerily bright. "I know there's nothing I can say or do that will make you feel more comfortable."

"For starters, we could not sneak into your friend's house."

A corner of his mouth lifted in a slight curl. "Maybe we'll grow on you."

And that made about as much sense as anything else he'd ever said. She followed him through the garage, where three more SUVs were parked. At the door to the house, he turned on the top step and put a finger to his lips, motioning her to silence. His eyes laughed, though, ruining his warning.

She followed him in, sticking closely behind him. As soon as the door opened, sound flooded them.

Women and children and men and dishes clattering. And oh, the delicious scent of breakfast.

"Is this a restaurant?" she asked.

He looked back and smiled. "You'd think so."

A middle-aged woman came into the kitchen with an empty serving dish. "Greer—you're back."

"Hi, Kathy," he greeted her. "This is Dr. Remington Chase. She's gonna be with us for a while." He looked at Remi. "Kathy's responsible for that wonderful smell you're enjoying."

Kathy smiled. "Dr. Chase. It's nice to meet you."

"Oh, please, you can call me Remi."

"Kathy's our housekeeper, cook, and jack of all trades. We'd be lost without her and her husband." Greer sent the older woman a smile, then glanced at Remi. "If you like, you can leave your things in here." He nodded, indicating her purse and laptop case.

"No. I'll bring them."

A swinging door separated the kitchen from the next room. He held it open for her. She stepped out into the dining room, which went silent as those assembled noticed her. Five women, seven men, and two children. The gathering looked familial. What the hell was going on here?

Greer slipped past her. He lifted his hand to indicate the group. "Everyone, this Dr. Remington Chase. Doc, this is everyone. Max isn't here, but you met him last night."

A redheaded lady who was helping a little boy straightened and held out her hand. "Hi. I'm Mandy.

I'm with Rocco." She pointed to one of the dark-haired men she met last night. "This is his son, Zavi. We heard you were helping the guys."

She nodded at Rocco and smiled at his boy. "I hope I can help them, but I'm afraid it may be an unequal exchange."

"Don't know if Greer told you, but the house you're staying at is where I live. Well, where I used to live." She flashed Rocco a look. "It was my grandparents'."

"Thanks for letting me stay there. It's very comfortable." Remi didn't bring up the huge black crater next to Mandy's house—she supposed it might be a sensitive subject in this group.

Another woman came over to them. Dark-haired with midnight blue eyes. "Hope you're hungry! Grab a plate and help yourself." She held out a hand. "I'm Ivy."

"Nice to meet you," Remi said.

"You've probably met my husband, Kit. That's our daughter, Casey."

Remi glanced across the table to Greer's team leader, who was regarding her with a measuring look. She nodded at him, then looked around the table. She'd met all the men, but none of the women—until now. Three more introduced themselves. Hope, Eden, and Selena, who was dressed like Greer in a black tee and cargo pants with a pistol strapped to her thigh. She had to be another mercenary.

Remi was curious about the group. They all

seemed healthy and happy and vibrantly alive…but happiness could be faked and fear hidden under masks of complacency—as she well knew.

Greer led her around the table to two open chairs. Once she'd put her things down, he gestured toward the long buffet overflowing with breakfast choices, hot and cold. "See why I wanted to come here?"

"You had me thinking we were sneaking into your friend's house."

"This *is* my friend's house." Greer nodded toward one of the guys. "Blade owns this fortress."

"It's a lovely home…Blade." She scoured her mind, trying to remember if the brown-haired, gray-eyed man had been introduced to her by his name or his nickname.

Remi filled her plate with eggs and fruit, then returned to her seat. There was a lot of movement in the room. People came and went.

Greer sipped his coffee as she finished the last bite of her fruit. The few remaining people in the room were having quiet conversations.

Out of the blue, Kit nodded and said, "Great. We're heading down now." He got to his feet and kissed his wife's forehead. "Lion's here. We gotta go."

She caught his sleeve. "Kit, let the boy eat first. Please."

Kit stared at his wife a long minute, then scowled. Looking into the middle distance, he issued an order. "Max, bring him up. Ivy wants him fed."

Remi leaned over and asked Greer in a whisper, "Who's he talking to? How?"

Greer pointed to his ear. "We wear a communication device. I'll have to join them in a meeting. I imagine you have some work you can do for a little while?"

She nodded and set her fork down.

"You can stay in here and do it, or use the living room, or park yourself on the patio. Please don't leave the grounds. If there's anything you'd like to eat or drink, help yourself from the kitchen." He gave her the wireless info she would need to connect.

Max came in with a young man close on his heels.

"Lion!" Hope hurried over to hug him, then led him over to the buffet table. The boy was nearly a man. He was almost as tall as Kit, with broad shoulders his lanky build didn't yet support. He wasn't dressed as any kid she knew; he wore a rustic and simple outfit of tan homespun pants and top.

The fabric looked terribly familiar. And his animal name…

She leaned over to whisper to Greer, "Is he a watcher?"

"You know about the watchers?"

"I know *of* them. I've never met one before."

The boy filled his plate then faced the table again as Casey came back into the room. She stopped next to her dad. "Lion! Hi." She smiled at the kid.

The boy's lean face remained stoic. The only

movement was the color rising on his cheeks. He looked at Kit, then dropped his gaze to his plate. "Casey," he said, as if even that was somehow trespassing.

Remi looked at Kit, caught his rigid expression. Ivy apparently did as well, for she tilted her head and widened her eyes, giving her husband the classic and silent order to stand down.

Kit's nostrils flared. He looked at his daughter. "Go about your business, Case."

"But Lion's here——" His daughter looked at her dad's imperious brow, then complied without further comment.

Kit nodded at Lion. "Greer, bring him with you when you come down," he said, then left the room.

Greer leaned back in his seat and grinned. "Roger that, boss."

Remi curiously tucked away that little exchange. She glanced over at Greer, who shook his head and mouthed, "Later."

Ivy reached over and gripped the boy's wrist. He'd quit eating and was about to rise. "Stay and finish. No harm will come to you here."

Max folded his arms. "Provided you stay away from the boss' daughter."

Lion looked up at the imposing man. "Casey is a child. Why would I be interested in her?"

Hope frowned at Max. "Don't you have someplace you need to be?" she asked. Max's gaze shifted to her. Whatever passed in their silent exchange had the woman coloring up—fast. Max pushed off the wall and started out of the room. "I'll see you in a few, Lion. Eat your fill. Ivy and your sister will protect you."

Lion set his fork down loudly. He looked over at the blond woman, his sister, apparently. "I don't need women to protect me."

"Of course you don't. Max is just pulling your chain."

"Lion," Greer said, redirecting the kid's focus. "I'd like you to meet my friend." He gestured her way. "This is Dr. Chase. She's a professor at the university in Laramie. You may address her as Dr. Chase, doctor, or professor."

Remi smiled at the boy, who looked about as far out of water as a fish could go. "Or you can call me Remi. It's nice to meet you."

He nodded at her, then returned his attention to his plate. In about thirty seconds flat, he cleared his plate, shoveling the food into his mouth with his fisted fork, then washed the meal down with a tall glass of juice. He wiped his mouth and stood.

Greer got up. "Call me if you need anything," he told Remi.

"I'll be fine. Like Lion, I don't need a babysitter."

Greer smiled and nodded toward Selena, who was coming in from the living room. "Well, you got one anyway."

"Fuck you, Greer. I'm not a babysitter," the woman snarled. "I'm coming down to the meeting."

Remi grinned, liking her instantly.

Greer laughed. "For real, Selena's kick-ass. She'll make short work of your baddies if they come here."

13

————

L ion followed Greer and the lady warrior downstairs to the big conference room in the bunker. All the guys were seated at the long conference table—even Owen, who stood as they came into the room. He gestured toward the empty seat at the far end of the table. "Lion, please have a seat."

The boy did as requested. To his immediate left sat Kit, then Max. Greer took the open spot to Lion's right. Owen nodded at Kit.

"Lion, as you know, we took a sample of your DNA a few weeks ago." Kit looked at him. "We have the results. They aren't what we'd hoped. We couldn't identify your father."

"What does that mean?" Lion asked, glancing from Max to Kit.

"It means your father, King, is either not in the system or has had himself removed from the system,"

Kit told him. "And it means we're back to ground zero in trying to identify him."

"Lion, let's go over the things you told me about your childhood and good ol' King," Max said.

Lion sent a glance around the table. "I've never met him in person."

"You may have, but without knowing who he was. Let's start at the beginning."

"My mother is Hope's mother. She died because of me, as you know."

Kit shook his head. "She died because King had her killed. Who raised you?"

"I was fostered with a family in the Friendship Community."

"Did your foster parents ever speak about King?"

"Frequently. He's someone all of us in the community were taught to revere."

"And he never made an appearance there?"

Lion was silent. His eyes took on a distant expression. "I believe he did come, when I was young. But I don't remember him. I left to be with the watchers when I was seven."

"And did King ever come to the watchers?"

"I think so, but he only interacted with Mr. Holbrook."

"You said he was revered in the community. Did you worship him?" Kit continued.

"It wasn't worship, but we all loved him. It was to him we owed our lives."

"How so?"

"He provided us with our homes, our fields, our community. He kept the outside world out."

"And you never questioned the sheep-think?"

Lion glared at Kit. "You judge me, but you don't know me."

"He's a kid, Kit," Greer snapped. "Cut him some slack."

"He's a warrior," Max said, "as lethal as you or I."

"Whatever his skill set"—Greer looked from Max to Kit—"he's still just a kid. We're asking him to remember things that might be painful to him, to question things he may not be ready to look at objectively."

Kit tossed his pen on the table and leaned back in his seat. "Take it, then."

"Lion, tell me about the things you do remember. It sounds like King was a legend among your people."

Lion nodded. "He was. It's said he has a thousand sons."

"Did you always know you were one of them?"

"Yes."

"Are other members of your pride his sons?"

"No."

"Have you ever met one of these brothers?"

"No."

"Do you know where we could find other prides like yours?"

"Find the other communities that are like the Friendship Community. King owns several of them.

Each is watched by a pride. Each is expected to play a different role in the coming Armageddon."

"And what is your pride's role in the Armageddon?" Kit asked.

Lion looked around the table. "We're engineers. We've been studying construction and destruction of bridges and waterworks."

"That was to be your pride's role in the Armageddon?" Greer asked.

"No. That was for after Armageddon. It's my pride's role to return rivers to their natural flow, to recover them from the societies who stole them from nature."

Max rubbed his forehead. "When is Armageddon going to happen, Lion?"

Lion shook his head. "I haven't been given any details. My gut says soon."

"Soon. That's all you got?" Kit snapped.

"That's all I know."

LION CAME out of the hidden staircase in the den, then crossed the room and went directly out the patio doors. He didn't stop until the sun was on him. Every time he was around Kit, he expected his skin to be peeled from his body. The fight between him and Kit was coming soon. And of course he would lose, because he couldn't bring further pain to Casey or shame to the warrior who was her father.

It occurred to him that he had nine hundred and ninety-nine brothers, if the legend was true. He wondered who they were, what they were like. How many had survived to adulthood? How many were watchers like him?

A movement out of the corner of his eye caught his attention. Casey was sitting on the rock wall that bordered the steps down to the lower lawn. She wore a T-shirt and shorts. Her blond hair was loose and waved in the breeze. Without intending to, he headed in her direction.

At the top step, he paused. "Hello, Casey."

She looked up at him, then away, then her gaze abruptly shot back to his. She straightened. "Hi." She looked around—as did he. Kit broke out in hives whenever he was near Casey. And after what had happened back at her camp, Lion couldn't blame him.

"Do you mind if I sit here for a minute?"

"No. Go right ahead."

Lion sat on the step. She folded her legs and turned slightly to look at him. His gaze fell to the book she held. "What are you reading?"

Casey glanced at her open book, then quickly hid it behind her. "Nothing. Just a book." Her face was washed with the color of guilt. He grinned at her. Her eyes widened.

"I've been wanting to apologize about what happened in the woods at your camp. I didn't mean for the lady warrior to be injured. And I didn't know how frightened you were."

"I wasn't scared."

He nodded. "I didn't realize exactly what we were involved in."

"Is my dad helping you?"

"Your dad would rather gut me than help me, but yes, he is. And I appreciate his help." He got to his feet. He'd said what he'd been wanting to say. He nodded at her, then started back toward the house. Selena was already halfway across the lawn. She met up with him fast.

"Listen, cat-boy, you don't need to be prowling around Kit's kid," she snapped.

"I wasn't prowling around anyone. I came to apologize. To her—and you." The woman wasn't quite as tall as he was, but she was a little older and had had more years to train. He was tempted to challenge her to see how she fought, but that would doubtless break another rule, and he was walking a fine line as it was.

"Yeah, well, you need to find a girl your own age." The warrior female gestured toward the house. "Shall we?"

Lion looked back at Casey, who was still watching them—hopefully they were out of earshot. "You think I'm interested in Casey?" He couldn't keep the full horror from his face. "She's a kid, no different from a boy yet."

The warrior woman laughed and shook her head. "I got news for you, Lion—girls are born different."

"She isn't even old enough to have done her tithe."

Selena gave him a sharp look. "What tithe?"

Lion stared into her eyes, conflicted about answering her question—or any of those posed by Kit and his fighters. He'd been raised to protect his people. Outsiders knew and understood nothing of the way they lived.

He shrugged and faced forward. "It's a service our young render our community when they first become adults."

Mandy walked toward the back of Ivy's diner. She'd made a lunch date with her to chat about hiring a teacher. They hadn't gotten much one-on-one time with each other in the last few weeks. With school scheduled to start soon, the time had come to decide what to do—home-school or send their kids to the local public school.

Zavi, at just four years old, was advanced for his age but too young for kindergarten. He needed special attention. Casey, just starting middle school, was attached to her friends; it would be a difficult adjustment for her to leave her regular life and be home-schooled.

Ivy smiled at her as she hung up from a phone call. "I'm so glad we made time for us." She stood up. "I'm afraid to think that we've found a new norm, that we've gotten used to the strange world we're living in."

"I know. I never saw this summer coming, that's for sure."

"Where do you want to have lunch? We can eat here or at Mama Rosa's." Her eyes sparkled. "Or we can slip down to Cheyenne like a couple of rebels."

Mandy smiled. "Don't think I'm up for an adventure. How about Mama Rosa's?"

"Works for me!"

They waved to Cord Ryker, Ty's dad, as they passed the kitchen. Out in the sunshine, Mandy felt her cares lift a little. It was nice to have time with her best friend—something they couldn't easily do at Ty's house. Ivy linked arms with her, and Mandy smiled.

They chose a table toward the back at Mama Rosa's. After ordering, Ivy leaned forward and looked at her. "Let's get business out of the way first. What's your thinking about a tutor for Zavi?"

"He needs one. He's too young for school, but he needs that intellectual stimulation. His maturity is that of a typical four-year-old, but he's ahead of the kids his age when you consider his reading level and linguistic skills."

"Wasn't Rocco just like him? How did his parents handle his abilities?"

"I asked him about that. He never knew his dad— he took off when Rocco was little. His mom was a cook on the ranch where they lived. The cowhands raised him. His mom would school him for a few hours each day, then he'd go tag along with the men. He learned various dialects of Spanish from the Columbian, Venezuelan, and Mexican hands. No one thought anything of it."

Mandy looked at Ivy. "Are you guys going to leave Casey in school? Or should we be looking for a tutor who can handle the full range of primary to secondary ed?"

Ivy drew a long breath. "It was a fight, but Kit and I have decided to keep her in the local middle school. For now. Provided she's safe there and her being there doesn't cause a safety issue for the other students. I'll drop her off and pick her up. So I think, for now at least, you should find a teacher who can focus on Zavi's special needs."

"Will you help me cull through the applications and interview the applicants? I have no experience with that. And I'm wanting someone who can be both tutor and nanny. Don't know yet if that's going to be one person or two."

"I'm an old hand at selecting staff. I'd be happy to help."

Their lunch was served. Mandy had a Caesar salad, and Ivy had chicken parmigiana. "How's Rocco doing? He seemed good at Ty and Eden's wedding." She grinned at Mandy. "Handled your belly dancing way better than I expected."

Mandy looked over at her friend, and slowly shook her head. "I don't know. I really don't. Sometimes he's so far away."

"I'm here for you, you know, if you ever want to talk."

Mandy pressed her lips together as she considered her friend. "Thanks. I don't feel as if I have anyone I can talk to." When Ivy looked a question at her, she said, "You're married to his boss."

"I'm married to his *friend*—and your *brother*. We both want you and Rocco to be well and happy." Ivy reached over to take her hand. "Look, we have to be there for each other. Our lives are not in any way normal. I promise not to pass along to Kit anything you tell me about Rocco, unless you specifically ask me to. I'm worried about you. And I'm your friend."

Mandy's eyes filled with tears. She blinked to clear Ivy's wavering image. "Thanks, Iv. I need you to be there for me."

"And I am."

14

R emi stared at the email from Clancy Weston. The questions he was asking were jarring—ones he shouldn't know to ask. Dr. Zimmers had probably filled him in. There was just something in the way he asked if she was going to park her work with the Friendship Community for good.

"…*The university isn't going to offer you a sabbatical. If you don't come back, they'll fire you. I'm worried about you. There are other groups to work on, you know. You have other studies in flight. Focus on them. Sometimes, you have to do what's good for you. You have to keep yourself safe…*"

"Remi?" It wasn't until Greer had called her twice that he caught her attention. "Doc?" She looked up, her mind still ensnared by her assistant's cryptic email. "Everything all right?"

"Yeah."

Greer looked around. "What are you doing in here?"

"Mandy felt it was a better place to concentrate. She was right."

"Owen has the things you requested ready for us. Let's have lunch, then pack up and head out."

Remi blinked, trying to clear her free-floating concerns from her mind. She put her laptop away. "Can I leave my things in here?"

A corner of Greer's mouth lifted in a one-sided smile. "You suddenly trust us?" Her hesitation was his answer. His face hardened. "Remember, I already have a mirror image of your laptop. If someone takes your laptop, I'll rebuild it for you."

"It's not that."

Greer frowned. "What else is eating at you?"

She shook her head. "Just an email from my assistant warning me about losing my job if I don't stop my research."

"Are you going to?"

Remi couldn't keep the wince from her face. "I can't." She was driven to do what she did. She could no more stop than she could make rivers flow up mountains. She shook her head. "I can't."

He held her gaze. "Look, how would they know if you continued to prepare your work for publication, as long as you don't publish anything? There's no reason you have to lose your forward momentum."

Remi looked at him. "You've heard of 'publish or

perish'? Well, it's a real thing. At least for an assistant professor in my field."

"So do what you have to do. Then do what you want to do. Make it happen."

Remi slowly smiled. The world seemed so simple from Greer's eyes. She nodded.

"You're okay for how long? A few days? A week? When does the semester begin?"

"I have a couple weeks before I have to be back at the university."

"We won't be with the Friends that long. And if you have to go back to work before we've put this to bed, you can crash here, help us on weekends."

"Is Owen going to tell the university I've gone back to the Friends?"

"I don't see why he would, but I can warn him."

"All right." Remi followed him down the long hall into the living room and up the steps into the dining room. Lunch was another selection of buffet options. The meal was as chaotic as breakfast. People came in, made a sandwich, and left. Others sat at the table. Owen, the team's boss, made a salad and took it someplace else.

The big blond guy sat next to her. Val, wasn't he? "Doc," he greeted her with a nod, then he leaned forward, looking around her to Greer. "It's so nice you have a playmate, G."

Greer chuckled, then blew a low whistle. "Unfortunate choice of words. I think I'll just sit back and watch her rip your head off."

Val arched a tawny brow as his Caribbean-blue gaze homed in on her mouth. "Oh?"

Selena joined them, a welcome tornado scattering the male bravado. "Give the professor a break. This is her first day with us." She set her plate on the table and took a seat next to Greer. "Doc, you're welcome to put them in their place or walk away."

"I take exception to that, Sel." Greer set a hand on his heart. "I've been a perfect gentleman."

Selena looked to her for confirmation. Remi met her guard's cinnamon eyes. Greer had been polite… but so demanding in bed. Remi felt her face flush. Val burst out laughing.

It was a huge relief when they were called into the after-lunch meeting. Lion and Max were absent, but Selena was present. Kit leaned against the front of a large desk. The other guys stood or sat on various pieces of furniture around the room. Owen leaned against the bookshelf behind the desk, his arms folded and feet slightly spread.

Remi glanced at Greer who was next to her, his face carefully blank. Looked as if this would be a short meeting…and everyone but she knew its agenda.

GREER MET Remi's nervous glance. He wondered how he would be handling things, were their situations reversed. His reaction to being dropped into the middle of all of this wouldn't be as calm as hers—

especially if it impacted his career as it had the potential to hit hers.

"Kit," Selena said, breaking the room's silence. "Lion mentioned a tithe he said the young adults of the Friendship Community do on behalf of the community. I don't remember hearing him say anything about that in the meeting this morning."

"He didn't." Kit looked at Remi. "Do you know anything about it?"

"Tithing has never come up in my interviews." She shook her head. "It is interesting that it's something common enough Lion would casually mention it, and yet absolutely none of the women I spoke to ever brought it up."

"Well, that's one more thing to figure out on your visit with the Friends. Are you ready to get out there? We have the things you requested." He nodded over at a few wooden crates full of goods the community would use that it couldn't generate itself: needles, pins, scissors, spools of thread, bolts of undyed cotton, pencils.

"Remi and I need a word with you before we head out," Greer said, looking at Owen and Kit.

"Get these crates loaded up in Dr. Chase's car," Kit ordered. When the room emptied, he looked at Greer expectantly.

"Remi has a week before she has to be back at the university."

Kit nodded. "Let's make it count."

"If things aren't stabilized by the time she has to

go back, I want her to stay here and commute to work."

Kit checked with Owen. "S'cool. I appreciate your help, professor. If you need Owen to have a chat with your people, we can make that happen."

"Don't do that."

"Won't they be worried if you just disappear for a while?"

Remi glanced at each of them, ending with Greer. "I let my department head know I would be visiting friends. I think it's best if they don't know I'm working with you."

"Why?" Owen said.

"This isn't the first time I've had someone come after me during a research project. Cults are closed and secretive for a reason. They like to keep it that way."

"I'm talking about telling your employer where you are, what you're doing, and that you're safe."

She hesitated. She didn't want to accuse her boss or assistant with something she couldn't prove. "I think I'm safer if they're not involved." She looked at Greer. "You are, too."

"You saying someone on your staff can't be trusted?" He asked.

Remi's lips thinned. "I have no proof. For now, no one has to be told anything. Let's leave it at that. Besides, the provost made it perfectly clear that I'm not to continue my research with the Friends. If you call them, they could well terminate my contract early."

Kit exchanged a glance with Owen. "All right. Let's try to get this wrapped up in a week."

REMI STOOD at the open hatch door of her car, her hand on one of the bolts of fabric, her mind lost in contemplation. Greer opened the tiny envelope Kit had given him and spilled its contents onto his palm. Two simple gold wedding bands lay against each other, shimmering in the sun. He picked up Remi's band. It was tiny.

Props, that was all, for a pseudo marriage. Probably the only way he'd ever have a wife.

"You got everything you need?" he asked. She nodded. "Then give me your hand."

Her brows lowered. "Why?"

"'Cause I'm gonna put a ring on your finger." He couldn't hold back his grin. Shouldn't make him so happy to have a fake wife. He slipped the narrow band down her finger, then made the mistake of looking into her eyes. He caught the flash of panic that sharpened her gaze before she could hide it.

He ground his teeth. "It's just a ring, Remi. A prop for the next few days. It has no meaning beyond that." He shoved the larger, wider band on his left ring finger. It felt foreign and constricting and warm. "There anything else you need from the house?"

She shook her head.

"Then let's get this show on the road."

She held her hand out. "Keys. I'll drive *my* car."

He set them in her hand without hesitation and went around to the passenger side.

REMI'S HEART drummed in her painfully constricted chest. Her hands tightened on the steering wheel. She looked at the wedding ring choking her finger. In fact, it was hard to stay focused on the road with that gold band glinting in the sun.

The road twisted around some hairpin curves. When it straightened out, she pulled off onto a scenic overlook. After putting the car in park, she got out and walked over to the half-wall, slipping the ring off her finger.

Greer followed her. Wind came up the cliff and over the wall, lifting her hair. She brushed it aside. "I can't do this."

"Do what?"

"Wear this ring. Pretend to be married. I'm never going to marry. Anyone who knows me knows that."

"How well do the Friends know you?"

"That's not the point."

"I get it. You like your independence. I do, too. But we don't have the luxury of indulging our fears right now. Something bigger than us is in play, and we need to figure out what it is."

"I'm fine with that. I'm okay with helping you. Just not as a married couple."

"If we don't go in married, I can't guarantee they keep us together. We need this so that I can protect you. It's very easy for people to quietly disappear. And we already know that's something they do. They've managed to lose a large portion of their youth."

Remi closed her eyes. "It's just a ring."

"Yeah. It's just a ring. You could wear it on your pinkie or in your nose, for all the significance it has to you and me. To the Friends, however, it means something entirely different." He held out his hand. "Give me your ring."

She set it in his palm.

He took the ring and turned it over a couple of times, then lifted her hand and put it on her ring finger again. "Why are you never getting married?"

She hated the feel of the ring on her hand. Hated that he always asked the worst questions. "Because I don't want to."

"What if you find the right guy?" His cinnamon eyes caught hers. His interest seemed legit, not more of the profiling she suspected he'd been doing since the beginning.

"I won't. Know why?" she asked. He lifted a brow. "Because I'm not looking."

"Not looking? Or hiding from the possibility?"

"Why do you think marriage is so important? It isn't everything."

"I never said I thought marriage was everything.

You're scared of something, and I'm trying to figure out what it is."

"It's none of your business. Haven't you been scared of anything before?"

His voice was a whisper. "Only ghosts. Only that." She had to strain to hear it above the wind buffeting the overlook.

Remi pressed her lips together. "We better get going."

15

Remi parked in the small dirt patch set aside for visitors a half-mile off the county road. The Friendship Community village was still another half-mile away, reached by a narrow buggy trail through a forest of aspen and ancient evergreens.

Greer looked around the parking area, noticing the treads from different motorcycles. He didn't mention it to Remi—she was tense enough as it was.

A bell began ringing before they were even in sight of the village. It had the sound of an old ranch bell hand-rung by someone. When they came out of the woods, the village was alive with kids and a few adults who were coming to greet them.

Greer had observed the village for several days, but watching it from afar and entering it were entirely different experiences. It was like walking back through time. The kids that surrounded them were white, with flushed faces and happy eyes. They wore the simple clothes of their people—homespun cotton shirts, trousers, skirts. Both boys and girls wore black boots with heavy socks.

Greer looked over at Remi to see her reaction to the kids. She had an easy smile on her face, but her tension showed when she looked at the adults. One of the women smiled at her, then gave him a curious once-over.

"Dr. Chase! How happy we are to see you!" the woman said as she shook Remi's hand vigorously.

Remi exchanged greetings then introduced Greer to Mrs. Dunbar and the Haskels. "Mrs. Dunbar's husband is the village's mayor. And the Haskels both serve on the town council," she told him.

"You're married? We didn't know that was in the works for you!" the first woman, Mrs. Haskel, exclaimed.

"Yes." She laughed like acting was first nature to her. "He talked me into it at last."

"That's wonderful! But you didn't take your husband's name?" Mrs. Dunbar asked.

Remi looked over at him, then shook her head. "I've established my professional reputation under my maiden name. We thought it best if I kept it."

Mrs. Haskel shook her head in a disapproving way. "Things are very strange in your world."

"Speaking of which, how is your article coming along?" Mrs. Dunbar asked.

"That's why we're here. I was hoping to wrap up

my research by spending a little more time with you, if that wouldn't be too much of an imposition."

"Not at all," Mrs. Dunbar answered for the group. "You know we've been looking forward to more visits with you."

"Thank you! I've been compiling my notes from our conversations and have a few more questions and things I'd like to have clarified."

Mrs. Haskel slipped her arms through Greer and Remi's and led them deeper into the village. She leaned over to Remi and whispered loudly, "Your husband's quite the beefcake."

Remi's blush made Greer laugh.

Mrs. Haskel squeezed Remi's arm. "Ask anything. You know we're proud of our community. I wish there were more like ours in the world." She gave Remi a sad look. "Every time we travel into Cheyenne for our market days, we learn such stories about murders and war and drugs and terrible things in your society. It's reinforcing our mission here in our own community. I think we're all excited for our story to be told."

Greer knew Max was hearing and seeing all of this from his magic sunglasses and comm unit. It wasn't the fearful greeting of a community who had anything to hide…which didn't necessarily mean they didn't have anything to hide, only that they were good at hiding it.

"You'll stay overnight, won't you? I'd hate for you to make the long trek here and back all in one day," Mrs. Dunbar said.

Remi looked at him, then answered. "We'd love to. Thank you."

"That's settled, then," Mrs. Haskel declared. "We have bread rising that we have to tend to. Our husbands can retrieve your things and get you settled in the guest cabin where you stayed last time. You come with us, dear. Ask us your questions while we work."

Greer looked to see if that suggestion caused Remi any concern. He took her hands and bent to kiss her cheek. "You okay with that?" he asked. When she nodded, he whispered a reminder about her alarm necklace.

Remi followed the women to Mrs. Dunbar's cabin, one of the larger ones in the immediate area. In the community, when a family had a lot of kids of both genders, the council permitted them to build additions that gave their daughters a separate sleeping space from their sons. And though the Dunbars' children were grown with families of their own, they remained in the large house because of their status in the community. The extra rooms were sometimes used for closed council meetings.

Mrs. Haskel directed Remi to a Windsor chair at the desk. A breeze filtered in from the open, screenless windows. The women put fresh aprons on, then washed their hands and turned out bowls of rising dough to be kneaded.

"Now you just go ahead with your questions," Mrs. Dunbar directed.

Remi pulled her notebook out of her laptop bag and opened it to a blank page. "We've spoken before about other groups similar in some ways to the Friends. In particular, about the Amish."

"Yes, I remember," Mrs. Haskel said without looking up from her dough.

"They have an event or activity called *Rumspringa*. It's a period of time where the youth in the Amish communities experience the outside world and then decide to stay in that world or return and commit their lives to their community. Do the Friends' youth participate in something similar?"

Mrs. Dunbar was using a great deal of force with the dough she was working. Mrs. Haskel said nothing, letting the mayor's wife answer for them.

"We don't have *Rumspringa* as you mention. There've been cases in our history where some of our citizens have left our community, but not very often. We've been growing, in fact. This year alone, we've built ten additional cabins for young couples."

"It was twelve, Mrs. Dunbar."

"Indeed. So it was." She looked at Remi. "There were many years, many in a row sometimes, where new families occupied cabins already emptied by citizens who had passed."

"To what do you attribute the recent growth?" Remi asked.

Both women kept their eyes on their work. "I would assume it's because our citizens feel invigorated by the nature of our community."

"And if someone wanted to go, could they?"

"Goodness, Dr. Chase," Mrs. Haskel said with genuine humor in her eyes. "Our community's not surrounded by armed guards. Any of us can leave at any time."

"And if they go, can they come back?"

"If they come back to stay, yes." Mrs. Dunbar paused and looked over at her, her palms resting on the soft dough. "Our community has a mission, Dr. Chase, one that is the center of our ethos. Everyone here knows it. Everyone who leaves, leaves because of it. It's what we're made of. If a citizen decides that what we're about is not a fit for him, there would be no reason for him to return for visits, would there?"

"I never heard it put that way," Remi said. "What is your community's mission?"

"We strive to live authentic lives focused on what matters. Family, community, peace."

"That's lovely." Remi jotted that down. "Do your citizens tithe?" If she hadn't been looking at the women, she wouldn't have caught the flash of tension that crossed their features.

"Of course we tithe. All Christians tithe."

"And how do your tithes work?"

"Same as anyone's," Mrs. Dunbar said, keeping her focus on her work. "We give back to the community. Because ours isn't a currency-based community, tithing is about service, not charity. Young people especially do some service for the community."

"What kind of service?" Remi asked.

"It varies. My husband, as the mayor, assigns them their task. It is a solemn event. The tasks are kept secret, out of humility. They are never discussed. But they are often challenging. And once they're completed, the young person takes his or her place in the community as an adult."

"Interesting. Are there any recent tithers I could speak to?"

"The Smiths' and Bennetts' kids just recently completed their tithes, as did the Johnsons'," Mrs. Haskel said, looking at Mrs. Dunbar, who gave her a stern look.

"They did—however, they're a bit under the weather."

"Yes, of course. And, truly, the tithes our youths do are sacred, doctor," Mrs. Haskel said in a soft voice, almost as if she was afraid they would get caught. "They aren't ever bandied about casually. It would be most impolite to ask anyone about their tithe."

"And beyond the youth tithes," Mrs. Dunbar continued, "we all tithe food or labor, as needed by anyone in the community. We take care of our own."

"That's admirable. Do you have any problems with the White Kingdom Brotherhood? I understand they have a large property that borders yours."

The two women exchanged charged looks. "I hate them," Mrs. Haskel hissed.

"We have as little to do with them as possible. They don't represent our community's values in any way." Mrs. Dunbar looked at Remi. "However, as you point out, they are our neighbors, and we do, sometimes, have interactions with them."

GREER CARRIED an armload of crates to the central storehouse where the community's shared goods were kept. The herd of kids brought the rest. While they began carefully unpacking the things Remi had brought for the community, Mr. Haskel clapped a hand on Greer's back and drew him outside. "I suppose you might like a tour of the town."

Greer looked over in the direction Remi had gone with the women.

"Oh, never mind about them. They're making bread today. They'll be hours yet. C'mon. We'll saddle some horses and go for a tour."

"Sounds good. I'd like to see what you're doing here."

They went down to a community stable. Mr. Haskel saddled a couple of horses. "You ever ride before?"

"Yeah. Summer camp years ago."

"Well, it ain't changed much since," Mr. Haskel said with a chuckle.

Greer mounted his horse and rode next to him down the dirt road that led through the village. Talk about a time warp. It felt like moving through a reenactment village.

The town had a population of three hundred adults and two hundred children, a number that jibed with the census Remi took and wasn't far off the last U.S. census. The community was extraordinary, and Greer enjoyed learning about its complexities.

Most of the unwed adult women lived with their parents. There was a long bunkhouse where unwed bachelors lived. Children were schooled from six to thirteen. When a kid showed a special interest in a topic, a resident who was a specialist in that topic furthered his education in the hopes of finding interns to help in his work.

There was a row of shops maintained by a barter system. Furniture for a side of beef. Candles for eggs. Veggies for candles. Ironwork for a horse. Horses for construction assistance. There were pottery shops, a seamstress, and an herbalist.

The community cut ice in the winter and stored it in great ice warehouses for use through the summer. Most cabins had old-time wooden iceboxes. There was a communal greenhouse. Everyone who wasn't a specialist found work in the fields, raising corn, wheat, and other crops for the community. Others were employed by taking care of the community's elders.

No one was idle. No one was superfluous. Even with the community growing, it grew in a balanced way. Greer learned there was no gender-based division of labor. If a woman wanted to be a smithy, she could be. If a man wanted to make candles, he could.

Town government permitted either gender in its leadership positions.

Mr. Haskel felt their community had survived because, unlike most other utopian societies that originated as theirs did in the nineteenth century, they allowed for variances of individual aptitude and interest. The community had a church and a minister, but was, by mission, a secular institution.

They visited the grain mill, with its storage silo, and the lumber mill, both powered by the river as they had been for close to two centuries. They visited the smithy, the icehouse, and shops for the butcher, cheesemaker, weaver, and apothecary.

Greer learned there was also an infirmary, just over the hill, set a little ways off from the main community. Their long-time doctor had recently passed and now the community was being served by his young intern, who was doing more than a passable job.

Greer asked if the new doctor, or even the former one, had a modern medical degree. Mr. Haskel frowned and said the community was extremely healthy. Most of their elders lived well into their eighties and nineties without medications and with their faculties intact. A community in balance, he reiterated, was naturally healthy.

They paused by the large schoolhouse. The population had grown so much in the last decade that a second one was being built.

"Do most of your children stay here in the community when they're adults?"

"Most do."

"What happens when they turn thirteen and their schooling ends?"

"By then, if the children have shown an interest in a specialty, their education is handed over to the experts in their interest area. Those who don't have a particular leaning toward one thing or another are shown how to work a farm or are brought into one of our other labor trades."

"Your community is efficient. Do you worry about your success outgrowing your resources?"

"We have five thousand acres up here. There are more we can buy. I think we are well situated now and for the immediate future."

"I understand from Remi that your youths perform tithes. Could you tell me more about that?" Greer asked.

Mr. Haskel's gaze flashed his way, his eyes widening briefly. "It is just another of our customs. When a young person decides he or she's ready to be an adult in our community—with the privileges and responsibilities that brings—he or she is tested with an act of service. If it's successfully completed, then the young person is regarded as an adult. Tithes come earlier for some and later for others."

"Are these tithes or services ever rendered outside your community?"

"Tithes are intensely personal, Mr. Dawson. We

never speak about the service we were asked to render."

"Would, say, committing murder be considered a tithe?"

The affability left Mr. Haskel's face. "I would expect such a question from an outsider. We have a very small population here, sir. Each of us has a specialty. There is little overlap. If someone were to commit murder, his actions would make life much more difficult for all of us."

"But not if the murder was committed in the outside world."

"What are you implying?"

"There was a girl from your community who tried to kill my friend."

"Impossible."

"I took her to the hospital, where they had to flush the drugs from her system. I met her parents. I saw the buggy they drove when they retrieved her. I saw the bench they left as payment. The closest other communities similar to yours are in Montana and Colorado, nowhere near here. Her name was Sally."

"Such an act defies everything we stand for. Everything. Describe her to me. I will question her myself."

"She's young. Sixteen or seventeen. Tallish. Long blond hair. Blue eyes."

He made a face, his lips tucked up on one side. "You've just described half of all our young girls.

None of them are named Sally. When you dine with us for supper tonight, tell me if you see her."

"Thank you. I will."

"Was your friend injured by this girl?"

"No. She was under the influence of some drug. I don't believe she was acting under her own will."

"I'm very sorry to hear this. Very sorry. It's shocking. I think you have my community confused with another, but you can help me investigate it during your stay." He leveled a look at Greer. "I would just ask that you keep your questions for the mayor and our council members. I don't want to alarm the greater community."

"I understand. Thank you." Greer couldn't tell if he was being played, but at least he hadn't gotten them run out of the community. The longer they were able to stay, the farther he might get in his discovery.

Looking around them, he realized they'd come to a stop at a long hall built from timber and mud. The sign over the front door read "Infirmary." A young man stood at the door, wiping his hands on a cloth.

Greer wondered how much of their conversation he'd heard. The man was in his mid-twenties. He was of medium height, with dark hair, and blue eyes. His complexion was a little gray. Greer wondered if he wasn't feeling well or if he was perhaps exhausted.

"Dr. Robinson, this is Mr. Dawson," Mr. Haskel said. "He's visiting with his wife, Dr. Chase, the sociologist from Laramie."

Greer nodded at the doc, who nodded in return.

"How is Mrs. Bennett today?" Mr. Haskel asked.

"She's stable, though still feverish. I would invite you in"—he gestured toward the open door behind him—"but I fear she may still be contagious," he said.

"We understand. She's in good hands. My wife will be sending over some soup and bread for you and the patients."

The young doctor looked relieved. "Thank you. We appreciate that."

Mr. Haskel faced forward and lifted his reins, but Dr. Robinson stopped him with a question.

"Have we opened our boundaries to any new resident, Mr. Haskel?" He sent a meaningful glance toward Greer.

"Nothing has changed, doctor. If a prospective citizen wishes to eschew modern civilization for the remainder of his natural life, and if such a person wishes to contribute in a beneficial way to our community, the council will review their application."

"No exceptions?"

"No."

"Good day, sirs." Dr. Robinson's wave was dismissive.

Greer looked at his companion as they continued on their way. "What was that about?"

"Mrs. Bennett has had a persistent fever. I doubt the doctor's had much sleep lately."

"I thought you said your community was extraordinarily healthy."

"We are. But we are only human, Mr. Dawson.

Sometimes we catch a bug that has a nasty way of running through the whole community. It's why we have an infirmary." He looked over at Greer. "I'm sure that happens in your community, too."

"Oh, it does. Probably far more often than here."

Here. In this strange Shangri-la that was almost too perfect to be real. No wonder they didn't want anyone visiting or observing or changing what they had going on.

Greer resisted looking back toward the infirmary. He definitely needed to have more words with the doctor.

16

——————

Owen looked up from his tablet as Casey came into the living room. Supper was still an hour away. No one else had come down for happy hour. He nodded at her and returned his attention to the article he was reading as she folded herself into the armchair next to him, her knees by her chin, her head propped on her fist as she faced him.

He continued to ignore for another few sentences. She didn't move. He looked at her again. "Something I can do for you, Casey?"

She frowned. "Do you like my dad?"

"I'm his boss."

She waved that away. "Yeah, but do you like him?"

"I do."

"Do you understand him?"

Owen studied Kit's daughter, wondering where she was headed with this. He looked out to the hallway, hoping for someone, anyone, to come into the room and spare him from this conversation. He glanced at her. "Maybe. In some things. Why?"

"Why is he so mean to Lion?"

"I think this is something you should ask him."

"I will. I'm just trying to understand him first, Uncle Owen. I can't ask Mom because her eyes get all big and soft anytime he's around."

Owen grinned, then cleared his throat and gave her a sober look. "Your dad holds the lives of all of us here in his hands—his entire team and now their wives and girlfriends. And kids, too. There's a lot at risk. Lion attacked you once—"

"Yes, but we got that all straightened out," she interrupted him.

"If you've already made up your mind about this, why ask me?"

She nodded. "Okay. Go on."

"Lion's primary loyalty is to his pride, not the team. Not the team's loved ones. He's young. He's dangerous. And he's still something of an unknown. As his trustworthiness becomes known, your dad's comfort level in him will grow. Or not. Until then, your dad can only go on the experience he's had with Lion, one in which you were exposed to grave danger and Selena was hurt—not something a team lead…or a dad…can easily overlook."

"Oh." She straightened in her chair, her eyes focused on nothing while she processed his explanation. After a moment, she nodded. "Okay. Makes sense." She looked at him. "Will he get over it?"

"Why does it matter?"

"Because I like Lion."

Owen arched a brow.

"As a friend. A brother. Don't get creepy."

Owen smiled. "Give your dad time. And talk to him about it. You should always talk to your parents."

"Okay." She got out of her chair and came over to kiss his cheek. "Thank you, Uncle Owen. This was a good talk."

Owen watched her leave the room, and felt a strange emptiness when she was gone. He'd never had a kid. Nor had anyone ever thought he owned the sun like she did her dad.

Chances were pretty damned slim he ever would.

WHEN GREER and Mr. Haskel returned to the Dunbars' home, Remi was sitting out front with a glass of water. She smiled at him, smiled as if she were truly a newlywed happy to see her husband.

Felt like a fist in his chest, 'cause it was all an act.

Knowing that didn't keep him from wishing it was real, wishing they had a shot at something. Talk about putting all your eggs in one basket. That basket had a paper bottom. And the eggs were wet.

He disabled his comm unit and shut down transmission from his glasses via his phone app. She lifted her water to him. The water was ice cold. He took a long swallow.

"Want more?" she asked.

He lowered the glass and looked at her. Yes, he did. A whole helluva lot more. He set the glass aside and held out his hand.

"Take a walk?" he asked.

She slipped her hand in his. The hand with her fake wedding band. The dream hadn't quite worn off, and he liked it that way. When they'd moved out of earshot, he told her about the tour. "It's like the town that time forgot."

Remi nodded. "But a little too Stepford Wives for me."

"Not everyone is a happy citizen. The doctor gave me the hairy eyeball."

"I haven't met the new doctor. I understand their old one recently passed away."

"I want to go talk to him later. He mentioned something about new residents. Might help us understand the community's population anomalies."

"Good."

"Anything from the women?"

"They admitted to doing tithes, but downplayed their importance. They said their community has little to do with the WKB. They looked scared as they said it, though." They'd stopped walking and now stood face to face. "Anyone know Sally?"

"Mr. Haskel didn't, but he invited me to look for her at supper."

"I'll help you."

Greer touched her cheek. She leaned toward him. He bent forward and closed the distance between them. Her mouth was soft beneath his. He kissed her slowly, as if he had all the time in the world. In this moment, in her space, he felt at home, felt an acceptance he'd never known from another woman.

The village was situated around a large center square. Trestle tables were being set up for supper. The sound of preparations filtered into Greer's mind.

"I brought our packs to the cabin. Let's go wash up for dinner." Greer wrapped his arm around her shoulders. She put her arm around his waist. God, he liked that simple touch.

The cabin they'd been assigned was no different than many of the others. There was a kitchen area at one end and a sleeping alcove at the other. The windows were open. A soft breeze blew cool alpine air through the house.

Something about the wood scent of the cabin and all the fresh air made Greer feel alive. He wanted to see Remi naked in the cabin's soft light. He closed the door behind them, then caught her around the waist in the middle of the room. He smiled as he kissed her, but his smile vanished as his kiss deepened.

"We could miss dinner," he suggested. "Tell them you were working on your notes."

Her arms went around his neck. Her little tongue slipped between his lips.

"We could, but we'd miss the chance to look for Sally."

Greer leaned his forehead against hers. His breathing was heavy. His dick was throbbing for her. He remembered he hadn't cleared the cabin of transmitting devices. He pressed his finger to his lips as he fished his phone from his pocket and swept the cabin with it.

"We're clear."

"Of course we are. We're in the nineteenth century."

Greer shook his head. "The Friends are in bed with WKB. Don't trust anyone."

Remi sighed. She went over to a bowl and pitcher, then poured out a small amount of water to rinse her hands with. She used the small bar of soap and rinsed again. Greer did the same. She handed him the linen towel.

"I wish this place was real," she said with a sigh. "I wish there really was a place like this where you could come for a break from reality. Get away from electronics. It's like being on a frozen lake high in the mountains, where time stands utterly still."

"Until you see just how thin the ice is. And how deep and dark the winter lake is."

She gave him a frustrated face. "Remember that thing I said about your reading fairytales to kids? Yeah, that. Do you see danger lurking everywhere?"

"Usually. Because it is. Things here aren't what they seem."

"Well, on that happy note, let's go have supper." She opened the door.

Dinner was a communal event. Families set up their own tables and brought their meal to share. Tablecloths, in varying shades of white, were clipped to the trestle tables. Handmade pottery dishes in earth tones helped pin the linens down in the stiff breeze that had come with the evening.

"You cold?" Greer asked Remi.

She smiled at him, which made him glad he asked. "I'm fine now. I might need my jacket later, though."

"I'll get it after dinner."

Greer took a backseat to Remi in conversations as the meal progressed. She was animated and engaged. He was enjoying watching her interact with the Friends. They sat at the Dunbars' table. While she chatted, he took a video of the gathering…and scanned some of the glasses of the people sitting around them.

Greer looked at the community's current mayor. Mr. Dunbar had been working in the fields when they arrived. When his wife introduced him, he looked less than pleased that they were there. Greer had thought he was going to send them packing, but Mrs. Dunbar reminded him of their commitment to Remi's project. Greer had overheard their conversation. Mr. Dunbar's main objection wasn't to Remi but to him. He'd seemed unconvinced about their recent nuptials.

Did Dunbar know who he was? If so, who had told him?

The families at the tables on either side of theirs seemed a little hushed, as if they were pretending to not listen to the conversations the Dunbars were having with Remi.

Greer wondered if all the families turned out like this on a routine basis or if they'd been ordered to present themselves this evening. He looked around at the gathering. There were several male and female teenagers. Some looked to be middle to older teens. But there were far more children than teenagers.

Sally wasn't anywhere to be seen.

When supper was over, the kids cleared the dishes and the men dismantled the trestle tables. In the middle of the busy activity, he looked up and saw the girl he'd seen at Remi's university.

He frowned. Was that one of Remi's assistants? Had she followed them out here?

Greer leaned over to Remi and whispered, "I'll be right back. Don't go anywhere."

He hurried away from the line of tables being broken down. The girl moved between two cabins. He jogged to catch up to her as she went around behind one.

When Greer stepped into the backyard, there was

nothing but a fenced-off vegetable patch that still had the desiccated remains of a long-gone garden.

Behind the other cabin was a mountain of firewood. A man was splitting wood. His ax slammed into the wood, cracking a half-log into quarters. He looked at Greer, then set up another half-log and swung hard.

He paused after that piece and stood silently staring at Greer.

Greer collected himself in time to not look like a fool. "Did you see a girl come this way?"

"You one of the visitors Mayor Dunbar invited for a stay?"

"I am."

"Well then, I wouldn't be chasing women here in our community."

"I'm not chasing women. I saw a girl I thought I knew. Long blond hair. Jeans. I think her name was Sally?" Of course, none of the females in the community wore jeans, he realized. Maybe this guy didn't even know what they were.

The woodcutter straightened, lowering his ax. "What did you say?" he asked, then glanced behind Greer.

Greer turned to see Mayor Dunbar coming along behind him. Greer smiled a welcome, then fell into benign chitchat as they headed back toward the dining tables. Greer looked back at the woodcutter, who was watching him with feral intensity.

When they reached the table, the women turned

to them. Greer smiled at Remi. "Take a walk with me? It's not often we get to enjoy a quiet sunset. I found the perfect hill while on my tour with Mr. Haskel earlier."

"No, I need to help with cleanup duties," Remi said.

"Nonsense. You go with your husband," Mrs. Haskel insisted. "No place in the world has sunsets like ours."

Remi stood and reached for his hand. "Well then, lead on."

"Where are we really going?" Remi asked when they'd gone a little way down the road.

"To see the doctor. I want to know what was up with him earlier."

"Why did you run off after dinner?"

Greer looked down at her, then away, wondering if what he was about to say sounded crazy. "I saw a blond who might have been Sally. Or someone who looked like her—I didn't see her face." In fact, he never saw the girl's face. Her hair was always in the way, or her back was to him. "Do you have a female assistant or intern?" he asked, watching her. "I thought I saw her at the university, too."

She shook her head. "Only Clancy, my teaching assistant. Were you able to talk to her?"

"No. She was gone before I could catch up with her."

"Well, if she is Sally, then at least you know she hasn't disappeared. She's here and safe."

ELAINE LEVINE

Greer said nothing, convinced of no such thing. How had Sally gotten down to Remi's university? What was she mixed up in?

They walked the remainder of the way to the infirmary in silence. Dusk was gathering, casting brilliant colors across the sky. Greer picked up the pace, knowing how the village shut down at night. He didn't want to miss this chance to talk to the doctor without one of the other villagers curtailing their conversation.

The infirmary was a long building made of rough-hewn logs, like most of the other cabins. This one looked like it might have once been a bunkhouse for ranch hands. The front door was ajar. Greer knocked and pushed the door open a little farther.

Motioning to Remi to wait outside, he stepped into the shadowy interior. To the right was a small waiting room with two wooden benches. To the left, a room that looked like a surgery room. Down the hallway were two more rooms—another surgery and a kitchen. Beyond that was the patient area.

Greer got a glimpse of several cots, three with patients who were resting somewhat uncomfortably. He wondered if the other two patients had the same ailment that Mrs. Bennett had.

"Can I help you?" Dr. Robinson came out of the kitchen. He looked beyond Greer, out the main door. "You came unescorted?"

Greer nodded. "I wanted my wife, Dr. Remington

200

Chase, to meet you." He led the way out of the infirmary and made the introductions.

"Since when does the WKB hire sociologists?" Dr. Robinson asked.

"What makes you think we're from the WKB?"

"You have the same pugnacious stance. And the WKB are the only outsiders allowed here."

"My wife is from the University of Wyoming. I'm just here to make sure she comes home safely. A place frequented by the WKB isn't a safe place."

The doctor searched Greer's eyes. Something shifted in his posture.

"And I'm looking for a girl named Sally."

The doctor's full attention sharpened on him. "How do you know Sally?"

"She tried to commit a crime while under the influence of drugs. My friends and I took her to a hospital. Her parents, who were from here, retrieved her."

Dr. Robinson sat on a bench in front of the clinic, dropping as if his legs wouldn't hold him.

"You know her, don't you?" Greer asked.

He didn't respond. "Where is she?"

"I just saw her—" Greer frowned. He had, hadn't he?

Remi sat on the bench next to the doctor. She touched his arm. "Talk to us."

Dr. Robinson lifted his head. His gaze was haunted. "I haven't seen her in almost two months.

She left to do her tithe and never came back. So many of them don't anymore."

"What are these 'tithes'?" Greer asked.

"Each young adult, when he or she or their family decide that it's time for them to go out on their own, renders a service to the community. The young who have a skill important to the community are exempted from tithing. As an apprentice to the doctor, I was exempted, so I don't know much about them. The tasks are secret, never to be spoken of."

He looked up at Greer. "Sally was her tithing name. Her real name was Rebecca Morris." His shoulders hunched, and he looked at his hands clasped between his knees.

"Most young women get married after their tithes," he continued. "If they return. Many are returning already married to WKB warriors. We're a pacifist community. These warriors are like infants." He waved his hand around. "They know nothing of life, nothing of our ways in the community. They have to be taught everything—building a fire, hunting, butchering, farming, home construction, our cere-monies. Everything.

"Rebecca and I were in love. But she'd been promised to the woodcutter. She hated him. I went to the council. I told them if they didn't overturn that decision, I would leave—with Rebecca. It's my fault she hasn't come back."

Greer realized the young woman he'd run after couldn't have been Sally. If she'd come back, he wouldn't now be talking to the doctor about her absence. "Have you talked to her parents? Do they know anything?"

"Rebecca was an orphan. She was raised by the village. And no, no one knows her whereabouts."

"Why does everyone avoid the topic of tithes?" Greer asked.

He lifted a shoulder. "Tradition. We are never to discuss them. We aren't to ask about how they went or what service they provided or what happened while they were away. Once a tithe is finished, the young person is treated as an adult, allowed to go to council meetings, allowed to marry, allowed to have children."

He was silent a moment. "I've watched these tithes change over the past twenty years. At first, while I was happy being the doctor's apprentice, I resented the fact that I didn't get my own tithe. When I was a kid, those who completed their tithes came back different. Wiser. More adult. Now they're coming back changed, but for the worse. Fearful. Broken temperaments. I don't know. I don't think the tithes are good things anymore."

Greer reached out to the doctor, resting a hand on his shoulder. "All right. Thanks. I'll get word to you when I find her."

Dr. Robinson stood and held out his hand. "I am in your debt."

"No. I've been worried about her since we met. I knew something wasn't right."

Greer took hold of Remi's hand again as they

headed back toward the village. The shadows were long. Night was close.

Greer looked down at Remi. "Am I pugnacious?"

Remi smiled. "You do puff up at times. Like when danger is near. Or you want sex."

He grinned. "So, all the time."

"No. Sometimes you're serious and introspective."

"And shrunken."

Remi laughed. "Is everything about size?"

He stopped and caught her up against him. "Does anything else matter?" He was about to kiss her when he noticed the woodcutter was placing chopped wood in the stand out front of their cabin.

Remi saw him, too. Greer felt her stiffen in his arms. "I want you to go inside and wait for me." Thankfully, she didn't argue as they neared the cabin.

They nodded to the woodcutter as they stepped up to the cabin. "I'll be in in a minute," Greer told her as he shut the door behind her.

"Need a hand?" he asked, grabbing a few split logs and setting them on the small stack.

"Sure."

"Thanks for the wood."

"Yep. I knew her." He flashed a look at Greer, followed by a quick one over his shoulder. "Sally. I knew her."

"How did you know her?"

"She was promised to me. We were gonna marry after her tithe." He carried over another log.

"Her tithe?" Greer asked, hoping ignorance

would lead him to say more about this mysterious service the teenagers rendered.

"We can't talk here. Meet me in the woods by your vehicle at two hours after midnight."

Greer nodded. "Will do."

17

———

Remi was standing in the middle of the room when Greer came into the cabin. "What did he say?"

He took hold of her shoulders and kissed her forehead. "He wants to meet with us in the middle of the night. Nothing good happens at meetings like that. I think you should stay here."

"Dr. Robinson said the woodcutter was from the WKB. Do you believe him?"

"I do. There's nothing about him physically that would point to the gang, but it's in his eyes, his voice. He knows something about Sally. I can't not go."

"What if it's a trick to separate us?"

Her hands were on his waist. She was looking up at him as if she believed in him, as if she knew he'd keep her safe. Made him feel ten feet tall. And he did puff up a little.

"All right. You're coming with me. I'm going to call the meetup in to the team."

He dialed Max, glad that the infrastructure Owen had had beefed up around the WKB compound reached the Friendship Community.

"S'up, bro?" Max answered.

"Just FYI. I'm meeting up with a former WKBer who's now a Friend here in the community. Said he knows Sally. Might have some info about the tithes, which no one else here will talk about in much detail. He wants to meet at two a.m."

"Copy that. I'll let Kit know. Where's the meet?"

"Near the entrance gate for the community. There's a small parking lot there."

"Okay. I'll send some of the guys your way, just in case."

"Don't need backup, Max. It's just one guy."

"Too bad. The guys here are bored and driving me crazy."

THE BED in the guest cabin was set in a deep alcove. Curtains that could be pulled across the opening were drawn back on either side. The dark, still sleeping bay was a perfect nest for spiders, Remi thought with a shiver. A quick check of the space showed it was as spotless as the rest of their cabin—and the outhouse behind it.

The community had provided a candle and a box of matches. They lit it and set it on the table a few feet from the bed. Remi took her boots off and climbed into the alcove. Leaning back, she watched Greer settle against the opposite wall.

The candle was dim and flickering, but once her eyes were used to the low light, she could see Greer clearly. He was the first guy she'd ever kept longer than a weekend. That should have panicked her, but it didn't for some reason she couldn't identify. Other than her professional cooperation with his team, Greer never asked anything of her personally. What would happen to them when this was all over?

In the dim light, for the space of a few heartbeats, his eyes seemed to darken as he said, "I want to still see you when this is over." It was as if he read her mind.

She folded her knees and brought them close to her chest. She wanted that, too. For the first time ever, she'd found someone she wanted in her life. The weight of that realization terrified her. "What if it's just the stress of everything bringing us together?"

He lifted a shoulder. "Maybe. But what if you're the one?" he asked. "What if I am? Do you want to quit before we know?"

"What if I'm not?" she countered. His silence was heavy in the space between them. "Do you really believe in finding the one perfect person?"

"Before you?" He shook his head. "I'd stopped believing when my fiancée left."

"I didn't know you'd been engaged."

"We met in college. I guess I just wasn't the guy she thought I was. At least not once the Army recruited me. I don't know. Maybe she didn't like Army life. I traveled a lot." He looked at her. "I don't want to be alone, Remi."

"What if I push you away, like I push everyone away?" She got off the bed and paced across the room. She opened the door and let the night wind in. Her back was to him; she didn't see or hear him move, but his arms slipped around hers like soft wings. He took her wrists and opened her arms, holding her hands at right angles to her body. The cool air slipped over and under their arms.

"What if…what if I am what you are for me—a soul hangover?" His rumbled whisper gave her a shiver. "What if I stay in your heart, and you ache for me as I do for you? Will you be brave? Will you fight for me?"

She did ache for him. Already. "I don't want to."

"But will you?"

"I've never fought for anything like that."

He turned his hands palm-up under hers. "Yes, you have. You've fought for your life. You've fought for your career." He pressed his face against her hair. "Will you fight for me?"

She turned and looked up at him. "Greer, you terrify me."

He nodded. "As you do me." He touched her hair.

"Will you fight for me?" she asked.

"Oh, yeah." His teeth flashed in a quick smile. "When this is behind us, we'll still be together. We're a long way from over."

KIT'S PHONE buzzed on the nightstand. He picked it up, checking Ivy to make sure it hadn't roused her. Casey was watching a movie with Mandy, Rocco, and Zavi, so they'd had the evening to themselves. Ivy was now in a deep, sated slumber.

Max was on the other end.

"Sorry to interrupt you, boss. The kid's walking into a situation you need to know about. He's meeting a former WKBer, who's now a card-carrying Friend, at the witching hour of two a.m. Want me to send a couple guys as back-up?"

"Yeah. Angel and Val. I'll go, too. Tell them to be downstairs at midnight."

He hung up. Ivy slipped her arm over his chest. "Where are you going?"

"Just a security patrol. Nothing to worry about. I don't have to leave for a while yet."

She smiled and reached up to touch his face. He kissed her as he rolled over her. Spreading her legs, he slipped inside her. This third time tonight was different from the others. Gentle. Slow.

She wanted another baby, and he wanted her to have everything her heart desired.

KIT WAS HUMMING in the passenger seat as they neared the turn for the Friendship Community.

"Jesus, Kit," Val grumbled. "Can you turn down the afterglow? It's hard to see the road."

"Sorry." He grinned. "We're working on kid number two, feel me?"

"Val and I are in the worst drought of our lives, and you're popping kids?" Angel grumbled.

Before Val could answer, a loud Harley roared past. Two more came over the hill they were climbing. All three of those slowed down, turned around, and rode up tight behind them.

"Hang on, guys," Val warned. "Looks like the party's starting."

"Max, we got ourselves a situation," Kit said over the comm unit. "The WKB's getting real friendly. Tell Greer we might be running late."

"Roger that. I'll send backup for the backup."

"Negative. Keep them at the house—on alert."

"Copy."

A line of bikes appeared ahead of them across the peak of the hill, blocking both sides of the road. Val executed a flawless J-turn, heading away from the bikes on the hill and into the three behind them. One of those whizzed by, but the other two didn't manage to evade his rapid acceleration. They laid their bikes down and slid off into the wayside amid a blaze of sparks.

The bikes on the hill, eight of them, screamed down the slope toward them, swarming both sides of their vehicle. None of them were paying attention to the road. One of the bikers pulled a gun and started peppering them with bullets. He was glad their vehicle was armored.

Val swerved into him, plowing him into two other bikers. Two more moved into position on either side of their SUV. Val swerved slightly, not to give warning so much as just to fuck with them. When they didn't back down, he bumped into one, then the other.

The remaining bikes followed them for a distance, then backed off, returning to their fallen brothers.

"Max, need another way up to the Friends. Stat," Val ordered over their comm.

"Roger that…take the next right turn. It's a rough road, so go slow. Hope'll have some choice words for you if you bring back her SUV fucked up."

"Yeah, a little late for that warning," Angel grumbled from the backseat.

"You guys okay?"

"You'd know it if we weren't," Kit snapped.

"Copy that. Follow the dirt road about ten clicks. There will be another dirt road heading west. Take that. It'll bring you to the dirt road that goes by the Friends. Take a right."

18

"**G**reer, *your tango's not alone. Proceed with caution,*" Max warned via his comm unit.

They were still a hundred yards from the woodcutter. The moon had finally risen, casting a pale light over the WKBer in the narrow dirt road used by the forest service and the residents of the Friendship Community.

"I don't see anyone else. Where are they? In the woods?" The road was flanked on either side by tall grass and scrub brush, easy cover for an ambush.

"No. Right next to him. I've got two heat signatures on the satellite."

"I'm looking straight at him, Max. You can see what I'm seeing." The amber glasses he wore not only transmitted back to headquarters, they also optimized ambient lighting, illuminating what Greer saw almost as effectively as night-vision goggles. "There's no one there but him."

"I can't explain it. I'm telling you what I'm seeing."

"Copy that."

"What's happening?" Remi whispered, watching him with tense eyes.

"Max says there's someone else with the woodcutter. Stay close to me." He nodded to her purse. "Keep your keys in your hand and get the fuck outta here if this goes south."

She scanned the area. "I don't see anyone else."

"Never mind," Max said. *"Whatever it was is gone now. Maybe he's got a dog with him."*

They approached the woodcutter, who stood like a tree stump in the middle of the road. Wide. Heavy. Resolute. The temperature was several degrees lower than the woods they'd just come through. Greer's breath made a thin puff of condensation. The woodcutter's hands were in his pockets as if he, too, felt the chill. Maybe this area was a low point and collected the cool night air.

Greer nodded at him, but neither man offered to shake. "This is my wife, Dr. Chase. We spoke earlier, but I didn't get your name."

"I didn't give it. You're going to publish what you see on your visit here, aren't you?" he asked Remi.

"Yes."

"When you do, you'll keep my name and profession out of it?"

"Yes. I'll keep your identity confidential. I won't publish anything that could identify you."

He shook his head. "Not good enough. This was a bad idea. I got nothing to say to you."

"No one's real name will be in anything I publish about this community. I promise to protect your identity, which means I won't use your name, and I won't describe you in ways that reveal who you are. I would like to be able to quote what you say, but I won't identify you with the quote. I'll know who you are, but I'm the only one."

He watched her for a minute. "Do I have your word?"

"You do. Protecting people's identity is something we take very seriously. Sociologists have gone to jail in order to protect the identity of the people they research."

With that assurance, he didn't waste any time getting to what he'd come to say. "Before we begin, you need to know what I am." He began unbuttoning his shirt.

Remi sent Greer a sideways glance. Greer didn't take his eyes from the woodcutter. A pattern of tattoos darkened his chest. Greer shined his phone light on it. Remi gasped when he fully opened his shirt, exposing the swastika and a pair of eagle wings flanking it. Below it, in five columns, were wide dashes...eighteen of them.

"You're WKB," she whispered.

"Was. I'm a yeoman in the Friendship Community. Wood's the only thing I ax now."

"How did you get from there to here?" Greer asked.

"The WKB retired me." He looked at Remi again. "I'm a confidential informant, right?"

"Right."

"I served the WKB for thirty years. I'm one of the few who lived to retirement. Holbrook gave me my cabin, job, and assigned a wife to me." He looked at Greer. "The girl you've been asking about. Sally. She was supposed to be my wife, once her tithe was finished."

"Fuck. Me," Max snarled in Greer's ear. *"We should have gotten you in there sooner, Greer."*

"What are these tithes? Payments made to the community?"

He nodded. "Payments in the form of a service. All the kids do a tithe before they can take their place as adults in the community—except artisans or crafts-men. They're forgiven their tithes. Many who leave to do their service never return. Most, even."

"So you think Sally just took off?"

"No." His lips thinned. His jaw bunched. "Nor-mally, an unhitched couple never gets time alone in this fucking nunnery, but I met Sally one day when I was cutting wood. She was alone and crying. The Friends consider their tithes sacred. Their details are never shared. Holbrook—now Pete—and the tithee are the only ones who discuss whatever task has been assigned, but we talked about hers."

"I thought the mayor assigned the tithe," Remi said.

"The mayor assigns the tithe that Pete orders. Anyway, Sally said she'd been ordered to kill someone. I told her that was no big deal. Wasn't any worse than slaughtering a pig. I even had her cut the throats of two of 'em so she'd get the experience first hand before carrying out her tithe."

Remi wrapped her arms around her stomach.

"She was sent to kill my friend," Greer told him.

"Oh, no. Really?"

Greer wondered if the woodcutter's concern could sound any more fake. "She failed. Did you drug her?"

He held up his hand. "I'm clean, man. Maybe it was that doctor she's been sneaking off with."

"Why did they give her that assignment?"

The woodcutter slowly smiled, showing a grin ravaged by crack and poor nutrition. "Why do you think? The Friends don't like so much attention. You and your buds just don't get the message, do you?"

"Greer, get outta there," Max's voice said via his comm unit. *"You got enough info from him."*

"Where's Sally now?" Greer asked.

"How should I know?"

"Someone from the community retrieved her from the clinic."

"Ask Dr. Robinson. He's been making plans for clearing out of here—with her."

"Do you think the WKB has her?" Remi asked. "Maybe you could go to them—"

"I can't," the woodcutter said. "I can't leave."

"Why?" Greer asked.

"G—the guys got ambushed and are rerouting. They're on their way but still fifteen minutes out," Max said.

The woodcutter pointed to the columns of dashes on his torso. "See these? They're my kills. I'm a liability to the WKB. I get to live only if I never leave the community. The terms of my retirement were quite clear." A sound in the woods made him jump. A nocturnal critter—whether it was a small one moving carelessly or a large one moving softly, was too hard to tell.

"I gotta go. I said what I came to say. If I was you, I'd forget all about the girl. Leave the Friends. Leave Wyoming." The woodcutter pointed at Greer. "You and all your friends." He slipped away, melting into the woods, moving more quietly than the animal they'd just heard.

The air in the hollow where they stood had only cooled since they arrived. Greer faced Remi. "That was chilling," Remi said. "And not very helpful. Do you think Dr. Robinson had more to do with Sally's disappearance than he let on? Maybe he's got her somewhere safe, and he's just biding time before he joins her."

"Maybe." Greer nodded. "That could explain her absence, but what about all the others that have gone missing? There are very few older teens here. No one seems worried about their missing children. I hate that." He turned back toward Remi's vehicle.

"Greer, get moving now! The woodcutter isn't heading back into the community. He's moving parallel to you," Max cautioned. *"I don't like it."*

"Roger that." He took Remi's elbow and hurried her toward her car.

"What's happening?" she asked, jogging to keep up with him.

"The woodcutter isn't as benign as he'd have us think."

"I never thought he was."

"We have to get out of here."

"But our stuff. My notes…"

"I'll come back for them. After you're safe." When they were almost to her car, Greer checked the woods, watching for the woodcutter. "Max, where is he?"

"Following along with you twenty yards to your right."

Remi unlocked her vehicle. "Turn the engine on. If I don't make it through what's coming, get down the mountain right back to Blade's house. Got it?" He wanted to send her home right away, but couldn't because whatever had waylaid the others could still be out there waiting.

"Greer, I'm scared."

"Some of the guys are already en route." He opened her door and hit the lock button as she got in. "Start it up and hunker down."

"Behind you, Greer!" Max warned at the same time

Greer heard the heavy weight of a man charging toward him.

Greer had enough time to duck the fast swing of his hand ax. It lodged in the door panel. Remi screamed, the sound muted behind the closed window of her car. Greer's senses narrowed to only the sounds that served in the fight—the woodcutter's breathing, his grunts as he retrieved the ax and raised it again, the silence of the road on either side of the small parking area where they'd left their vehicle.

Greer kept his body between the woodcutter and Remi's car. The guy was about the same height as Greer, but bulkier. The skin of his face was pulled back from his teeth and eyes, presenting a formidable mask of horror. Such a face was the last thing the eighteen lives carved into his chest had seen.

Greer considered shooting the woodcutter, but discarded that option as fast as he thought it. The guy was more useful alive than dead. And so he danced with him, dodging to the left, to the right, moving closer so that the woodcutter had to step back in order to get a good swing in.

Greer let him tire himself, then he caught the woodcutter's hand, stopping it on a downward swing. He punched the guy's face, stunning him long enough to twist the ax from his grip. The woodcutter drew his knife from the sheath at his waist and jabbed at Greer, who blocked the thrusts with the flat side of the ax.

When that bored Greer, he shoved the flat head of the ax into the guy's solar plexus, knocking the wind from him. His arms went wide and he teetered on the edge of his heels, then dropped backward like a felled tree.

Dully, Greer became aware of Remi still screaming in her vehicle. The lights from Remi's car and the other that now faced him illuminated the WKB's hitman. Greer left him to the guys who were rushing from their SUV. He had to get to Remi.

He tried to open her door, but the ax had messed it up too much. He hurried around to the passenger side. She was already scrambling over to him, then panicked when she couldn't open the door. Greer set his hand on the window, against hers.

"Unlock it, Remi."

She fumbled with the button. As soon as the lock released he yanked the door open and grabbed her up against him. She was holding him so tight, he thought she might crawl inside of him.

"I'm sorry about that. So sorry." He rubbed her back.

"He could have killed you!" she said, looking up at him, unaware that her nails were digging into his side.

"Naw. He just looked scary."

"He had an ax, Greer. He chopped up my car."

"Yeah." Greer winced. "Sorry about that. We'll get it fixed." Angel had secured the woodcutter. Kit was calling it in to Lobo.

"Let me take you home," Greer said.

"My notes. Our things."

"I'll go get them. Wait here." He looked over toward the guys. "Val."

"Yeah, man?"

"Stay with Remi. I'm going to go get our stuff."

"You got it." Val went to the back of the SUV and grabbed a blanket, which he put around Remi's shoulders.

"I'm not cold," Remi said.

"You're shaking. I don't want you to get shocky."

"Thank you." She looked into the woods toward the village. "I'm fine here. I think you should go with him. What if there are others like the woodcutter?"

Val met her gaze, then nodded. "Angel—"

"On it." He jogged after Greer.

19

Remi stared at the timber facade of Blade's house. She got out and waited for Greer to climb out her side. She didn't move. She couldn't. He stood quietly next to her. Perhaps, being here in the lap of this luxurious home, there was no need to rush anymore.

"I knew the woodcutter." She looked at Greer. "I saw him on my other visits. If you hadn't come this time…"

"But I did. Don't think about what might have been. It wasn't. It couldn't have been. It happened as it was intended."

"He's from the WKB."

"Yeah. And they'd given Sally to him."

"Do you think the doctor has her hidden someplace?"

"No. He looked too panicked about her." He lifted

a big hand to her shoulder and gave her a light squeeze. "Let's go in."

"Are we staying here?"

"Yeah. I think it's for the best. I'll bring your other things over from Mandy's tomorrow." He grabbed their packs and led her to the house.

Lights were on but dimmed in the entranceway and living room. Greer led her upstairs and across the bridge. One door was open, its light spilling out into the hall.

"Kathy got this room ready for you." He looked farther down the hall. "My room's the middle one at the end of the hall." He left his bag in the hall and took her things inside. "There's a list of numbers on the nightstand. Call any of us if you need anything."

He set her stuff on the bed. He reached for her arm. His hand slipped down to hold hers. She blinked as a wave of exhaustion and fear wracked her spirit. "I don't know what end is up anymore."

His mouth tightened. "I know. You're safe here. And I'll help you figure it out." His brown eyes studied her as he fought for the right words.

"Are you guys feuding with the WKB?"

"No. This fight is bigger than that. It has no beginning and no end. Good and evil never triumph, Remi. They only keep each other in balance." His hand left hers. "The dark side is very dark. Most people never have to see what we see. The world we live in is nothing like your civilian world. You have the world you have because we do the work we do." His expression held no emotion. Not anger or remorse. Not belligerence or sorrow.

She knew about dark and hidden worlds. Thanks to her mother, she'd survived hell itself.

A KNOCK SOUNDED on Remi's bedroom door the next morning. "Dr. Chase? You there?" a woman's voice came muffled through the door. "I have your things."

Remi opened the door. A brunette with short hair was standing in the hallway…Eden, wasn't it? Remi opened her door. A huge tan dog sat on the floor next to Ty's wife.

"Hi. Greer asked me to give these to you," she said, handing Remi her suitcase with her things from Mandy's house. Eden and her pup came into her room. "Greer and the guys were having a meeting and will be late to breakfast. You'll get used to that, if you stay around here long. The hours they keep are irregular at best. If you want, I can go down to the dining room with you. I know what it's like being new to the group and thought maybe you could use a friend."

"I could use a friend." She met Eden's eyes. "You're new here?"

"Sort of new. I've been here most of the summer."

"How long have the guys been here?"

Eden gave that some thought. "A couple of

months? Three, maybe? I think Mandy said Rocco came out in May. I got here in June. Why?"

Remi shrugged. "Just trying to understand more about the group. Can I ask you something?"

Eden nodded. "Sure. Anything."

"Can you leave, if you wanted to?" She wondered how deep the cult of Greer's team ran. If the non-fighters could come and go at will, perhaps this group wasn't as much of a cult as she feared.

"Leave what?"

"Here. This group of guys, fighters. Whatever they are."

"I could." Eden smiled and gave a little laugh as she sat on Remi's bed. "But I'm married to Ty."

Remi sat on the edge of the bed and faced Eden.

"Look, I'm sorry you're here, sorry you got involved in all of this," Eden said. "I remember how overwhelmed I was when I was first brought in to it. I wasn't at all sure what to expect. Who would think that all of this is going on in the middle of America?"

"How were you brought into it?" Remi asked.

"I came up from Cheyenne to visit a couple of my longtime girlfriends who were staying at a guy's house that one of them had been internet dating. Turned out it was the leader of the WKB's house."

Remi was shocked to hear that.

"We ran in to Ty and the team. They discovered what I do and hired me to have Tank check out Ty's house. This house. After that, things just fell into place. Owen has me training some dogs for him."

"What happened to your friends?"

"They were roughed up pretty bad. Owen sent them home on his private jet." She looked at Remi. "Greer hasn't said why you're here, but knowing what I do, I imagine it's bad. You were at Mandy's. You saw what the guys are dealing with. Their enemies blew up her equestrian center and they kidnapped her. They mobbed this house, fought a battle here. One of their leaders came in and tried to shoot Kit and Ivy's daughter. If you're here, it's for a good reason. And it's best that you're here and not somewhere else."

Eden studied Remi. "So, to answer your question, yes. We can leave. Any of us can. But there is no safer place for us than right here."

And that was the crux of it all, wasn't it? The secret to maintaining cult members' adherence to the community culture. Convince them no one would understand them in the real world, no one believed as they did, none would be safe separate from the group. It was so easy to keep people subjugated. Geez. She'd gone in search of one secret society and found herself sucked into an entirely different one.

Remi looked at Eden's dog absently as she tried to find holes in her observation about the group.

"This is Tank. He's a working dog and my best friend."

Remi smiled. "He looks like he eats baby hellcats for his meals."

Eden laughed. "I thought that when I first met

him, too. He's a pit bull/bullmastiff mix. Now I just see a teddy bear. Unless you make him mad."

Remi looked from the dog to Eden. "Are you happy, Eden?" she asked.

"Yes." Eden smiled. "Meeting Ty, getting involved in the team, it's the best thing that ever happened to me—both professionally and personally. I can show you around, if you want, while you wait for Greer. This is a ridiculously big house. And I want you to see my kennels and Mandy's stable."

"I'd like that."

REMI AND EDEN came back to the living room at the end of their tour. Ty and Greer were just coming into the dining room. Greer checked her over critically, his eyes serious. He came down the steps into the living room. Eden said something as she went the opposite way, up to greet Ty. Remi didn't take her eyes from Greer. He looked tired.

He walked right over to her, stopping so close to her that his body blocked the dining room.

"Hi," he said.

She tried to smile, but the attempt was lost in the intense way he was regarding her.

"How are you this morning?"

"I'm okay," she said.

"Did you sleep?"

"I did. Eden gave me a tour."

"Good. Hungry?"

"I could eat."

He started to turn, but she stopped him.

"I need to go to Cheyenne this morning."

"Why?"

She sent a quick glance around him to the dining room. "I have my archives in an apartment there. I need to check something out."

"We'll go after breakfast."

"I want to go alone. No one knows about the apartment, except my assistant. I'll be safe there."

"The WKB wants you dead. You don't leave here without me."

"Greer, my research is secret. I have a ton of files of confidential information. I swore to the people who provided me with their information that I would keep their identities confidential."

"Like you did with the woodcutter."

"Yeah."

"You saw how much he cared about your high morals."

"That's not the point."

"It is the point. What do you want from there anyway?"

"After the shock of the night wore off, I remembered I have info on other white supremacist groups. I'd like to see how many have relationships with isolationist groups like the Friends."

Greer nodded. "We'll go after you eat."

She shook her head. "I don't want to lose my data.

I don't want it sucked into this—" she waved her hand as she searched for the word.

"Let's take a look at what you've got. If it's something that will help the mission, we need to bring it in."

"No. No, Greer. My data can't be used for other things. I promised people that only I would have access to it."

A muscle bunched in the corner of his jaw. "Are you going to support the woodcutters over us, over your country?"

"That isn't a fair question. I have to apply the elements of trust equally across all informants and sources—I have to treat everyone the same or I have nothing. If I find something in my files that can help, and if I can keep my sources protected, I'll share it."

"Let's see what you've got, then we'll talk about it."

20

R emi's apartment was on the top floor of a brick building in Cheyenne's Old Town. It wasn't a large building, only three apartments on each floor. She put the key in the lock, then looked at Greer before she turned it.

She felt more nervous now than she had the first time she got naked in front of him.

She'd never brought anyone here. In fact, her teaching assistant was the only other person who even knew about her archives.

Greer lifted his brows, waiting.

She steeled herself for his reaction.

Opening the door, she walked in first so she wouldn't have to see his expression. Off to the immediate right was a short hallway with a door into the kitchen on the left, a bathroom on the right, and a bedroom at the end of the hall. Straight in front of them was the living room...and a lifetime of research in neatly stacked boxes where furniture should have been.

"What is all this, Remi?"

She flashed him a look as they navigated their way through rows of boxes. "It's my research archives. I've been studying cults a long time." She made her way to the kitchen, where she set her purse down. "Want something to drink? Water or coffee?"

"I'll take some coffee. Looks like we've a long day ahead of us."

She put the grinds in the coffeemaker, then fetched two mugs. When it was ready, she poured two cups. "How do you like it?"

"Black. Straight up."

Greer leaned against the kitchen island and sipped the hot brew. She avoided looking at him. "Talk to me, doc."

"About what?" she asked, staring at her mug.

"About why you chose the field, the specialty you did. Why cults?"

She looked at his throat, then dragged her eyes up over his jaw, over the hollows in his cheeks, to his cinnamon eyes. "I was under the impression there was nothing about me you guys didn't know."

"I know you on paper. I don't know the whys and hows of you."

She set her mug aside. "I grew up in a cult in Colorado."

He nodded. "The Grummond Society. But you

got out. So why are you still fighting the fight? Why the rabid desire to continue existing in that world?"

"Because I want to raise awareness of communities like the one I grew up in."

He sipped his coffee. "What's wrong with people living how they wish, grouping together according to their ideals?"

"I don't have a problem with adults who self-identify with certain schools of thought and build communities around them. I do have a problem when those groups use fear to impose rules that harm the welfare and freedom of their residents. I have a problem when women are owned by men. I have a problem when children are taught to fear and hate and judge and condemn."

"And marry at fourteen."

Her heart skipped a beat. "And that." Especially that. Oh, God. Did he know? Or was that just a random comment?

"What happened to your mom? She seems to have disappeared after you turned eighteen."

"She got me out when she learned that I didn't want to be Prophet Josiah's fifth wife." Remi looked at the floor, remembering those idyllic four years with her mother after they'd left the Grummonds—the only time the two of them had ever been alone.

Her mom had put a brave face on, but Remi knew she didn't like being separated from her group. She lost weight and grew fatigued over the years. The day Remi graduated high school was the day her mom returned to the Grummond Society. Communication between them became sparse, then stopped. In the autumn of her freshman year at CSU, Remi contacted one of her mom's friends when she couldn't get a hold of her mom, only to learn that she died of a chest cold that went to pneumonia the summer she was back with the group.

Her mom's friend warned her never to contact the group again. A warning she'd heeded for more than a decade…until this year. She'd reached out to them a few weeks ago. She hadn't used the name she'd been known by while she lived with them; she'd used her real name. She had street cred now, a professional reputation that she could stand behind. She'd come far enough as a researcher that she'd decided it was time to look at the Grummonds with the eyes of an academic.

Remi looked at Greer. "She stayed with me until I turned eighteen, then she returned to the Grummonds, where she died." Silence settled between them.

Greer reached for her hand. "Can I ask you something?"

She looked up at him, waiting, dreading his question.

"You and your mom picked new names when you got out and set up your current identities. Why did you pick the names you picked?"

Remi smiled, remembering those frightening first days, wondering if the Grummonds were going to come after them. "My mom picked Joan for her name because she thought it sounded like a warrior's name." She leaned her head as she glanced at him. "You know, Joan of Arc."

"And you?"

"I picked Remington because I thought it was about as polar opposed to Chastity as I could get. I was going to be an ender of things...and a protector."

Greer slowly smiled, though his eyes looked sad. "I told you that you were a warrior. Why Chase?"

"Mom wanted us to never forget that we might be targets of Grummond retribution, that we might always be chased."

"Did they come after you?"

"No. But we changed our names, blended in quickly, disappeared into mainstream society."

"Who set up your IDs?"

Remi looked at Greer. "Are you asking as a Fed?"

"I'm not a Fed. Just curious."

"There was an underground network of people who'd left the Grummonds. Mom used them. One of them helped us establish all of the historical paperwork we'd need."

"Do the Friends have a network of ex-members like that?"

Remi shook her head. "I looked for one, but couldn't find it."

His hand tightened on hers. "About your identity... your mom had your new profiles set up illegally. I don't know if he picked a social from a deceased person or one that hasn't yet been assigned, but the fact that it isn't legitimate is a wrinkle our enemies could exploit."

Remi pulled her hand from him and gripped her mug. "What does that mean?"

"It means we need to file the proper documentation so your past can't come back to haunt you."

"Oh my God. If the WKB knew…if the provost were to find out…"

"Right. We'll get it squared away."

"I've passed so many background checks, it never occurred to me that Mom might have done it illegally."

He set his cup down, then eased hers from her tight hold so he could pull her into his arms. "I'll help you."

"Thank you." Remi hugged him. "You know everything about me." She flashed him a look. "Tell me something else about you."

He lifted a shoulder. "Not much to tell. I'm the oldest of three kids, well four, but you know about the baby. Both of my sisters are married. Like I said before, my parents are both schoolteachers. We lived in a suburb of D.C."

Remi smiled, feeling a little jealous of his life. "That's all so normal."

Tension shimmered across Greer's features. "Yeah. Until you wash away the shine and look at the ugly beneath."

"Do they know what you do for a living?"

His gaze locked on hers. All softness vanished from his face. "They know. I stay away to spare them."

Remi's eyes widened. She'd loved her mother. Always. Without fail. She even felt that her mom had surrendered her life for Remi's. What kind of relationship did Greer have with his family if it was easiest to simply stay away from them?

"Can you control it—the thing you do?" She closed her eyes and shook her head. "When you fight, it's like nothing I've ever seen. What happens when you get mad, really mad at something?"

"Nothing makes me flip, Remi. I am always aware, always on, always watchful. There is nothing without self-control. You learn to rein in your fear and anger, to hold all of your emotions in check. Every step, every movement is calculated."

"So you're not like a mad dog that flips into snarling beast mode without warning?"

"I didn't say that. I move fast, but never without cause or provocation. If you're worried that I'll turn on you, I won't. Unless you're one of the bad guys, in which case you can kiss your ass goodbye."

"What if I am a bad guy? What if I brought this on myself?"

"What, like a rape victim who asks for it?" He shook his head. "The victim is never the one to blame."

Remi slowly smiled. It was so easy talking to

Greer. He never pretended to be something he wasn't; he never expected her to, either.

"Let's go through your stuff here and find out why they're after you." He walked into the living room, where boxes were stacked on top of boxes. "So what is all this stuff?" he asked.

Remi knew it looked like some hoarder's nirvana. She'd long meant to tidy it up, but instead she'd just kept adding boxes to the stacks. "When my mom and I first got out, I started to do some research on the group we'd just left. It led me to info about other similar groups. And then I was lost. I studied all of them, collected files on them, built portfolios on them. This is all my early research and my more recent stuff."

She reached into one of the boxes and pulled out a blue folder thick with lined paper and handwritten notes. "I analyzed each group, summarizing their culture, management, membership requirements, philosophies, benefits, punishments, family structures. Everything." She ventured a look up at his warm eyes, then put the folder away. "It helped me understand what happened to me, that I wasn't the only one who'd been raised in the way I was."

He smiled down at her. "You were born to be a sociologist."

She shrugged. "I guess. I certainly knew what I wanted to be when I entered college. One year, I learned about groups that admitted former white supremacists into their communities."

She started rearranging boxes, handing the upper ones to Greer to set somewhere else. "That discovery sent me down a summer-long rabbit hole of research into white supremacist groups." She straightened and looked over at him. "I wasn't your normal, hormone-driven teenager."

Greer smiled and said, "A deficiency that you're making up for now."

"I like the freedom to do what I want to do now."

"So do I."

She looked at the odd jumble of boxes. "These were my friends. These kept me sane." She glanced at Greer, but looked away before she said, "I was the weird one at school."

He touched her arm, capturing her attention. One side of his mobile mouth lifted in a sexy, masculine curve. The corners of his eyes crinkled. "I would have liked you."

A warmth slipped down her spine, coiling between her hips. She turned back to the boxes she was rearranging. "I would have shut you down. My life plans don't include settling down."

"I'm still trying to figure that one out."

She straightened and looked over at him. "It's cult-like, tying yourself to someone else, expecting your interests to head in the same direction…or surrendering your own life plan for your spouse's when things don't turn out as planned. I've earned the right to be me. I'm not giving that up."

"You're lucky."

"How so?" It didn't feel like luck. It felt lonely.

"I am what I've become, but you are what you've intended to be. That's powerful."

That observation took her by surprise. "Are all mercenaries as self-aware as you?"

He grinned that sexy, male smile of his that made her breath hitch. "The ones I know are." He shrugged. "The ones I've ended weren't."

Remi returned her attention to finding the cases she was looking for. Two more boxes down, she found it. "Here they are. A group in Montana and another in Utah. They seemed similar, so I put them in the same box." She looked around at the other boxes. "There might be others that are part of what's going on, but I haven't made that connection yet."

GREER WATCHED Remi sleep hours later, caught up in the innocence of it. They'd been digging through the files for twelve hours. She had to be exhausted to let her guard down enough to crash in front of him.

He went into her room and turned down her covers, then came back into the kitchen for Remi. She didn't stir when he lifted her legs and eased his hand around her back. God, he liked the feel of her in his arms. She curled into him even tighter, lifting an arm around his neck, pressing her face against him. He felt the cool draw of air as she pulled in his scent.

"How is it that an assassin can smell so good?" she mumbled as he stepped into the shadows of her room.

"It's a lure I use to draw my victims in close."

She sniffed him again. The hairs tightened on the back of his neck. "Mmm. Do you kill many women?"

"I haven't yet, but I have no gender preference when it comes to victims. I kill enemies. Period. So far, though, they've all been male."

"Maybe you should specialize."

"Why?"

"Because you smell like a snickerdoodle. An assassin cookie. Women would be helpless to fight you."

He chuckled, wondering now if she was really still asleep. He eased her down to the mattress, reluctantly emptying his arms. "I'll give that some thought. Might be a good strategy." He pulled the blankets over her. She rolled onto her side, away from him. "Night, doc. I'll lock the door behind me so you won't worry about me coming back in."

Greer went back to the living room and started rummaging around in the other boxes. Remi needed to get this info scanned and stored in a systematic, retrievable system. Maybe he'd help her with that when this was all over. He discovered a pattern of symbols she used as meta category labels. Some had peace signs. Some had crosses. Some had swords. And some had swastikas.

He checked all the boxes, then pulled out the ones with the swastikas. He got through three more boxes before fatigue made his eyes jump across the pages, scrambling what he was reading. He'd sent some of the information—the stuff Remi had approved, anyway—back to Max. They could work on finding the links, if there were any, between those groups and the Friendship Community when he got back to Blade's.

He returned those boxes to the stacks and was about to quit for the night when the label on one of the boxes snagged his attention. The Grummond Society. Greer stared at the box. It pulled and repulsed him. He checked over his shoulder to see if Remi's door was still closed.

He'd read everything he could find online about the group that was still active in southern Colorado. It was a reclusive group. Even the Feds had little data on them. The only pictures that he'd seen of the residents were taken with telephoto lenses from a good distance away.

He lifted the box and carried it over to the table. He flipped through the different folders, scanning Remi's notes, newspaper clippings, a handful of photos, photocopies of permits the group had pulled for wells, and other public documentation.

He went back to look at the few photos. Some showed women in pastel hand-sewn dresses standing on balconies on the upper floors of various houses. Their hair was pulled back in neat buns and covered with white caps of some sort. There were lots of kids.

The men wore white cotton shirts, black trousers, suspenders, and black boots.

A photo dropped out of the file onto the floor. He picked it up. It was a pic of several men, in traditional garb, standing in a cluster talking while women brought food to what looked like one of their celebration feasts. Hard to tell what time of year it was. The trees were green. Sometime in summer or early autumn.

His gaze drifted off, settling in an unfocused way on Remi's kitchen island before returning again to the picture. It was hard to imagine Remi in this setting. She was intelligent, independent, self-sufficient. He wondered how he was going to get her to open up to him about her experiences there. He wanted to hear the story about how she got out.

He focused on the picture, looking at each community member's face. "Sonofabitch!" he snarled, tilting the pic to hold it under better light. He snapped a picture of it and sent it over to Max in a text.

A minute later, he had a response. *"Fuck. Me."* And then his phone rang. *"What the hell is Senator Whiddon doing in the Friendship Community? It is the Friendship Community, isn't it?"*

"No. This is from Remi's group—the Grummonds. I think we know why they're coming after Remi. The photo came from the file Remi made on the group she grew up with. You think King knows about this?"

"Don't know. Does Whiddon have the power to mobilize the WKB without him?"

"Another good question. Look, Remi has an apartment full of research she's been doing for more than fifteen years. I think we need to get it transferred up to headquarters so that we can go through it and see what else is lurking in the files."

"She gonna let you do that?"

"I'll convince her."

"I'll let Kit and Owen know. Can we fit it in the SUVs, or do we need to rent a truck?"

"I think we can get it in the vehicles."

"Copy. I'm out."

Greer leaned back in his seat as he stared at the picture in his hand. A familiar chill crept down his spine. Without moving, he lifted his eyes and sent a look around the shadowy interior of Remi's apartment, searching for the source of dread filling him. He saw nothing, but he knew he wasn't alone. If Remi had come out of her room, he would have heard her unlock her door.

A sound outside the window caught his attention. He ditched the light in the kitchen. Remi's apartment was one of three on the fourth floor of a nineteenth century red brick building. It overlooked the roof of the building next door. It was two a.m. No one would normally be out and about. Her building was two streets off the main drag—nowhere near the bars.

He pushed aside the curtain. What he saw on the roof next door lifted the hairs on his neck. That damned girl he kept seeing was standing there, looking up at his window. *What. The. Fuck.* How did she find him?

He went back to the papers spread across the kitchen table. He stacked them and put them back into the box, then set it with the others in the living room.

He went to the window again as a chilling realization jelled. This girl wasn't human; she was a ghost. She was the one haunting him. He lifted the curtain to take another look, but she was gone.

He glanced around the apartment, checking to see if she appeared. All was quiet…until an orange-red ball smashed through the kitchen window and spread flames across the table where he'd just been sitting.

21

Greer grabbed the fire extinguisher that Remi had on the kitchen wall. He'd barely gotten it in hand before men dressed in black, their faces masked, slammed into the apartment. The smoke alarms sounded from the fire on the kitchen table. In only seconds, Remi would be up and out of her room and open to attack. He had to end this fast.

Greer made his way over to the hallway beside the kitchen and met his attackers at a spot of his choosing. The first to charge him got an iron canister to his forehead, dropping him in place. The next lifted a gun with a silencer as the first guy fell. Greer ducked behind the wall as a bullet thudded into the jamb of the kitchen door.

Another thug was waiting for him just inside the kitchen. The guy caught him by the neck and banged him against the wall. Greer sprayed the guy's face with the pressurized spray from the extinguisher, causing him to step back. Greer kicked him in the gut, followed by one to the head, the force of which landed him against the kitchen island. Stunned, he slumped down the side of the island.

Greer was vaguely aware of Remi rushing out of her room. She reached for the fire extinguisher. He handed it to her and shoved her to the ground behind the kitchen island.

"Forget the fire. Stay down."

Remi stayed on her knees but began spraying the fire anyway. Two guys were left—one had a gun. They both came into the kitchen. One went for Remi. Greer ran then slid feet-first into the gunman. Twisting his legs through the gunman's, he dropped him fast. His gun skidded across the floor. Greer slammed his fist into the guy's face, incapacitating him.

He turned to help Remi. She had sprayed the other guy with the fire extinguisher, freeing herself. He scrabbled for the loose gun. Greer reached him first and flipped him over, then slammed his head against the floor until he we went limp.

Greer looked back to make sure the fire was out. Smoke, steam, and the stink of retardant foam blanketed the room. He sought out Remi. "Shout out, Remi. You okay?"

"I'm not hurt."

Greer smiled. Even in the middle of a shitstorm,

she still managed to properly qualify her answer. "Stay put."

Searching under the sink for the plastic trash bags, he grabbed a couple. He had to immobilize the guys fast, else they'd be gone long before the cops got there. He cut two bags in half longways, then used the makeshift strips to bind their arms behind them.

"Max, read me?" he said into his comm unit. "We got a situation."

"Go, Greer," Max's voice came over his comm unit loud and calm.

"The doc's apartment was just hit by a handful of thugs. I've secured them, but the cops are on their way. Lobo's going to want these guys."

"Roger that. You or Remi hurt?"

The sirens got loud out front, then stopped, leaving only flashing emergency lights. "No. Tell Kit I'm gonna need bail money."

"Team's on their way. I'll have Kit call Lobo."

"Copy."

"Get their IDs?"

"Not yet."

"On the ground! On the ground, now!" the first couple of cops through the door shouted. "On the ground!"

Greer put his hands on the back of his head and slowly knelt. The cops were all over Remi, who was stiff with shock and didn't follow the instructions fast enough.

Greer looked around the room, calibrating an

escape plan in case any of the cops were on King's payroll. He and Remi were at their most vulnerable right then. He stayed quiet, however. Any argument he put up might have the effect of getting them separated.

Two of the cops pulled them to their feet and led them roughly over to a spot in the hall. One of them picked up the gunman's weapon.

He looked over at Greer. "You want to tell me what happened?"

Greer shrugged. He nodded toward Remi, who was almost as white as the wall. "We were getting ready for bed when these bozos broke in."

"What were they after?"

"How the hell would I know?" Greer snapped.

"This your apartment?"

"No. It belongs to my girlfriend." The cops cleared the apartment, then let the firemen in. One of them lifted the remains of the glass bottle that had come through the window and started the fire. "Looks like it might have been thrown from the fire escape."

The cop frowned. "Why raid a hoarder's apartment? What's in all these boxes?"

"Stuff," Greer snapped.

The cop questioning him was summoned out to the hallway. Greer checked Remi. Her face had gone from white to gray with shock. At least she wasn't screaming hysterically.

Jesus. He hoped she wasn't getting used to this.

"Remi, come here."

Her haunted eyes lifted to his.

"Now, Remi."

Her gaze caught on the broken window in her dining room. Greer looked down the hallway and out the front door. There were a lot of fucking men crawling around her apartment now. He didn't know if any of them were dirty. He wanted her next to him in case they tried to take her. King had friends in high places.

"Come closer." Her eyes got bigger and her face paler. "Do it," he ordered, his voice soft but firm. "Lean against me. Take my strength for yours." His hands were still clamped behind him in the cuffs. He turned slightly at an angle, giving her space to lean in behind him. Letting him shield her slightly. "Put your face against my shirt."

He drew a long, fortifying breath when he felt her body meld to his. She was so little. Her indomitable spirit made him forget how fragile she was. And cold. She was too fucking cold. He wished he could wrap his arms around her. She pressed her face against his shoulder blade. At least her breath was still warm.

"Everything's going to be fine. This is the end of it," he whispered.

She shook her head against his back. "This isn't the end of it. It's not even the middle."

"Yeah, it is. I figured out what's happening. And you're coming back with me to Blade's place."

"What's happening?" she asked.

"Can't talk here."

"What about all of this?" She started to look around the loft, then quickly put her head down again. "I can't leave my research."

"We're bringing it with us. The guys are on their way down." He looked at the broken kitchen window. "And we'll get someone in to repair this place, too." He grinned at her over his shoulder, then shivered when her face pressed against his shirt a little harder.

A short while later, Greer heard Kit's voice in the hallway. A pissed Kit was a thing to behold. He was glad the cop was getting the first wave of his steam.

Speak of the devil. He entered the apartment, took one look around, then walked right up to Greer's face. "What the fuck's going on?"

Greer lifted his shoulders. "What? I didn't kill anyone."

"Is it too much to ask that you take a low-key approach?" He growled between clenched teeth.

Greer ground his jaw before answering. "They weren't in a negotiating kind of mood, Kit. They came in guns blazing. They wanted to set fire to Remi's things and kidnap her. Next time, if they're more polite, I'll offer them tea so we can chat about it first."

Kit's eyes narrowed. He tucked his lips against his teeth, then ordered one of the policemen to take off their cuffs. As soon as his hands were free, Greer steered Remi toward her room. He made a quick sweep of the room, then ordered her to get dressed and collect her things. "I'll be waiting outside. No one's coming in until you come out."

She stood in the middle of the room, looking at him, adrift in the chaos of her life. He shut the door —with him on the inside—then walked back to her. He took hold of her cheeks, and his thumbs brushed the soft skin of her face. His heart clenched at the fear in her eyes. He almost wished it was still him she feared.

He bent down and touched his lips to hers. He meant only that small touch, nothing more, but her hands gripped his sides. She lifted up on her toes, reaching up to him, pushing her mouth against his. She was drawing from his strength as he'd told her to do. He felt it transfer from him to her. All of it. Leaving him no reserves, nothing to guard his heart.

He kissed her again. It wasn't a simple thing, their embrace; it was a wave of motion. Her hips against his thighs, her waist to his hips. They were like two vines caught in the wind, leaning, rubbing, entwining. His hands were on her face, pressing against the pocket of her open jaw in his palms. Hungry for more, he wrapped his arms around her body, locking her to him, feeling his strength in her as his mouth moved over hers in soft kisses, then opened-mouthed tongue-to-tongue kisses.

She did the most dangerous thing then—she opened herself to him. And he was lonely enough to take all she offered. It was a chilling thought, 'cause this would end like all the others. It had to. He bent his forehead to hers, then slowly eased her back to her feet, unaware he'd been holding her above the ground.

"Remi, get changed. Get your stuff together, but don't come out until I tell you. I don't know if the WKB owns any of the guys here."

She didn't step away, and he didn't let her go. She bowed her head to his chest. "Can you stay with me?"

"No. I need to go help them. We're going to bring your stuff up to Blade's. We'll talk to Kit and Owen about how sensitive it is. Okay?" He expected more arguments, but maybe the dire nature of her situation finally hit home, because she nodded.

He pulled away. "One of us will guard your door." He looked back at her when he reached the door, then shut her from his mind and stepped into the hall.

THE GUYS WERE LUGGING the last of the boxes out of Remi's apartment. Arrangements had been made to fix the shattered front door, broken window, and fire damage. Lobo had taken custody of the thugs.

Dawn was a hint of lavender in the eastern sky when Greer brought Remi down to one of their SUVs. Val was driving her Forester home, which for once, she was grateful for; she didn't have the strength to drive back.

The constant danger had worn down her defenses. Maybe Greer and his team could find whatever it was in her files that the WKB was after. They had respected her work so far. They weren't going to pry it wide open and let her protected sources out willy-nilly. They were going after something specific. She had no choice but to trust them.

Not if she wanted to live.

Were it not for Greer, she would have been dead long before now. Even before the woodcutter. She would have been killed during the home invasion at her townhouse or in the parking lot of the university. She looked across the middle row bench seats to her self-appointed bodyguard.

He was looking at her. She thought of the way he'd kissed her at the apartment. Her gaze lowered to his lips, soft and kissable in his fierce face. He stole her breath. She swallowed and looked away, burying her gaze in the empty prairie outside Cheyenne.

She felt a tug on her seatbelt. Greer had reached over to unfasten it. The sensor alarm sounded. Angel looked in the rearview mirror at them. Greer ignored him as he pulled her onto his lap, then draped a soft throw that he'd taken from her apartment over her shoulders. Reaching up to her neck, he pulled her head down to his shoulder. "Sleep," he ordered quietly. "We'll talk when we get to the house. You'll know what we know. You're gonna be safe, Remi. I promise you that."

Remi hadn't realized how cold she was until Greer covered her. Her eyes were heavy, lulled by the steady, strong beat of his heart. She worried she was too heavy, but he locked his arms around her and stared straight ahead as if he were barely aware of her on his lap. She closed her eyes and breathed in his soothing scent.

How could she feel so safe in his arms? She'd sworn off any serious relationships her entire teen and adult life. She'd picked lovers for short and intense interludes, always with the clear understanding that it would never be more than a weekend with any of them. If they'd called her afterward, wanting more, she shut them down. Greer made her feel as if more might actually be possible—perhaps because he was a warrior, not a benign professional.

And that scared the hell out of her. Assassins likely didn't live long enough to keep their promises.

"Doc, we're here." Greer's voice slipped quietly into her mind, waking her. The door closed as Angel got out of the SUV.

Remi pushed against Greer's chest, sitting up. She couldn't believe it, but she'd actually slept for most of the ride home. *Home.* She pulled the throw off her lap and ducked out of the SUV. Greer followed her, carrying her purse and laptop bag. The guys were already hauling her boxes into Blade's home.

Staring up at the big timber house, she thought the *déjà vu* she was feeling was stuck on repeat. Only now she really had nowhere else to go.

"Where are they taking my boxes?" she asked when they went inside.

"To our conference room."

Remi sent a glance around the sprawling mansion, wondering where that was and if she'd ever get her research back. The guys were carrying boxes down the hall to the right, but she thought there were only bedrooms in that direction. Greer led her up the stairs.

"Everyone's going to crash for a few hours. We should do the same," he said as they paused outside her bedroom. He was speaking quietly because the rest of the household was asleep.

She didn't go into her room, didn't move at all. She wanted him to stay with her. She wished she could put her life in reverse and get off at a different stop.

He must have read the confusion in her face. "C'mon." He put his hand on her back and directed her into her room. After shutting the door behind them, he set her things on the floor beside her desk, then took her hand and led her into the bathroom.

He stripped, then turned the shower on and focused on helping her peel off her clothes. There was no lust in his eyes, only concern. Her clothes were pooled on the floor in no time. He tested the water, then stepped into the shower stream and drew her in with him.

Remi closed her eyes and let the hot water soothe her. She didn't resist when Greer poured shampoo into his hands and lathered her hair. He shifted in the shower stall so that he could rinse her hair. When the shampoo was gone, she filled her palm with conditioner—it wasn't a process she gave any thought to. It was just the next thing to do.

She could live like this, in automaton mode. She could exist. Numb was nice. Numb didn't hurt. Numb didn't fear. Numb didn't bleed.

Greer leaned back to look into her face. He must not have liked what he saw, for he scooped the conditioner from her hand and smoothed it over her hair.

His knuckles looked bruised. There was a dark line of blood stuck beneath his short nails from the fight at her apartment. The shower hadn't yet washed it away. She took up the bar of soap and ran it directly over his hands, digging his nails into it.

The soap scent smelled foreign on him. She wanted his cinnamon scent back. She lifted the ball of aqua netting and attacked the stains on his hands, scrubbing and scrubbing.

GREER WATCHED REMI. She looked wrecked. Exhausted. Lost. She was scrubbing at phantom dirt on his hands. No, that wasn't true. He knew she was trying to get the blood off his hands. He held still, though it had begun to hurt. He could tell she was weeping, even though her face was in the stream of water.

"Baby, don't cry. Please, don't cry."

She paused her fevered motions, and slowly lifted her face to look at him.

"You'll never wash me clean. You can't. The blood isn't on my skin. It's in my soul."

And there it was. The truth. The thing his fiancée had run from so long ago. The thing his parents and sisters condemned him for.

His soul was stained. And he didn't care. Someone had to protect the good from the bad.

She turned his hand over in her palm and looked at his skin. He braced himself for her to turn from him. It had to come. Light like hers couldn't exist in his darkness.

She lifted his hand to her mouth. Dropping the scrubby, she held his hand against her face and cried.

Oh. Fuck. This hurt. He loved her. He fucking loved her. A love so deep and bright, he realized he'd never loved like that before.

"Greer." Her voice broke. She leaned her head into his chest.

He pushed free of her and got out of the shower. "I'll go."

She followed him out without turning off the shower. "Why? Why are you going?"

"I'm tainted, Remi. You know that. You've seen that."

"I am, too, Greer."

He lifted his head and frowned at her. "No, you're not."

"Don't leave me." Her eyes welled with tears. "I'm tired of standing alone."

He stepped back into her body space. Catching her chin, he lifted her face to his and kissed her. He reached over and shut off the shower, then wrapped a towel around her, and carried her to her bed.

He went back into the bathroom and found the drawer with the carton of condoms he'd put there for their use. He covered himself as he walked back into the bedroom.

Lifting the covers, he moved over her, between her legs, entering her without prelude. She opened to him, holding nothing back. Her eyes were locked with his. He stared down at her beautiful face, grounding himself in her arms, in her body. He felt impossibly hollow. She would go, quit him, as all the others he'd loved had, his family included.

He rocked over her slowly, deeply, watching her the whole time. Color began to blossom on her face, the beautiful, beautiful red of her life force. Her eyes closed and her lips parted as her body rose to meet his. He gripped the edge of the mattress above her head and leveraged it to move deeper inside of her, spreading his thighs, spreading hers.

He felt her body convulse beneath his as he drove her over the edge into ecstasy. As her body quieted, his began to peak. He jammed himself deep inside her, holding her hip still as he banged out his release.

When the last wave left him, he leaned his head on the pillow, against hers, waiting for his breath to even out. She was stroking his back, trying to soothe him. He lifted his head and looked at her. Her eyes mirrored the trouble in his heart.

He got up and removed the condom, then left it in the bathroom trash. He went over to her window and drew the light darkening drapes over the sheers. Then he went back to her bed and slipped between the covers, pulling her close.

"Sleep now. When we wake up, we'll figure out what's next. I've got you. You've got me. We're safe. So sleep." *My love.* The last were words he thought but didn't say. He couldn't. He couldn't bring himself to clip her wings by limiting her choices.

She nestled into him. He felt her body relax as her breathing evened out. When she slept, he allowed himself to shut his eyes and drift away.

22

Bright light slashed across Remi's face. She scrunched her eyes up, then cracked one open. Greer was standing next to the bed with a tray of food. Whatever was on it smelled divine. Remi was starving.

"Morning. Well, afternoon. Kathy made a big meal for lunch since so many of us missed breakfast."

Remi held the sheet to her bare chest and sat up. Her hair was dry, but since it was wet when she went to sleep, it now looked like a rat's nest. She pushed some of it out of her face.

"That was my fault," she said.

"No, it wasn't. Shit happens." He set the tray on the dresser, then lifted the steel cover and snagged a fry.

"What's in there?"

"Cheeseburger, fries, and side salad. With iced tea. Couldn't remember if you liked your tea sweet or used mustard or mayo on the burger, so I brought some of it all." He plopped himself down on the armchair near the window and grinned at her.

She smiled back. For no reason other than it felt right.

"What happens now? What's next?" she asked.

"Next, you get up, dress, eat, wrangle your hair into some kind of order"—he looked at her and cocked his head to the side—"or not. It's kinda sexy like that."

Remi shoved the covers aside and walked into her closet.

"No one would know if we went back to bed for a while," Greer suggested. "We'll just tell them you're a slow eater."

Hearing the grin in his voice, she laughed. She pulled on some underwear and clothes—jeans and a white cotton blouse. "We could," she said as she came out of the closet. "But your self-satisfied smile would give us away."

She lifted the tray and brought it over to the bed. "Did you eat?"

"I did. I wanted to put off waking you until I couldn't delay any longer."

"Last night, you said you knew what was happening." She fixed her burger and took a big bite. After swallowing, she said. "So tell me what it is."

"We'll talk about it with the team in a few. You've been a big help, let's just say that."

"I have?"

"Huge. It's actually a big breakthrough."

She smiled as she chewed another bite. That was a relief. Maybe they were close to the end of this fiasco after all.

"Stairs or elevator? You have a preference?" Greer asked when they went down the south staircase to the main floor.

"No." She looked down the hall where she'd seen the guys take her stuff. "My boxes went this way."

Greer nodded. "Then let's go that way."

He led her into the bedroom with the secret elevator. They went into the empty closet. She looked at him warily. He smiled at her and popped a compartment open in the paneling. There was a single button, which he hit.

"I always feel like 007 when I do this." He opened a sliding panel in the back of the closet, revealing an elevator gate. She gasped. That was the very last thing she'd expected to see. He pushed that open when the elevator arrived. Stepping inside, he held the doors open for her, then shut the hidden panel, then the gate.

The ride was short. When the doors opened, they stepped out into a state-of-the-art weapons room. Each wall had lighted glass and steel cases with row upon row of long guns, pistols, knives, accessories. There was a steel island in the center of the room that looked like a work surface. Below the weapon cases were more locked steel cabinets. The room had the acridly sweet scent of gun cleaner and oil.

Greer sniffed the air and smiled at her. "That smell always gives me a flash boner."

Remi blushed. He laughed.

She followed him out of the weapons room into a dim room lit by a dozen computer screens with a couple walls of floor-to-ceiling servers. Cool air moved up from vents in the floor. Max got up as they came in. He looked too rangy to be a computer geek, but he also looked at home in the ops area.

"Glad you're here. Was gonna go look for you. Kit's ready to start. Doc." He nodded toward her, then led the way out of the ops room.

They passed a bunkroom, a bathroom, a kitchen, then went into a long, wide room. Greer's team was seated around a huge conference table. Two smart screens the size of blackboards were suspended on one wall.

Owen was standing at the back wall. His arms were folded over his chest. His eyes were as chilling as the steel weapon cases. Remi looked away as soon as she could. Greer led her over to two open seats next to Selena. Remi sent a glance around the table. None of them were looking particularly welcoming. Course, none of them had gotten much rest over the past few days, either.

"Soon, Professor, you'll be able to return to your regular life," Owen said.

Remi's mind replayed a slice of her life before her world imploded. As much as she missed the routine of daily life in academia, the sociologist in her was intrigued with the alternate realities Greer and his team had shown her. She realized her work so far had only scratched the surface of hidden human societies.

Owen nodded toward Kit, who began his explanation. "There are terrorist cells lying dormant in our country. Recently, some of those have been activated for various purposes that include taking revenge against our warriors and introducing chaos to undermine our country. Some of those cells have connected with the criminal elements in our country to traffic drugs, making money to fund their activities in hot spots here and abroad. It's an effective network we're in the process of discovering. They're working with the WKB, and the WKB are hiding in some of these utopian or cult societies. Hence the intersection of our interests."

Remi got up and started pacing around the conference room. She walked past stacks of her boxes, organized by the symbols she'd marked on them. "You've got my files, all my data, but you don't have my eyes. I've been studying these groups for years, looking for their similarities and differences. Let me help you find the patterns you're looking for."

"Agreed," Kit said. "Sounds like a good place to begin. But first, Max, put up the senator's picture."

Remi looked up at the big smart screen. The image she saw was the stuff of her nightmares. Her hands covered her mouth, but didn't block her gasp. She recognized the picture—and the man. Oh, sweet Mother Mary. Was he behind all that had been happening to her? She was twelve when that picture was taken.

She realized the room had gone silent. She ripped her gaze from the big screen to the table full of people who had turned and were now staring at her.

"Remi—do you know this man?" Greer asked.

Her heart was pounding in her ears. She felt cold and terrified and numb. She nodded.

"Who is he to you?" Greer asked.

Oh, God. She needed to vomit. Not a good reaction here, in front of these mercenaries who probably ate crybabies like her for breakfast.

She pulled a long draw of air in through her nose, then another, fighting back the bile. These people knew her secrets, knew her shame. Her eyes watered, but she didn't blink.

"He was one of the prophets in the community where I grew up." Her voice was a whisper. She wasn't even certain she'd spoken aloud. No one spoke. No one moved.

Greer exchanged glances with Kit. "Motherfucking sonofabitch," he growled, and got up from the table. She was afraid for a second that he was going to pull her into his arms. If he did, she would break.

Instead, he came to stand in front of her, blocking her from the team—and from the picture of Prophet

Josiah. *"I'm tainted,"* he'd said. He wasn't nearly as soiled as she.

"Baby, breathe," he whispered as he hunched his shoulders, cupping her inside their wide span. She lifted her terrified gaze up to him, latching on to his calm eyes. "Breathe, baby." He took his hands from his pockets and peeled hers from her face. The heat in his hands made her realize how cold she'd gone. He kissed her fingertips, then looked at her and said something that sounded like, "I will end him."

She couldn't have heard that right.

"Remi," Kit said, his voice softer than she'd ever heard it, "was the WKB involved with your community?"

She pulled a long breath at last, then leaned her forehead against Greer's chest. Two more slow breaths, and she was ready to talk. Greer stepped aside but stayed near.

"No," she answered Kit. "But I left when I was fourteen. Maybe they are now."

Kit turned back to Max. "Bring up the finger-prints," he ordered.

Max added images to the screen—two finger-prints and an image of the burned-out shell of a car.

"You sent us scans of three fingerprints," Kit said, glancing at Greer.

"You did?" Remi asked him.

"Yeah. Remember when I was 'videoing' the table? I used an app we have on our phones to scan fingerprints from the Dunbars' and Mr. Haskel's glass-es." He shrugged. "Just out of curiosity."

"We had two hits from those scans," Max told them, "for crimes that have been unsolved for decades." Over the top of the burned car, he showed a pic of a gangbanger whose lifeless body was slumped over his steering wheel.

"Two different fingerprints, two different unsolved crimes from thirty, almost forty years ago. The car bomb was in Los Angeles and the gangbanger in San Diego."

"There must be some mistake," Remi said. "The Dunbars and the Haskels are natives of the commu-nity. They've never left it."

"Except…during their tithes," Greer said.

Remi stared at him, then shook her head. "No. They don't travel anywhere except by horse or horse and buggy. It's a two week round-trip to go to the market in their buggies."

Greer shrugged. "Someone's helping them. Sally had to have help getting down to Wolf Creek Bend the night she came to kill Kit. Not to mention, how did her 'parents' come after her so quickly when we took her to the clinic? No way could they have come that far that fast. And who contacted them anyway? They don't have phones. No, the Friends aren't as isolated as they would have us think."

"You saying that was her tithe? Killing me?" Kit asked.

"Yeah. The woodcutter wasn't surprised that she'd been assigned that task. He said he even had her practice by slaughtering some pigs. She said that that night, too. Remember?" Greer reminded Kit. "The Friends aren't supposed to ever talk about their tithes—"

"Because they're committing crimes," Remi finished for him.

"Yeah. And both Dr. Robinson—the village doctor," he explained for the others, "and the woodcutter knew Sally was her fake name for her tithe service."

Remi walked over to her chair and sat down. Greer followed. "I don't understand why they would do that," she said. The Friends are a pacifist society. They don't have any designs on taking over the world. They just want to be left alone. Why go out into the world to do a crime? How is that a service to their community?"

The group silently considered that.

"So what's happening with the teenagers who've gone off to do their tithes and aren't returning?" Blade asked.

"Have Lobo look into adolescent John and Jane Does who're showing up in morgues," Kit told him. "It isn't a large number we're looking for, is it?" He looked at Remi and Greer. "Maybe twenty? Twenty-five? Fifteen?"

"True. But from a community of five hundred, that's sizable. What are they up to in the outside world?" Greer asked. "Kids slip under the radar so easily."

Kit nodded. "You need to get out there and get more fingerprints. Let's see what washes out. But first"—he jerked his head toward the stacks of boxes —"let's get a handle on what we know and what we don't."

"I don't know if we can go back," Remi said, glancing from Kit to Greer.

"Why not?" Kit asked.

"Because of what happened to the woodcutter."

"Unless the WKB told someone, the Friends don't know anything more than that he disappeared."

23

After supper, Remi carried a couple of boxes up from the bunker. She wanted to spend the evening reading through the files, but didn't want to stay in the cavernous meeting room down below.

Hope was coming down the stairs as she was going up. "Hey, Remi—I've ordered replacement parts for your car. They should be here tomorrow. The shop in town will let me use their paint booth. I'll have you back on the road in no time. If you have to go somewhere, use one of the guys' cars or grab mine."

"Thanks, Hope. That's awesome."

"Yeah. Val's SUV can't be as easily fixed. They're going to have to trade it out for a new one while it goes back to the armor shop."

"Why? What happened to it?"

"It was peppered with bullets the night Greer fought the woodcutter."

Remi's eyes widened. "I didn't know."

"Yeah. They got an earful from me." They smiled at each other. "By the way, I'm new here, too. I know how overwhelming it can be. These are good people. They'll help you. If you let them."

"I don't think I have a choice. Greer's saved me more times than I can count. I obviously don't know what I'm up against."

Hope reached out and squeezed her arm. "I'm here, if you need me. Even if you just want to talk. Generally, I'm messing around in the garage. But they have a great pool here, too, and I'm often in it."

"Thanks. I appreciate it."

A FEW HOURS LATER, Remi leaned back against the pillows and stretched her legs out over the papers on her bed. She wondered how much longer she could delay going back to the university. If things didn't change fast, there was no way she could do that. Even if she put a very public halt to her work on the Friendship Community, it was already too late—she was in too deep.

She wouldn't survive a return to the university at this point. And how many others would she be endangering simply by being on campus when the WKB came for her again?

She'd have to let things play out for a few more days, then decide what to do. Maybe the provost would be understanding if he thought she was attempting to comply. Maybe Clancy could start her classes for her for a short while.

She listened to the sounds in the house. She could hear mumbled voices of the guys in the billiards room downstairs. There was a faint buzz from the TV down the hall in the south bedroom wing. It all made her feel comfortable. And not alone. Bad things always seemed to happen when she was by herself lately.

She changed into a pair of flowery boxer briefs and a tank top, then brushed her teeth and got ready for bed.

"Hey, Remi." Greer's voice came into her room as he knocked on her open door. "You okay?"

"Yeah. Greer?" she called out. "Can we talk for a bit?"

"Sure." He walked down the short hallway sandwiched between her walk-in closet and bathroom. She didn't know if all the bedrooms were set up the same way, but hers felt a lot like a hotel room—except the furnishings and linens were top grade.

Greer leaned against the corner where the hallway met her room. "S'up?"

He wore a white T-shirt that looked sprayed on. It conformed to his muscles, leaving nothing—and everything—to the imagination. His brown hair was mussed, as if he'd run his hands through it, making it spiky and unkempt. A day's growth of beard shadowed his square jaw. He looked as tired as she felt. Neither of them had gotten much sleep lately.

"Nothing. Nothing new, anyway. I'm tired, but I don't think I can sleep."

"Might help if you close your door."

"I like the noise. I like hearing people around me."

He came into the room and started stacking the papers spread out on her bed. "Remi, you gotta leave this stuff downstairs." He put everything back in the box and carried it over to her dresser.

"Why?"

"Because it's ugly shit. You need your room to be a refuge. In my world, you learn to keep a space that feels peaceful."

They were in his world now, weren't they? In her world, she'd lived her work, 24-7. It defined her life, as she'd intended. Greer wasn't just a wrinkle she hadn't planned for—he was a cliff she was terribly afraid he was going to ask her to jump off.

He sat on the bed, folding his legs as he faced her. "Want to tell me what happened downstairs when you saw Whiddon?"

"No." The shock had been terrible. Prophet Josiah had lectured long and passionately about the spiritually corrupting power of the secular world, but all the while he was living in both worlds, rising in the ranks of the nation's political leadership and keeping a harem in the Grummond Society.

She would never forget the day he selected her for

his wife. All the twelve-year-old girls had been presented to him, in their little white dresses…the only dresses to that point in their lives they'd been allowed to adorn with lace and ruffles.

They'd stood in line in front of him. He'd picked three of them. She had no real understanding of that event's significance. Her mom had gone pale when the news was delivered to her.

"You said you would end him," Remi whispered, hoping she'd misheard him.

He neither confirmed that promise nor denied it. "What did he do to you?"

"I don't want to talk about this."

He took hold of her hands, threading his fingers between hers. "Remi, we haven't known each other long, but we've been through a lot together already. You know you can trust me."

"He isn't worth the cost of ending him," she said, watching Greer. "Let's just leave it at that."

Greer didn't answer, but his face said it all. She could tell his mind had already been set. She shook her head. "Sometimes, you look like a college student, like any of my students. And other times you look like an ancient warrior with eyes that see the fire that made the glass, never the glass itself."

"You can turn the conversation away from yourself, but the question remains, and I will get an answer."

She ignored that. "I don't want to talk about me. Let's talk about you. What happened after the home invasion you told me about when you were a kid?" She rubbed her thumb over his. "Having been through that now—more than once—that had to be devastating as a kid."

"It was. After Gramps and I got my parents and sisters into the panic room, we took care of the bad guys." He sighed. "When my family came out, there was blood everywhere, all over me, Gramps, the walls, the floors. A baptism in hell."

"You had to be in shock."

He shook his head. "Two of them got away. I wanted it finished. Gramps and I went after them. They showed up dead a few weeks later. One had a lethal allergy to bee stings. Sadly a bee got in his car and stung him. The other wrecked his car, wrapped it around a tree."

"Did you kill them?"

"That would be illegal." He shook his head, giving her a look that said he was shocked she thought he was guilty. "They were on Interpol's top hundred wanted. I suppose karma caught up with them." He brushed his thumbs down the sides of hers. "After that, my parents became skittish around me. Like you, they thought I was guilty. I was allowed to go to my sisters' weddings, years later, but only if I promised no one would die."

Remi's eyes widened. "Did anyone die?"

"No." He grinned like they weren't talking about murder and assassinations. "It was a wedding." He looked at their hands. "Gramps was gone by then. I think he outlived his enemies, for none came to make trouble." He looked at her over their hands. "My folks threw a welcome home party when I got back from Afghanistan. They were so careful to keep up appearances. They wore their fake smiles and perfect clothes and all the neighbors came."

"I'm sure they were happy to have you back in the States."

He shrugged. "Would have been cleaner for them had I not returned." He looked at their joined hands. "When my fiancée left, it was as if a divide was carved between me and them, like if she couldn't even stand me, then they'd been right in their judgment of me."

"Doesn't mean they're right. I think you're pretty awesome." Tears distorted the seam of his sleeve, where she'd locked her eyes. "Besides my mom, you're the only other person I've ever felt safe around."

He looked into her eyes. "I'm glad I got to meet you. You're different from any woman I've known."

She blinked and met his eyes. "I've never known anyone like you, either."

Greer smiled. "That's probably a good thing."

Her gaze lowered to his T-shirt, then she met his eyes and asked, "Does it bother you, what you do?"

"No."

"What happens if you make a mistake? Kill someone who's innocent?"

"Karma works the same for everyone. But I can usually tell the guilty from the innocent when I'm standing at the business end of a knife or a gun." He held her gaze. "We're going to be lovers, you know, not just fuck buddies."

Remi started and almost pulled away, but his hands tightened.

"If that means you want one of the other guys posted on your guard duty, let me know, but it won't change our fate."

Remi slowly smiled. "You seem rather certain of yourself."

"I am."

"How do you know?"

"Besides the way you kiss me?"

She nodded.

"Because you're the first woman who's willing to touch me without being paid."

Remi frowned. "You frequent prostitutes?"

"No. I hire women to sleep with me. No sex. Just sleep. They're sleep partners."

She studied his eyes. "Why?"

"I don't like being alone when I sleep."

"You could just find yourself a girlfriend."

"It's not that easy. You've seen why. I'm not exactly an asset to a woman interested in building a future."

"You think I'm not interested in a future with a guy?"

"If you were, you would have already."

"Maybe I've been busy building my career."

"Or maybe you've been busy hiding from relationships. Why would that be?"

She pulled her hands free, stung by how close he came to her reality…and how neatly he circled back around to the subject of her freak-out in the conference room. She stood up, silently inviting him to leave.

Greer stood up too, rising next to her, towering over her, breathing her breath, which now came in fast, shallow pulls of air. He lifted his hand to her neck, capturing her rapid pulse. He lowered his head, holding her gaze until he was too close for her to focus on, watching her lips as his mouth brushed hers.

She shivered at the contact. Her body tightened from her breasts to her thighs. Breathing became a struggle. She wanted to press in to him, wanted to feel his arms around her, wanted to prove to him she hadn't been hiding from men…just from every man who wasn't him.

She caved first. Tiptoeing as she leaned in to him, she wrapped her arms around his neck and drew him closer. She moaned. He growled in answer. His hands moved over her, touching her shoulders, her neck, lifting her chin. His lips parted and his mouth opened. She wanted to feel his tongue inside her, to know the taste of him. She was glad when he backed her up against the wall; she needed its support.

He broke from the kiss. He kissed the space between the corner of her mouth and her chin, then her throat, then the curve from her shoulders to her neck. She arched in to him. He pressed his lips to the soft flesh below her collarbone. Her hands were on his biceps. She felt them bulge as he lifted her.

She wrapped her legs around his waist. Gripping his face, she lifted it for a kiss. She started to tug at his shirt. He set her down so she could pull it up. She stood between his bare feet to push it up. He leaned forward, catching her mouth with his, his shirt still fisted in her hands. He wrapped his arms around her body, surrounding her in his strength.

She moved her body against his, reveling in the waves of movement they shared, body to body, mouth to mouth.

Too soon, he paused, drawing a long breath as he leaned his forehead to hers, the back of her head hard against the wall. He took his shirt all the way off. Gripping it in one hand, he set his fists against the wall, caging her between his arms.

She watched his face as her hands slipped down his neck, over his collarbone to the light fur on his chest.

"Admit you will be mine," he demanded.

She smiled, shocked that he'd gone all primitive. "I'll admit no such thing."

He made a small predatory smile as he caught her throat in one hand, then slid his fingers around the nape of her neck and lifted her chin up with his thumb. He kissed her, his mouth open, hungry. "Admit it. Because you will."

"No."

"Mine to protect, mine to cherish, mine to hold, mine to lift up." He looked at her. "Mine to follow."

She shook her head. "What kind of man says things like that?" She frowned. "What kind of man even does those kinds of things?"

"The kind of man I am. A man who's been alone so long that he isn't really living."

"You really scare me, Greer. You don't want the part of me I can give you. You want all of me."

He nodded. "I do. I want all of you."

"I can't do that."

"You can't do that *yet*." He drew back. Heat rolled off him like a tin roof in the summer. "I've waited this long; I can wait longer."

She watched him walk out of her room, taking his heat and leaving her hunger.

24

G reer startled awake. It was still dark out. He'd opened his window before he went to bed. The fresh air calmed him; it was a normal temperature.

His body was hot, but the sheets were cool. He spread his legs to find the places his body hadn't heated. The cool cotton against his bare skin gave him a hard-on, which only increased his heat. The hunger Remi had started was spreading like a coal fire through his body. And he knew she wouldn't be coming to help him.

He checked the clock. Two a.m. He leaned his head back on his folded arms and closed his eyes, clearing his mind, emptying it of any content, then slipping into the forced nothingness. He could sleep on demand. It was a skill he'd developed long before the Army, one his grandfather had taught him in his early teens. He used it tonight, as he did most nights.

GREER SAT in Sally's room at the clinic in town. The machine monitoring her vital signs quietly beeped, its green screen illuminating the dim room. He looked at the bed where Sally lay. A sheet had been drawn up over her face. The machine began to scream as the beeps merged into a solid flat line.

Greer jumped up and grabbed her shoulders through the sheet, shaking her, shouting at her. The monitor went silent. Sally reached up and pulled the sheet down. She stared at him from empty eyes. No, not empty. Where her eyeballs should have been were white, glowing beams of light. Her hands reached for his. They were like ice.

"Sally, stop it. You're not dead," he shouted at her.

She sat up and pointed to her parents, who'd come to collect her from the clinic and bring her back to the community. She silently mouthed, "Help me!"

GREER SHOT OUT OF BED, stumbling across the room, more asleep than awake. His heart was beating as if it had stopped for a time and was racing to catch up. His body itched with sweat and fear. He realized finally he'd been having this dream for a while now. It was her eyes he'd been seeing. Sally's dead eyes.

He pulled his jeans on and grabbed a T-shirt on his way out of his room, but didn't pull it on until he was in the elevator heading to the bunker.

His fast stride rapidly moved him out of the weapons room and into ops. The room's fans and the quiet whirring sounds coming from the servers were a balm to his ravaged senses. He sat in one of the wheeled office chairs and leaned forward, bracing his elbows on his knees so he could hold his head.

Safe in the presence of comforting technology, he let his mind replay his dream.

Was Sally dead? Or was her death only imminent? Geez, was the ghost he'd been seeing Sally, too? She seemed scared of her parents in the dream, but hadn't been in real life. The woodcutter had said she was an orphan. What was the truth? After talking to Doc Beck about the bench they left in payment for Sally's care, and then seeing the homespun clothes they'd dressed Sally in, Greer hadn't been surprised to see their black buggy ride off into the night, taking her back to the Friendship Community.

Fuck. That should have set off alarms right there. Forty miles separated Wolf Creek Bend from the Friendship Community. And while they did sometimes come into town—or traveled even farther down to Cheyenne—that long of a trip would have been spread over a few days when done by horse and buggy. They would have had to camp somewhere along the way, unless they had a place to change out horses…or someone had helped them, someone with a couple of trailers, one for the horse and one for the buggy.

For them to make it down so quickly, they had to have been told Sally failed in her mission to kill Kit.

Sally hadn't been alone the night she came into Winchester's to kill Kit.

Greer felt a hand on his shoulder. He looked up to see the girl of his nightmares standing right there, with real eyes now. She wasn't a ghost. She was corporeal. Relief washed through him. She smiled at him, then walked away. He followed her into the hallway. She opened one of the heavy steel doors that led to the delivery tunnel.

He hollered at her to wait, but she didn't. She stepped through the door and into the absolute darkness beyond.

Greer rushed after her, but before he could get to the door, someone slammed him back against the wall between the bunkroom and the kitchen.

"What the hell are you doing, bro?" Max frowned at him.

Greer blinked, surprised by Max's sudden appearance. "It's Sally. She's here."

"No one's here but us."

"No, she was here. She just went out—" He looked over Max's shoulder to the steel doors, both of which were closed. "She went into the tunnel."

"That door hasn't been opened in a couple of days. Check the logs." Max's eyes narrowed. "You're sleepwalking, Greer."

Greer sighed and leaned his back against the wall. Hell. Maybe he was. Maybe he'd been asleep the whole night. Was he still asleep? It felt so real, all of it.

Seeing Sally just now. His nightmare before. "How do I know I'm not still asleep?"

Max slapped the flat of his palm against Greer's forehead, banging his head against the wall. "Feel that?"

"Ouch."

"I'd pinch you, but you're not my type."

Greer shoved free of Max's hold. Stepping away, he set his hands on his hips and lowered his head, forcing himself to take a few long breaths.

"C'mon. You need some joe." Max went into the kitchen.

Greer followed him, taking the mug of black coffee he was handed. "When did you make this?"

"While you were snoring in ops. I walked right past you."

"What are you doing down here?" Greer asked.

"I was curious. We have a visitor in the house. I don't like anyone making midnight trips to the bunker." They both sipped the coffee. "What the fuck's going on, Greer?"

"Sally's haunting me."

"She the ghost you were talking about when we were in the WKB silo?"

Greer nodded. "Yeah, but I didn't know it then. You saw her on the satellite feed the night we met with the woodcutter."

"No. I saw a glitch."

"Whatever. She was there. I've seen her several times. I was chasing her through the woods when I met Remi. She was on the roof at Remi's hideaway. She was here tonight."

Max set his mug down on the counter and folded his arms. "Okay. Whether it's your own brain trying to get a message to you or her ghost is actually talking to you, I'll play along. What does she want from you?"

"I think she's dead."

"And how does this help us?"

He shook his head, shoving his fingers through his hair. "There's something we're not seeing."

Max gave a humorless chuckle. "There's a whole lot we're not seeing."

Greer started to pace the small area of the bunker's kitchen. "The woodcutter said she was doing her tithe when she came to kill Kit." He looked at Max. "The people who took her out of the hospital weren't her parents."

"Sorry, G. I don't see her as a threat. She isn't where our focus needs to be."

"Except that every time shit's going down, she pops in." He looked at Max. "She has a message. An important one. I have to find out what it is."

GREER CAME up the stairs through the secret access in the den. He could smell the delicious breakfast Kathy was making. He sniffed the air, catching a hint of cinnamon and coffee. His stomach growled. He almost made a detour to get the first taste of whatever that was, but he didn't. He desperately needed a shower to wash away the strange night he'd spent.

He walked down the main hall on his way to the stairs in the south bedroom wing. Remi was coming down. She paused on the bottom step. Even a step up, she was a little shorter than him.

She looked so alive. Her eyes were bright, not hollows of searing light. Her skin was flushed. Her hair was shiny and loose. She smelled sweet, like an apple tree. Like springtime. Like life. She stepped down. He made a little room for her. They turned at the base of the stairs, still facing each other, only inches apart.

She reached up to touch his face. She left her hand there as she looked into his eyes. "Did you sleep well?"

"No."

"I'm sorry," she said.

"Not your fault."

"We might have both slept better had we been together."

"Mm-hmm." His left hand reached for her hand as his right hand captured her jaw and neck. He stroked her skin softly with his thumb. "Do you keep your promises, Remi?"

She nodded. "I try to. I've learned not to make ones I can't keep."

"I promised Sally I would keep her safe, but I didn't. She haunts me now."

"Is that who you've been seeing? She's Sally?"

"I think so."

"You think she's still alive?"

"No."

"Then let's find out what happened to her, give her justice, at least."

"It's gonna get bloody," he warned.

Remi gave a nervous laugh as she looked up at him with her dark green eyes. "Are you afraid, Greer?"

His gaze moved back and forth between her eyes. "Afraid of the bad guys? No. Afraid I'll never know what happened to Sally? Yes. Afraid of ghosts? Hell yes." He released her and started up the steps.

"Greer," she said when he was halfway up the stairs, "I believe you'll keep your promise to me."

He studied her over his shoulder, then pivoted and headed back down the steps. Without a word, he caught her face in his hands and crushed his mouth to hers. Her hands moved up his arms to hook over his shoulders. She opened to him, held herself against him.

Her touch chased the shadows away. He pulled back to look at her. He'd said he wouldn't rush her, but giving her the space she needed to make up her mind about them was a whole lot harder than he'd expected.

25

M andy was in the living room with Ivy later that morning, waiting for the latest prospective teacher to arrive for an interview. Max phoned her.

"Wynn Ratcliff's here. Eddie's on her way with Tank. Let her check the teach out before she brings her inside."

"Is that really necessary?" Mandy asked.

"It's not optional. You want Rocco to come up?"

"No. Let us chat with her first. If she's a good candidate, I'll call him up to talk to her."

"Copy that. Selena will be with you for the visit."

"Thanks, Max."

"Yep. Hope she's the one."

"Me too!"

The search for a live-in tutor/nanny had been more difficult than Mandy would have expected. Rocco was offering an amount considerably higher than the going salary for a public school teacher in rural Wyoming. They should have had an adequate pool of applicants to choose from. Over a hundred had applied, but only eight were worth interviewing. The first seven, while highly qualified on paper, had been absolute no-gos. The skill sets for a teacher and that of a nanny didn't seem to exist in a single individual. Mandy had begun to think they might have to hire two people for the different roles she and Rocco wanted to fill.

The woman they were meeting today, Wynn Ratcliff, was the eighth candidate so far. Her application had come in after the initial batch, but she was highly qualified. She'd graduated a year earlier from the University of Wyoming with a degree in elementary education. Since then, she'd only been working as a substitute teacher—something concerning to Ivy. That might work in their favor; if they liked her, she would be available quickly.

Selena went to the door as Eden brought the teacher inside. Tank seemed absolutely uninterested in her, which was a good thing. Mandy and Ivy stood up.

"Ladies, Ms. Ratcliff is here for her interview," Selena said as she brought the young woman into the living room.

"Wynn's fine," she said.

Mandy liked her instantly. She was tall—same height as Selena but with a zaftig build, soft and feminine. She had long brown hair, an oval face, blue-brown eyes that smiled when she smiled. Mandy hoped she sailed through the interview; she was certain Zavi would love her.

Mandy handled the introductions. Kathy brought in a tray of coffee, ice water, and cookies. They made small talk for a bit, then covered most of the interview questions she and Ivy had compiled.

"One last question, Wynn," Ivy said. "Can you tell us why you're subbing and not working a full-time position?"

"My grandmother had a stroke toward the end of my last semester. She was in intensive care when I graduated. She's just recently been moved to a long-term care facility. She seems to be responding well to treatment and rehab. I did receive several great job offers, but they were all out of state. I just couldn't bring myself to be very far from her. She raised me. We're the only family we have. Also, subbing allows me adequate time to work on my masters in gifted education. That's why your position here sounded so interesting." She sipped her coffee. "Can you tell me about the students I'll have?"

Mandy nodded. "Zavi is four. He's a linguistic savant, like his father. His dad will handle teaching him languages. We're looking for someone who can keep up with him, present him with intellectual challenges, keep him from getting bored. Ideally, we'd like someone who's comfortable being both nanny and tutor."

"I feel I'm equipped for that challenge. Is he the only student?" Wynn asked.

"There's also my daughter, Casey, who's twelve. She goes to the local public school. You won't be tutoring her, unless she needs help with homework, and her dad and I aren't around. For the most part, you'll only be teaching Zavi, with some babysitting duties for both kids within your forty hours a week."

Wynn nodded and sent another nervous glance toward Selena—and her gun. "If you don't mind my asking, can you tell me what it is that you do here?" she asked Mandy. "I'm not used to armed guards."

"Zavi's dad works for a private company that provides security services, which is run out of the house here. I'm a physical therapist. I'm working on establishing a hippotherapy center."

"What's that?"

"It's an approach to physical and emotional therapy centered around horses—riding them, caring for them, sometimes just being near them. Every client has different needs and uses different types of interactions with horses."

Wynn smiled at Mandy. "That's wonderful. I had no idea there was such a thing."

Mandy nodded. "Ivy runs the diner in town. And you met Eden. She and her husband own this house. She's a dog trainer."

"There are a few more of us," Ivy added. "Fiona is a student at CSU. Hope's a mechanic…"

"So there are several families living here?"

"Right," Ivy said.

"What are the position's hours?" Wynn asked.

"Eight to five, Monday through Friday," Mandy said. "You'll have weekends off."

"It's a long drive up here from Cheyenne. Do you know what the rental market is like here in Wolf Creek Bend?"

"No need to rent," Mandy said. "Your position comes with room and board. We eat together. Breakfast and lunch are buffet style, but dinner is a sit-down meal. There's also a small kitchen in the apartment we have for you, so you could have some privacy if you wanted to make your own meals." Mandy looked at Ivy. "Let's show her the apartment."

"Good idea. If you'll follow us, we'll just go upstairs. The apartment is over the garage."

"Zavi's up that way with Casey." Mandy picked up her phone. "I'm going to have Rocco meet us up there."

They went upstairs and down the hallway. At the bedroom wing, they turned right to go down the hallway that led to the apartment. It was a modest space. The kitchen, dining room, and living room were all in one large area. A short hallway led to a bathroom, laundry room, and bedroom.

Wynn walked through the apartment and seemed pleased when she came back to them. "This is included with the position?"

"It is," Mandy answered. "If you like, we can furnish it for you."

"Yes. That would be very helpful. With this, I can

keep my apartment in Cheyenne for when I visit my grandmother."

Rocco came into the apartment, Zavi on one side, Casey on the other. Mandy made the introductions, watching Rocco's reaction to Wynn.

"Nice to meet you," Rocco said.

Wynn nodded. "It's nice to meet you as well."

"This is my son, Zavi, and Ivy's daughter, Casey."

Wynn smiled at both kids. Zavi stood between Rocco's feet, his left hand tangled with his dad's shirt.

"Hello, Zavi," Wynn said as she knelt down, bringing herself to his height.

Rocco nudged his shoulder. He straightened and held out his hand. "How do you do?"

Wynn's smile widened as she shook his hand. "Quite well, thank you."

"Is she going to be my teacher?" Zavi asked as he looked up at Rocco.

"Possibly."

"Will I have to do what she tells me? Will she be the boss of me like Casey?"

"Yes. And she'll be Casey's boss, too," Rocco answered.

"Will she belong to you?" Zavi asked.

Mandy felt herself blush as Wynn's wide eyes went first to Rocco, then to her.

"She'll be my employee," Rocco clarified. "There's a difference between an employee and a wife."

"Oh."

"Zavi has lived in Afghanistan until recently," Mandy explained to Wynn. "He's more familiar with a family relationship that exists in a tribal structure. He likes to put the pieces together in a way that he understands."

"Makes perfect sense." She stood up. "I think we all do that."

Zavi reached for her hand. "Uncle Ty is going to build my classroom in the basement. Mandy says school will be in one of the other rooms until then. Do you want to see my bedroom?"

Wynn looked over at Mandy, who nodded. "Sure," Wynn said as he led her out of the apartment. "Are you excited for school to begin?"

Rocco nodded toward Selena, sending her after them. Zavi's voice faded behind them. "Do you like her?" Rocco asked Mandy and Ivy.

"I do. She has a kind face. She seems patient," Mandy said.

"Her grandmother is ill, which is why she's been subbing," Ivy added.

"If you guys approve, then I approve." He took Mandy's hand and kissed her forehead. "Thank you for taking the initiative and doing the interviews. I trust your judgment. Will she need help moving in?"

"I'll ask her. I'm excited for this next step."

"Me too. I'm going to head back to work. Need anything else before I go?"

"Not immediately, but I would like to move the

furniture out of the third bedroom by us and into her apartment. Then we can set that room up as a classroom until the construction's finished in the basement."

"And you'll need some things for the classroom. Let's talk it over tonight."

Mandy nodded. "Okay." She smiled at Ivy. "I think we found our teacher."

A KNOCK SOUNDED QUIETLY on Greer's door. Had he not been lying awake, he would have missed it. He turned on a light, then slipped into a pair of jeans but didn't fully fasten them. He went barefoot to the door. Remi stood there, wrapped tight in a white terrycloth robe.

Greer pushed the door open wider. "Hi."

She came inside, then stood, white-knuckling her robe as if she were torn between ripping it off and running out of the room.

He really hoped she picked the former.

"Can I sleep with you?"

Greer felt his nostrils widen, even as his body tightened. He didn't immediately answer. He waited until the breath she held came out in broken puffs, as if she expected his rejection. He shut the door.

Looking into her eyes, he eased the sides of her robe apart. She wore an old T-shirt and a pair of plaid boxers. He fought a smile, wondering if she'd chosen the least seductive attire she owned, thinking it would save her.

As if she wouldn't light up his world even in rags.

He pushed the robe from her shoulders, letting it fall to the floor as he reached for her waist. She flattened her hands against his chest and lifted a brow as she looked up at him. "I think we could both use a night of sleep."

He leaned forward, bracing his fists on the wall behind her. His heat circled her like a coil. "Sleep…afterward."

"Sleep, Greer. Just sleep." Her gaze lowered to his mouth and lingered there, undoing her words.

"So a try-out of sorts? See if I snore?"

"You're angry."

"Yeah. I am." He tore his eyes from her and stared at the wall behind her, trying to cool his senses. "But not at you." He met her eyes. "I'm angry that I'm so far ahead of you. The least I could have done was go slower so you could catch up."

"I'm catching up now."

He waited for her next move.

"I've been trying to see us from a rational, non-hormonal frame of mind," she said.

"Why do we need so much thinking about us?" He took her hand and flattened it against his heart. "Logic has nothing to do with the way I feel. I don't have to think why my heart beats. I just have to know that it does and because it does, I live."

She held her hand where he put it. "Because we're

amazing together in bed, but that can't be the only thing our relationship is made of. Passion fades."

"Mine won't."

"We're happening so fast—how do you know?"

"Because truth is truth, Remi."

"Can you give me tonight, one night, no sex, to help me feel my way through this?"

"One night or a thousand. Nothing is going to change what is." Unless, of course, she realized she'd let a monster inside her body. God help if that ever happened. If it did, while nothing would have changed for him, for her, everything would have. And lucky him, he would get to hold her while she took the night to withdraw completely from him.

Even so, he had no choice but to give her the space she needed. "Sleep it is." He pulled a long draw of her scent into his nose, then straightened and led her by the hand into his room. "Shall I grab more pillows?"

She looked up at him for a prolonged moment, then shook her head.

"You care which side?" he asked. Again she shook her head.

"I'll take the side closest to the door." He lifted the blankets. She crawled across his mattress to settle on the far half. He went to the dresser and took out a pair of gray boxer briefs. With his back to Remi, he dropped his jeans down his hips and kicked them off, then pulled on the briefs and arranged his raging boner to the side. It pushed against the elastic waistband. Whatever. At least packaged like this, she wouldn't think he had other ideas about their night together.

He walked over to his side of the bed. Remi's gaze moved down his chest and stuck to his crotch.

"Greer…"

He lifted the covers. "I finally have my woman in my room, in my bed, and you think my body's not going to react to that windfall?"

"We're just sleeping." Her grip tightened on the fold of the sheet she held tightly to her chest. "And I'm not your woman."

Greer got in bed, then turned off the light. "You are. You just don't know it yet." Like an enemy who, shot through the heart with a 9mm, still fought for a few dangerous seconds after his death. She was his— she just hadn't fallen.

She pulled a long and audible breath, but didn't follow it with words. He held himself still and waited for her to settle in for the night. But she didn't and he didn't, and neither of them slept. It was like living in the space between breaths.

"What did you pay them?" Remi asked, breaking the dreadful stasis.

"Pay whom for what?"

"The women who slept with you."

"I didn't pay them. I paid their employers. Two to three hundred, depending on how long I needed them."

"Did they just sleep?"

"They sure didn't talk."

"What if they had lice?"

Greer grinned. Was she jealous? "They didn't."

"Did you touch each other?"

"Yes." He looked over at her. Her head was tilted toward him in a shaft of blue light from the window. "That's kinda the point of hiring a sleep buddy. So you know you're not alone."

"Did you hold them?"

"Sometimes."

"Did you kiss them?"

"Never. It was just sleeping, Remi."

"What if I want you to hold me?"

"Do you?" he asked, looking at her. She nodded. He lifted his arm so that she could scoot in to him. She came up close, her body lying against his, her arms folded between her chest and his.

She drew a breath to ask another question, but he beat her to it. "Did you know that the part of your brain that handles speaking opposes the part of your brain in charge of sleeping?" he asked.

She sighed. As close as she was, her breath skittered across his chest hair. "I'm sorry. I chatter when I'm nervous."

"Sleeping with me makes you nervous?"

She nodded.

"Why?"

"Because it means I'm letting you inside my walls." She stroked his chest for a while. He hoped she couldn't feel his cock pulsing with each innocent touch. "So how do you sleep when you're having trouble?"

"I hire companions." He grinned at her.

She frowned. "You should get a dog."

"I'll talk to Eddie about that."

Her hand made a fist, which she banged gently against his chest. He chuckled. She unfolded a bit, nestling more comfortably in his hold.

"Good night, Greer."

"Night, Remi."

"Greer?"

"Hmmm?"

"What happens if I want to talk all night?"

His arm tightened around her. His hand rubbed her shoulder. "Then we'll talk all night." He moved her up over his body, leaving her legs to drape over his hips. "I'm not in a hurry for what's coming. Well, I am, but I don't want to be. You're far too fragile—and too precious—to bulldoze. Soon enough, you'll accept what we are to each other."

Her arms folded over his chest. He drew her body forward with his hands round her ribs, then kissed her gently, lips to lips, taking only what she offered. When she opened her mouth to him, he did the same. Their tongues met halfway, sliding, pushing, dancing. His head lifted off the bed as his leaned to the side to deepen the kiss.

He fisted her hair as he pulled away slightly, then kissed her lips twice more. "In case you hadn't noticed, I'm breaking down your walls."

She shook her head slightly. "It's like they weren't ever there with you."

"You don't need them with me, Remi. I won't fail you." He gritted his teeth, trying to pause long enough to get some control over his emotions. "But I goddamned sure would like to kick the ass of the bastard who made you put them up in the first place."

She pushed back from him, studying him with solemn eyes in the dark room. "I did that on my own. For my own protection. Until you, I never let anyone inside."

He took a couple of breaths and pushed a bit of hair behind her ear. "Walls are hard to build and harder to maintain. No one puts them up on a whim. They're only ever needed for defense. What caused you to need them?"

With her splayed over his body, he felt the shift that came over her. Her body cooled, stiffened. She pushed up and sat on the bed. "I don't want to talk about this."

He sat up too. "Okay."

She stared at him, a silent silhouette against the ambient light from his window. Without a word, she scrambled off his bed and crossed his room. He caught up with her as she slipped into her bathrobe. Wrapping an arm around her from behind, his hand crossed her body and caught her hip. "Don't go. Please. Give us a night of sleep. Let me hold you. Just that. Nothing more. We'll both quit talking."

She caught his hand and brought it up, pinning it

against her heart, which beat against her ribs like a caged refugee. "I can't talk about those things, the things you want to know."

Greer pressed his face against the side of her head. "I'll stop asking."

"You slip under my skin and into my secrets so effortlessly."

"I was trained to do that. I don't even do it consciously anymore."

"I'm not your mission." She tilted her head up and looked back at him, frowning. "Or am I?"

"You aren't." He locked his jaw, to keep the truth from rolling out, but it just came out anyway. "And you are."

"Which is it?"

He turned her in his arms, moving so that faint light from his window across the room hit his face. He wanted her to read the truth of his words. "There are things you know that I need to know…for your own safety. I'm not using you. I can't use you. I won't use you."

She held his intense gaze for a minute, then pulled free. "Good night, Greer."

He didn't move, didn't try to stop her this time as she left his room, quietly shutting the door behind her. His breath escaped his lungs in a long hiss. When he'd mentioned the difficulty maintaining walls, he'd spoken from experience. He'd let her inside his walls, and all he had to show for it was a blistering pain in his heart.

26

Greer was at breakfast before Remi. As the others came in, they filled in around the table, leaving the seat next to him open. Remi usually sat next to him, but he knew she wouldn't this morning. Not after last night. This morning—if she even came in—she'd pick a seat at the end of the table, leaving a big empty spot in his heart and a question in the minds of the guys. They hadn't exactly hidden the fact that they were hooking up.

When Remi did finally come in, the room was noisy with chatter. Their eyes met, so briefly, then she headed over to the buffet table to fill a mug with coffee.

She looked at him as she faced the table. He held her gaze, his expression blank, his eyes hard. She walked right over to the empty seat beside him. He stood and pulled out her chair. She set her coffee down, then faced him, still on her feet.

"Sorry I'm late." Her lips curled upward in a slight smile. "I had a hard time sleeping until a few hours ago."

He lowered his head so she alone would hear his words. "So you're still talking to me?"

She laughed. Fucking laughed. And touched his chest. "Of course. I repaired my walls overnight."

Greer's brows lowered. "Doesn't matter. They're coming down. Very soon."

She stepped away with a smile, terminating their quiet convo as she went to fill a plate from the buffet. He sat down again, watching her, then intercepted hard glares from Owen and Kit.

Fuck. It. All.

His heart was his to give. Even if it came back to him bruised and battered.

Minutes later, before the guys started to leave the table, Kit called the team down to the bunker for a meeting. Greer and Remi were among the last to clear out. She started toward the living room. He caught up with her. She hooked two of her fingers with his. His body tightened.

"I'm going to work in the billiards room. Call me if you need me in the bunker." She took a step away, smiling at him over her shoulder.

He tightened the hold his fingers still had on hers and pulled her back to him. Pivoting, he put his back to the camera he'd installed in the corner of the room months ago, shielding her.

"Remi, when you fixed your walls, did you build them with me inside or outside?" Not that it mattered, because he was damned serious about taking them down; her answer would just indicate how hard he was going to have to work.

"I might have left a door for you…" She smiled and walked backward until their fingers broke apart.

"Yo, Greer!" Max shouted from the hallway outside the dining room. "You coming? Or do you need an engraved invitation?"

Greer watched Remi disappear around the corner, then went back into the dining room. "Geez, Max. When did you take up caterwauling?"

Max grimaced. "When you stuffed your balls in your ears, I guess."

Greer grinned and walked past him. It wasn't going to be an easy siege, his fight for Remi, but it wasn't going to be a long one either, and that left him feeling optimistic.

VAL STEPPED out of the diner, into the stairwell that led up to the apartments above Ivy's restaurant and down to her storage area. The downstairs light was on. The basement was dark, despite the fact that it was still midmorning.

"Ivy?" he called, though he wasn't there for Kit's wife. He'd come to talk to Ace again. "Yo, Ivs. You there?" he asked, halfway down the basement stairs.

Ace came to the door of the storeroom. "She's not here. Hi, Val."

"Hey, Ace." He went down the stairs. "She took her car into the shop and needed a ride. What're you doin'?" Val went down the remaining steps.

"Laundry. Ivy said I could use her machines."

"Oh. That's nice."

Ace shrugged. "Better than the laundromat." She lifted a full hamper, leaving another behind.

"Want a hand with that?"

She looked at the hamper, then at Val, hesitating longer than such a decision should take. Finally she shrugged. "Sure."

Val grabbed the second hamper and followed her up the stairs to the second floor. "Didn't know you lived here."

"Yeah. Ivy's been a lifesaver. The job. The apartment."

"The washing machines."

Ace gave him a reluctant smile over her shoulder. At the door to her apartment, she dug into her pocket for her keys, though why she'd locked her door when only she and Ivy's employees had access to the stairwell, he didn't know.

She pushed the door open and shoved her basket inside, then grabbed the one he'd carried. He looked into her apartment, seeing its Spartan furnishings. A couple of folding camp chairs, a blowup mattress, and a few boxes comprised the sum total of her furniture.

Val looked at Ace. *Pain.* He rubbed his chest. Who was she? Who had done this to her? "Talk to me."

"What for?"

"I can help you."

"I don't need your help."

He pushed the door open, exposing her austere circumstances to his full vision. "Don't you?"

"Look, I don't even know who you are." She turned from the door and walked into her apartment. "I'm poor. So what? You think rich people are waitresses?"

Jesus. The vibe coming from her was clawing at his heart. He walked over to look out the front bow window.

"It's not a big deal. I travel lightly," she said behind him. "This shit fits in my car."

He turned slightly from the window, looking at her. "Who are you running from, Ace?"

"Who says I'm running?"

"You did. You said you 'travel light.' Only people who need to move fast travel light."

She went back to the still open door. "I think you should go."

Val didn't move. "Are you bringing trouble to my friend's restaurant?" He could have sworn he saw her chin tremble.

"Please leave."

"It's a simple question."

Ace folded her arms and buried her gaze in the shadows of the stairwell. Val crossed the room to stand in front of her. "Let me help you."

"No. You can't." She huffed a little laugh, flashing her crooked fangs that were so sexy to him. "No one can."

He handed her one of his cards. "Call me. Please. We'll talk it through."

She took the card but didn't look at it. She didn't look at him, either. "Later."

WHEN VAL LEFT, Ace shut the door and stared at his card through vision that wavered. "Special Consultant to the Department of Homeland Security," the card read. She blinked her tears away. Taking out her phone, she dialed a number she rarely used. When the call connected, she didn't waste words.

"I think I found them…"

MANDY USED the house phone in the kitchen to call down to Greer. "*S'up, M?*" he answered.

"Is Rocco in the house? I can't find him."

There was a brief hesitation on the other end,

then, "Yep. He's in the spare bedroom in your wing. Everything cool?"

Mandy wasn't sure how to answer that. She spent a lot of time standing between Rocco and his team when he was at his weakest. She didn't know how else to assist him, except to help shield the worst of his dark moments from the guys. The team was a lifeline to him. Without them, she feared he'd completely spiral downward. This latest bend was bad.

She wondered if she should talk to her brother. But she didn't, because she didn't want to jeopardize Rocco's place on the team. Maybe she should go see the shrink in town. Maybe he could give her pointers. Or maybe even help her find a way to get Rocco in to see him.

"Yeah. It's fine. I just couldn't find him. Thanks a bunch, Greer." She could find his body, but God alone knew where his mind had gone.

She walked up the stairs, grateful that Casey and Zavi were out playing. She stepped into the third bedroom and scanned the empty space. If Greer said he was here, then he was, but where? She went over to the closet and opened the door. It was empty of clothes and any stored items, so it was easy to make out the man crouching in the corner.

Rocco didn't look up when she stepped into the small space. She shut the door behind her, then crossed to the back wall to sit beside him. Other than sitting so that their bodies touched, she didn't reach out to him or try to hold his hand. She didn't speak to him, didn't do anything other than lend him her strength. It was like standing near an unbroken horse, working on trust. Or maybe more like an unbreakable horse, one that needed to be gentled every time it was ridden.

The times when Rocco was out in the light, he was brilliantly alive, a great father, lover, friend, and teammate. But increasingly, those moments were fewer and farther apart.

She locked her gaze on the bead of light leaking in under the door and told herself the darkness would end. Soon, she would have to leave, but she would stay as long as she could. She had a client coming up from the VA hospital in Cheyenne. Her first client. She hoped she could get Rocco to assist, but she didn't know if he'd break out of his shadows in time.

She heard Rocco sigh. The bright light under the door let her see well enough to know he leaned his head against the wall. "You don't have to do this, you know."

She considered his words. "It isn't a matter of 'have to' anything. I'm your sidewalker. It's what I do." She drew a long breath. He'd said he'd be hers. "I have my first client today."

"That's great," he said, as if it were the first he'd heard of it. They'd talked about it all week. It was like the darkness ate his mind and all his values and left only the pulp of him behind.

"I could use your help," she said.

He didn't answer immediately, then, "Not today."

"Okay." There was no point arguing. "I'll come back when I'm done."

"Don't bother. I'll be downstairs. I'll see you at dinner."

Mandy fought back her tears. At least he let her be near him in these moments. She wondered if the guys knew he was faking living. "See you then."

She pulled herself to her feet and silently left the closet and the empty guest room. He wouldn't be able to hide there soon, once Wynn started. They were going to use this spare room for Zavi's classroom until the basement rooms could be built out.

Mandy was lost in thought as she moved down the hallway and collided with Angel, who stepped out of the den. He reached a hand out to steady her.

"Whoa. Sorry about that, Mandy." She nodded and tried to smile. "Hey, what's goin' on?"

"Nothing. I'm heading out to get ready for a client."

"Oh yeah, you mentioned that. Your first, right?"

"Yeah." And of course she stood there too long. His brows knitted. She spoke up before he could ask more questions. "Can I ask a favor?"

"Name it."

"Do you have an hour you could spare?"

"I think so. What's up?"

"My client is a disabled vet. He has prosthetic legs. He'll be able to use the ramp we have to mount. He's bringing out a friend to walk on one side, and for moral support, I think. I've been communicating with him about our setup here, and that I'm not fully staffed. I'm not charging him for his sessions yet, as I still need to work out the kinks. He was excited to help me, but I need someone else to be a sidewalker. I thought I might be able to get Rocco to help, but he's not ready for that."

"I got your back, Em. I'd be happy to help."

Mandy smiled up at Angel and nodded. "Thank you. I'm heading out that way now. Come out when you can."

THE HOUSE WAS SILENT AGAIN, the quiet no balm to Rocco's frayed nerves. He sighed, remembering his shock when Mandy joined him in his black hole. She didn't try to talk to him, didn't try to touch him, simply sat next to him as an anchor, tethering him to the light beyond the door.

He pushed to his feet and exited the empty closet. Where had Mandy said she was going? A client? He walked down the hallway, across the bridge that joined the two upper bedroom wings of Blade's house, and stopped at Val's door. He knocked, though he didn't expect to hear an answer. Val had been in the bunker when Rocco came upstairs, however long ago that was. There was no answer.

Rocco let himself inside. Someone was showering in the bathroom. He didn't care about that. He crossed the room and went to the window that overlooked the south side of the house, where the stables and paddocks were. He pushed a panel of the window sheers aside and looked out to see Mandy. And Angel. And a guy who had to be a vet, judging by the straight grade of his shoulders and his grace with crutches. Another guy was with him, wearing fatigues.

Mandy and Angel shook hands with them, then chatted a moment. When they moved away from the car, Rocco could see that the guy with crutches had prosthetic legs. He got around pretty good. The crutches were almost not needed.

The water shut off in the bathroom behind Rocco, but he didn't move from the window. "Hey, Rocco," Val said.

Rocco didn't answer him. He was vaguely aware of him dressing, but he never took his eyes from the scene in the corral.

"What are you looking at?" Val asked as he joined Rocco at the window. "Oh. That's right. She said at breakfast she had a client today. Her first. Pretty cool."

As they watched, Mandy showed the visitors around, introduced the wounded vet to one of her horses. Rocco knew that sorrel. A middle-aged mare, she was docile as hell. Perfect for therapeutic uses. Boring as fuck for anything else.

Val looked from the window to Rocco. "Why don't you join them?"

Rocco still didn't answer. Mandy was walking her client up the mounting ramp. She took the crutches from him, then his friend helped him balance as he got on the horse. Angel was on the horse's other side. Apparently Mandy had shown him what to do as a sidewalker, for he held his position while the vet got settled. Mandy set the crutches aside, then led the horse forward as she moved down the ramp.

For this exercise, she was leading the horse. They walked the circle of the corral. Mandy must have said something to the vet, for he straightened his posture and looked up, ahead of where they were walking. And he was smiling.

"Mind if I use your window?" Rocco asked Val without looking at him.

Val laughed. "Sure. Better yet, why don't we go down there?"

"No."

"It's a big day for Mandy."

"Yeah." And wasn't that the fuck of it? It was a huge day for her, and he'd already let her down. He couldn't get that back, even if he went down now. He let the curtain drop, then leaned against the wall, watching the murky shapes through the sheers.

"What's going on, Rocco?" Val asked.

"I wish I knew." He looked over at the blond giant. "I thought this would end when I remembered the day I lost Zavi. And when I got him back, I thought it was over for good." He made a face. "But I can't shake it." Val listened in silence. He didn't reach out to him, didn't offer useless suggestions. Made it easier to talk to him. "Kit wants me to see the shrink in town."

"Maybe you should."

Rocco lowered his gaze, staring at nothing. "She asked me to stand with her today. I said no."

A heavy hand fell on his shoulder. He looked over at Val. "Maybe the worst thing isn't wading through the black. Maybe it's losing Mandy. How far you willing to go for her? Far enough to fix yourself?"

"I can't even see the edges of it, Val. What if I'm not fixable?"

Val lifted one of the curtain panels. "You see that guy out there? He lost his legs. They're gone. No way is he ever getting them back. But you know what? He's learning a new normal." He looked at Rocco. "Maybe this thing following you around is your new normal. Maybe it isn't. Maybe it'll end. Maybe it won't. The shrink should be able to guide you through it. You know that. If you don't want to see him, then talk to us. Talk to Mandy. You can't cave in to it, Rocco. Not when you got all of us behind you."

Rocco sighed. "There's not a lot left of me, Val."

"That's okay. We'll re-gen you like some freaky sci-fi project. Grow a new you—better, faster, stronger. We could inject your cells into a lab rat and see what happens."

Rocco laughed. "I'd kill the rat. Or become it." He pushed aside the curtain again and looked out. Maybe he already was the rat, leaving Mandy to her triumph alone as he had.

WHEN THE SESSION ENDED, Mandy's client was as wobbly-legged as a new foal…and happy as all get out. Angel and the guy's friend bookended him down the mounting ramp.

"That was amazing. I've never been so happy to walk in circles. Well, I wasn't walking. The horse was. But it felt like me. I felt free again. First time since this happened." He looked at Mandy as she joined them. "I want to come every day."

She shook her head. "Let's work up to that. How about twice a week for a couple of weeks, then we'll reevaluate? We can work up to a full trail ride, when you're ready."

"Yeah. I'm ready." They chatted about his next visit, then both men shook hands with Mandy. "I'm going to tell them about this, the others at rehab. You're going to be busy as all hell."

Mandy kept her sigh to herself, thrilled with the work, yet saddened that it was needed. "I'm here to help. Bring a few of them out with you next time."

Her client grinned. "Don't think I won't!"

Angel stood beside her as they watched their visitor's car roll down the drive. "Thanks for your help, Angel."

"Anytime."

He looked at her as the silence stretched between them. Mandy wished she'd not let the silence speak for her.

"I'll talk to Rocco," he said quietly.

Mandy blinked and focused on breathing so she wouldn't cry. "There's no point. You can lead a horse to water, and all."

Angel's face was like stone as she moved past him to head back to the house.

27

F iona was at the Swinging Monkey Tiki Bar in old town Fort Collins with her friends. The giant green stamp on her hand warned servers she was too young to drink. It didn't matter. She was there as a DD anyway.

The bar was slammed, the jungle-beat music throbbing. It was hard to hear her friends. But she saw that something—or someone—had captured their attention. She looked to see what it was, and a familiar pair of deep brown eyes met hers. Her breath hitched in her chest. Kelan was here! He'd said he was going to come down and spend the night with her at their apartment.

The music switched to a different, quieter song. One of her friends slapped a five-dollar bill in the center of the table and announced, "Five bucks to the first of us who can get him to come join us."

Fiona grinned. "Guys. Not a good idea—" It was

too late. Her friend was already making a beeline for Kelan. Fiona watched, feeling a strange mixture of jealousy and worry. She hadn't told them much about her summer, only that she'd met an amazing guy during her babysitting gig.

Kelan crossed his arms and glared down at her friend, saying nothing. Her friend stayed long enough to try to extricate herself without losing her composure. When she came back to the table, the next one made her attempt. This time she got a raised black eyebrow.

"Guys, stop this. Really—" Her words fell on deaf ears, drowned out by a new, louder tune. The third attempt made Kelan lift his gaze across the room and pin her with the blackest look she'd ever seen.

"My turn," she announced before his patience broke.

KELAN SAW FIONA APPROACH HIM. The noise of the bar receded, drowned out by the sound of his thundering blood. His gaze narrowed on his woman, only her. Everything else in the room faded away.

Don't touch her. Don't touch her, he ordered himself. It had been days since he'd seen her. He'd been having severe withdrawals.

She didn't stop until her toes touched his. He didn't move, didn't acknowledge her, didn't take his eyes off her. All he allowed himself was to breathe her scent deep, deep into his lungs, giving his soul a nibble of the woman it craved.

She reached out and touched his chest, letting the flat of her palm stroke his pec. A shiver ripped along his spine. His cock speared to life, lying sideways and swollen in his jeans. She moved closer still, stepping between his spread legs. Both of her hands were on him then. He watched her, his gaze intensifying every second she stayed so near him.

She reached up and hooked her hands on his shoulders. Standing on her tippy toes, she kissed the bare skin at his open collar. He bent his head slightly, dragging the sweet fragrance of her hair into his nose, his lungs, his whole goddamned body.

Her tongue peeped out and licked where she'd been kissing. Her mouth worked its way up as high as she could reach. "Kiss me, Kelan," she whispered harshly.

He wrapped his arms around her, one around her narrow waist and the swell of her hips, the other up under her shoulder blades, lifting her. Pinning her body to his. He took her mouth, fucking it with his tongue, performing the only sex act allowed in such a public place.

A small mewling sound came from deep in Fiona's throat, rippling into his mouth as if they weren't separate beings. She gripped the back of his head, tightening the seal of their lips while he ate at her mouth.

"Pull back, Fiona. Pull back now. Or I swear I will

find a bare stretch of wall to take you against. I will claim you right here. Right now."

Fiona did pull back a little, but only to smile at him. "Will you? We can end this waiting?"

His nostrils flared and his eyes narrowed. He set her a few inches from his body. "Are you twenty-one yet?"

Of course he knew she wasn't. She held up her fist, showing the ugly green stamp. "No. And everyone here knows it."

"Then don't start a game you can't end."

She grinned, certain of his self-control. "I want to end it."

"As do I." He looked beyond her to the table where she'd been with others. "Are these girls your friends?"

"Some of them. Will you join us?"

"Only if you sit on my lap to protect me from them."

"Deal!"

REMI SHUT her laptop and listened to the quiet in her room as she leaned back in her desk chair. The silence made her edgy. She didn't want to be alone. She wondered what Greer was doing. Funny; she'd gotten so used to having him around that she missed him when he wasn't there. He'd kept his word about not rushing what was happening between them, giving her the room she needed for the past few days.

She wondered, when this was all over, where would they stand? Did they have a chance at a relationship, as he believed? And would they still—once he found out the truth about her?

She showered, then dried her hair and put makeup on as if she were going out. In truth, she was just going down to the billiards room. She stepped into her closet and tried on a few different combinations of tops and pants, then decided to go slouchy, choosing a fitted tee, her jeans, and her simple leather sandals.

It wasn't like her to be so insecure about what she wore. It was just that she only had a subset of clothes here, and she'd worn them all. Big deal. Everyone knew she was just visiting. Greer in particular never paid much attention to what she wore, though granted, most of the time, they were running somewhere or he was fighting someone or they were dropping their clothes on the floor.

She stepped out of her room and went down the hall to his. She knocked twice, waited, then knocked again. No answer. Turning around, she supposed he could be anywhere. She heard voices coming from somewhere downstairs.

She went down the staircase in his wing, then headed toward the sound of people. They were in the billiards room. She looked around the masculine space with its wood-paneled walls and leather furniture. At one side of the room was an antique bar, made from mahogany featuring densely carved panels and classic columns. An age-stained beveled mirror was its central focus.

Almost everyone in the household was there. Looked like a private club open only to adults living in the house. The Jacksons and the kids were absent. Greer was nowhere to be seen. Was he still below, in the bunker? He wasn't in his room.

"Hey, doc! Come on in!" Eden greeted her in a friendly way, waving her deeper into the room.

Remi smiled and nodded. She was looking forward to the chance to get to know the women better. For most of the time she'd been here, she'd been working—in her room, in here, or in the bunker.

Val was behind the bar pouring what looked like a whiskey. Eden and Angel were at the pool table. Selena was with them, ready to take on the winner. Kit, Owen, Rocco, Max, and Ty were playing a hand of poker. The rest of the women were seated on the burgundy leather sofas and armchairs, having a friendly discussion.

The guys nodded, smiled, or just ignored her as they concentrated on their activities. No one seemed concerned or resentful that she'd joined them.

Remi sat at the end of one of the sofas. "I thought maybe Greer would be down here."

"He'll probably be along soon," Mandy said. "Did you want something to drink? Val can mix any drink you can think of. Or maybe a glass of wine?"

"Name your poison, professor," Val called from the bar.

Remi smiled. "I'll have what you're having."

"Good choice! One Balcones coming up."

Owen looked over at them. Val smiled at her. She didn't understand that exchange, but there was a lot about these people she didn't get.

"Thanks," she said as Val handed the drink to her.

"Greer mentioned you've been working on an academic article," Ivy said.

Remi nodded. "Every couple of years, I select a different isolationist group here in the U.S. to study. Lately, I've been focusing on the Friendship Community."

"Are there so many different ones in the U.S.?" Hope asked.

"I don't think there's a good estimate on a number. I would guess there's upward of a thousand. The government puts it somewhere north of four hundred."

"I had no idea there's so many."

Remi shrugged. "Groups like the ones I study are elusive. New ones form all the time. Old ones disband or dissolve. It's a constantly changing landscape. The Friendship Community is one of the older ones. It started in the nineteenth century as a utopian society. It had all but died out until the Great Depression kicked it into gear again. Every wave of fear that passes through the main U.S. population infuses it with new vigor. It's now stronger than it's ever been and has been growing steadily for thirty years. My paper focuses on what's made it survive—and now thrive—for so long. The social cohesion at its core."

"That sounds fascinating," Mandy said. "Will we be able to read your finished paper?"

"Of course."

"I'd like to read it before you publish it," Owen said. Remi hadn't been aware that he'd joined their group.

She looked into his cold blue eyes. "You said you weren't interested in my research."

"I'm interested in your analysis."

"What makes a cult a cult, Remi?" Ivy asked.

Remi smiled. "That's an easy question to ask and a hard one to answer. Depends on the group's ideation. It could be centered around religion, hate, fear. Anything could be a unifying thread that pulls a group together. Once together, however, it uses fear, dread, and mind control to keep the group together."

"God, that sounds like us," Ivy said. Kit had come over to their group. Remi didn't miss the way his hand tightened on her shoulder.

Remi shook her head. She understood this group so much better than she had just days ago. "This isn't a cult. Maybe an enclave, but not a cult." She smiled at Kit. "You identify with a mission, but your lives aren't centered around a leader." She looked at Owen, whose pale blue eyes showed no emotion, then back to Ivy. "You're careful about who comes into your midst, but you also exist in the wider external society. You don't eschew science. You embrace different races and religions."

"Good save," Val said, chuckling.

Remi realized the entire group was standing around them, listening. "It's no save at all. I don't hold back. If I thought this group was a cult, I'd say it." And that was the truth. She realized, now, there were big differences between this group and a cult.

Someone came into the room. Remi turned to see Greer heading toward them. He wore flip-flops, tight jeans, and a gray V-neck T-shirt. The black leather and silver bands made a wide cuff on his right wrist, and were balanced by the tactical watch on his left wrist. His hair was still damp and wavy. He hadn't shaved, but his stubble didn't soften his hard jaw or that cleft in his chin that Remi found so fascinating.

He looked at her, almost as if checking her well being, then glanced around at the group, his gaze hitting on Owen and Kit. "S'going on?"

"Late to class, as usual," Blade said, grinning.

"Remi's teaching us about cults," Mandy said.

He crossed his arms as he came to stand behind the sofa next to Kit. "Oh."

Max frowned at him. "You okay, man?"

"Yeah." Greer looked at him, then looked away. "I just crashed for a bit. It's all good."

Val brought him a beer, then turned some country music on. Everyone returned to where they were before.

"Selena! Get over here and dance with me!" Val ordered.

She was leaning over the pool table, about to take a shot. She straightened and called out, "Val, go fuck yourself."

He sighed, throwing his arms out to his sides. "See? I've lost my mojo," he said to the room at large.

Hope set her beer on the coffee table and went over to him. "I'll dance with you."

Val's face lit up. "Are we sharing?" he asked Max.

"Oh, hell no," Max answered with a flash of teeth.

"Course not." Val gave a disgusted face.

"I thought you gave up sharing," Owen said as he set a card on the table.

"Yeah. Forgot about that. Well, just the dance then, Hope." He reached for her, and they started a slow movement across the floor.

Hope laughed. "I understand. You have an awfully pretty face. I'd hate for Max to rearrange it."

Val huffed loudly. "As if."

Remi was watching Val and Hope, smiling at his antics, when she felt Greer's fingers slip into hers. She looked up at him, into his haunted eyes. Her smile faded.

"Dance with me?" he asked.

She let him lead her to the area where the carpet ended and the wood floor made dancing easy. The song was a slow one. He set his big hands on her waist and drew her close to his body. She ran her hands up his chest to circle his neck.

For a long moment, he stared into her eyes. She watched the shadows in them, surprised that he didn't try to hide them from her. "You saw her again when you slept, didn't you?"

He didn't answer for the space of a breath. "This isn't about Sally. It's about us." He touched his hand to her face.

She ducked her head. "Greer, what will your friends think?"

"I don't see anyone here but you."

She smiled at that, but she wasn't as oblivious to those in the room as he was.

He touched his thumb to her lips. "And it occurs to me, the way I'm looking at you leaves little to the imagination."

"You're okay with their knowing about us?"

"Yeah. 'Cause I really don't give a fuck about them right now." He leaned forward and kissed her gently on the lips. "In fact, I think we should go up to my room. Now."

"Now?" She bit her lower lip, holding it between her teeth.

He leaned forward and used his teeth to pull it free. "Yeah. Got a problem with that?" he asked, his lips brushing hers as he spoke.

She shook her head ever so slightly. "No, I don't."

28

Greer shut the door to the game room, then faced Remi. His desire felt like a vise around his ribs, compressing his chest. He didn't touch her. She stepped back against the hallway wall. He moved with her.

"I've been thinking about us," he said.

She smiled. He didn't. "What are your thoughts?"

"My head said you look like a heartbreak. My soul said you might be the one. My mind said shut it down, get out now. My heart said open up." He shrugged. "And after that, there's nothing, 'cause the heart's spoken. So I'm in, Remi. All the way."

She reached over and fingered the leather wrapped around his wrist. Just that slight touch made his body quake. He shoved his hands in his pockets to keep from grabbing her. She stepped closer to him, her face lifted to his. He leaned into her, his head bent to hers.

"I'm in, too, Greer."

She flattened her hands to his chest, for balance, not resistance. His rigid cock made his jeans too freakin' tight. He met her halfway, holding himself from actually connecting their mouths. He wanted to freeze this moment, remember everything about the night. Watch it like he did the glycerin bubbles Casey and Zavi blew into the wind.

Her hands moved up his body, to his shoulders. His lips parted. God, he wanted her. She looked at his throat as her hands captured his neck. Muscles in his cheeks clenched. His nostrils flared. And then her lips were there, on his throat. When she licked his Adam's apple, he was undone.

He tore his hands from his pockets to hold her, pulling her with him as he fell back against the heavy wooden door to the game room. His legs parted, and she moved between them.

He fisted her hair and brought their mouths together. The first touch of her tongue sent a shiver down his spine. He didn't let go of her hair, even as his other hand circled around to her hip. He lifted her slightly, rubbing her body against his. He wondered if she could feel the hard ridge of his boner, even through their clothes. He could sure feel the softness of her body.

The kiss slowly ended. Her eyes opened, looked into his. He straightened, backing her into the hallway. He held her waist and leaned over to kiss her cheek, her chin, that space behind her ear.

She groaned. He pushed her against the hallway wall. Taking hold of her hands, he lifted them above her head, then pushed a knee between her legs. She arched against him. He leaned forward and caught her chin between his teeth, meeting her eyes as he drew his teeth over her skin.

Her breath was coming fast in short puffs. "Greer, I want you so badly, I don't think I can stand much longer."

He grinned. "We should get you off your feet, then." Bending slightly, he scooped up her legs across one of his arms. She wrapped her arms around his neck, holding tightly as he took long strides to the stairs.

"Where are we going? Your room or mine?"

"Mine. Kiss me," he ordered.

Remi caught the side of his face, pulling him to her as he went up the stairs. Her lips were soft on his. She owned his mouth. He gave himself over to the sensations she stirred in him. His arms tightened around her. He stopped midway up the second turn of stairs to focus on kissing her.

When his tongue, teeth, and lips had leisurely tasted hers, he lifted his head to look at her. "Open your blouse."

She bit her bottom lip, almost hiding her slight smile as she looked around them. "What if someone sees us?"

"Then they'll know I'm about to fuck the most beautiful woman in the world. Do it."

She still had an arm around his neck, so she could only release the buttons with one hand. Her fingers moved clumsily, opening her shirt just past her bra. He watched the flesh she slowly bared, his gaze lingering on the white lacy material of her bra. The difference in color between the crisp white and the creamy color of her skin was fascinating.

He lifted her body to his mouth. She was lighter than the weights he lifted. Her skin was like velvet. He pressed one side of his face to the soft flesh above her bra, pulled a long breath of her scent. It must have sent a current of air along her skin, for her ribs lifted upward.

They reached the top of the stairs. A few long strides brought them to his room. She opened the door. He walked inside and kicked it shut. The pale, late evening light spilled through the sheers, casting a lavender blue glow about the room.

He lowered her to her feet, keeping an arm around her. Her hands moved over his body as if she needed to touch all of him. His waist, his chest, his shoulders, his arms, never breaking the kiss. Her warm breath, puffing near their mouths, excited him.

He loved the way she responded to him. She was never still in his arms. She moved hungrily, taking and giving, experiencing the feel of her body against his. He pulled her shirt up and off. She lifted his tee, pushing it up his chest until he tugged at the neckline and dragged it over his head, discarding it on the floor.

She kicked off her sandals. He did the same, then reached for the waist of her jeans and unfastened them. She moved his hands away and pushed them down her hips, exposing a pair of white, stretchy boy briefs.

His hands felt unsteady as he touched her shoulders, feasting his eyes on her bared body. He ran his palms down her arms, then up again to slip them down her back.

She was the most intense, intelligent, complex woman he'd ever known, and she was giving herself to him. *To him.*

She reached for his jeans and popped the waist button, then started on the zipper. He tightened his stomach. "Careful," he warned with a grin. Going commando had its benefits…and its risks. She pulled the material away from his body and lowered the zipper. Her fingers bumped his cock. He jumped. She looked up at him in a quick glance. Her pupils were huge and black. She pushed his jeans down his hips, exposing his dick.

He stepped out of his jeans. She took him in her hands and leaned forward to kiss his chest. He didn't have a lot of chest hair, but he had a dark line that led from his navel down to his crotch. Keeping him in one hand, she used the other to trace that line of dark hair.

He shoved himself against her hand. She groaned and hissed on a sharp inhale. He bent his head down to nuzzle her face.

"Hurry," she urged.

"I don't want to hurry. I want to remember all of this."

Her hand tightened on him. "We'll remember next time."

"We will. And the next time and the next time." He palmed her through her panties. Her lips parted on a sharp breath. Her hands shifted to his shoulders, her nails digging into his skin.

He pulled her against his body, feeling his erection press against the soft flesh of her belly. His arms wrapped around her. His hands moved restlessly over her back, down her hips, over her ass. He lifted her so that he could taste the curve where her neck and shoulder met. He ran his teeth over the ridge of her shoulder, then lifted her thigh so that he could push himself between her legs. When he lowered her, she wasn't tall enough for him to stay there. He bared his teeth in frustration.

She unfastened her bra and slipped it off her arms. The distraction worked. Her nipples pointed at him from the soft globes of her breasts. He cupped them in his palms, his thumbs brushing their dusky tips. He moved his hands to her sides, stroking downward until they caught on the lip of her panties. He dragged them down her hips, luxuriating in the feel of her skin against the back of his thumbs.

Remi lifted her knees and pushed her underwear all the way off. Her body was pale except for her nipples and the small auburn column of hair between her legs. She reached for him, pressing her body against his. She seemed so slight in his arms. Incredibly soft.

He walked her backward to the bed. She held on to him as he leaned over her. He wanted to taste every part of her, learn her with his mind and his mouth and his hands and his eyes.

Already, the light was growing dimmer in the room as dusk gave way to night. She lay beneath him in the lavender wedge of light that spilled over the bed.

He kissed her mouth. Her lips smiled under his. He was too far gone to return the smile. He kissed her again, barely able to believe she was in his room, in his arms, giving herself to him…after everything she'd seen and learned about him.

He kissed her chin, her neck, her collarbone. Her legs were together between his as he knelt over her, feasting on her body. He palmed her breasts, kissing one just beneath her nipple, the other just to the side of it. He looked at her as his tongue circled one taut peak. Tension flashed across her features as she pushed herself closer to his mouth.

He ran his hands down both sides of her ribs, then caught her hips and kissed them. Burying his face in her belly, he drew a breath.

"Holy hell, you smell good."

She smiled and forked her hands into his hair. "Not as good as you do."

He grinned at her. "I'll let you use my soap in the morning when we take a shower."

Humor left her face. "I don't want the morning to come for days and days."

"Me either."

He bent down to kiss the tender area between her hips, just next to the strip of auburn hair at the top of her legs. He separated her legs and pressed kisses all along the inside of her upper thigh. He hadn't shaved, so he knew the stubble of his beard prickled along her skin.

"How can you be so soft?"

She bit her lip, then smiled. "I was hopeful tonight would end this way."

Greer's nostrils flared. He nipped the inner flesh at the top of her thighs. "Every night could have been ending this way. Every morning starting this way. I can't believe you made me wait so long."

"I gave us a lot of thought."

He felt himself tighten. "You think too much." He gripped her ass and lifted her to his mouth. He ran his tongue over the seam of her core, then stroked her feminine folds for a while before he thrust his tongue inside of her. "So am I?"

She frowned. "Are you what?"

"Right for you." He licked her clit. Her body responded sharply. Her only answer was a heavy breath. He laved her some more, circling her opening, then focusing again on the sensitive swell of flesh. He lifted his face and looked at her. "Answer me."

"Don't stop."

He slipped a finger, two fingers, inside of her, stroking, stretching her. He thumbed her clit. "Am I?"

Her body had begun moving against his hand. "I don't want you to be," she answered in a breathless voice.

"Why?"

"Greer!"

He mouthed her clit, almost sending her over the edge. "Answer me!"

"Because I'm falling for you, and it scares the hell out of me."

He thrust his fingers in and out of her, in and out as he pushed his tongue against her clit. She cried out as her control broke. She braced her feet on either side of his shoulders and let the spasms take over. As soon as they began to fade, he replaced his fingers with his tongue and started them off again. Her eyes locked with his as her orgasm took her.

He put his hands on her hips, his face against her belly as her tremors eased. The passion was slow to leave her body. Every move he made sent another ripple through her. She was breathing fast. He kissed her ribs, her breasts, her throat.

"Greer—" Her quiet moan was filled with frustration.

"I know. We're not done."

He reached over to the drawer of his nightstand and took out a Trojan. Covered, he spread her legs with his knees and held himself against her opening.

He pushed in just the tip. She was tight, but still very wet. She bent her knees. Her hand wrapped around his on her hip.

He eased himself in a little deeper, watching her. He wasn't a small guy, and he was stiff like a marble rod. Her hips moved to accommodate him. She wanted all of him, but he still went slowly, in a little deeper, a little more, letting her body get used to him.

"You're torturing me," she complained.

He grinned. "I don't want to hurt you."

"Kiss me." She took hold of his face, lifting up to match her lips to his. His arms circled her body, his elbows braced on the bed. She arched up beneath him, taking all of him. He felt her satisfied smile against his mouth. He began to move in her, pumping, in and out with slow strokes. She was already so heated, so ready for him, that she couldn't take much of his gentle rhythm.

"Harder. Now," she ordered.

He complied, pulling out and slamming in. He gripped the pillows under her and spread his legs—and hers—wide. He pushed in and out, holding her body to his, grinding himself against her clit, willing her control to break.

She cried out, a loud, guttural sound. He pumped against her, hard, his own release so close. Her third orgasm set him off. He leaned up, holding her hips to his as his release shot from him.

Slowly, slowly, sanity regained control of his mind, sooner than it did for Remi, whose body was still pulsing over his cock. He eased her hips back to the bed and settled down on top of her, holding her until her body cooled.

She was sweating—they both were. He loved the smell of her passion. As she came down, a strange pallor came over her face. Her breathing sped up. She dug the heels of her hands into his shoulders and pushed at him, locking her elbows.

"Get off me. Get off. Get off, Greer."

He pulled back, withdrawing from her body. As soon as he sat up, she made a beeline for the bathroom. The door slammed shut.

Greer knelt on the bed, feeling a little shattered. What happened? What had he done? Jesus, had he hurt her?

He discarded the condom, then followed her to the bathroom. The door was locked. "Remi—what's going on?" There was no answer, only the sound of running water. "Open the door." He knocked again. He could hear her sobbing. "Open the goddamned door, Remi, or I will kick it down."

He was just about to do that when the door swung open. She was standing with her back to him, her shoulders hunched, crying into a wet hand towel.

"Did I hurt you?" he asked, coming close to her. He didn't know what to do. He looked for blood on her legs, but there wasn't any. "Remi, talk to me. What's happening? I thought what just happened was amazing...I thought I brought you with me."

"It was amazing."

"Can I hold you?"

She shook her head. "No."

He did anyway. He stepped up to her body and wrapped his arms around her. "Why are you crying, then?"

She turned in the circle of his arms and leaned her forehead against his chest. After a minute, she looked up at him, the stupid towel obscuring half her face.

"I'm married."

29

R emi grabbed the fluffy white terrycloth robe hanging on a hook at the back of Greer's bathroom door. Shoving her arms into it, she hurried into his bedroom. She should go. She really should, but she was too dizzy to leave. She dropped into the armchair near his window and put her head between her legs.

Greer knelt in front of her. His hands were warm on her knees. She was trying to breathe slowly, but she kept gasping. Oh, hell. She didn't want to vomit now. Here.

He put his hand on the back of her head. "Look at me," he ordered. She didn't. "Remi, you aren't married."

She did look up then. "I was there. I think I know what happened."

"I compiled your profile. You have no marriage license in this state or any other."

"It happened before I left the Grummonds."

"I hacked their system. They had no marriage listed for you—under this name or the one you used as a resident there."

"They didn't file marriage licenses."

"Wait a minute. You were fourteen when you left. You weren't old enough to be married, even with parental permission."

Bile rose to her throat. She tried to fight it back down, but the memories she'd struggled so hard and long to avoid exploded into her mind. She covered her mouth and shook her head, mumbling from behind her hand, "I was twelve."

The look of horror on Greer's face matched the disgust roiling in her belly. She shot up from the chair and ran to the bathroom, emptying her stomach violently into the toilet.

Greer followed her back into the bathroom. He pulled her hair from her face and held it behind her until her stomach had calmed down. When she was finished, he handed her a towel. She went to the sink and washed her hands, holding cold water to her face for long moments.

Greer turned on the shower, holding his hand under the stream of water until it reached the right temperature. He pushed his robe from her shoulders, leaving it in a pile at her feet, then drew her with him into the shower.

All she felt was numb. She never wanted to fall in love. Never wanted to bring a man she cared about into her crazy life. Most of all, she never wanted to see his affection flip from caring to disgust, as Greer's just had.

He was just being nice now, because what else could he do? Curse at her messed-up life and boot her from his room? That would probably come next.

She stepped into the shower stall with him, but kept her eyes averted. He shut the door, then reached for the shampoo. She tried to move out of the way so that he could access the jets of water, but he stopped her. He poured a bit of shampoo into his palm, then lifted her chin so that he could wet her hair.

She flashed a look at him. His eyes caught hers and wouldn't release them. He was somber. Fierce. His eyes had the same edge in them that she'd seen when he looked at enemies. She blinked and looked away, grateful for the streaming water that camouflaged her tears.

He rubbed the shampoo in her hair, kneading her scalp. Some of her tension eased at his touch. He didn't speak, didn't ask questions. She was grateful she didn't have to talk. She had no words left with which to defend herself.

She'd let them come to this point in their relationship without warning him away. Some things you just didn't recover from.

He rinsed her hair and repeated the steps, this time with conditioner.

Things had moved so quickly, bringing them to

this point so very fast. Reason never had a chance to catch up with her heart.

No, that was a lie.

She'd known from the night at her secret apartment that he was the only man who stood a chance in her life and in her heart. He was made of steel, absent any imperfections like fear or doubt.

He was a good man, and she'd trapped him in her hell.

Greer wetted a washcloth and poured a dollop of liquid soap on it. The delicious scents of cinnamon and vanilla filled the shower stall. At least she had that. When he was gone, she could always pull those from her cabinet and remember him. The bittersweet moments with her assassin cookie.

She didn't resist as he washed her. When he was finished, he did a quick pass over himself, then rinsed both of them. He shut the water off. Cold air filled the shower as he opened the stall door. He grabbed a thick towel and wrapped it about her body, then handed her another for her hair.

He gave himself a quick rubdown, then took her hand. When they reached the bed, she started to collect her clothes. "I should go."

He took her things from her and dropped them back on the floor. "No. We're not done."

"Greer, I told you I'm married."

He lifted the corner of the covers. "You've said a lot of things. Now you're going to listen to me. In." He pointed to the bed.

She didn't comply. Her feet were locked in place.

"Remi, I want to hold you in my arms when I say what I have to say."

She blinked at the liquid in her eyes. He still held the covers open. She lowered her head, then ditched the towels and crawled into his bed. He followed her, then scooped her up and brought her close.

"This is what I have to say."

Remi kept her arms folded between them, bracing herself to hear words he could never take back and she could never forget.

"You're an educated woman. You know as well as I do that no twelve-year-old can get married, least not here in the U.S."

She nodded. "I know."

"So you know, too, that whatever bullshit they told you—"

"There was a ceremony. I signed my name in a Bible."

He drew a breath before continuing. "Baby, listen to me. They could have had you walk upside down around the compound dressed in rainbows. It doesn't matter. Whatever they said, whatever they had you do, has no bearing on reality. It has no foundation in logic, ethics, morals, reason—or any other measure of human behavior and intellect. You know this. You've helped deprogram former cult members."

She gulped too much air. "But I...I can't deprogram me."

"Okay." She felt him nod. "You're not in this

alone. I got my arm around you." He kissed her forehead. "And you know I'll slay your dragons. Or even just clean your weapons after you vanquish them."

"I don't know why you would."

He laughed. "I told you before, the bad guys don't get to fuck with the good guys." He tightened his hold on her. "Take me through that time. Help me understand what happened. Who did what and when?"

"I've never told anyone this."

"Maybe it's time you shined a little light on it. You're safe here with me. I'm not goin' anywhere."

"You should go, Greer. They will kill you."

He chuckled. She felt that small puff of breath on her face. "I would love for them to try."

"They killed my mother. They said she died of pneumonia, but she was healthy when she went back to them. Thin, but healthy."

"Go ahead. Start your story."

She sighed. "When I was twelve, the Prophet—"

"Josiah. AKA Senator Whiddon."

"Yeah. He decided to take me and two of my friends as his wives. Wives number four, five, and six. I learned later, once my mom and I were away from the group, that he did that to trap us in the community. She thought he knew she was wanting to get me away. Once I became his bride, we were elevated in status. It became very difficult for either of us to ever be alone…or unguarded.

"Custom dictated that the prophet not consummate the marriage until two years after his wife began menstruating. My friend reached that threshold a year before me. She told me what happened during the consummation ceremony.

"There was a chamber above our worship hall. No one but the prophets and the male elders were allowed up there. It was considered sacred. The consummation ceremonies took place there.

"My friend told me the room was all white. There was a large bed made from white wood, with white linens. It was far more luxurious than anything she'd ever seen. It was up on a dais."

She paused. Greer's hand on her arm gave her strength. "There were restraints of some sort at each of the four corners of the bed. She was cuffed to the bed. The prophets took her first. Then they let the elders have her. Then the men had a feast as she watched them—and they her.

"My friend risked her life to tell us this. My mother broke into the chamber shortly after learning about this. I was terrified for her. When she came back, she packed a small bundle of food and clothes, and we left."

"So the prophet never touched you?" Greer asked.
"No."

"They have a different head prophet now. I don't know what happened to Esrom Stanton, the top guy in your day. I didn't think to search for him." He stroked her arm. "Where was your father in all of this mess?"

"My mom was one of seven wives. My father was

much older. He didn't live much past my fifth birthday."

"Do they know polygamy is illegal?"

She shrugged. "They don't care. Each husband has only one legal wife. The rest are his wives within the community only. In the eyes of the law, they aren't doing anything wrong. Earlier this year, I'd decided that I had to go back and face them, face my terrors. And I wanted to visit my mother's grave."

"How'd that go?"

"They wouldn't let me in."

"Bastards. I'll get you in. And if you like, we can have your mother moved to a cemetery in Laramie. Then you can visit her grave whenever you wish."

Remi frowned as a new thought took root in her mind. She pushed herself up to see him better in the dark room. Greer also readjusted himself, sitting up so that he was at her level.

"I just thought of something. It might be coincidence."

"What?"

"I've been studying the Friendship Community for three years. With no problems." She felt Greer tense.

"I hate the thought of that, and all it means. You were there unguarded around the woodcutter." He ran his hand down her arm. She took hold of his hand.

"Nothing happened, none of this trouble, until after I visited the Grummonds earlier this summer. What if...what if everything that's happening has nothing to do with the Friendship Community? What if it's because of me and Senator Whiddon—Prophet Josiah?"

Greer thought of that for a minute. He nodded. "Makes sense, at least, in the beginning. It's caused us to discover things about the Friends that now implicate them as well. The senator's deeply involved in King's infrastructure, else he wouldn't have been able to send the WKB after you. The WKB's gotten real cozy with the Friends. From the sounds of that, it's a new change. Something's going on. What happened with you is just a symptom of something much, much bigger."

He smoothed some hair from her face. "We're going back to the Friendship Community tomorrow. Let's see what more we can find out."

30

W ayne Dunbar had shifty eyes, Greer decided. And he looked anything but pleased to have him and Remi back in his community. He could simply demand they leave, but he didn't, which fired off warning signals for Greer.

The number of people who came out to greet them was far fewer than before. He looked around at them, wondering what had changed in the community and if whatever it was meant he and Remi were in danger.

He couldn't put his finger on it, but something was different.

Remi was bartering the use of their cabin again in exchange for additional supplies the community might need. She made it sound as if she was close to finishing her article and wanted a quiet place, off the grid, where she could focus and be isolated to wrap it up. She was non-threatening, grateful, and offered a lucrative trade that had a firm end date: she told them she needed to be back at the university before the semester began.

"Where is your wife, Mr. Dunbar?" Greer asked.

The man blinked, and the pause before he answered was interesting. "She's under the weather at the moment."

"Oh no," Remi replied. "I'm sorry to hear that. If there's anything I can do—"

"Thank you, but I think it's best not to disturb her. She has what she needs."

LION CARRIED Sparrow's feverish body through the woods. He hated going to the Friendship Community in the daylight; watchers were rarely ever seen. It couldn't be avoided now—the boy's condition was worsening fast.

The wool blanket he carried Sparrow in made Lion's arms itch, but it kept the boy from shivering. When they reached the clinic, Lion set Sparrow down on the bench outside, then went in search of the healer. Inside, all but two of the cots were filled, though upon inspection, Lion realized that only half the patients still lived. He pulled sheets over the faces of those who'd passed. Whatever illness Sparrow had had come with him from the community. Most of those in the cots and all of the dead patients had the same sores on their skin as the boy.

One of the patients was watching him. "Thirsty," the man hissed.

Lion fetched a cup of water and held it to his lips. "Where's the healer?" Lion asked.

The man lifted his hand and tried to point to the two empty cots. "The creek."

Lion nodded. He straightened to go, but the man's hand shot out to hold him. Lion could feel the tough blisters on his palm and fingers. "Don't leave us. Please. Don't go, watcher."

"I'll bring help back. I'll be back. I promise."

He filled a fresh glass with water, then took it out to Sparrow, who looked at him with sad eyes, as if he knew his fate. Lion clamped his jaw, locking his emotions away.

"You're going to be fine," he told the boy. "You're going to pull through this. I am Lion, and you are in my pride. You will live." The boy wasn't listening; he'd already slipped back into his fevered sleep.

Lion took out his phone and dialed Mad Dog. The phone ran only once. *"S'up, Lion?"*

"They're dying."

"Who's dying?"

"Sparrow. The community."

"What do you mean they're dying? Where are you?"

"I took Sparrow to the Friends' healer. He has a fever that I can't break. And sores all over his skin.

The infirmary is filled with the same sickness. Four of them are dead."

"*Okay. Stay put. Greer is there. I'm sending him down to check things out.*"

~

"*GREER.*" Max's voice came over Greer's comm unit.

"Go, Max."

"*Get over to the infirmary.*"

Greer got to his feet. "What's up?"

"*I don't know. There's an outbreak of something that's filled the infirmary. Lion's there with one of his boys. Have Remi stay in your cabin. We don't know what we're dealing with.*"

"Roger that." He turned to Remi, who was watching him with anxious eyes. "I have to go check something out."

"I'll go with you."

"No. There could be an outbreak of something infectious. I don't want you exposed." He looked at her. "I mean it. Promise me you'll stay here."

Her eyes widened. She nodded. He went over to shut and lock the windows. "Swear you'll stay in here."

"I swear." She came over to walk him to the door. "Be careful."

He touched her cheek, then kissed her cheek. "Lock the door after me. No matter what, don't open it to anyone other than me or someone from the team."

Again she nodded. "I won't. Be safe. Hurry back."

Greer jogged toward the infirmary on the far side of the community. He was glad they'd had the foresight to put their small clinic a distance from the main section of homes.

Lion was standing outside the building. He looked relieved to see Greer. Without preamble, he turned and showed Greer the little boy lying on the bench, lifting the blanket covering him. The boy wore only his boxers. His head, arms, hands, legs, and some of his torso were covered with blisters.

"Oh, motherfucker." Greer snapped a pic and sent it off to Max, then dialed him. "I've only ever seen pictures of smallpox, but I think that's what's happening here. It's some kind of pox, anyway."

"Find the healer. Get me a picture from inside the clinic."

Greer stepped into the small infirmary. There were ten cots lined up on the long walls in the big back room. He saw sheets drawn over four of them. He pulled back the sheet from one patient, revealing a face swollen and so full of blisters, there was no skin to be seen. He snapped a picture, then covered him up again. He repeated that with three of the other corpses, sending all of them to Max.

None of the other patients objected to his presence or his taking pictures. Only one of them was conscious. The man coughed. He was too weak to cover his mouth. Greer took a picture of the whole room. "Help is on the way. Where's the healer?"

"Creek," the man said, but that little effort caused him to cough.

Greer left the clinic. "Lion, the healer went to the creek."

Lion nodded. "It's a common remedy to douse a feverish patient in cool water. He may not have wanted to take the time to fill a tub. The creek is easier—and colder."

"Show me where he would have gone."

They walked downhill through a steep draw, to a mountain stream. There, perched in a natural pool, were the healer and two boys. The healer's dead arms still clutched the boys' bodies. Greer snapped a picture, then went in the river to pull them out. Lion followed him.

"No! Stay back. My smallpox vaccine is current. You can't come in contact with them."

"I've already been in contact with it from Sparrow. And I was in the clinic."

"Lion." Greer leveled a hard glare at him. "Stay back. That's an order."

Greer pulled the three bodies from the stream and settled them several yards from the bank. He took another picture of them on the bank, and one more downstream shot from the spot where they'd been.

Lion looked down at the three dead community members.

"I suspect this is smallpox," Greer told him, "a

deadly disease that was thought to have been eradicated a long time ago." He looked at Hope's brother, searching for the pox on him. "How are you feeling?"

"Tired. I've had little sleep since Sparrow became so ill."

"What about the other boys?"

"They seem fine so far. Once Sparrow became sick, I sent them to sleep outside."

Greer shoved his hand through his hair. If this was smallpox, and if it had jumped from Lion's pride into the WKB compound, they could be looking at national—even international—pandemic in no time. Where did it come from, though? Smallpox was no longer a naturally occurring disease.

"Let's head back. I have to warn the village."

"What about these three?"

"Leave them."

Back at the infirmary, Lion checked on Sparrow.

"It's best if you stay here, Lion. Warn anyone else who comes not to go inside the clinic. Max is sending help this way. Doctors from our world will be able to help you, your pride, the community. Even the WKB. Call me or Max if you have any problems. I'll be back as soon as I can."

Greer moved quickly back to the village. He stopped at the cabin he shared with Remi. She opened the door and stepped outside as soon as he neared the cabin.

Greer held up a hand. "It may be smallpox. Don't come closer."

Her eyes widened. "Oh my God."

"Do you have any hand sanitizer?"

She nodded.

"Throw it out to me, then get back inside and lock the door again."

She did as he requested. He slathered it over his hands, arms, and face—all of his exposed skin. The disease was still on his clothes, but there was nothing more thorough he could do at the moment. He stashed the little bottle in his pocket, then hurried to the mayor's cabin.

When Wayne Dunbar opened the door, Greer stepped back. The Haskels came outside with the mayor. "I've been down to the infirmary," Greer told them. "Your people have contracted a deadly fever. The healer and six of his patients have passed. The others there are close to dying."

Dunbar's lips thinned and his eyes hardened. It was almost as if he wasn't surprised by the announcement. Mr. Haskel didn't show a reaction either, but his wife gasped in shock.

"Mrs. Dunbar is down there," she said, speaking through the hand that she still held over her mouth.

Greer nodded. "We need to warn the village and ask them to return to their cabins, to stay inside until help can come."

"No help is coming. No outsiders are allowed on our property," Dunbar said.

"You don't let them in, then your people—every

man, woman, and child, will become sick. A third or more will die, slow, painful, horrible deaths."

The mayor didn't blink. "I'll send some of the women down to the infirmary." Mrs. Haskel started forward, ready to round up the women to help.

"No." Greer stopped her. He looked at Dunbar. "Help is already on the way. What's happening here can spread beyond the borders of your community fast. The government has no choice but to send doctors, medicine, and soldiers to set up a perimeter. Don't make this worse than it already is. If we can get your people back into their cabins, isolated from those who are sick, there's a chance they will live."

Mr. Dunbar stood like a statue. Maybe he was in shock.

Mrs. Haskel grasped the situation far more clearly. "We'll use the bell to summon them. It will be heard all the way down to the fields, where there is another one to send the call out farther."

"Ring it," Greer ordered when the mayor said nothing.

Mrs. Haskel looked at the mayor and her husband, waiting for their confirmation. When they remained silent, Greer repeated his order. "Do it now, Mrs. Haskel."

Greer went over to the cabin he shared with Remi. She was standing at the front window, watching the village anxiously. He put his hand up to the glass. She held hers to the other side of the glass. Her hand was small enough to fit entirely inside the windowpane.

"What's happening?" she asked.

"All hell's breaking loose." He was close enough to the window that he didn't have to shout. "The CDC's flying in some doctors for an initial assessment. They should be here any minute. The Army's sending soldiers to establish a perimeter. If it is smallpox, I don't know what will happen."

"I don't want these people to die."

"Nor do I. The farmers are being recalled to their cabins." He looked around, making sure no one was in earshot. "I think the mayor, and/or the council, may have had something to do with this. The men, anyway. They didn't look surprised by this."

She frowned at him through the glass. "You've been exposed to whatever it is."

"If it's smallpox, I've had a recent vaccination for it. The whole team has. But anyone not vaccinated, or whose vaccination is older than a decade, is at risk."

"What's going to happen?"

Greer lifted his shoulders. "Don't know for sure. The CDC may decide to quarantine the community. Or they may evacuate everyone."

"But there's no running water, no electricity… they'll have to move them."

"They can bring in generators and water trucks. Field hospitals can be set up anywhere."

"I'm scared."

"I know. I'll get you out of here as soon as possible." He started to turn away, but she banged on the window. She held up both hands this time. He covered hers with his.

"I love you, Greer."

I love you. She'd said the very thing he'd been feeling. But was it real? Or was it simply a reaction to the stress they were under? "Remi, this is all going to be over soon."

"I know that. That's not why I said—oh, forget it."

"Did you mean it?" His fingertips pressed into the glass until his nails were white.

"Yes."

"Good. 'Cause I had no intention of letting the woman I love slip out of my life when things return to normal."

She slowly smiled. "You love me, too?"

"Fuck yes." He heard the first helicopter approaching. "Gotta go. I'll be back. Stay put."

Max was having the doctors land in the field nearest the hospital. Two men disembarked. Greer waved them over toward the infirmary. They both paused long enough to pull on masks, gloves, and surgical covers over their clothes. One of them went inside. The other knelt beside Lion.

He pulled the edges of Sparrow's blanket apart. Seemed the boy had even more sores than before. Greer watched as the doctor checked his pulse, then drew his hand down over the boy's eyes.

"I'm sorry, son." He looked at Lion. "Are you his brother?" the doctor asked in a calm voice.

Lion squeezed his eyes shut, then looked away. "Yes."

"He's no longer feeling pain. He's dead, son. Where are your parents?"

"I am—I was—his guardian." Lion covered Sparrow up, as if the kid still needed the warmth. A tear spilled down his cheek.

"Do you know if anyone from your family has been over here to the clinic?"

Greer braced himself for whatever Lion would say. The doctor understood nothing of Lion's world or his pride or the Friendship Community.

"No one has been here. When Sparrow became so sick, I had the rest of the pride sleep outside."

Greer silently sighed as the doctor sent him a questioning look. "There are unique living arrangements in this community. Leave it at that. For now, it's enough to know that no others from Lion's family have come over here."

"I did go into the clinic," Lion told them.

"Then you'll need a vaccination."

"What is that?"

"It's a shot. In the arm," the doctor said.

"I had one of those."

"When?" Greer asked.

Lion eased himself from under Sparrow and stood. He pulled his sleeve up and showed the doctor his arm. "Is it this shot?" There was a mark on his arm of a recently healed sore.

"That's it."

"When did you have that?" Greer asked.

"Six weeks or so. Before Sparrow came to live with us."

Greer and the doctor looked at each other. Someone had known about the outbreak…and they'd been preparing for it.

The other doctor came back out from the clinic and confirmed Greer's worst fears. It was smallpox. They stepped a short distance away and called in their assessment.

Greer set a hand on Lion's shoulder. "I'm sorry about your cub."

Lion's nostrils flared. He nodded. "He came to us because his mom died. Do you think she had this illness?"

"It's possible. The doctors will do an investigation."

STRUCTURED MAYHEM TOOK over in the next hours. More helicopters arrived. Tents were set up for a morgue and others to triage sick patients. Sparrow's body and the others from the clinic were put in body bags and transferred to the temporary morgue.

Greer showed the doctors where the healer and his two patients were, then he and Lion went up to the guest cabin. Kit was there, with Lobo and the other guys.

"Lion and his pride were inoculated against smallpox about six weeks ago," Greer told Kit. "All except the newest member."

"Does his boy have smallpox?"

Greer nodded. "He did. He died."

Kit set a hand on Lion's shoulder. "I'm sorry, Lion. Jesus. Tell me about the shots you and your pride received. Who authorized it? Who did them?"

Lion shook his head. "King ordered them. A man showed up one night a while back and administered them. We were told if we discussed the shots with anyone, we would be arrested by your government, that the pride would be dissolved, the cubs separated."

"We're not going to let that happen." Kit looked at Greer. "I need you to take one of the physician assistants to the house to vaccinate everyone there. Take Lion and let him clean up. You guys need to stop at the station over there to change into a pair of scrubs. Put your clothes in a laundry bag. They're giving out instructions for washing…which only apply to us and the other responders, since there are no washing machines in the community. While you clean up, the PA will vaccinate everyone else—including the Jacksons. Doc Beck is going to be at the house, too. He needs a vaccination in case this spreads wider than the Friendship Community."

"I want to get Remi out of here."

Kit sighed. "She can't go. No one who was exposed and unvaccinated is allowed to leave."

"Then I'm coming back to stay here with her."

"Good. We could use you here." He looked at Greer. "Listen, Greer—Ivy can't get the shot."

Greer frowned. "Why?"

"She may be pregnant. We've been trying, anyway."

"I'll be sure the PA spells that out for her and the others."

31

G reer changed, then went to say goodbye to Remi. The silence inside the small cabin was deafening after the chaos outside.

"I can't take you home yet, Remi. As an unvaccinated person, you're caught up in the quarantine."

"I know." Her mouth tightened. "I'm dreading calling the university. The semester will be starting before my quarantine is over. They told me to stop, and I didn't. And now look what happened."

A thought occurred to Greer. He looked at her, almost hoping she'd shut him down. "Shit. Remi. Do you know if Senator Whiddon had anything to do with their changed opinion of your research?"

She shook her head. "He's a Colorado senator. Why would he be involved with the University of Wyoming?"

"Because he figured out who you were. Sweet little

Chastity grew into a major threat to him. As a senator, he could pull strings."

Her eyes widened. "Do you think he did?"

"I can find out."

She bit the tip of her thumb as she turned from him, deep in thought. "You could be right. When I went down to the Grummond's earlier this summer, I gave them my academic credentials. When they wouldn't let me in, I asked to speak to some of the women I grew up with." She looked at Greer. "I told them I used to live there." Panic grayed her face. "I told them I used to be known as Chastity."

"Oh hell. That's it. The senator is still plugged in to that community."

"I did bring this on myself."

Greer took hold of her arms. "No, you didn't. You had no idea Prophet Josiah was Senator Whiddon. And you had no knowledge of his connection to the WKB." God, he wished he could hold her tight and tell her everything was going to be fine, but even that contact might endanger her.

"I'm going to do a little digging when I get back to the house. Kit or one of the guys will stand guard over you here until I return. Don't call the university yet. Let me talk to Kit and Owen first."

She gripped his wrists. "Okay. Let me know what you find out. I'll walk with you part of the way. Kit said they're doing vaccinations now. I need to get mine."

"I'm afraid to kiss you. I don't want to contaminate you. I'm taking one of the medics home so he can vaccinate everyone there. Is there anything you want from the house?"

She shook her head. "I have everything I need."

They crossed the main square. Already, it looked like a war zone. Military trucks were driving across the property, carrying troops and supplies. Residents were standing in small groups, holding each other, watching the goings-on with frightened eyes. Remi's hand tightened in his.

"This isn't going to be forever, Remi. Just a few months. Half a year. Only as long as it needs to be. Soon they'll clear out. Next summer, this will all be a memory."

She shut her eyes and nodded.

Mayor Dunbar was standing on one of the picnic tables in the community square. His arms were raised and fists clenched. Sweat cloaked his face. A truck went past, keeping them from hearing what he was saying. People from the community were gathered around his table in a half-moon throng.

Off to the right side of the square, a neat line of residents was queued up for their shots, their numbers and complacency in sharp contrast to the rabble the council leader was whipping up.

Kit caught up to them. "What's going on?" Greer asked.

"The CDC can't vaccinate the residents involuntarily." He gestured toward the mayor. "This portion of the community doesn't want the inoculation."

"What's with the construction vehicles?"

"The powers that be decided it was best to quarantine the virus here. They're setting up a field hospital with separate concrete tents for exposed and feverish, individuals with the poxes, and those in recovery." He looked at Greer. "There's also going to be a morgue." He gave the crowd a baleful glare. "There's pushback on the fact that those who pass from smallpox need to be cremated."

Greer shook his head. "It's a lot to take in. It was a shock for us, and we've been somewhat prepared for a biological attack."

"Do you think this was an attack?" Remi asked.

Greer nodded. "Yes. Someone infected these people."

"Kit—let me talk to them," Remi said. "Of all the outsiders here, I'm the most familiar to them."

Kit nodded. "Go for it." He looked at Greer. "Keep with her."

No sooner had they started into the dense throng than Mayor Dunbar called them out. "This is all their fault. They brought this disease to us!"

Greer's nerves sharpened as they became the focus of the mob. He wanted to pull Remi back with him and get her behind the line of soldiers that had quietly surrounded the square. Before he could act, the crowd separated, opening a path for them that led straight to the mayor.

"None of this happened until they came here," Dunbar said, pointing at them.

Remi jumped onto his picnic table without hesitation. She held up her hands, commanding silence from the crowd in a way that made Greer wonder just how unruly her classes at the university were.

"Smallpox doesn't occur naturally anymore and hasn't since before 1980," she said. "For it to show up now, and here, it had to be intentionally released."

"That's what I said! You released this into our community."

"No. We didn't do that. In fact, I will need to get the shot myself. If I had released it, I would already have had the vaccine. The vaccination is not a big deal. It makes a very tender sore, which becomes a blister. It'll need special care for a few weeks, but then you won't get the terrible, terrible disease that is already ravaging your village. If you don't get the vaccine, history shows us that thirty percent of you will die. Many of you will have terrible scarring for life. Instead of one sore from the vaccine, you'll be covered in itchy, painful, pus-y sores. They'll be all over your face, in your nose, your ears, your mouth. Down your throat. In your lungs. In your eyes. You'll go blind."

The crowd went quiet. They began to look at each other. "How is that preferable to one shot?" she continued. "One sore. No disease? Greer, show them your vaccination scar."

Greer stood on the picnic bench so his arm could be seen across the crowd. He lifted his sleeve to show them the white, puckered scar that was smaller than a dime.

"You have that," Mrs. Haskel said, pointing to her husband. "I had to take care of your sore." To the crowd, she said, "Dr. Chase is right. It just makes one sore. We've seen our loved ones in the infirmary. They have the sores all over their bodies."

"Silence, Mrs. Haskel," the mayor snapped.

Mrs. Haskel's eyes narrowed as she looked from the mayor to her husband. "You knew this was coming. You knew it. You got that shot long before Mr. Dawson and Dr. Chase came to us."

Greer cautiously watched the crowd. Another woman spoke up. They'd been introduced to her— she was the wife of another councilman. "My husband also got the shot." She shouldered her way through the crowd and came to stand near to Mrs. Haskel. "Like you, I cared for it. He said it was a spider bite."

She stepped up to the picnic bench and faced the crowd. "Who else has already had this shot? Who?" She pointed to another councilman. "You?"

Everyone turned to face the man she called out. He shrugged. "The mayor said it was mandatory. All the councilmen took the shot."

"But not the councilwomen. I didn't have the shot." Mrs. Haskel turned wounded eyes on her husband.

He tilted his head and lifted his hands. "He owns us. He knows everything about us. We were told we couldn't come out with the news. We weren't allowed to tell you."

"Who owns you?" Greer asked, his question heard across the suddenly quiet assembly.

"King."

Greer looked back at Kit and the guys. Lobo was watching them, too. "How does he own you?"

Mr. Haskel looked at the mayor, whose face was hard as stone. "Your own wife may be dying," he said to the mayor. "We can't keep this up. It has to end."

The mayor said nothing.

"King knows our sins," Mrs. Haskel said.

Greer shook his head. "I'm not following."

"The sins we committed during our tithes. Our payment for the privilege of being allowed to live here," Mr. Haskel said. "It's why no one talks about their tithes."

"See what it got us?" Mrs. Haskel said. "We've brought this terrible day to our own community. I told the council it needed to end. I begged you to let us change our policy."

Greer looked at Kit, then back at the three leaders. "All right." He nodded. "So this terrible outbreak is the result of your choices. What happens next is up to you. Tell your people to get the vaccination. Live to tell your stories. Live, so you have the chance to straighten this out."

Mrs. Haskel sent a glance around at those gathered, then nodded. She climbed down from the picnic table and went over to stand in line for her vaccination. When the others followed her, Greer helped Remi down.

She crossed her arms and lifted sad eyes to Greer. "That's the end of this community. The adults who survive will do time for their crimes. The kids will be taken away to foster care if there aren't enough remaining adults to care for them. It's the end."

"We don't know that. The FBI will have to investigate."

She blinked tears away. He pulled her into his arms. "It doesn't answer the question of what happened to their teenagers," she said.

"It doesn't." He nodded toward Lobo. "Maybe the FBI can get that out of them." He looked at her, lingering longer than he should have. "I wish I didn't have to leave."

"It's important. Go. I'll be fine until you get back."

He waved Kelan forward. "Stay with Remi."

Kelan nodded. "You got it."

MANDY'S STOMACH tightened and a cold sweat broke out on her face and arms. She looked around the room at the women who had become her friends, along with the Jacksons and Doc Beck. She was breathing too fast. She crossed her arms over her stomach and tried to calm herself, but the moment she'd been dreading had come, as it had to sooner or later.

"Mandy? You okay?" Ivy asked, frowning at her.

Mandy stood, then felt faint. The room got wobbly. She ran out of the living room, past confused and worried faces. She tried to make it to her room, but her stomach only let her get as far as the hall powder room on her way.

She bent over the toilet and lost her lunch. Someone came in with her. She didn't look over that way, couldn't face whoever it was. When her stomach quit fighting her, Mandy took the cool wet towel she was handed, then looked up.

Ivy was leaning against the sink. Mandy flushed and washed her hands, splashing cold water over her hands and face. She took a dry towel and mopped her face.

"Hey." Ivy put an arm around Mandy's shoulders. And then the tears came. Foolish, useless tears. "What's going on, Em?"

"I can't get the shot."

"Why?"

Mandy looked over at her friend as she tried to draw enough air to tell her.

"Oh, God. You're pregnant."

Mandy squeezed her eyes shut and held the towel to her face with shaking hands.

"Does Rocco know?"

Mandy shook her head. "I've tried to tell him half a dozen times. I can't tell him when he's stressed. And

I don't have the heart to tell him when he's happy. Those moments are so few."

"Maybe this will be good news."

"Maybe. Maybe not. How can I know?"

"You have to tell him."

"I'm scared, Ivy. I'm such a coward."

"I can be there with you, if you want."

"I didn't do this on purpose."

"I never thought you did. But honey, what happened? I thought you were on birth control."

Mandy shook her head. "I was, but it was making me sick. I kept spotting. I've tried several different doses and brands—since long before Rocco. When none of them worked without problems, Rocco and I decided to just use condoms." She met Ivy's eyes. "One of them broke."

Ivy didn't even try to fight her smile. "This the best news ever. I'm so happy for you both. I know it's stressful now, but it will work out. Trust Rocco. Trust yourself." Ivy rubbed her arm, dispelling the persistent chill Mandy had been feeling.

"You think it will?"

"I know it will."

"But Rocco still has issues…"

"That man loves you. He'll pull it together." Ivy's smiled widened. "And you aren't the only one who can't get vaccinated."

Mandy's eyes widened. "Are you pregnant, too?"

"I don't know for sure, but we've been trying, and

I'm a few days late. I can't risk the shot right now, until I know for sure I'm not."

Mandy laughed. She hugged Ivy. "I would so love to be pregnant with you!"

"We'll get through this. I promise you. Should we go break the news?"

Mandy shook her head. "I don't want to tell anyone before Rocco."

"Don't think that can be avoided now. We'll make them take a vow of silence until you and Rocco talk. Same for me with Kit. He doesn't know either."

Mandy took a fistful of tissues, then faced Ivy and nodded. "Let's go."

Max stood in the hallway right outside the bathroom, his arms crossed, his legs spread. "S'up, ladies?"

Ivy giggled and Mandy started crying. "We can't have the vaccine right now," Ivy told him.

His brows lowered. "And why would that be?"

Ivy wrapped her arm around Mandy. "We're pregnant."

Max's brows shot up. "You're fucking with me, right?"

Mandy shook her head, looking at him over the wadded tissue she held to her nose.

"Aw, hell. Do the guys know?"

Again Mandy shook her head.

Max sighed. "Fuck. Me. All. To. Hell. You know I gotta tell Kit."

"No, don't! I want him to hear it from me first," Ivy said.

"We don't have that luxury now. I don't know what his plans are, but he needs to know I couldn't get the entire household vaccinated."

"Then let me talk to him when you're finished."

Max dialed Kit. There was a pause. He looked at Ivy. "We got a situation here at the house. There's two people I can't get vaccinated. Seems one's pregnant and the other's sorta pregnant and their men don't yet know." He grinned. "Yeah… Basically my reaction. Who? Uh. Well. The confirmed pregnant one is Mandy… Yeah… I'll let you talk to the other."

Ivy took the phone Max handed her. "Kit?"

There was a long silence. *"Oh, hell. I gotta sit down, Iv. Hold on."*

She could hear him walking somewhere. She gave a shaky laugh. "Look I didn't mean for you to learn this way." Ivy drew a jagged sob. Mandy rubbed her back. Max shook his head and folded his arms. "I-I had a whole fun reveal planned. I just wanted to make sure I really was pregnant first—"

"Baby, I was hoping it was you."

"You were? Kit, I'm so sorry."

"Don't be. We're ready for this, feel me?"

"But now, with the smallpox—"

"Just means we take extra care of you. It'll work out, Ivy mine. Tell me, though, what makes you think you're pregnant?"

"I'm a few days late. And I took one of those over-the-counter tests, which showed positive. I just won't believe it until I see a doctor. I didn't want to get your hopes up until I knew for sure."

Kit chuckled. *"Goddamn. This makes me so happy. You can't even know."* She heard his sigh. *"I need to ask something of you. A couple of things."*

"Okay."

"I need you to stay put at the house. My sister, too. Just until we know for sure this thing is contained here at the community."

She looked at Mandy, who was watching her tensely. "We will."

"And I'd prefer if we could keep this on the down-low until Rocco's gotten his news. I don't know how he's going to react to being a dad again. I don't want our joy to affect him in an unintended way."

"Of course."

"I'm going to send him home. The sooner we can break the news, the better." He sighed again. *"Honey, I wish I could be there, but I can't come home right now."*

"I know. I know. It's all right. Everything's fine here."

"No hugging Casey, now. At least, not for the next month or so until her shot has fully healed."

"That's going to be hard."

"Yeah. I'll give her your hugs for you until then."

"I love you, Kit."

He huffed a little breath. She could just see his expression. *"I love you, too, babe. Hand the phone back to Max."*

She handed it over to Max. He arched a brow at her as he asked, "So, boss, we cool?" A big grin split his face. "All righty, then. Roger that. I'm out."

Max looked at the two of them. He smiled and held out his arms for them. "It's going to be okay. I'm happy for you both. Mandy, I think you know you've got a challenge with Rocco, just because of everything he's been through. We'll help you through it, though."

Mandy sniffled and nodded.

He looked down at her terrified face. His thumb forced her face upward. "Be full of joy. This is good stuff. Everything else will fall into place."

Ivy reached across Max's chest to squeeze her wrist.

Mandy dabbed at her red eyes. "I am happy."

Max laughed. "I can see that."

HOPE HURRIED to catch up with Max before he took the elevator to the bunker. "Hey, Max!"

He stopped outside the bedroom with the secret bunker entrance. He smiled, then frowned at her bandaged arm. Holding her elbow, he bent and kissed the edge of her shoulder. "These shots hurt like a sonofabitch. Sorry you had to have one."

Hope shrugged. "No worries. It's better than the alternative."

"S'up?"

"I wanted to talk to you about Lion. Have he and his boys been vaccinated?"

"They have."

There was something he wasn't telling her, but she knew better than to ask for details he couldn't give her. "Good. I was thinking, if we were to ever get him and his pride off the WKB compound, now would be a good time to do that, under cover of everything that's happening."

Max stared at her. She could tell his mind was running through various scenarios. "You're right. I'll bring it up with Kit and Owen."

She squeezed his hand, wanting to say more, wanting assurances he couldn't give. "Thank you."

Max smiled and leaned over to kiss her. "I'll take your mind off your sore arm later," he said, still grinning.

"I'm counting on it!"

32

Mandy was in the corral, brushing Kitano, when Rocco came looking for her. Though the horse was still skittish as hell, her being able to groom him was a big step forward. He had an uncanny ability to sense her moods. He didn't seem to mind her brushing him when she had something she needed to think through.

"Keep that up, and Kitano will be one ugly horse. You'll have brushed him bare."

Mandy spooked at the sound of Rocco's voice. Kitano gave an agitated shake of his head. She patted his shoulder, releasing him, then walked over to greet Rocco. She stepped on the lowest plank of the corral fence and leaned up to kiss him.

He was just showered. He'd shaved. His cheek was soft. His hair was still damp. His eyes were wrecked. "Was it bad out there today?" she asked.

"Very. Smallpox isn't a naturally occurring

disease. Hasn't been since it was eradicated worldwide. Someone infected the people of the community. It was like a war zone, with the CDC and other medical staff, the FBI, and Army there. When I left, they were setting up a field hospital inside the community. They'd decided it was best to keep the outbreak contained in place, at least until they better understand the full extent of it."

He touched her arms carefully, just above her elbows. "What's got you upset? Did the vaccination hurt?"

"I didn't get the vaccination."

"Why?"

Mandy stepped down from the fence and started toward the stable. Rocco followed her inside. She set the brush down on a shelf, then turned to face him. "Because I'm pregnant."

For a moment, his face looked like marble, pale and hard. She wondered where his mind slipped away to. Perhaps to his wife, Kadisha, and the last time he'd been given similar news.

"Okay," he said at last.

"Okay? That's it?"

"How are you feeling?"

She folded her arms and dropped her gaze to the middle of his shirt. "I'm a wreck, honestly. I cry at everything. I'm starving, but when I eat I get sick. And I'm terrified of losing you."

She felt his arms slip around her as he moved closer to hold her. "That makes two of us."

She wrapped her arms around him and leaned her forehead against his chest. "You aren't going to lose me."

"Marry me."

Mandy didn't answer immediately. "No."

"Why?"

She leaned back so that she could see his face. "Rocco, you'll be an amazing dad to our baby. I've seen you with Zavi. I know this for a fact. But marriage needs to be for us, about us, not an obligation because of an unplanned baby."

"That doesn't make sense. I'm asking for us. You, our baby, Zavi—you're my family. I want us to be together."

She put a hand on his chest. "I don't know how to explain it. Could we just take this slow?"

"No. I want you to be my wife before the baby comes." When she held firm, he pulled back, then shoved a hand through his hair as he turned away from her, facing the entrance to the stable.

He looked at her over his shoulder. "Have you seen a doctor yet?"

Mandy nodded. "I went to the OB/GYN at the clinic."

"How far along are you?"

"About seven weeks."

He turned toward her slightly, his hands on his hips, his head bowed. "Can I…participate in your pregnancy?"

"Of course." Mandy smiled. "I want you to."

"I couldn't with Kadisha. Those were women's things. And I was a warrior and out fighting."

"You're still a warrior and still fighting. But I want you with me the whole way, as much as you can." She went over to stand in front of him. Lifting his hand, she set it on her belly.

"You don't seem different." He gave her a tentative smile.

Her eyes teared up. "You've had so much on your mind. And honestly, I was terrified of telling you...I couldn't let you see how it affected me."

His face hardened. "Is that why you don't want to marry me? Because I'm a freak?"

Mandy frowned. "Rocco Silas. When have I ever thought you a freak?"

He drew his hand away from her and scrubbed it over his face. "So what now?"

"Nothing." She shrugged. "Nothing changes. Except my body. And maybe we should get some nursery furniture." She ventured a smile, but he was miles away from her, even though his body was inches from hers.

"Can I go to the doctor's with you next time?" he asked.

"I'd like that."

He nodded and looked at the dirt under his feet. "Have you eaten today?"

"I had lunch, but lost it a while ago when the vaccinations happened. I couldn't face dinner."

He held a hand out to her. "Then let's go get you something to eat. Something small and light."

She took his hand. "I don't want small and light. I could eat an entire village suddenly."

He gave her a lopsided grin as he looked at her sideways. "Maybe I should sleep with Zavi at night, just to be sure neither of us goes missing."

Mandy laughed. "Maybe you should."

He caught her up against him as they faced the bright afternoon sun, then kissed her forehead. "I love you. Don't ever doubt that."

She wrapped her arms around him and held him tight, communicating her love in the only way he'd believe—through touch.

33

M ax went into the conference room in the bunker. Owen sat at the long table with his laptop. "Hey, boss."

Owen looked up.

"We've been looking for the right time to get Lion and his pride out of the WKB. Now is that time, under cover of all the chaos happening near the Friends."

Owen met his eyes, considered it a moment, then nodded. "Do it. We can set up bunks in the basement until we find a permanent situation for them."

Max went upstairs to break the news to Lion. Dr. Beck and the medic were taking the medic's cases outside. Max pulled Lion aside, out of earshot. "It's time we got you and your pride away from the WKB. With everything that's happening, no one will notice our vehicles. I'll pick you up at ten tonight on the forest service road above your dorm."

"You'll take all of us?"

"Yes. But only bring what you have to. There won't be room in the vehicles for you and a lot of baggage."

Lion nodded. He started toward the door, then stopped to look back at Max. "Is this the beginning of Armageddon?"

Max took a deep breath. "Good question. It might have been, had Greer and Doc Chase not been there right when they were."

"If this disease gets out, what happens?"

"A lot of people die. But it by itself isn't enough to collapse our country."

"What if this is happening in multiple countries at the same time?"

Max walked over and set a hand on Lion's shoulder. "Don't borrow trouble. We stopped this in time. And whoever started this will be brought to justice."

It was a quarter to ten that night when Max turned his small convoy onto the dirt road that led behind the pride's bunkhouse on the WKB compound. They'd passed several vehicles near the Friendship Community, but no WKBers anywhere.

He pulled to a stop and shut his lights off. At ten o'clock, there was no sign of the boys.

"What time did you tell Lion?" Angel asked via their comm system.

"Now. I'm going down there."

"Want company?" Val asked from the third SUV.

"No. Best if it's just me in case I run in to anyone."

Max walked down the hill and across the backside of the WKB compound, heading toward the Quonset hut where the pride bunked. He stepped inside the dark interior. His eyes had acclimated to the dim ambient light outside, but it was even darker in there.

The bunks were all made. Nothing seemed out of order. He opened one of the footlockers. It was empty. He checked another. Same thing.

"Looking for something?" Pete said, stepping out of Lion's room.

"Pete," Max greeted him. "Was looking for Lion. He's hard to get a hold of except in person."

"He's gone. What are you doing back here anyway?"

"King sent me for Lion and the pride."

"No shit."

"Yeah."

"Can't say I'm sad to see them go, but it's odd that he sent you."

"Why's that?"

"Because King already took them."

"That a fact?"

"Yeah, it is. So you want to tell me who you're really working for?"

"Does it matter? We're both in the same war."

"I liked it better when you had my back."

"What makes you think I don't?"

"You sneaking around my compound at night."

"We had a deal, if I remember," Max reminded him.

"How close to the end is it?" Pete asked.

"Close. Did you know about the smallpox the Friends are infected with? Have your guys been exposed to the virus?"

"No. We got shots recently. I don't know that everyone here has been vaccinated, but most of us have. I didn't know why that happened."

"You aren't going to win this war, Pete."

He shrugged. "I don't expect to be alive long enough to care."

"So be on the right side of it. Help me get to King."

"That would be instant death."

"There's only the two of us here. No one else will know."

"Can I count on you to keep your word? You'll give me sufficient warning before the end so that I can go out my own way?"

"Yes. Now where are Lion and his pride?"

Pete shook his head. "I really don't know. King took them."

Max shook his head. Lion and the boys were gone. That was going to be some hard news to break to Hope. They were savvy kids. They'd find a way to get in touch with him. But why would King have taken them—taken the only alarm system he had in place to guard his gold?

What was the bastard up to?

Max walked to the door, then looked back at Pete. "Look, the CDC is going to come knocking on your door. Let them in. They don't give a shit about your drugs. They just want to vaccinate the ones who need it. Let them do their thing."

"Sure. Why not?"

"Call me if you hear any news about the boys."

"Maybe."

Max smiled. "If you hear something and I learn later that you didn't tell me, I'll revoke our agreement."

"It's not like King tells me anything. But if I hear something, I'll tell you."

KIT'S PHONE rang when he was on his way back to Blade's house that night. He didn't recognize the number. "Bolanger here."

"Hello, Mr. Bolanger. It is I, Jafaar. How are you this fair summer night?"

"What do you want, Jafaar?"

"I merely wished to tell you how aggrieved I am to see so many citizens of the mighty United States brought so low so quickly by an antique germ many thought extinct. Of course, it was never eradicated. It simply withdrew into labs and other dark corners. It has been tenderly cared for by specialists for

decades, while it waited, patiently, for its appointed time to reap-pear. Like so many who are truly loyal to the cause."

"Why am I not surprised you're calling me tonight?"

"I couldn't help but speculate how things might unfold. Who would suspect an eradicated virus when members of a certain motorcycle gang spread their illness across all states in the U.S., across the northern and southern borders? How quickly terror will spread when it hits the southern border, especially.

"It will be fun to watch. Your country will be overrun with panicked immigrants, demanding a cure for their loved ones. A cure for a disease your country unleashed upon them. The U.S. may have enough vaccinations for every one of its citizens, but it doesn't have enough for its neighbors.

"But do not think I am responsible for this. I am merely an amused bystander—how is it you say 'popping popcorn.' I believe the smallest first domino spilling into the next, and the next is all that will be needed to end the oligarchy that is America.

"No wall along your southern border will be high enough when millions start climbing it at once. While the border patrol along with local and national law enforcement have their hands full, the next domino will be falling."

Kit laughed. "Ah, Jafaar, you've been watching too many zombie movies. The CDC already has this under control."

"No, my friend. It is not I who is lost in the fiction told to us by our leaders. I deal in facts. I have workers in key labs whose only function has ever been to help disburse the appro-priate lab samples at the appropriate time. Have you not noticed

how many samples lately have been mishandled, inadvertently shipped internationally? Live bacteria, spores, and viruses. From American labs.

"You see, our cells are not comprised of the disorganized and disenfranchised few. Oh no. They are far more complex than that. Our foundation is made up of multigenerational members who've waited for years to be called upon. They remember the wounds of their ancestors. Their blood is red with hate and white with patience."

"Holy hell, that's depressing, Jafaar. Our people spend generations lifting each other up, not plotting doom. Clearly you're mismanaging your breeding program."

"We do not have an issue with your people, my friend. I do not blame them for the country they were born to. They are merely fodder for the fire. We must pass through them to get to your leaders. It is them I blame."

"Hate is a perfidious motivator, Jafaar. It not only bites the hand that feeds it, it consumes its entire food source, then dies of starvation. You'll botch this just as you've botched every other attempt to end this country. So keep running around, singing big songs. Just makes it all the easier to root you and yours out." Kit dropped the line.

34

———

Greer came awake fast. Too fast. Without opening his eyes, he tried to get a sense of what roused him. He and Remi weren't alone. He drew a long breath, testing the air. Nothing unusual. No stink of a hitman. No chill of a specter. He opened his eyes, surprised to see that morning had already come. A soft blue light radiated from a spot near the door. He looked at the window and realized that it wasn't daylight illuminating the cabin.

The glow came from the ghost girl who'd been following him around. He eased himself free from Remi and sat up. The girl turned and stepped through the closed door. Greer walked across the room and looked out the front window. She looked at him from the middle of the public square.

Greer dressed. He felt an illogical urge to go after her. Was she warning him? Or guiding him toward something?

The glow returned to the dark cabin. Greer touched Remi's arm. "Remi. Wake up."

She smiled at the sound of his voice and stretched, then opened her eyes and shrieked, instantly pulling the covers over her head.

"You see her too?" Greer asked.

A lump under the covers nodded.

"We have to go with her."

Remi lowered the covers enough to expose her eyes. She looked over toward the floating, human-sized blue orb, then shook her head and covered back up.

Greer pulled the covers back. He handed Remi's clothes to her. "Get dressed. I don't want to leave you behind." She dressed in hurried jerky movements, keeping her eyes on the apparition. He geared up, strapping on his Kevlar, stowing his weapons. When Remi came to stand behind him, he turned and helped her into her protective vest.

"Don't be afraid."

She glared up at him. "Do you hear yourself? We're going out into the night in an area where we know mass murderers are loose, wearing Kevlar, you're armed to the teeth, to follow a *ghost*. The only sane thing to do *is* be afraid."

Greer grinned. "That's my girl."

The ghost disappeared. Greer took Remi's hand and led her through the front door and out into the night. The village was buzzing with activity, as it had been since he and Remi quit for the night. He checked his phone to see if something more had happened while they slept. No alarms or messages.

The ghost had jumped all the way to the edge of the forest, on the far side of the village. Greer and Remi jogged after her.

When they reached the edge of the community, Sally's ghost slipped into the woods. Her glowing light dimmed, then disappeared, only to reappear whenever they had to make a course correction.

Two miles into the national forest, Remi stopped Greer. The path they'd taken wasn't a well-defined hiking trail. No, it was over steep, rocky outcroppings and through underbrush dense with ancient scrub pines. They'd just topped another jagged ledge when Remi snagged Greer's shirt. She needed a short break…and they needed a reality check.

"What are we doing? Think about it. This is crazy."

Greer set his hands on his hips and peered into the dark woods in the direction where they'd last seen the blue glow. "Have you ever seen a ghost before?" he asked.

"No."

"But you saw the ghost tonight, right?"

"Yeah."

"I saw her the night I ran into you up here. I saw her at your office. I saw her on the next rooftop over the night your apartment was hit. It's no accident that we're seeing her tonight."

"Greer, where is she going? What's ahead of us in

this direction?"

He pulled out his phone and opened an app Owen had provided the team. Beyond a topographical map, this one had layers for roads and trails, residences and commercial buildings, energy and telecommunication resources, underground gas, sewer, and water lines.

"The only man-made structure around here is another mile east of us," he said.

"Do you think that's where she's leading us?"

"I don't know. According to my info, there's no power or telephone to the site. Either they're running on generators or it's an abandoned building." He sent their coordinates to Max. There was no reason to wake the team—yet. When they arrived at what the ghost was leading them toward, he'd be better able to assess the situation and know what kind of help he needed.

He looked at Remi, proud of her fortitude and attitude. He wished, as much as she was keeping up with him and staying calm, that he'd had a safe place for her to wait. He had no idea what they were getting into up ahead. This whole thing may not pan out at all...or it could be an important discovery in the mystery of what had happened to Sally and the others.

He cracked open a bottle of water and handed it to her. She guzzled half of it and handed it back to him. He finished it off, then put the empty bottle in his backpack. They started off again, following the terrain shown by his phone app. He hadn't gone but a few hundred yards when he realized Remi wasn't behind him.

"Greer, over here! She went this way!" he heard her call.

He doubled back and followed Remi. He couldn't see her or the ghost, but he could hear her moving at a fast pace through the woods. On the side of the mountain where they were, there was less underbrush to obstruct their way. Jagged rocks pierced the ground, sticking out at sharp angles.

He was about to call out to Remi to slow down and move carefully—he didn't want her injured by missing a step and slipping down into the ravine below them—but a sharp cry from her told him he was too late.

Her flashlight was dancing around in a tight pattern as he reached her side, then it locked on one thing. "Oh, God. Oh, God. What is that? Greer, what is that?" Remi held the flashlight on the decomposing flesh of an arm.

The ghost stood where the feet of the body would be, a little down slope, and wept, the ethereal sound surrounding them as if it came from the hills themselves.

Greer knelt beside the body. He had no doubt the body was Sally. He'd found her at last. "Aw, hell. I'm so sorry, Sally. Rebecca." He looked at the corpse's dirtied blond hair, her head at a strange angle against a rock.

Remi scooted away, tucking her heels tightly against herself. "Is that her?"

"Yeah. I'm willing to bet it is." He texted the coordinates and info to Max.

"What do you suppose she was doing out here, so far from the community?"

"I wish I knew."

The ghost's blue glow dissipated. Greer looked up to see if she was leaving them now that she'd accomplished her mission. She was walking away, heading toward the building site he'd identified on his app.

"I don't think she's done with us," he said. He looked at Remi. "Are you all right?"

"I tripped on her arm. I-I'm fine."

He gave her a hand up. "Then let's get a little closer to that building."

About a hundred yards out from the building, Greer found a hiding spot for Remi. "Stay here, stay hidden. I will come back for you. If for some reason I don't, wait until the guys come for both of us. Be quiet. Keep your phone on silent."

"Greer, don't go in there. I have a really bad feeling about that place."

"Yeah, so do I." He caught her elbow, then moved his hand down her arm to the flashlight she held. He switched it off. She stood before him, shadowy and solid. He wondered if Sally and the healer had told each other the truth of their feelings. Had she died wondering if the man she loved loved her back?

"Remi." He caught her face in his palm. She

could no more see him than he could her. "I love you."

She grabbed his wrist in both of her hands and moved her face into his palm. "Don't you dare die in there, Greer Dawson. I have plans for you, ones that involve long years of me being afraid for you and you laughing at me."

"I never laugh at you."

"No, you don't. And that's why I love you."

He leaned forward and kissed her lips, then pressed his mouth to her temple. "You are the best thing that ever happened to me, Remi."

He took out his phone and dialed ops.

"Go." Kelan's voice came over the line.

"We found Sally's body."

"We?"

"Remi and I. It's near a collection of Quonset huts. They look abandoned, but I'm going to check them out."

"I got your coordinates. I'll send some of the guys your way."

"It could be nothing, K. Let me check it out first."

"Negative. Hold your position. Max, Val, and Angel are already near you. I'll send them your way."

"What were they doing?"

"Retrieving Lion and his boys. King got to them first."

"Were they hurt?"

"No. Just gone."

"Shit."

"Hang tight, bro. The team's on its way."

"Copy." Greer dropped the connection. He felt Remi's hand slip into his. Though he couldn't see her face, he felt the question she wasn't asking. "King got Lion and his pride."

"No. That is not good. Do you think they'll be all right?"

Greer shook his head. "King's a fucking hotwire. Who knows." He and Remi went up the hill to the nearest forest service road to wait for the team.

Their big SUVs pulled up a few minutes later. They parked in a way that would let them head out fast if needed. Greer took Val's keys and handed them to Remi.

"Get in the back and stay down. No one can see you through the tinted windows. If there's a problem, get the hell out of here. Drive back to the Friends and wait for us. It's too far to go back to headquarters alone."

"Okay. Be careful." She reached out for Greer's hand. He held it for the length of a step, then let go. He watched until she was safely locked inside the SUV, then caught up with the guys.

"I heard about Lion," he said to Max.

"Yeah."

"We'll find them."

Max didn't answer at first, but it was ugly when he did. "Your girl Sally's dead. We didn't find her in time. Half the kids from the Friendship Community are missing. We haven't found them. King's a fucking expert at disappearing people."

"So we find King and get our answers."

"Oh yeah. Bet your ass we're gonna find him."

"What's going on here, G?" Angel asked.

"Remi and I followed a ghost here. There's a girl's body on the hill below. I think it's Sally's remains. She's near three Quonset huts that look abandoned. I haven't checked them out. Could be nothing. Could be something."

"A ghost brought you here?" Val asked. "What've you been smokin', G?"

Max pursed his lips and shook his head. "He's been getting visits from a ghost for a while."

"Shit." Val smiled at him. "Maybe you should read my cards or something."

Greer waved his hand. "I'm over it. Let's go." He started down the hill.

The forest was dark. None of them had night-vision goggles. They walked the perimeter of the site. The windows in each of the buildings were boarded up. The huts were dark and quiet. They switched on their flashlights and immediately saw fresh tire tracks.

"Doesn't look exactly abandoned," Angel muttered.

They split into two teams, Max and Greer taking the nearest hut, Val and Angel the farthest. Greer and Max flanked the door at one end. On Greer's signal, Max opened the door. Greer raised his gun and flashlight, pointing both into the cavernous space. Long sheets of plastic hung from rods, separating cots. The cots weren't empty. The monitors attached to the occupants were dark. The place had a rancid odor of death and human waste.

"Shit. Shit. Shit," Max snapped. "Greer, get outta here. I think we found where the smallpox came from."

Just as Greer started to retreat, he noticed one of the bodies move. "They're alive."

Max grabbed his arm and pulled him out of the building. "We'll call it in. We aren't equipped to deal with it. We don't know what they've got."

Halfway to the other hut, they met up with Angel and Val, who'd made the same assessment. Max called it in to Kit. Greer went to the third hut. There were no cots inside. What he saw was a thousand times worse. It was a deep pit half filled with bodies in various degrees of decomposition. He backed outside and shut the door.

What the hell had happened here? He thought of Sally's body just up the hill. Had she come from here? Was she trying to get away? Were these the missing Friends kids?

"Max." Greer's voice was raw. "We got a mass grave, too."

"Aw, hell."

GREER HELPED an emergency worker haul the last victim up the hill to a waiting emergency vehicle. He was strapped to a backboard so they could navigate the steep hill. The guy began to rouse and struggle against the restraints and blanket.

Greer freed a hand to set it on the guy's leg. "Be calm. We're here to help you."

The guy started to weep silently. What a terrifying experience he'd come through. Hopefully, the hospital he was being transported to would be able to reverse whatever had been done to him.

A paramedic with a gurney was waiting at the top of the steep slope. Greer hoisted his half of the backboard onto the mobile cot. He was about to turn away when the victim stopped him.

"She did it."

"Who? Did what?" Greer asked as the medics wheeled him away.

"Sally. She found help. She left to bring back help."

Greer slipped his gloved hand into the young man's. "Yes. She did. She was very brave. I'm sorry it took us so long to get to you."

A tear slipped over the guy's cheek. Greer watched as he was stowed inside an ambulance. When the ambulance pulled away, he moved down the slope to the spot where they found Sally. Her remains were being bagged for removal. She hadn't come far, physically, from the site of her torture, but she'd moved worlds to reach out to him.

Maybe she had believed his promise of help after all.

35

———

Greer knocked on the Haskel's door. Mrs. Haskel opened it. Fatigue shadowed her eyes. In just the few days since the outbreak was discovered, she'd aged a decade. It was as if she'd stepped outside the walls of her Shangri-la world and time caught up with her.

"Mr. Dawson."

He tried to smile, but he didn't have it in him. He knew she was hurting. She and several others in the community had spent the day pouring over forensic reconstructions made of those found in the mass grave in order to give preliminary identifications for the families missing loved ones.

He was there to burden her with yet another young face needing a name—Sally.

Mrs. Haskel stepped aside and invited him in. Sitting at her table were half a dozen people he hadn't seen around the village. The community was crawling with outsiders now, so there were lots of people coming and going he didn't recognize.

Mrs. Haskel made the introductions. He was stunned to learn that her visitors were former Friends who slipped away during their tithes rather than commit crimes. They were adults now, in ages ranging from early twenties to mid-thirties. She knew them, knew their families. Some had come back too late— their parents and siblings had passed from the smallpox.

All of them wanted to stay for good. Mrs. Haskel had had them checked out by the FBI. Greer couldn't wait to tell Remi. This new development meant that these returning members could help the village navigate the current crisis, perhaps even offset the numbers of adults needed to foster all the kids orphaned by the disease or the arrests of their parents.

Why wasn't Mrs. Haskel smiling? "This is good news," he said.

She nodded. "It's wonderful news. I spent the day with parents who got the terrible confirmation that their children will never be returning." She looked at her visitors. "And now others who lost their kids long ago have them back again. It's a gift."

"I'm sorry to add to your burden, but I have one more girl I hope you can identify for me." Greer showed her the reconstruction of the girl he and Remi found on the hillside.

She took the large photo. Her hands shook as she looked at it. "Yes. I know this girl." She looked up at Greer. "Was she also in the mass grave?"

"No. She was outside the building, on the hill. She fell and broke her neck. We think she had gotten out and was going for help."

Mrs. Haskel nodded. Tears filled her eyes. "This is —was—Rebecca Morris. She has no one to mourn her. She was an orphan when she left for her tithe." She handed the photo back to him.

Sally.

"She has me. I will see that she has a proper headstone for her ashes."

Mrs. Haskel nodded. "She and the doctor wanted to marry, even though it had been decided that she would marry the woodcutter because the WKB demanded it." She shook her head. "So many lives ruined so needlessly."

"What will happen to the Friends now?" Greer asked, though he doubted enough time had passed to answer that.

"We will continue," one of her visitors said as he came to stand next to Mrs. Haskel.

Another from the group joined them. "We'll return to our core values. We'll still do tithes, but they will be visible to the whole community, in service to our community. They won't be sin tithes anymore."

"That way we'll keep ourselves from becoming blackmail fodder for anyone like the WKB," a third returning member said.

Mrs. Haskel gave Greer a sad smile. "Many of us wanted to end the way we were doing things. Especially when the WKB got so involved in our community. We didn't know how to stop it without destroying ourselves. In the end, it destroyed us anyway." She looked at him. "We should have fought sooner and harder—" she nodded toward the picture he held "—before so many innocent lives were thrown away just so we could protect our guilty ones."

"The FBI hasn't associated you with any crime, Mrs. Haskel."

She shook her head. "I was a coward. I got pregnant early so that I wouldn't have to do my tithe. But don't mistake me. I'm as guilty as everyone else. I knew and did nothing."

Greer sighed. He looked from her to each of her visitors, hoping they could in fact put the village back together again.

"Thank you for ID'ing Rebecca. I'll see that she and the doctor are laid to rest together in your cemetery."

GREER STEPPED in to Remi's cabin. She looked up from her laptop, then hurried over to him. "What's wrong?"

He showed her the photo of Sally's reconstruction. "I asked several people if they knew her. They all did. She was Rebecca Morris."

Remi reached out and touched his arm. "I'm sorry. I was hoping she was one of the ones who just ran away."

"She was a fighter." He shook his head.

"She came and got you."

Greer huffed a rushed breath. "Man, did she. First time a ghost has ever been useful."

Remi's phone rang. She picked it up from the table, then sent Greer a panicked look. "It's my department chair." She wrapped a hand around her stomach as she answered the call.

He felt her fear. This was the week she should have returned to work. He went over to the bowl and pitcher, then brought back just the bowl. "Just in case," he whispered with a grin, hoping the call didn't make her puke.

She held a finger to her mouth as she put the call on speaker.

"Dr. Chase."

"Dr. Zimmers. Thank you for returning my call. I need to give you an update."

"Yes. And I have some new information for you. There have been some developments in our investigation that affect your situation. Can you please come meet me at the provost's office?"

Her panicked eyes zipped over to Greer. "I can't right now."

"Where are you?"

She pinched her eyes shut. "I'm at the Friendship Community…and I'm stuck here under quarantine."

"Ah. Do you by any chance know Senator Whiddon, from Colorado?"

Remi looked at Greer. He held his breath, waiting for her answer. "Yes."

"Mm-mmm. So much has happened since we last spoke. I was hoping to tell you in person. The FBI has been here."

Remi's mouth and eyes opened as she waited to hear more.

"Dr. Crawford has been arrested."

"Board member Dr. Crawford?"

"Yes. We discovered he paid the thugs to tag the building. And it was he who broke into your office."

"Oh my God. Why?"

Dr. Zimmers skipped that question and went back to his own. *"How is it that you know Senator Whiddon?"*

Remi was silent for a long moment. Greer wondered how she would answer. She sat heavily on the edge of the bed. "He was a prophet in the polygamist community where I was raised. The Grummond Society." She met Greer's eyes. "I was married to him when I was twelve."

"Ah. It all makes sense now. Dr. Crawford, apparently, was being blackmailed by the senator, who had some ugly dirt on his extra-marital affairs. Dr. Crawford was pressuring your assistant to get you to stop working on your Friendship Community research. Your assistant did the right thing. He reported the situation to me immediately, and I brought it to the provost.

"When things escalated, and when the FBI started talking to us, we brought the issue to you. It was our hope at the time, when we

didn't know everything that was happening, that having you put some distance between yourself and your project might have kept things from taking a disastrous turn. I'm sorry that we couldn't give you a better explanation at the time. We, too, were kept in the dark."

"I understand. I never faulted you for your decision. I just couldn't figure out what I had done to lose your support."

"You never lost my or the university's support, I assure you. Agent Villalobo has filled us in regarding your pivotal role in helping spot the perfidious activities being conducted through the Friendship Community. He's going to be recommending you for the Presidential Citizens Medal because of the danger you put yourself in so that a national and international crisis could be averted."

Greer grinned. He'd found the link between Whiddon and Dr. Crawford. Lobo had taken the info and run with it. He was glad to hear that Dr. Crawford had been arrested.

The stress in Remi's voice yanked him out of his thoughts.

"Dr. Zimmers, I don't want that medal. Absolutely not. I did not do this for personal glory. I don't want to become known as the person who destroyed this community so that I could make a name for myself. I would never again be able to establish rapport with any other groups I want to study. And I will lose all standing with the Friends, which I cannot do at such a critical juncture. Please have him withdraw his nomination."

"Dr. Chase, you did not destroy that community. It was their own actions that secured their downfall."

"I insist, Dr. Zimmers."

"Very well. I can't say I agree with your decision, but I will see that it's honored. When will your quarantine be finished? And, of course, I should have asked first—how are you feeling?"

"I believe I should be in the clear in about two more weeks. I feel fine. I've had the vaccination. I don't think I was exposed, so I'm not worried about the quarantine, other than what it will do to my position at the university."

It seemed to Greer that he heard a little chuckle in Dr. Zimmer's voice. *"Put your fears to rest. The provost encouraged me to consider putting you up for tenure early."*

Remi looked up at him with a stunned expression. He bit his lip to keep from shouting out.

"As you know," Dr. Zimmer continued, *"going up too early isn't good for one's career, but it shows how deeply the provost supports you. I only mentioned it so that you would have no worries about your position here. We're far more concerned about losing you to more competitive universities, though of course you didn't hear that from me. Mr. Weston will be covering your classes until you can return. And by no means am I implying that you need to rush. You have before you an extraordinary opportunity as a sociologist to document this event and its impact to the Friends' community."*

"Thank you, Dr. Zimmers. You just made my day."

"Stay well, Dr. Chase. And stay safe. I would love to hear

more about your time with the Grummonds. I can imagine it being a very formative experience."

"It was."

"You were brave to tell me. I'll keep that information confidential. By the way, are you in a safe place where you are?"

"Yes. Why?"

"The FBI informed us the senator has gone missing."

36

Senator George Whiddon lowered the sun visor. It was so hot outside that his Mercedes had a difficult time keeping things cool. He'd plugged the location coordinates into his GPS. It hadn't rained in weeks out here in the remote Colorado plains. Months, even. The dirt road he was on sent a plume of dust high into the air. He was going to have to get his car detailed after this trip.

But it would be worth it.

He hated this half of his state. It was a barren wasteland, fit only for oil rigs and rattlesnakes. The plains were brown with dead grass. Even the sage and rabbitbrush looked skeletal. He came this far east in his state only during campaigns. The rest of the time, he sent his employees when something needed his attention.

He tried to adjust the air conditioning again, but it was already as cool as it would go. Maybe it wasn't only the August heat making him sweat. Maybe it was the fact that he was finally going to meet King. For more than a decade, they'd been partners, building a future fit for world leaders like themselves. For ten years, he'd pulled strings for King from inside the government, run interference for him, smoothed the way for him. Whatever King wanted, King got—and not only from George.

None of his peers, the few of them who were going to survive the coming Armageddon, knew what King looked like. None of them had met him in person. He would be the first. He already suspected he was King's highest-ranking operative. For that's really what he was. An operative. A rebel. An instrument in the making of a new world order. A founding father of the new country.

His place in history would never be forgotten.

He smiled, then guzzled a long swallow of water from his plastic bottle. The fine dust from the road left grit in his mouth—even with the windows closed and the air on recycle. He looked at his GPS. Twenty-three more miles to go. This part of Colorado slid seamlessly right into Kansas. He wasn't surprised this was where King had picked for the meet. King was a man who fiercely protected his privacy. Out here, there were no cameras. And the appointed meeting time was conveniently between satellite rotations.

George watched his progress on his phone's map. He'd reached his destination. He slowed, then stopped. There was nothing out here, only miles and miles of brown earth, dead grass, and wind. It was a great ocean of parched land.

The only thing that told him he was in the right spot was a black SUV parked facing away from him on the low slope of a hill. He drove across the dry field and pulled up next to it.

His phone rang. *"Leave your keys in the ignition and your phone in your car,"* the electronically altered voice ordered. George complied, feeling ripples of excitement.

"Very good. Pick up the wand and scan yourself."

Again George complied. Of course he wasn't wearing any transmitting devices. He wasn't a fool. He knew everything he'd done for King could come back and bite him in the ass.

"Very good. Pick up your phone and come forward."

George could feel his heart speed up. This was a day he'd never forget. This day made everything he'd done for King worth everything it had cost him. George walked up over the hill. His palms were damp.

A man sat in one of two folding chairs. Between the chairs was a cooler.

George walked up to the man, who was younger and more fit than he'd expected King to be. The man wore glasses, so it was hard to tell his age. Somewhere between twenty-five and forty, he guessed.

George held out his hand. "It's a pleasure to meet you at last, King."

King didn't look at him or return the handshake.

Instead, he turned and retrieved an ice-cold bottle of water from the cooler. George's mouth watered in anticipation.

King cracked the seal and guzzled the refreshing liquid. "Sit down," he ordered.

George sat.

"You've broken my trust," King said. Somehow, even in person, his voice was being electronically altered.

"I don't know what you're talking about."

"Yes, you do."

"May I have some water?"

"In time."

They sat in the bright afternoon sun. The dry air evaporated George's sweat as soon as it appeared on his skin, leaving it salty and itchy. He licked his lips, a rough drag over dry skin.

King lifted his face to the sun and smiled. George took note of all of his features. His legs were long and muscular, his waist lean, his shoulders broad. George had the feeling that King was six inches or more taller than he was. A few days' growth of beard shadowed the ridge of his jaw. There was a cleft in his chin. His hair was a warm brown, reddish in the bright sun. Black nitrile gloves covered his hands, partially covering the tactical watch on his right wrist.

"You're not King."

The man smiled. "How would you know?"

"You're too young."

The man's head slowly tilted his way. "Maybe I have a clear conscience and therefore age slowly."

"I'm fine with what I've done. It's for a greater good. A new beginning for this country and the world."

"One where prophets marry twelve-year-old girls and rape them before an audience of like-minded religious fanatics?"

The first whisper of panic flicked through George's mind. "Who are you?"

"Your life, as you know it, ends today, in the way of your choosing."

George tried to lick his lips again, but this time his tongue stuck on the first patch of skin it reached. He pulled it back into his dry mouth. "Did King send you?" His voice was raspy. He needed water.

Silence. The man reached into the cooler and brought out a fresh bottle of water. He set it on the cooler, then handed George a clipboard with pieces of white paper and a pen tied to the clip.

"Confess your sins. I hear it does a body good."

"No."

The man smiled. "This is the end of the road for you. Did you not notice?"

"I want water."

"When you finish. Start with the animals you tortured as a boy. The girl you raped in high school. The one you murdered in college. Spend plenty of time on your sprint of pedophilia as a prophet in the Grummonds. Does your wife know how many girls are in your harem? List whose palms you greased to start your career as a politician. Don't leave your association with Amir Hadad out. Or your part in earmarking funds for the research facility that was testing bio weapons on underage volunteers from the Friendship Community. Such a fascinating life you've lived. Write it all out. I have time."

The man smiled. Only King knew those things about him. He had to be King.

"Oh, and be sure to note how you mobilized the WKB against the girl who was one of your twelve-year-old brides, ripping open a wedge in my organization wide enough for the whole fucking federal government to step into. That, my friend, was your biggest sin. Now write, before your water gets hot."

"I had to stop her."

"Not at the cost of my kingdom. Write. It. Down."

George wrote down the things King listed. He wasn't King. He couldn't be King. He was too young; George had been working with him for more than half this guy's life. Perhaps there was more than one King? Maybe this King had inherited the job from the previous? He wrote the things the man mentioned, no more and no less, though there were more. Too much for the sheets given him.

He handed the clipboard to the man and reached for the water.

"Ah-ah-ah. A moment, please." The man read over the confession. "Sign and date it."

George took the clipboard back and did as he requested.

"Very good. Now, we just have your decision about the rest of your life. I am not going to kill you." King smiled, the expression anything but benign. "Here are your choices. Option A, you turn yourself in, with this, and accept your punishment."

"That will end my career. I'm far too useful to you. I know things about you."

"Very true. Hence Option B." He nodded toward the still-cold bottle of water. "Drink the entire contents of this bottle."

"Why that bottle and not a different one from the cooler? What's in it?"

"LSD. Not enough to kill you, though your death will follow shortly. Of course"—King touched his heart—"I am not without empathy. The LSD will prevent you from feeling anything."

King removed the papers from the clipboard and slipped them into a sealed plastic bag. "What is your choice?"

"My life's over either way."

"Very true."

George reached for the water bottle. He opened it and looked at King as he guzzled most of its contents.

King smiled and settled back in his chair.

Instead of the pain George had expected, a comfortable, warm sensation slipped through his veins. He laughed. This wasn't death. King had just been scaring him. He had overstepped in sending the

WKB after that bitch. There wasn't anything on that paper that King didn't already know about him, obviously. He couldn't believe he'd fallen for King's bullshit. Thank God he hadn't lost his head and begged.

He looked at the huge ravine in front of them. It was an odd geographical feature that seemed to appear out of nowhere. There wasn't a river causing the draw to develop. It was just a massive crack, about a half-mile wide and several miles long. Maybe at the bottom, there was a small creek running through it. Trees and sage had claimed tenuous spots on either side of the rocky walls.

The heat made George's skin itch. He scratched his forearm. The collar of his golf shirt rubbed his neck in an irritating way. He scratched there, too, then held the ice-cold water bottle up to his forehead. He was feeling just a little queasy. He looked over at King, who was watching him with concerned eyes.

"Sorry. This heat," George mumbled. "I have a hard time with it. It's much better when Colorado's cold than hot."

King smiled. It was a kind smile. "I understand. It's the heat, you think?" He looked over toward the ravine. George followed his gaze. "Or is it the vultures?"

George looked on in shock as huge turkey vultures flew out of the ravine. Three of them. Their six-foot wingspans kicked up dust as they perched on the ravine's edge. It was a beautiful and horrible sight.

"Drink some more water. It will cool you down. The smell of sweat attracts them. Drink."

George lifted the bottle to his lips and drained the remaining liquid in it, all while watching more and more vultures pop out of the ravine. One came close. King calmly shooed it away. He was brave. Shit.

"Remind me, when did we first meet?" King asked.

George laughed. "You forgot? You came to me. The Senate ethics committee was launching an investigation into my alleged misuse of official resources. You made it go away. I've been your faithful servant since. Even my son is in your debt. He'll serve you as well."

King smiled. "That pleases me."

"I'm not the only high-ranking official in your service, but I was the first."

"Ah. And who are the others? Tell me their names."

George did, pleased he knew so much. He knew too much to be easily disposed of.

King stood and took his folding chair, then the cooler and put them in the black SUV. George swiped his forearm against his forehead. One of the vultures hopped toward him, then spread its wings and flew closer, landing only a couple of feet from him.

George shouted and jumped up, then backed away. He tripped and fell, scrabbling away as he kicked backward. King put his chair into the black SUV as well.

"King! Help me!"

King waved the demon vultures away.

George was going to say something, but just then, a vulture landed on King's shoulder and ripped his ear right off his head in its massive beak. George screamed. King screamed. They ran to George's car. King leaned in and started the engine.

"Get in, quick!" King ordered, saving George before himself. "The only way you can disperse them is to drive toward them. Do it! Do it now! Hurry!"

KING WAS PLEASED George didn't hesitate. He watched as the senator floored the accelerator. Dirt spun out from his tires. He weaved about, as if running off the imaginary vultures conjured by the LSD trip. As he neared the ravine's edge, he had to be going close to ninety. His pretty Mercedes soared into the air, then nose-dived to the bottom with a loud explosion. A black ball of smoke shot up from the rim of the canyon.

REMI FOLLOWED Greer into the den. She sent him a nervous glance, wondering why Owen had summoned them. She'd been away from the team for most of her quarantine, and she'd forgotten how intense the bosses were. Kit nodded to Owen, silently giving him the floor.

"I wanted to bring Dr. Chase up to speed," Owen said. "Your help in uncovering the hidden reality inside the Friends Community has been invaluable." He looked around the table. "As you know, most of the people we discovered in the Quonset huts were the missing teenagers from the community, though some were Jane and John Does, taken from the streets elsewhere. There were forty-five in all, twenty dead, twenty-five very close to death."

"What were they doing to them?" Remi asked. She'd heard some of this news from Greer, but not the official version.

"The investigators found evidence of slow- and fast-acting bio agents, from brucellosis to hemorrhagic infectants in the labs and in the dead in the mass grave. They were testing bio weapons."

"On the kids?"

Owen nodded. "Seems the nature of their tithes changed from committing crimes to being victims. The living patients have been moved to Denver, the dead to special labs for analysis. DNA from each corpse is being matched to those in the Community so that their families can be notified."

"Will the ones who survived pull through?"

Owen lifted his shoulders. "Time will tell. They are receiving the very best care now. I don't know whether you've heard, but Senator Whiddon has evidently committed suicide."

"He killed himself?" While it was a relief he was no longer a threat to her, Remi had a hard time getting her head around that news. Men as arrogant as the senator rarely felt remorse for their crimes.

"It appears he was overcome by guilt. He enumerated his crimes in a detailed suicide note." Owen gave Greer a penetrating look.

Greer shrugged. "I can't say that's much of a loss. He and his son had been under FBI scrutiny for some time."

Remi couldn't help the shiver that ripped down her spine as she remembered his whispered promise, *I will end him*. Greer was smiling at her.

She shifted her gaze to Owen. "Do you think the WKB will leave me alone now?"

"The WKB have their hands full dealing with the FBI and the CDC and various other agencies. You'll be the last thing on their minds for a long time," Owen told her.

Remi reached for Greer's hand, realizing what the other side of the coin meant; she was now free to go. Free to return to her old life. She looked to see if Greer had made that connection yet. If he had, it didn't show on his face. Her heart hammered uncomfortably in her chest as they left the den.

She was quiet as they walked down the hall. "I never thought I could open my heart the way you've shown me to. Now that I have, if you aren't in it, I'll just feel broken."

He smiled and stopped to face her. "Go on."

"I need you to be with me. Here. At my place. Whatever."

Greer touched her cheek. The humor slowly slipped from his face. "I wouldn't have it any other way, Remi. I love you."

"I love you, too."

He caught her hand and pressed it to his chest. "Marry me."

"We have complicated careers. How will we make it work?"

"I think my team's going to be here a long while. And it sounded like your university's never going to let you go. I'll put you first. You'll put me first. We'll make it work."

She smiled at him. "I like that."

"I do, too." He laughed and kissed her. They walked down to the living room, where everyone was gathering for supper. Kelan's phone rang.

Greer smiled as Kelan said, "Hi, babe. What's up?" There was a pause. "Fiona? Fiona?" Another pause. The guys went quiet, hearing a note in Kelan's voice that set them on edge. Remi felt the tension that rippled through the room.

Kelan straightened and frowned. "Who is this?" He lowered the phone slowly, then looked at Greer. "They have Fiona."

OTHER BOOKS BY ELAINE LEVINE

RED TEAM SERIES

(This series must be read in order)

1 The Edge of Courage

2 Shattered Valor

3 Honor Unraveled

4 Kit & Ivy: A Red Team Wedding Novella

5 Twisted Mercy

6 Ty & Eden: A Red Team Wedding Novella

7 Assassin's Promise

8 War Bringer

9 Rocco & Mandy: A Red Team Wedding Novella

10 Razed Glory

11 Deadly Creed

12 Forsaken Duty

SLEEPER SEALS

11 FREEDOM CODE

MEN OF DEFIANCE SERIES

(This series may be read in any order)

ABOUT THE AUTHOR

Elaine Levine lives in the mountains of Colorado with her husband and a rescued pit bull/bull mastiff mix. In addition to writing the Red Team romantic suspense series, she's the author of several books in the historical western romance series Men of Defiance. She also has a novel in the multi-author series, Sleeper SEALs.

Be sure to sign up for her new release announcements at http://geni.us/GAlUjx.

If you enjoyed this book, please consider leaving a review at your favorite online retailer to help other readers find it.

Get social! Connect with Elaine online:
    Reader Group: http://geni.us/2w5d
    Website: https://www.ElaineLevine.com
    email: elevine@elainelevine.com

Made in the USA
Coppell, TX
26 April 2022